D0780402

JUVENAL AND PERSIUS

LCL 91

JUVENAL
AND PERSIUS

EDITED AND TRANSLATED BY

SUSANNA MORTON BRAUND

HARVARD UNIVERSITY PRESS
CAMBRIDGE, MASSACHUSETTS
LONDON, ENGLAND
2004

Library of Congress Catalog Card Number 2004042213
CIP data available from the Library of Congress

ISBN 0-674-99612-7

Composed in ZephGreek and ZephText by
Technologies 'N Typography, Merrimac, Massachusetts.
Printed and bound by Edwards Brothers, Ann Arbor, Michigan
on acid-free paper made by Glatfelter, Spring Grove, Pennsylvania.

CONTENTS

CONTENTS

PREFACE

My aim in translating the Satires of Juvenal and Persius for the Loeb Classical Library has been to produce a translation that is vivid and vigorous and accessible, without compromising accuracy to the Latin text. Ramsay's 1918 Loeb translation has lasted remarkably well, but it is clearly time to update it and to incorporate advances in scholarship since then. One central difficulty of preparing a translation which is designed for a long shelf life is that of contemporary idiom. There is no doubt that when we look back at translations of Juvenal that were in vogue in the 1960s, such as those of Rolfe Humphries (1958), Hubert Creekmore (1963), Jerome Mazzaro (1965), Charles Plumb (1968), and above all Peter Green's 1967 Penguin, they seem very dated, not just because of their covers, but because they indulge too much in ephemeral expressions. I have tried to strike a balance between their strategy of trendiness and the clumsiness that results from trying to reproduce the structures of an inflected language like Latin in a largely uninflected language like English.

The intrinsic problem of the Loeb Classical Library is that of turning poetry into prose. In this particular case, it is highly rhetorical poetry, which self-consciously resonates with intertextual allusions to earlier satire and to epic and other classics of the ancient literary canon. I hope that in the case of Persius I have not made his Latin too easy. He is one of the hardest poets any student of Latin literature is likely to meet, and I believe that to "dumb down" the intensity and obscurity of his idiom would be to do him an injustice. In the case of Juvenal, I have tried to convey the verve and energy of his rhetorical impetus in the early Satires and his tone of superiority in the later Satires. Particularly in his case, I have designed my translation to be read aloud, because I consider it crucial that we reconnect with the oral presentation and the performative aspect of these poems.

A central difficulty is presented by the emphasis created by word order in Latin. To convey the effects of word order in Persius and Juvenal, I have at times recast sentences. Another problem is that some kinds of question and exclamation clause sound unnatural in our English; for example, relative clauses with the possessive genitive "whose." I have taken liberties in such situations, aiming for a result that will sound at least possible for a native speaker. Another difficulty arises over connections between clauses and especially with words like *nam* and *enim*, conventionally translated "for," and similar words, such as *itaque*, "therefore." No one I know actually uses the connectives "for" and "therefore" in spoken English, so I resolved to avoid them in my translation, sometimes omitting them, where the thought connection seemed self-evident, but more often spelling out the connection of ideas more explicitly than may seem warranted in the Latin. And in terms of choice of vocabulary, I have tried to provide a judicious blend of Latinate roots with the more periphrastic expressions that currently dominate spoken English. I hope that these strategies combine fidelity to the Latin with a vitality which can last a long time. That, after all, is the crucial aim of the Loeb Classical Library: to make these fascinating and provocative authors accessible to students of Roman culture for years to come.

Both Juvenal and Persius have been well served by their editors in the twentieth century and I was consequently in the happy position of being able to rely to a considerable degree on the judgement and imagination of some eminent Latinists. I based my study of the text of Juvenal on Wendell Clausen's 1992 Oxford Classical Text and on James Willis' new Teubner (1997), and I had frequent recourse to the editions of A. E. Housman (1931), Edward Courtney (1984), and J. R. C. Martyn (1987) and to articles on the text of Juvenal by Robin Nisbet. I also had access to the conjectures of the scholar Guyet and to the annotations made by Markland on a MS in St John's College, Cambridge, thanks to the generosity of J. N. Adams. When I met him in Perth, James Willis kindly supplied me with the *Testimonia* prepared for his Teubner edition, which they had declined to print. With Persius I am likewise indebted to the scholarship exemplified by Clausen's Oxford Classical Text; I also used Bo's 1969 edition, Harvey's 1981 commentary, and Lee's 1987 edition, although none of these differs hugely from Clausen. For both authors, I follow the Oxford Classical Text fairly closely, although I offer a number of repunctuations and adopt some different readings and conjectures. These are listed in the rudimentary apparatus, along with other MSS variants and critical emendations that struck me as worthy of mention. I have translated in my notes all the lines that I propose to remove from Clausen's 1992 OCT if they appear unbracketed in Clausen, along with a selection of the lines that Clausen brackets. My aim has been to produce the most plausible text and translation of Persius and Juvenal, while making it possible for the reader to identify textual cruces that might affect interpretation.

In terms of translations, there were four stalwarts beside me throughout my work on Juvenal: Ramsay's 1918 Loeb, Niall Rudd's translation for Oxford World's Classics (1991), Steven Robinson's idiosyncratic 1983 translation from Carcanet Press, and an old and lasting favourite of mine, the Rev. J. D. Lewis' prose translation of 1873, my copy of which I purchased in 1975, just after I completed my B.A., at a bookshop in Hay-on-Wye. John Henderson's lively rendition of Satire 8 (1997) also proved provocative. In the case of Persius, Niall Rudd's Penguin Classics translation (revised version, 1987) and Guy Lee's 1987 translation published by Francis Cairns were my first resort, along with J. R. Jenkinson's 1980 Aris and Phillips translation.

Acknowledgements

I started work on this new translation of Persius and Juvenal for the Loeb Classical Library, at the invitation of George Goold, during a welcome semester of leave at the University of Bristol in spring 1995. Progress slowed when I moved to the Classics Department at Royal Holloway, University of London, in September 1995. I finished the substantive version in November 1998. In hindsight, it seems amazing that I did finish—and, indeed, that anyone working in the British university system ever finishes anything—and I am grateful for the patience extended to me by those at the Loeb Classical Library. The ensuing delay can be attributed to changes within the Loeb Classical

PREFACE

Library and to my move to Yale University in 2000. The new General Editor, Jeffrey Henderson, has devoted painstaking attention to every level of detail and improved the result immeasurably. I cannot express myself adequately about his contribution. Margaretta Fulton at the Press has been marvelous from beginning to end.

I wish to thank all those friends and colleagues, in Bristol and London, at Yale, and in the wider academic community, who supported me in this project. Vital assistance came from Dr Stephen Harrison, who took time during his Research Leave to trawl through my text and translation of Juvenal, and from Brother Paulinus Greenwood, O.S.B., who performed the same task for my translation of Persius. To both I am hugely grateful. I would also like to thank the entire Department of Classics and Ancient History at the University of Auckland, where I spent July and August of 1998 as a Foundation Visitor "finishing off" Juvenal, especially Marcus Wilson, for all his time and continuing friendship and support. J. N. Adams, John Barsby, Duncan Cloud, Michael Hendry, Harry Jocelyn, John D. Morgan III, and James Willis all gave me advice on specific passages and problems. My London colleague Nick Lowe gave invaluable technical help, and John Jacobs, a Yale graduate student, was a marvelous proofreader. Where none of the above could persuade me of my ignorance, I take full blame. I cannot conclude without naming the friends who have supported me during this project: Lene Rubinstein, Jonathan Walters, Patricia Moyer, Carole Newlands, Ted Kenney, the three Christophers—Carey, Gill, and Rowe—and above all Adam Morton.

New Haven
August 2003

JUVENAL AND PERSIUS

INTRODUCTION

"Satire" seems a seductively straightforward term, because everyone can think of satirical forms of writing. But any attempt to define "satire" shows it to be a slippery term. "The playfully critical distortion of the familiar" is Feinberg's attempt.[1] This pinpoints four features common to most works of satire, usually distributed along two axes: the spectrum of playfulness and criticism, and the spectrum of the familiar and its distortions, ranging from suppression to exaggeration. Satire, moreover, is "an urban art,"[2] "set in the city, particularly in the metropolis with a polyglot people."[3] These definitions work well for Roman satire. They offer a reminder that these texts are not streams of angry consciousness but highly crafted artefacts written for a sophisticated audience. It follows that the uncritical use of the texts of Roman satire as evidence for Roman social practices is highly problematic: the apparent realism of these texts should not blind us to the degree of distortion exerted in the interests of entertainment. In particular, the habit of attributing what is said to the poet himself (the biographical fallacy) has been countered by an awareness

[1] Feinberg *The Satirist* 7.

[2] Hodgart *Satire* 129.

[3] Kernan *The Cankered Muse* 7–8.

1

that the satirists create a range of satiric mouthpieces, conveniently called the satirist's mask or persona.[4] The dramatic dimension of these poems would have been readily appreciated by the Roman elite audience, who were thoroughly accustomed to the creation of characters from their rhetorical training.

So the first Satire of Juvenal may seem familiar. Juvenal presents a character who seems to be an ordinary citizen of the metropolis of Rome, ranting at the excesses and outrages that surround him, a simple man who is so frustrated at society's hypocrisy and corruption and at its failure to address burning issues of inequality and immorality that he is driven to deliver a scathing condemnation of that decadent society. This fits modern ideas of "satire" rather closely. The fact is that Juvenal has had such a profound and lasting influence on the development of satire that it would be surprising if our concept of satire did not match his. But the story of satire is much more complex. This introduction will briefly review the origins and development of the genre of Roman satire through more than three centuries, from the first experiments of Ennius in the late third to early second century B.C., through the establishment of the standard features of the genre by Lucilius in the late second century B.C., the refinement of the form by Horace, close associate of both the emperor Augustus and his "minister of culture" Maecenas, to the radically different treatments of the genre by the satirists of the

---

[4] Highet *Juvenal the Satirist* was chiefly responsible for popularising the biographical approach; Anderson *Essays on Roman Satire* was crucial in shifting the parameters of the debate. All subsequent work on Roman satire is indebted to him.

early Principate, Persius and Juvenal. This diachronic overview is crucial to a proper understanding of the individual poets and poems.[5]

Greek and Roman literature operated within a framework of genres with their unwritten rules. Although "genre" itself is a relatively modern word, the ancients clearly found ways of classifying their literary productions into family groups. It was expected that a writer would acknowledge his debt to his predecessors by imitation, which was regarded as the highest form of compliment. This element of imitation needed to be blended with innovation, to avoid stagnation and to develop the genre. This makes it important to be aware of the history of any Greco-Roman genre: later writers invariably demonstrate an intimacy with earlier writers by reworking and adapting and even at times overturning their ideas.

The rules of the genre of Roman verse satire prescribed the metre and form, material, presentation, and language. The metre was the dactylic hexameter, and the form required compositions of short to middle length, usually in the range 50–250 lines long. The content included matters of morality, education, and literature. The type of presentation was generally the autobiographical monologue, with occasional excursions into dialogue, epistle, or narrative form. The language ranged from mock-epic grandeur, through everyday discourse, to moments of explicit crudity. These features emerged in the Satires of Lucilius, who is regarded by later satirists as the founder of the genre: Horace actually calls him its inventor at *Satires*

---

[5] For a fuller account see Braund *Roman Verse Satire* and Freudenburg *The Walking Muse*.

1.10.48. From the few surviving fragments of his Satires, Lucilius' influence upon later satirists is palpable. Horace, for example, reworked his predecessor's diary-type poem depicting a journey to Sicily in his journey to Brindisi (*Satires* 1.5), and presented himself as a new Lucilius for a more sophisticated era (*Satires* 1.4, 1.10, 2.1). In the case of the relationship between Horace and Persius we fare better. Virtually every line of Persius' Satires demonstrates his deep familiarity with Horace's satirical writings.[6] He takes individual words, phrases, patterns of thought, and material from Horace and reworks them into something distinctively his own which all the same is indelibly Horatian. Juvenal shows more independence, but is nevertheless indebted to Horace and Persius throughout his Satires—and, doubtless, to Lucilius too. Persius and Juvenal both include in their opening, "programmatic," satires indications of their literary pedigree. Persius opens his first Satire with what is probably a quotation from Lucilius, and he later asserts the right to express his views because he is following the precedent set by Lucilius and Horace (1.114–18): "Lucilius ripped into Rome—you, Lupus, you, Mucius—and broke a molar on them. While his friend is laughing, the rascal Horace touches every fault in him and, once he's got in, he frolics around his heart, clever at dangling the public from his cleaned-out nose." Similarly, early in his first Satire Juvenal cites the precedent of Lucilius, "the great protégé of Aurunca" steering his chariot across the plain (19–20), and later that of Horace's "Venusian lamp" (51); he reworks from Persius a scene of death in the bath (142–6, cf. Persius 3.98–106); and near the end

6 See Rudd in *Lines of Enquiry* 54–83.

of the poem he parades Lucilius blazing and roaring "as if with drawn sword" (165–6).

The Origins of Roman Satire

For the Romans, there were two types of satire, one in prose and one in verse.[7] The two share many characteristics, yet ancient discussions of the genre privilege the verse form. This may be because the prose form, often called Menippean satire, had its roots in Greek culture, specifically in the diatribe, a kind of sermon associated with the Hellenistic philosophical schools such as Cynicism. In contrast, the verse form was claimed as Roman.

The origins of the genre of satire and the significance of the word *satura* have been much debated, in antiquity and since. The most famous Roman statement about satire is Quintilian's: "Satire is entirely our own" (*Institutio Oratoria* 10.1.93, *satura quidem tota nostra est*). This seems to mean that there is no original Greek form which the Roman satirists are imitating, unlike the rest of Latin literature, which is heavily influenced by Greek literature. This view is supported by Horace when he calls satire "verse never handled by the Greeks" (*Satires* 1.10.66, *Graecis intacti carminis*) and by the fact that this is the only genre discussed by Quintilian which is identified by a Latin name. This does not, of course, mean that Greek literature never uses a satirical or critical or aggressive tone—the genres of comedy and iambus offer plenty of examples—but it does mean that there is no Greek satire in the form used by Lucilius, Horace, and Persius.

[7] Coffey *Roman Satire* discusses both genres of satire.

Quintilian, writing in the late first century A.D. (earlier than Juvenal), groups together Lucilius, Horace, and Persius as the chief exponents: "The first to win renown in *satura* was Lucilius, who has some devotees who are so dedicated to him that they without hesitation prefer him not just to other authors in the same genre but to all poets. I disagree with them as much as with Horace, who thinks that Lucilius is a muddy river with a lot of stuff that you could remove. His learning is remarkable, as is his freedom of speech and the sharpness and abundant wit which derives from it. Horace is much terser and purer and, unless I lapse because of my affection for him, the best. Persius has won a considerable and legitimate reputation, although he wrote only one book. There are eminent satirists today who will be celebrated in the future" (*Institutio Oratoria* 10.1.93–4). When he goes on to mention a more ancient form of satire, "an older kind of *satura*, composed by Terentius Varro, which has a mixture variegated not just by verse" (*Institutio Oratoria* 10.1.95), he is clearly referring to Menippean satire, which later develops into all kinds of prosimetrum compositions.

Apart from Quintilian's comments, we find *satura* appearing incidentally in the historian Livy's discussion of the history of Roman drama and directly in the writings of Diomedes, a fourth century grammarian. Livy, writing early in the Augustan era, presents an elaborate theory of the development of Roman drama. He mentions a dramatic form which he calls *satura*, a scripted musical stageshow with no organised plot (7.2.4–10). What relation this bears to the polished literature that survives as hexameter satire is hard to say, but it supports a view of satire as a form of drama.

The only theoretical discussion of *satura* from antiquity is that of Diomedes, who may have derived this material from Varro, the late Republican antiquarian scholar and author of Menippean satires. Diomedes offers four possible explanations of the word *satura* (Diomedes, *GLK* I.485): "*satura* takes its name either from satyrs, because in this form of poetry laughable and disgraceful things are said in the same way as if produced and performed by satyrs; or from a full dish which, stuffed with many varied first fruits, was offered to the gods in religious ritual among the ancients and was called *satura* from the abundance and fullness of its material; . . . or from a certain type of sausage which, stuffed with many ingredients, Varro says was called *satura* . . . Others think that its name came from the *lex satura* [lit. "full law"], which combines together many provisions in a single bill, because in the poetry form *satura* many poems are combined together." The connection with satyrs (*satyri*) seems tenuous (although Petronius clearly plays on it in his *Satyrica*): Roman satire does not have the ribald and obscene nature of Greek satyr drama. The other three explanations hinge upon the notions of mixture and variety: the derivation of *satura* from the *lanx satura*, "mixed dish" of offerings to the gods; the association with a kind of stuffing or sausage made from many ingredients; and the derivation of *satura* from the *lex per saturam*, a law with mixed provisions of Republican times.

Although it is impossible to make a firm choice, these ideas of abundance and variety dominate. Maybe the poet is offering a "mixed dish" to the inspiring deity; or he is like a moral legislator; but it is most appealing to view the satirist as a cook, serving up to his audience a sausage stuffed full of varied ingredients, ingredients that include a substantial quantity of feasting and food. This explanation gives a piquant taste to Juvenal's description of his work as a *farrago* (1.86): by styling his poetry as "mixed cattle fodder," he may well be alluding to and debunking learned speculation on the origin of the word *satura*.

Diomedes provides an overview of the genre and its practitioners (*GLK* I.485) which resembles Quintilian's: "Satire is the name of a form of poetry among the Romans and not the Greeks that is abusive and composed to criticise the faults of men in the manner of Old Comedy, such as Lucilius and Horace and Persius wrote; but formerly satire was the name of the poetry which consisted of a variety of poems, such as Pacuvius and Ennius wrote." Two things are striking: the link with Greek Old Comedy, mentioned by the satirists themselves (Horace, *Satires* 1.4.1–5, 1.10.16, Persius 1.123–4), and the division of the genre into, on the one hand, the form written by Lucilius, Horace, and Persius and, on the other hand, the older form written by Pacuvius and Ennius.

Nothing is known of Pacuvius' satirical works. Quintus Ennius (239–169 B.C.), his uncle, from Calabria in the south of Italy, made many literary innovations. He was the first to write Latin epic poetry in hexameters; his works in other genres also reflect his inventiveness. It is hard to judge his *Saturae* because only 31 lines survive from the four books he wrote. But it appears that they were a miscellany written in a variety of metres and sometimes using autobiographical presentation (21W = Warmington's Loeb). They include a multiple word play (28–31W), a debate between Life and Death (Quintilian, *Institutio Oratoria* 9.2.36), a fable of Aesop (Aulus Gellius, *Attic*

Nights 2.29), with a tone sometimes critical (23W) and sometimes humorous (21W). This is not much to go on. We have to accept the judgement of the ancients in pronouncing Lucilius and not Ennius the inventor of the genre of satire.

Lucilius and Horace

Gaius Lucilius (180 or 168/7 to 102/1 B.C.) was a wealthy member of the Latin aristocracy (an *eques*) in Campania and connected with the intellectual and political elite in Rome through his association with Scipio Aemilianus, a general, politician, and patron of the arts. This gave him a powerful position from which to write his satires, which are highly engaged politically and culturally in their exposés of those who do not reach the desired standards of conduct.[8] Cicero describes him as "an educated and highly civilised man" (*De Oratore* 3.171, *homo doctus et perurbanus*), a comment on his blend of knowledge of Greek culture with assertion of Roman ideology.

Lucilius wrote his Satires from about 130 B.C. onwards. Only 1300 lines of fragments survive, mostly preserved by later grammarians for their linguistic interest. He initially experimented with different metrical forms before settling on the hexameter, hijacking the metre of epic poetry, the highest genre, which recorded the exploits of heroes, kings, and generals. The inherent conflict between form and content must have been striking to the Roman ear. Although it is hard to reconstruct the content of the thirty

[8] See Raschke in *Hermes* 115:299–318 and *Latomus* 49:352–69.

books of Lucilius' Satires, some evidently contained medleys of several short poems, while others consisted of a single longer poem. He clearly used monologue, dialogue, and the letter form in his poems, with monologue the most prominent.

Lucilius established the repertoire of the genre. Most striking is his criticism of individuals. He attacks both eminent men and the more lowly for a variety of faults ranging from incompetence to arrogance. Elements of what may be termed "everyday life" feature prominently: the hustle and bustle of city life (1145–51W); feasting and drinking (1022–3W, 601–3W); morality, philosophy, and religion, including the longest surviving fragment, on *Virtus* ("excellence": 1196–1208W; also 1189–90W, 805–11W, 524–9W); literary issues (1085W, 1079–80W, 401–10W); and even matters of spelling (394–5W and 384–7W).

His Satires have a distinctive autobiographical presentation (for example, 650-1W), sometimes including criticism and irony at his own expense (as at 1183W, 635W, 1039W, 1131W), a characteristic to which Horace draws attention at *Satires* 2.1.30–34 (tr. N. Rudd, Penguin Classics, 1979, cf. 2.1.71–4): "In the past he would confide his secrets to his books, which he trusted like friends; and whether things went well or badly he'd always turn to them; in consequence, the whole of the old man's life is laid before us, as if it were painted on a votive tablet." In all these respects—form, content, presentation—Lucilius' Satires established a model which later satirists imitate, emulate, and develop.

His diction, however, is informal and unelevated, sometimes blunt and even obscene (354–5W, 1081W,

1183W), particularly in his descriptions of women, bodies, disease, and sex. A conversational flavour, highly suited to these "chats" (*sermones*), is generated by a repetitiveness and looseness of structure, features for which Horace criticises him (*Satires* 1.4.9–13, 1.10.50–64). Particularly distinctive is his use of Greek words and quotations, for a variety of effects (1048W, 267–8W). His characteristic vigour and aggression, which are represented in physical terms by later satirists (Persius 1.114–18, cf. Horace, *Satires* 1.10.3–4, 2.1.62–70; Juvenal 1.19–20 and 165–6), articulate a forceful assertion of Roman ideology, which his successors do not replicate.

After Lucilius, the next exponent of satire was Horace (Quintus Horatius Flaccus; 65–8 B.C.), writing at the end of the Roman Republic and beginning of the Principate. Although from a much humbler background—his father was a freedman, as he reminds his audience in *Satires* 1.6.45–6—he too moved in a politically charged environment by his association with Maecenas and Octavian (the future emperor Augustus). His poems in the genre of *satura*, which span his poetic career, *Satires* Book 1 (published 35–4 B.C.) and Book 2 (published 30–29), *Epistles* Book 1 (20–19) and Book 2 (hard to date), cover the same broad range of subjects as Lucilius, but have a more limited and refined vocabulary as well as a more modest tone and character.

In *Satires* Book 1, he presents himself as the new Lucilius, in literary and political terms, articulating the ideology of his circle. He takes Lucilius' autobiographical mode for a series of monologues in a conversational tone which presents a narrative sequence exploring issues of friendship, freedom, and power, and their relation to and expression in literature.[9] *Satires* 1.1–3 present Horace as a street-corner philosopher delivering strident lectures on popular morality. In *Satires* 1.4 he explicitly situates himself within the genre of satire: he claims to be following Lucilius' practice of criticising people's faults, but not his style, which he condemns for its verbosity; and he attributes his frankness to the upbringing he received from his father, thus marrying literary with moral credentials. This manifesto of his worth is portrayed as bringing the desired result: acceptance into the coterie surrounding Maecenas (*Satires* 1.4–6). He immediately adopts the values of his new friends and defends those values in social and literary matters (*Satires* 1.7–10). In the last poem of the Book he refines his earlier assessment of Lucilius and offers his own poetic manifesto: he values terseness, linguistic purity, humour, and appropriateness (*decorum*).

In *Satires* Book 2, Horace takes the dialogue form from Lucilius and develops it in a sophisticated way which places the onus of interpretation upon the audience. In this series of dialogues, Horace takes a passive role while the "wisdom" of others on the topics of literature (2.1), philosophy, and morality (2.2, 2.3, 2.5, 2.7) is exposed in sermons, lectures, and conversations. He plays "the Roman Socrates,"[10] in that he resembles Plato's portrayal of the philosopher who allows his interlocutors to pursue their ideas to the point of folly or impossibility. While friendship, freedom, and power remain important con-

[9] See Zetzel in *Arethusa* 13:59–77 and DuQuesnay in *Poetry and Politics in the Age of Augustus* 19–58.

[10] Anderson's expression in *Essays on Roman Satire* 41–9.

cerns, food is the dominant theme (2.2, 2.4, 2.6, 2.8), re-
working a prominent theme of Lucilius.

After writing his famous lyric poems, the *Odes*, Horace
returns to satire by adopting the letter form in *Epistles*
Book 1, producing an artfully arranged assemblage of
twenty "letters." This is a vehicle for a mature and worldly
adviser to share his wisdom on questions of education, phi-
losophy, literature, friendship, leisure, and etiquette with a
variety of addressees mostly junior to him in years or sta-
tus, but also including his friend and patron Maecenas.
The chief positive ideals which emerge belong to no single
philosophical school: tolerance, tranquillity, and indepen-
dence.[11]

Epistles Book 2 is similar, but shifts towards a more di-
dactic pose by Horace. *Epistles* 2.1, addressed to Augustus
himself, *Epistles* 2.2, addressed to Florus (a young man of
Tiberius' circle of friends), and also the so-called *Ars poeti-
ca*, addressed to members of the Piso family aspiring to be
poets, feature themes familiar from *Satires* and *Epistles*
Book 1: morality, education, literature and philosophy,
friendship and right conduct. *Epistles* Book 2 can be read
as a celebration of the Augustan ideal, continuing the ear-
lier unelevated, conversational tone and incorporating il-
lustrations from many varied activities together with the
autobiographical mode of presentation.

Horace has taken the genre he inherited from Lucilius
and refined it to be an instrument of contemporary ideol-
ogy. The aggression of Lucilius lies well beneath the sur-
face in Horace, covered with a veneer of humility which

[11] See McGann *Studies in Horace's First Book of Epistles* and
Kilpatrick *The Poetry of Friendship*.

has persuaded or seduced many readers into acquiescence with his perspective and his standards. Horace's subtlety and indirection are adeptly characterised by Persius in lines 116–18 from his first Satire quoted above.

Persius

Aules (or possibly Aulus) Persius Flaccus (A.D. 34–62) was born a Roman *eques* in Etruria into an important family of high status. A plausible-looking biography (*Vita*) transmitted among Suetonius' *Lives of the Poets* perhaps derives "from the commentary of Valerius Probus," a first century grammarian from Berytus. Persius received his education at Rome as a pupil of the Stoic Lucius Annaeus Cornutus, who was a freedman of the family of Seneca, and he was linked with other important individuals of Stoic leanings, including Thrasea Paetus, who was married to Persius' relative Arria. The epic poet Lucan, nephew of Seneca, a younger but precocious contemporary, greatly admired Persius' poems. His book of fewer than seven hundred lines of Latin, probably unfinished when he died, consists of six Satires preceded by a prologue in the choliambic metre. The poems are packed with literary echoes and allusions, showing an intimate familiarity with the satirical works of Lucilius and Horace. At the same time they are fresh and original, thanks to Persius' creation of the character of an angry and alienated young man. His friend Caesius Bassus, addressee of Satire 6, published Persius' Satires posthumously, apparently after a little tidying up by Cornutus, which most famously involved the replacement of line 121 in Satire 1, allegedly "King Midas has donkey's ears," with "Is there anyone who does not have donkey's ears?" to avoid the risk of insulting Nero.

Persius presents a stance of scornful isolation in the Prologue, where he depicts himself as not a full member of the guild of bards and rejects their poetic imagery of inspiration. His rebelliousness is marked by his choice of the choliambic metre, associated with a long Greek tradition of invective dating from the seventh and sixth centuries B.C. in the hands of Archilochus and Hipponax, renowned in antiquity for the damage they could inflict with their words, even to the extent of driving people to suicide. This stance is confirmed by the opening lines of Satire 1, where Persius appears content with a tiny audience, and is maintained by his wholesale rejection of contemporary poetry on the grounds that it is too smooth, weak, and artificial. This develops into a broader attack on the moral spinelessness of contemporary society.

The rejection of society and its standards is maintained throughout the Satires. Frequently the ideal of independence and self-reliance is expressed in the uncompromising terms of extreme Stoicism, which is Persius' idiom. The intolerance of contemporary literature and morality expressed in Satire 1 is followed by an intolerant condemnation of the hypocrisy and foolishness of people's prayers in Satire 2. In the third Satire an angry young student who appears to have lapsed receives a lecture on the madness of people who will not allow philosophy to help them. Satire 4 uses Socrates as the voice of self-knowledge in conversation with his young pupil, the politician Alcibiades, whose glibness and lack of exprience is attacked. The poem's central message is a graphic illustration of the ancient Delphic maxim "Know Yourself." Satire 5 is the longest in the book. It begins in a strongly autobiographical mode with a personal tribute to Cornutus, Persius' instructor in Stoicism, closely modelled in literary terms upon Horace's presentation of his relationship with his father (*Satires* 1.4 and 1.6), and incorporates a substantial sermon on the theme of freedom (treated in Horace, *Satires* 2.7), delivered from an extreme Stoic viewpoint. The sixth Satire is presented as an epistle (following the tradition of Lucilius and Horace) in which withdrawal from Rome to the coast is the logical consequence and physical realisation of the isolation proclaimed throughout the book. The aggressive attitude Persius adopts in the poem towards his heir continues the theme of independence and detachment to the end of the book.

Persius' Latin is extremely difficult. It is marked by a dense literary texture and startling and at times humorous juxtapositions of images. He puts into Cornutus' mouth at 5.14–16 a characterisation of his style:

> verba togae sequeris iunctura callidus acri,
> ore teres modico, pallentis radere mores
> doctus et ingenuo culpam defigere ludo.

"You pursue the language of the toga, skilled at the pointed combination, rounded with moderate utterance, clever at scraping sick morals and at nailing fault with well-bred wit." The crucial phrase here is *iunctura callidus acri*: Persius' compressed language and startling images frequently overturn or rejuvenate literary and philosophical clichés and commonplaces. For example, in the Prologue and the opening of Satire 5, he satirises the conventional

language of poetic inspiration through an overly literal interpretation of the metaphors of founts of inspiration and dreams and voices, mouths, and tongues. Some of the images are designed to ridicule their victims by puncturing pretentiousness and unveiling the hypocrisy of people's behaviour and aspirations. Another function is to provide a source of unity to individual poems. The theme of Satire 1—Style is the Man, a Stoic notion also explored by Seneca in *Epistle* 114 (e.g. *talis hominibus fuit oratio qualis vita*, 114.1), which argues that literary style is an indicator of morality—is conveyed through images drawn from disease, clothing, food and drink, homosexuality and effeminacy.[12] Sexual imagery equates the politician with the male prostitute in Satire 4. The dominant metaphor of Satire 3 is that of disease, spiritual and physical, while in Satire 5 the central theme of freedom and slavery is explored with imagery drawn from shadow and substance, food, astrology, and numerology.[13] In Satire 2 the theme of bribery of the gods is associated physically with food, and Satire 6 again uses imagery of food, including the banquet of life. Throughout, the imagery is an important element of Persius' rejection of society: his subjects are deglamourised by the startling, shocking metaphors. Persius' angry young man and his graphic language are his most original contributions to the genre. Whether he exerted an influence on the writings of Turnus, a poet writing under Domitian whom Quintilian perhaps includes in his category of "eminent satirists today who will be celebrated in

[12] As Bramble has demonstrated in *Persius* esp. 26–59.
[13] See Dessen *"Iunctura Callidus Acri"* on Persius' imagery.

the future" (*Institutio Oratoria* 10.1.94), we cannot tell. But it is evident that, another generation later, Juvenal was familiar with his Satires.

Juvenal

Virtually nothing is known for sure about the life and circumstances of Juvenal. It is not even certain that the name we use, Decimus Iunius Iuvenalis, is correct. The ancient biographies and their more recent counterparts seem worthless, offering simplistic constructions from details in the Satires, a method which fails to take account of the generic convention of using the first person. For example, there is no convincing evidence for his alleged exile to Egypt by Domitian, nor can his poems be used to deduce that he was an impoverished client or a misogynist.[14] An inscription found at Aquinum which was believed to depict Juvenal as commander of a Dalmatian cohort cannot be regarded as reliable evidence either. The inscription, which disappeared long ago, recorded the dedication of an altar to Ceres by one Iu**** Iuvenalis, a tribune in a Dalmatian cohort, *duumvir quinquennalis* and *flamen* of Vespasian (*CIL* 10.5382). Those who have wanted to identify this individual with our poet have made much of the passage at the close of Satire 3 in which Umbricius talks of coming to Aquinum to visit him and "Helvius' Ceres and your Diana"(3.319–20). But apart from the problem of the partial preservation of the name and the disappearance of the inscription, the dating is difficult, since all other indicators suggest a significantly later date for Juvenal.

[14] See Highet *Juvenal the Satirist*.

18

Yet there are a few fixable dates that occur in the Satires. He refers to the murder of Domitian (A.D. 96) at 4.153. At 1.49–50 he mentions the condemnation of Marius Priscus for extortion (A.D. 100). Satire 7 seems to celebrate new possibilities of patronage, and may be associated with Hadrian's accession to power in A.D. 117. In Satire 13 his sixty-year-old addressee is said to have been born when Fonteius was consul, which could be the years A.D. 58, 59, or 67, giving a dramatic date for the poem of 118, 119, or 127. Finally, Satire 15 refers to events which took place "recently," in the consulship of Iuncus, that is, in A.D. 127, and though Juvenal uses the term *nuper* with exceeding fluidity (e.g. at 2.29 it refers to an outrage committed perhaps twenty years earlier), this could give a date in the late 120s or into the 130s for Juvenal's last complete Satire. It is prudent, then, to remember that, as Syme says, there is a "scarcity of facts" in this field, although that has not prevented its being "infested with credulity and romance."[15] Syme's own assessment of the little evidence afforded by Juvenal's name and the poems leads him to suggest, tentatively, an African origin.

Juvenal is the addressee of three epigrams by Martial (7.24, 7.91, 12.18) which were written in A.D. 92 and 101–2. Martial refers to Juvenal's oratorical skill (7.91.1: *facundo*) and depicts him living a hectic life in Rome (12.18.1–6). This is appropriate, since his Satires certainly reflect the rhetorical training received by members of the Roman elite. The fact that the Satires are not dedicated to any patron may indicate that he was of relatively high social status, like Lucilius and Persius. The few dateable ref-

[15] Syme in *Roman Papers III* 1133–34.

erences mentioned above confirm Syme's view that the five Books were written during the second and third decades of the 2nd century A.D., at about the same time as Tacitus was writing his *Annals*, which seem strikingly similar in their biting tone.

Juvenal is chiefly renowned for his savage indignation, *saeva indignatio* (Scaliger's phrase), a tone of voice which he perhaps developed from Persius' creation of the angry young man; from the maniacal fanatics in Horace's *Satires* Book 2; and from Lucilius' aggressiveness. It is this that has determined the essential idea of "satire" ever since. Juvenal's particular innovation is to forge for his satire a "Grand Style" very different from that of the lowly "conversations" of Horace.[16] He thus makes his satire challenge and rival epic discourse. But it is less often appreciated that Juvenal experimented with satire as he continued to write and that he was continually developing and modifying his satiric persona. The simple anger of the early persona (Satires 1–6) gives way to a more ironic view of the world which perceives two sides to any issue (Satires 7–12); this ironic view finally dissolves into a superior cynicism (Satires 13–16). The condemnation of humankind in Satires 1–5 and Satires 13–16 has to some seemed similar—but Juvenal has not simply come full circle. Rather, the condemnation of humankind in the later Satires is delivered from a higher plane of aloofness than that in the earlier.

Juvenal's Satires were written for a sophisticated audience well educated in rhetoric and Greek and Latin literature. The influence of rhetoric and declamation is obvious

---

[16] On the Grand Style see Scott *The Grand Style*.

in his tone of indignation and in the many "commonplaces" (*loci communes*) which pepper the Satires. On a larger scale, too, the poems are shaped by standard types of declamatory speech,[17] for example, speeches of persuasion to or from a particular course of action (Satires 5 and 6) and speeches of welcome (Satire 12), departure (Satire 3), and consolation (Satire 13), although usually with a parodic intention. The strongest literary influence, apart from earlier satire, is that of epic, with tragedy, comedy, elegy, and epigram important, too. The intertextual relationship with epic is most obvious in the parodic narratives which Juvenal incorporates into Satires 4 and 12, but also in other features such as the apparently unprecedented size of Satire 6 and the frequent interface with classic moments from ancient epic, such as the Underworld scenes in Satires 2 and 3. The striking presence of rhetoric and epic in Juvenal's satire puts it in a different category from previous satire.

There is no reason to doubt that the Satires were written and published in Books. Books One and Two of Juvenal's Satires, probably written in the second decade of the second century A.D., towards the end of Trajan's reign or, possibly, soon after Hadrian's accession in 117, present the angry persona for which Juvenal is best known. Book One, which contains Satires 1–5, handles a number of familiar themes of Roman satire with a particular emphasis on public life, the male sphere of action. Central themes include the patron-client relationship (Satires 1, 3, and 5), the

17 On the influence of declamation, see Cairns *Generic Composition* and Braund *Juvenal Satires Book I* 18–21. On Satire 6, see Braund in *Journal of Roman Studies* 82:71–86.

disappointments, inconveniences, and dangers of life in Rome (Satire 3), the hypocrisy and moral bankruptcy of the aristocracy (Satire 2), and the horrors of life in the court of the emperor Domitian, including the courtiers' craven flattery and the emperor's abuse of his most eminent citizens (Satire 4). In Book Two, by contrast, which consists of one enormous poem, Satire 6, the focus is upon private life and family life, with women as the primary victims of the satire. The central argument against marriage builds a fantasy picture of the folly and depravity of Roman wives. The two Books together make a complementary pair presenting a massive indictment of Roman life broader in scope than anything attempted by Horace or Persius. Juvenal's satiric mask or persona in Books One and Two is essentially that of an extremist and a chauvinist who sees every issue in stark black and white and who becomes passionate in his condemnation of those who offend his simplistic morality. Juvenal indicates the limitations of this character by exposing the contradictions between his view of himself as a morally pure and superior being and the more objective view of him as a narrow-minded bigot.

Book Three (Satires 7–9), which appears to have been written early in Hadrian's reign, presents a shift away from the earlier angry personality. Juvenal's new satiric persona takes a complex, double view instead of the simplistic outlook in the first two Books, while continuing the central themes of the earlier Satires. Satires 7 and 9 develop further the treatment of the patron-client relationship explored in Satires 1, 3, and 5, while Satire 8, on the uselessness of pedigrees without morality, develops the theme of corruption at the centre of Roman life, reminiscent of Satires 2 and 4. All the poems have an ironic and detached presentation, with Satire 7 hardly arousing sympathy for the inept poets and teachers Juvenal describes and with the disgusting Naevolus in Satire 9 alienating any remaining sympathy for downtrodden clients.

In Book Four (Satires 10–12), Juvenal declares a new program and approach. At the beginning of Satire 10, the philosophers Democritus and Heraclitus are presented as antithetical models of viewing the world: Juvenal clearly endorses the cheerfulness of Democritus over the tears of Heraclitus. Satire 10 is a carefully constructed condemnation of the foolishness of human prayers; Satire 11 shifts into epistolary mode to deliver an invitation to dinner after a satirical condemnation of human inconsistency; Satire 12 celebrates a demonstration of true friendship in contrast with the false friendship exhibited by greedy legacy-hunters. The familiar topics of the first three Books—friendship, power, corruption, wealth—appear again, but significantly altered. Juvenal's satiric persona is an explicit advocate of Democritean tranquillity and ironic detachment.

Juvenal's fifth Book (Satires 13–16, the last unfinished), which dates from after A.D. 127, takes the experiment further. He rejects anger in Satire 13—the addressee's petty overreaction to being defrauded by a friend of a small sum of money—and Satire 15, in the form of a religious feud which leads to a horrific act of mob cannibalism. In Satire 14 he offers an elaborate disquisition on the inculcation of avarice in children by their parents; and in the incomplete Satire 16 protests against the privileges enjoyed by military men. Juvenal's satiric personality here is more cynical than in Book Four, and the strong overlay of philosophy in his discourse conveys a superiority over the whole of humanity.

All the characters whom Juvenal created to deliver their epic- and tragic-style condemnations of the world have moral flaws. In the case of the chauvinist or the misogynist, the flaw is obvious; in the case of the more complex ironic personalities in the later Satires, their aloofness, nihilism, and cynicism are repugnant. Juvenal in effect has set up a tension between his first person approach, which tends to draw the audience into sympathy with the opinions expressed, and the audience's realisation that the things they are assenting to are morally dubious or even reprehensible. This tension, so characteristic of satire, makes it dangerous and exciting: there is always more than one way of reading satire.

The Influence of Persius and Juvenal

Of the many personae of Roman satire, it was Juvenal's articulation of *indignatio* that exercised the strongest influence on subsequent satire. Once satire was regarded as the angry unmasking of faults and vices rather than anything more complicated, it became acceptable to Christian ideology. Both Persius and Juvenal contained much in the way of instant moralising that could readily be assimilated to the Christian point of view, and it is clear that Christian writers such as Jerome and Augustine were familiar with the Satires. Consequently, Latin satire is well represented in the Middle Ages. Charlemagne's library in the ninth century possessed copies of both Persius and Juvenal, and from then on the satirists feature in the educational curriculum. The influence they exercised was enormous. Juvenal, for example, was called a sage by Chaucer and was a source of epigrams for Erasmus. In Italy, Boccaccio imitated his sixth Satire, and in France and Spain there were poets writing close adaptations of passages from Juvenal. Gradually the hexameter form was abandoned and "satire" came to include poetry with a satiric tone in a variety of forms. An important exception to this is the formal verse satire that flourished in the Elizabethan and Jacobean periods. Poets including John Donne, John Marston, and Joseph Hall all wrote satire recognisably in the Roman tradition, heavily indebted to Persius and Juvenal in the uncompromising aggression and violence of their attacks. In the later seventeenth and eighteenth centuries, Dryden, Boileau, Pope, and Samuel Johnson all reflect the powerful influence of Juvenal in their translations, imitations, and original satires. Juvenal also influenced dramatists including Ben Jonson, Molière, and Corneille. Since then, the idea of satire has widened from the narrow framework of Roman hexameter satire to denote essentially a fiercely critical tone of voice. Even though the genre of Roman verse satire no longer enjoys any currency, its legacy in unmistakable.

The Text and Transmission of Persius

Persius' little book of Satires, if the testimony of the ancient biography can be believed, was edited, after his early death at the age of thirty, by his mentor Annaeus Cornutus, and handed over for publication to another friend, the poet Caesius Bassus. It is reported as an instant hit. Certainly, within a generation his book won high praise from the rhetorician and literary critic Quintilian (*Institutio Oratoria* 10.1.94: *multum et verae gloriae quamvis uno libro Persius meruit*, "Although he wrote only one book Persius has won a high and well-deserved reputation") and from the epigrammatist Martial (4.29.7–8: *saepius in libro numerantur Persius uno / quam levis in tota Marsus Amazonide*, "Persius more often wins credit in a single book than trivial Marsus in his whole tale of Amazons"). Clearly, the transmission of the Satires was assured from an early time. The stability of Persius' reputation is demonstrated by his influence upon the Church fathers, such as Lactantius, Augustine, and Jerome. In the fourth century Ausonius imitated him, in the fifth Sidonius Apollinaris contrasted his *rigor* with the charm of Propertius, and in the sixth the Byzantine critic John Lydus commented on the obscurity of his writings. Manuscripts of Persius survived through the Dark Ages into the Carolingian Renaissance, from which point the Satires were a staple on the curriculum, a fact that is borne out by the abundance of manuscripts from the ninth century onwards.

There exist perhaps more than one hundred and fifty MSS of Persius, according to D. Bo in his 1969 edition (page vii). Of these, the most important are the ninth-century MS known as P and, from the same period, the closely related pair known as A and B. P (Montpellier 125) is the Pithoeanus, the MS owned by Pithou which also contains the Satires of Juvenal, which for some time stole the limelight in the textual criticism of Juvenal. In this MS the choliambics of Persius are added in later handwriting, before the text of the Satires. The pair A (tenth century, also in Montpellier) and B (ninth century, in the Vatican) are so closely related that they must derive from the same source, here designated α. Both present the choliambics after the Satires, and both include a record of the text having been edited by someone called Sabinus in Barcelona in 402. Of similar age and reliability is the ninth century MS from St Gall which excerpts 40 lines from Persius along with 280 from Juvenal. Older than all the above is the palimpsest fragment from Bobbio written in the sixth century, probably in Italy, which unfortunately contains only some 50 lines of Satire 1 along with a similar portion of Juvenal. Two other significant MSS, both also held in the Vatican, are V, which contains part of Satire 3, Satires 4–6, the Life (*Vita*) of Persius, and a fragment of the so-called *Commentum Cornuti*, an ancient commentary; and X, which contains the choliambics and most of Satires 1–5. Though the above offer a sound enough basis for the establishment of the text, Clausen selects a further seven of the inferior MSS as worthy of mention, all of which contain the choliambics and the Satires, and several the Life and the *Commentum Cornuti*. There is a clear consensus that the construction of a stemma for the MSS of Persius is impossible because of the complexity of the process of transmission. Here is a list of the MSS mentioned above:

P	Montpellier medical school 125 (ninth century, Lorsch)
A	Montpellier medical school 212 (tenth century, French)
B	Vatican, Arch. S. Pietro H. 36 (ninth century, French)
α	Denotes consensus of A and B
Sang.	St Gall 870 (ninth century florilegium; includes 40 lines of Persius)

Bob.	Vatican 5750, a palimpsest fragment containing Satire 1.53–104 (sixth century, probably Italy)
V	Vatican, Reg. lat. 1560 (tenth century, Fleury/Auxerre)
X	Vatican, Pal. lat. 1710 (second half of the ninth century, Tours area)
C	Paris Lat. 8055 (tenth century, southern France)
G	Berne 257 (early tenth century, France)
L	Leiden, B.P.L. 78 (eleventh century; includes *Vita* and *Commentum Cornuti*)
M	Munich 23577 (eleventh century; includes *Vita* and *Commentum Cornuti;* but parts of Satires 4 and 5 are missing)
N	Munich 14498 (eleventh century, written in the monastery of St Emmeran in Regensburg; includes Vita)
R	Florence, Laur. 37.19 (tenth–eleventh centuries; includes abridged *Vita*)
W	Munich 330 (tenth century, Germany)
S	Denotes consensus of the lemmata

In addition the ancient scholia, Σ, found in L and M above along with U (Munich 14482, from the eleventh–twelfth centuries), can sometimes assist in textual matters.

The first edition of Persius was published in Rome in 1470, and (as in the case of Juvenal) Pithou used his superior MS P as the basis for his 1585 edition in Paris, which set the standard for the future. During the seventeenth century Isaac Casaubon produced three editions (culminating in his 3rd, dated 1647, published in London). The next major advance was Otto Jahn's edition of 1843 (Leipzig), to which modern scholars still refer. John Conington's

edition (3rd edition, 1893, Oxford) is of interest more for
its parallel translation and commentary than its text, and it
was not until W. V. Clausen turned his attention to the text
that further significant progress was made. Clausen has
been able to take into account a wider range of evidence
than Jahn in his editions, first in a separate text of Persius
(Oxford, 1956) and then in the Oxford Classical Text of
Juvenal and Persius published in 1959 and revised in 1992.
This new edition for the Loeb Classical Library is closely
based upon the 1992 OCT.

For fuller accounts of text and transmission, see the ar-
ticle "Persius" by P. K. Marshall in *Texts and Transmission*
ed. L. D. Reynolds (Oxford, 1983), the introduction to D.
Bo's 1969 edition (Paravia), and above all the relevant sec-
tions of Clausen's OCT.

The Text and Transmission of Juvenal

The early reception of Juvenal seems very different from
that of Persius. Martial is the only contemporary to men-
tion him. Whether or not this implies that his Satires were
badly received is difficult to say. From then he virtually
disappears until the fourth century, when Lactantius (c.
240–320) quotes him by name (*Div. Inst.* 3.29 = *PL* VI
443B). He is cited more than seventy times in Servius'
commentaries on Virgil, and at some time between 352
and 399 the Satires were edited and published with a com-
mentary. By the end of the fourth century, he was very
popular, as indicated by the imitations of Ausonius (died
c. 395) and others. The historian Ammianus reports that
at the end of the fourth century he was read by people
who read no other poetry (28.4.14: *quidam detestantes ut*

venena doctrinas, Iuvenalem et Marium Maximum cura-
tiore studio legunt, nulla volumina praeter haec in profun-
do otio contrectantes). Thereafter his survival was not in
jeopardy. The Satires were present in the library of Charle-
magne, which was established during the ninth century,
and, together with the Satires of Persius, manuscripts cir-
culated widely. More than five hundred MSS of Juvenal
survive. The first printed edition appeared in the late
1460s in Rome, and in 1486 Valla's transcription of the
commentary on Juvenal by "Probus grammaticus" was
published in Venice. Many more editions of the Satires fol-
lowed during the next hundred years, but it was not until
1585 that Pithou published the text based on the superior
Pithoeanus MS (P below).

As early as the fourth century, a number of spurious
lines were present in the text and therefore persisted in the
later MSS which form the majority in the transmission of
Juvenal. A much smaller group of MSS and fragments are
freer from interpolation, although corrupt in other ways.
Between them, these provide a broad basis for establishing
the text. In the smaller group are the following:

P: Montpellier medical school 125. This MS was writ-
ten at Lorsch in the ninth century.

Arov. Fragmenta Aroviensia, five leaves of a tenth-
century German MS containing parts of 2.148–
7.172, virtually identical to P.

Sang. St Gall 870. A ninth-century florilegium includ-
ing 280 lines of Juvenal and the ancient scholia.

S: Lemmata of the ancient scholia preserved in P,
Arov., and Sang. The older scholia have been edited
by P. Wessner in his 1931 Teubner (Leipzig).

R: Parisinus Latinus 8072. A tenth-century MS, possi-
bly French, containing 1.1–2.66, 3.32–6.437.

V: Vienna 107. A ninth-century MS containing 1.1–
2.59, 3.107–5.96, but influenced by readings from
the interpolated category of MSS.

The larger group of MSS showing interpolations cannot
easily be organised into a stemma because of the degree of
contamination. Clausen uses the following representatives
of this class in his Oxford Classical Text, calling the consen-
sus of these Φ:

A   Munich 408 (eleventh century, Germany)

F   Paris Lat. 8071 (ninth century, France)

G   Paris Lat. 7900 (ninth–tenth century)

H   Paris Lat. 9345 (tenth century, Cluny)

K   Laurentianus 34.42 (eleventh century,
Florence)

L   Leiden B.P.L. 82 (eleventh century)

O   Oxford, Bodleian Library Canon. Class. Lat. 41
(eleventh–twelfth century, south Italy)

T   Cambridge, Trinity College 1241 (O 4.10) (tenth
century, England)

U   Vatican, Urb. Lat. 661 (eleventh century, Ger-
many)

Z   London, British Museum/Library Add. 15600
(ninth century, France)

In addition, some ancient readings are preserved in frag-
ments of ancient books, as follows:

Ambr., containing 14.250–6, 268–91, 303–19 (sixth
century)

Ant., containing 7.149–98 (c. 500)

Aur., containing 2.32–89, 3.35–93

> Bob., containing 14.324–15.43 plus a similar amount
> of Persius in palimpsest (Vatican 5750, sixth cen-
> tury, probably Italy)

Finally, there is the 1486 edition in Venice by George Valla
of what he claimed to be the commentary of the grammar-
ian Probus on Juvenal (Probus Vallae); and Σ denotes the
scholia.

After Pithou's publication of the P MS in the sixteenth
century, the next landmarks were Ruperti's commentary of
1801 and Jahn's 1851 text, based upon the rediscovered P.
Two events called the authority of P into doubt. In 1859
Ribbeck labelled about one third of the transmitted text as
spurious, thus provoking closer scrutiny. And in 1899 an
Oxford undergraduate discovered thirty-four lines of Sat-
ire 6 in a MS of the eleventh century in the Bodleian Li-
brary (O) which do not survive in any other existing MS.
But most scholars, including Bücheler (1886, 1893) and
Friedländer (1895), continued to accept the transmitted
text and to accept the authority of P implicitly. In response
to this, Housman in the Preface to his magisterial edition
(1905, second edition 1931) explicated the issues facing
editors of Juvenal (and of other Latin texts) in typically
trenchant form. The central decision is the balance be-
tween P and Φ: the reading of P may be corrupt but that of
Φ may be an interpolation. Another issue is the identifica-
tion of spurious lines, some of which are present even in
the P class of MSS. It would be rash to say that a consensus
has arisen since Housman's edition, but Knoche's text
(1950), based on his full collation of all the important
MSS, the Oxford Classical Text of W. V. Clausen (1959, re-
vised 1992), and the editions of E. Courtney (Edizioni
dell'Ateneo, Rome 1984) and J. R. C. Martyn (Hakkert,

Amsterdam 1987) show few significant differences except in matters of punctuation. One dissenter from this unanimity is J. Willis whose Teubner edition (Leipzig, 1997) invites a more thorough and radical rethink. Though he cannot quite be styled a new Ribbeck, he excises or casts doubt over many lines and passages. Most notable is the suspicion he raises over the whole Crispinus section of Satire 4 (lines 1–36) and, following Reeve, over the most famous words from Juvenal, *mens sana in corpore sano* (10.356). This new edition for the Loeb Classical Library is broadly based upon the 1992 OCT. In a number of places, I have adopted different readings and punctuations and these are noted in the apparatus. For a fuller apparatus, I refer the reader not only to Clausen's OCT, which is often very sketchy, but also to Willis' much more compendious edition.

For fuller accounts of the text and transmission of Juvenal, see the article "Juvenal" by R. J. Tarrant in *Texts and Transmission* ed. L. D. Reynolds (Oxford, 1983) and the relevant sections of Clausen's OCT, Courtney's commentary, and Martyn's edition. This account of the text and transmission of Juvenal is expanded and updated from my account in my Cambridge Greek and Latin Classics commentary on Juvenal Book One.

SELECT BIBLIOGRAPHY

Editions and Commentaries

Bo, D.: *A. Persi Flacci Saturarum Liber* (Paravia, Turin, 1969)

Braund, S. M.: *Juvenal Satires Book I* (Cambridge, 1996)

Clausen, W. V.: *A. Persi Flacci et D. Iuni Iuvenalis Saturae* (Oxford, 1959, rev. edn. 1992)

Clausen, W. V.: *A. Persi Flacci Saturarum Liber* (Oxford, 1956)

Conington, J.: *The Satires of A. Persius Flaccus,* ed. H. Nettleship (2nd ed. 1874 Oxford, 3rd ed. 1893, repr. 1967 Hildesheim)

Courtney, E.: *A Commentary on the Satires of Juvenal* (London, 1980)

Courtney, E.: *Juvenal the Satires* (Rome, 1984)

Duff, J. D.: *Fourteen Satires of Juvenal* (1898, repr. Cambridge, 1970)

Ferguson, J.: *Juvenal. The Satires* (New York, 1979)

Friedländer, L.: *D. Junii Juvenalis Saturarum Libri V* (Leipzig, 1895)

Harvey, R. A.: *A Commentary on Persius* (Leiden, 1981)

Housman, A. E.: *D. Iunii Iuvenalis Saturae* (Cambridge, 2nd edn., 1931)

Jahn, O.: *Persii, Iuuenalis, Sulpiciae Saturae* (Leipzig, 1843)

Jenkinson, J. R.: *Persius: The Satires* (Warminster, 1980)

Knoche, U.: *D. Iunius Juvenalis Saturae* (Munich, 1950)

Lee, G., and W. Barr: *The Satires of Persius* (Liverpool, 1987)

Martyn, J. R. C.: *D. Iuni Iuvenalis Saturae* (Amsterdam, 1987)

Mayor, J. E. B.: *Thirteen Satires of Juvenal* (3rd and 4th edn., Cambridge, 1881–6)

Wessner, P.: *Scholia in Iuvenalem* (Stuttgart, 1967)

Willis, J.: *D. Iunii Iuvenalis Saturae Sedecim* (Stuttgart and Leipzig, 1997)

INTRODUCTION

Translations

Gifford, W.: *Juvenal Satires with the Satires of Persius* (1802 and 1821, new edn. London, 1992)

Green, P.: *Juvenal. The Sixteen Satires* (Penguin Classics, 1967, revised 1999)

Holyday, B.: *Decimus Junius Juvenalis and Aulus Persius Flaccus Translated* (Oxford, 1673)

Lee, G., and W. Barr: *The Satires of Persius* (Liverpool, 1987)

Lewis, J. D.: *D. Iunii Iuvenalis Satirae* (London, 1873)

Ramsay, G. G.: *Juvenal and Persius* (Loeb Classical Library, London and New York, 1918, rev. 1940)

Robinson, S.: *Juvenal: Sixteen Satires upon the Ancient Harlot* (Manchester, 1983)

Rudd, N.: *Horace: Satires and Epistles. Persius: Satires* (Penguin Classics, 1987)

Rudd, N.: *Juvenal. The Satires* (Oxford, 1991)

Warmington, E. H.: *Remains of Old Latin Vol. 1: Lucilius and The Twelve Tables* (Loeb Classical Library, Cambridge, Mass. and London, 1938; rev. 1967)

Books and Articles on Satire

Elliott, R. C.: *The Power of Satire: Magic, Ritual, Art* (Princeton, 1960)

Feinberg, L.: *The Satirist* (Ames, Iowa, 1963)

Frye, N.: "The Nature of Satire" *University of Toronto Quarterly* 14 (1944) 75–89

Frye, N.: *Anatomy of Criticism: Four Essays* (Princeton, 1957)

Hodgart, M.: *Satire* (Verona, 1969)

Kernan, A.: *The Cankered Muse: Satire of the English Renaissance* (New Haven, 1959)

Books and Articles on Roman Satire, Lucilius, Horace

Adams, J. N.: *The Latin Sexual Vocabulary* (London, 1982)

Anderson, W. S.: *Essays on Roman Satire* (Princeton, 1982)

Braund, S. H. (ed.): *Satire and Society in Ancient Rome* (Exeter, 1989)

Braund, S. H.: *Roman Verse Satire* (Greece and Rome New Surveys in the Classics no. 23, Oxford, 1992)

Braund, S. M.: *The Roman Satirists and Their Masks* (London, 1996)

Braund, S. M., and B. Gold (edd.): *Vile Bodies: Roman Satire and Corporeal Discourse, Arethusa* 31.3 (1998)

Cairns, F.: *Generic Composition in Greek and Roman Poetry* (Edinburgh, 1972)

Classen, C. J.: "Satire—The Elusive Genre" *Symbolae Osloenses* 63 (1988) 95–121

Coffey, M.: *Roman Satire* (1976; 2nd edn. Bristol, 1989)

DuQuesnay, I. M. Le M.: "Horace and Maecenas: The Propaganda Value of *Sermones* I," in *Poetry and Politics in the Age of Augustus,* edd. T. Woodman and D. West (Cambridge, 1984), 19–58

Edwards, C.: *The Politics of Immorality in Ancient Rome* (Cambridge, 1993)

Fiske, G. C.: *Lucilius and Horace* (Madison, 1920, repr. 1970 Westport)

Freudenburg, K.: *The Walking Muse. Horace on the Theory of Satire* (Princeton, 1993)

Freudenburg, K.: *Satires of Rome: Threatening Poses from Lucilius to Juvenal* (Cambridge, 2001)

Gowers, E.: *The Loaded Table. Representations of Food in Roman Satire* (Oxford, 1993)

Kilpatrick, R. S.: *The Poetry of Friendship: Horace Epistles I* (Edmonton, 1986)

Kilpatrick, R. S.: *The Poetry of Criticism: Horace, Epistles II* (Edmonton, 1989)

Knoche, U.: *Roman Satire* tr. E. S. Ramage (Bloomington and London, 1975)

Lafleur, R. A.: "Horace and *Onomasti Komodein*: The Law of Satire," in *Aufstieg und Niedergang der römischen Welt* II.31.3 (1981) 1790–1826

McGann, M. J.: *Studies in Horace's First Book of Epistles* (Brussels, 1969)

Miller, P. A., and C. Platter (edd.): *Bakhtin and Ancient Studies: Dialogues and Dialogics, Arethusa* 26.2 (1993)

Ramage, E. S., D. I. Sigsbee, and S. C. Fredericks: *Roman Satirists and Their Satire* (Park Ridge, New Jersey, 1974)

Raschke, W. J.: "*Arma pro amico*—Lucilian Satire at the Crisis of the Roman Republic" *Hermes* 115 (1987) 299–318

Raschke, W. J.: "The Virtue of Lucilius" *Latomus* 49 (1990) 352–69

Richlin, A.: "Invective Against Women in Roman Satire" *Arethusa* 17 (1984) 67–80

Richlin, A.: *The Garden of Priapus. Sexuality and Aggression in Roman Humor* (rev. edn. New York and Oxford, 1992)

Rudd, N.: *The Satires of Horace* (Bristol, 1982)

Rudd, N.: *Themes in Roman Satire* (London, 1986)

Rudd, N.: *Horace Epistles Book II and Epistle to the Pisones ("Ars Poetica")* (Cambridge, 1989)

Sullivan, J. P. (ed.): *Critical Essays on Roman Literature, Vol. II: Satire* (London, 1963)

Van Rooy, C. A.; *Studies in Classical Satire and Related Literary Theory* (Leiden, 1965)

Witke, C.: *Latin Satire: The Structure of Persuasion* (Leiden, 1970)

Zetzel, J. E. G.: "Horace's *Liber Sermonum*: The Structure of Ambiguity" *Arethusa* 13 (1980) 59–77

Books and Articles on Persius and Juvenal

Bramble, J. C.: *Persius and the Programmatic Satire* (Cambridge, 1974)

Bramble, J. C.: "Martial and Juvenal," in *The Cambridge History of Classical Literature II: Latin Literature* edd. E. J. Kenney and W. V. Clausen (Cambridge, 1982) 597–623

Braund, S. H.: *Beyond Anger: A Study of Juvenal's Third Book of Satires* (Cambridge, 1988)

Braund, S. H.: "Juvenal—Misogynist or Misogamist?" *Journal of Roman Studies* 82 (1992) 71–86

Cloud, J. D., and S. H. Braund: "Juvenal's Libellus—A Farrago?" *Greece and Rome* 29 (1982) 77–85

De Decker, J.: *Juvenalis Declamans: Etude sur la Rhétorique Déclamatoire dans les Satires de Juvénal* (Ghent, 1913)

Dessen, C. S.: *"Iunctura Callidus Acri": A Study of Persius' Satires* (Urbana, Chicago, and London, 1968)

Gerard, J.: *Juvénal et la Réalité Contemporaine* (Paris, 1976)

Griffith, J. G.: "The Ending of Juvenal's First Satire and Lucilius, Book XXX" *Hermes* 98 (1970) 56–72

Henderson, J.: *Figuring Out Roman Nobility: Juvenal's Eighth Satire* (Exeter, 1997)

Highet, G.: *Juvenal the Satirist* (Oxford, 1954)

Kenney, E. J.: "The First Satire of Juvenal" *Proceedings of the Cambridge Philological Society* 8 (1962) 29–40

Kenney, E. J.: "Juvenal: Satirist or Rhetorician?" *Latomus* 22 (1963) 704–20

Lafleur, R. A.: "*Amicitia* and the Unity of Juvenal's First Book" *Illinois Classical Studies* 4 (1979) 158–77

Lindo, L. I.: "The Evolution of Juvenal's Later Satires" *Classical Philology* 69 (1974) 17–27

Luck, G.: "The Textual History of Juvenal and the Oxford Lines" *Harvard Studies in Philology* 76 (1972) 217–32

Martin, J. M. K.: "Persius—Poet of the Stoics" *Greece and Rome* 8 (1939) 172–82

Romano, A. C.: *Irony in Juvenal* (Hildesheim, 1979)

Rudd, N.: "Imitation: Association of Ideas in Persius," in *Lines of Enquiry: Studies in Latin Poetry* (Cambridge, 1976) 54–83

Scott, I. G.: *The Grand Style in the Satires of Juvenal* (Northampton, Mass., 1927)

Smith, W. S.: "Heroic Models for the Sordid Present: Juvenal's View of Tragedy," in *Aufstieg und Niedergang der römischen Welt* II.33.1 (1989) 811–23

Sullivan, J. P.: "In Defence of Persius" *Ramus* 1 (1972) 48–62

Syme, R.: "The *patria* of Juvenal," in *Roman Papers III* ed. A. R. Birley (Oxford, 1984) 1120–34

Winkler, M. M.: *The Persona in Three Satires of Juvenal* (Hildesheim, 1983)

PERSIUS

NOTE ON PROLOGUE

Persius presents himself as a rebel right from the start. His choice of a non-hexameter metre for his prologue (if it is a prologue and not an epilogue) signals his break with tradition. He uses the choliambic metre (or scazon, "limping" iambic) to mark a more aggressive stance, relying on its associations with its inventor, Hipponax (6th century B.C.), and with the Hellenistic poet Callimachus (3rd century) who presents himself as a new Hipponax in his iambics. Persius presents a stance of scornful isolation, by rejecting the traditional poetic imagery of poetic inspiration (1–5)— drinking from a holy spring or dreaming in a divine location—and by representing himself as "a half-caste" (*semi-paganus*, a word coined for here; the neologism refers to the Paganalia, the communal rites of village communities, *pagi*), that is, not a full member of the community of poets, here called bards (*vates*) (6–7). He asserts that money and greed are their inspiration, and compares them unflatteringly to parrots, ravens, and magpies (8–14).

PROLOGUE

Nec fonte labra prolui caballino
nec in bicipiti somniasse Parnaso
memini, ut repente sic poeta prodirem.
Heliconidasque pallidamque Pirenen
5   illis remitto quorum imagines lambunt
hederae sequaces; ipse semipaganus
ad sacra vatum carmen adfero nostrum.
quis expedivit psittaco suum "chaere"
picamque docuit nostra verba conari?
10 magister artis ingenique largitor
venter, negatas artifex sequi voces.
quod si dolosi spes refulserit nummi,
corvos poetas et poetridas picas
cantare credas Pegaseium nectar.

5 remitto αLNWP: relinquo CGMRX

44

PROLOGUE

I neither cleansed my lips in the nag's spring[1] nor recall
dreaming on twin-peaked Parnassus[2] so as to emerge an
instant poet. The Heliconians[3] and pale Pirene[4] I leave to
people with their statues licked by clinging ivy.[5] It's as a
half-caste that I bring my song to the bards' rites. Who
equipped the parrot with his "Hello"[6] and taught the mag-
pie to attempt human speech? It was that master of ex-
pertise, that bestower of talent, the belly—an expert at
copying sounds denied by nature. Just let the prospect of
deceitful money gleam and you'd think raven poets and
poetess magpies were chanting the nectar of Pegasus.

[1] Hippocrene (Greek = "horse's spring"), the source of po-
etic inspiration created by Pegasus' hoof on Mount Helicon in
Boeotia.

[2] A mountain near Delphi, sacred to the Muses.

[3] The Muses, who lived on Mount Helicon.

[4] A spring associated with the Muses in Corinth, where Bel-
lerophon captured Pegasus.

[5] The busts of famous poets, displayed in libraries, with ivy
crowns.

[6] *Chaere* is Greek for "Hello!"; by Persius' time it had become
naturalised.

NOTE ON SATIRE 1

Satire 1 is a programmatic poem placed at the start of the book, following the precedent set by Lucilius and Horace in *Satires* 2.1, and later followed by Juvenal in Satire 1: see Courtney, *Commentary on Juvenal* (1980) 82–3 and Braund, *Juvenal Satires Book I* (1996) 116–19. Persius' attitude towards literary activity in the Prologue is confirmed at the opening of Satire 1, where he appears to be content with a small or nonexistent audience (1–3). He maintains this independence throughout the poem and at the end describes his preferred audience: the devotee of Greek Old Comedy, who approves of "boiled-down" poetry, and not the silly and superficial person who mocks education and philosophy (123–34). The poem takes the form of a dialogue between the poet (P) and a fictitious interlocutor (I), addressed as "whoever you are" in line 44, and is a programmatic statement in which Persius establishes his isolationism by a wholesale rejection both of contemporary poetry for being too smooth, weak, and artificial, and of contemporary morality, which produces such effete literature.

Persius starts by rejecting the conventional standards of assessing poetry (1–7), on the grounds that he has a special insight which frees him from convention. He feels justified in articulating his insight because of the hypocrisy of society (8–12). The poem then catalogues the particular forms of hypocrisy and decadence he sees around him. He depicts a poetry recitation as if it were a sex show in which the audience are brought to orgasm (13–23). He diminishes the poet's desire for praise by ridiculing his criteria of success—to become a set book in the schools or to win the approval of the great men of Rome at a dinner party (24–43). He declares that he shrinks from praise (44–7) and refuses to subscribe to contemporary standards of approval, because they lack discrimination and cannot offer up the truth (48–62). In response to the interlocutor's question about public opinion (63), he depicts a society convinced that poetry can be measured by a plumb line and keen for poets to stray beyond their capacity into heroic themes (63–75). He criticises the vogue for archaic poets (76–83) and the desire for approval even in the inappropriate context of law-court speeches (84–91). His interlocutor then defends contemporary poetry and condemns Virgil's *Aeneid* (92–7). In reply, Persius spits out some of the "effete stuff" which he regards as a betrayal of the manly Roman inheritance (98–106). The interlocutor then warns him against offending the great and powerful (107–10). At first, Persius pretends to heed this warning (110–14), but he then cites his predecessors in the genre, Lucilius and Horace, as his precedent and justification for writing satire (114–18). He insists on his right to articulate his secret, the insight he started to express earlier (8)—that everyone has the ears of a donkey, that is, that no one has any critical judgement whatsoever (119–23). Finally, he indicates his ideal audience and dismisses the narrow-minded people who enjoy mocking intellectuals (123–33): their reading matter is advertising hype for popular entertainments and romantic novels (134).

SATIRE 1

O curas hominum! o quantum est in rebus inane!
"quis leget haec?" min tu istud ais? nemo hercule.
    "nemo?"
vel duo vel nemo. "turpe et miserabile." quare?
ne mihi Polydamas et Troiades Labeonem
5 praetulerint? nugae. non, si quid turbida Roma
elevet, accedas examenve inprobum in illa
castiges trutina nec te quaesiveris extra.
nam Romae quis non—a, si fas dicere—sed fas
tum cum ad canitiem et nostrum istud vivere triste
10 aspexi ac nucibus facimus quaecumque relictis,
cum sapimus patruos. tunc tunc—ignoscite (nolo,
quid faciam?) sed sum petulanti splene—cachinno.
    Scribimus inclusi, numeros ille, hic pede liber,
grande aliquid quod pulmo animae praelargus anhelet.
15 scilicet haec populo pexusque togaque recenti

---

[1] Probably a quotation from Lucilius, thus establishing the genre as satire.   [2] I.e. his critics: an allusion to Hom. *Il*. 22.99–130 where Hector fears criticism from Polydamas and the Trojan men and women. "Dames" is a sneer at the alleged Trojan ancestry of some of the Roman elite.   [3] Attius Labeo was a poet under Nero who translated Homer's *Iliad*.   [4] The "secret" that P cuts short will not be revealed until line 121.

[5] Lit. "took on the flavour of."

SATIRE 1

P "How troubled is humanity! How very empty is life!"[1]

I *Who'll read that?*

P Are you talking to me? No one, for God's sake.

I No one?

P Perhaps one or two.

I That's disgraceful and pathetic.

P Why's that? Because Polydamas and the Trojan dames[2] might prefer Labeo[3] to me? Rubbish! If muddled Rome disparages something, don't step in to correct the faulty balance in those scales and don't search outside yourself. The reason? Is there anyone at Rome who doesn't[4]—oh, if only I could say it—but I may, when I look at our grey heads and that gloomy life of ours and everything we've been doing since we gave up our toys, since we started sounding like strict uncles.[5] Then, then—excuse me (I don't want to, I can't help it), but I've got a cheeky temper—I cackle.

We shut ourselves away and write some grand stuff, one in verse, another in prose, stuff which only a generous lung of breath can gasp out. And of course that's what you will finally read to the public from your seat on the platform, neatly combed and in your fresh toga, all dressed in white

et natalicia tandem cum sardonyche albus
sede leges celsa, liquido cum plasmate guttur
mobile conlueris, patranti fractus ocello.
tunc neque more probo videas nec voce serena
20 ingentis trepidare Titos, cum carmina lumbum
intrant et tremulo scalpuntur ubi intima versu.
tun, vetule, auriculis alienis colligis escas,
articulis quibus et dicas cute perditus "ohe"?
"quo didicisse, nisi hoc fermentum et quae semel intus
25 innata est rupto iecore exierit caprificus?"
en pallor seniumque! o mores, usque adeone
scire tuum nihil est nisi te scire hoc sciat alter?
"at pulchrum est digito monstrari et dicier 'hic est.'
ten cirratorum centum dictata fuisse
30 pro nihilo pendes?" ecce inter pocula quaerunt
Romulidae saturi quid dia poemata narrent.
hic aliquis, cui circum umeros hyacinthina laena est,
rancidulum quiddam balba de nare locutus
Phyllidas, Hypsipylas, vatum et plorabile siquid,
35 eliquat ac tenero subplantat verba palato.
adsensere viri: nunc non cinis ille poetae
felix? non levior cippus nunc inprimit ossa?
laudant convivae: nunc non e manibus illis,
nunc non e tumulo fortunataque favilla
40 nascentur violae? "rides" ait "et nimis uncis

23 articulis *Madvig*: auriculis PαXΦSΣ
24 quo PGLMRS: quod αXNS

---

6 Titus designates an ordinary Roman.

7 The wild fig tree was renowned for the power of its roots to dislodge stones.   8 Two inconsolable heroines.

and wearing your birthday ring of sardonyx, after you have
rinsed your supple throat with a liquid warble, in a state of
enervation with your orgasmic eye. Then, as the poetry
enters their backsides and as their inmost parts are tickled
by verse vibrations, you can see huge Tituses[6] quivering,
both their respectable manner and their calm voice gone.
What, you old reprobate, do you compose morsels for
other people's ears, morsels which would make even you,
with your joints and skin decayed, say, "Enough!"?

I   What's the point of studying, if this yeast, this wild fig tree,[7]
    once it's taken root inside, can't rupture the liver and burst
    out?

P   So that's why you are so pale and decrepit! Appalling! Is
    your knowledge so worthless unless someone else knows
    that you know it?

I   But it's splendid to be pointed out and to hear people say:
    "That's him!" Is it worth nothing to you to be the dictation
    text of a hundred curly-headed boys?

P   Look—the sons of Romulus, stuffed full, are enquiring
    over their cups what's new from divine poesy. At this point,
    someone with a hyacinth wrap around his shoulders, snort-
    ing and lisping some nauseating stuff, filters his Phyllises
    and Hypsipyles,[8] the typical tear-jerking stuff of bards,
    tripping up the words on the roof of his delicate mouth.
    The great men nod in approval. Are your poet's ashes not
    blissful now? Does the tombstone not rest more lightly on
    his bones now? The guests applaud: will violets not spring
    from those remains, from that tomb and from that blessed
    ash now?

I   You're mocking me, he says, and letting your nostrils sneer

51

naribus indulges. an erit qui velle recuset
os populi meruisse et cedro digna locutus
linquere nec scombros metuentia carmina nec tus?"
    Quisquis es, o modo quem ex adverso dicere feci,
45 non ego cum scribo, si forte quid aptius exit,
quando haec rara avis est, si quid tamen aptius exit,
laudari metuam; neque enim mihi cornea fibra est.
sed recti finemque extremumque esse recuso
"euge" tuum et "belle." nam "belle" hoc excute totum:
50 quid non intus habet? non hic est Ilias Atti
ebria veratro? non siqua elegidia crudi
dictarunt proceres? non quidquid denique lectis
scribitur in citreis? calidum scis ponere sumen,
scis comitem horridulum trita donare lacerna,
55 et "verum" inquis "amo, verum mihi dicite de me."
qui pote? vis dicam? nugaris, cum tibi, calve,
pinguis aqualiculus propenso sesquipede extet.
o Iane, a tergo quem nulla ciconia pinsit
nec manus auriculas imitari mobilis albas
60 nec linguae quantum sitiat canis Apula tantum.
vos, o patricius sanguis, quos vivere fas est
occipiti caeco, posticae occurrite sannae.

    60 tantum W: tantae Φ

---

   9 Cedar oil was used to preserve books.
   10 A reference to the traditional fate of bad poetry (cf. Cat. 95.9, Hor. *Ep*. 2.1.269–70): to be used as wrapping paper by shop-keepers.
   11 For "horn" we would say "cast iron."
   12 See 1.4n. above.
   13 Hellebore was taken to clear the head and to cure madness.

too much. Is there anyone who would disown the desire to earn the praise of the people?—or, when he's produced compositions good enough for cedar oil,[9] to leave behind him poetry which has nothing to fear from mackerels or incense?[10]

P   You, whoever you are, whom I've just created to put the opposite case—when I write, if by chance something rather good results, and that would be a rare bird, if, though, something rather good results, I have no fear of praise. My guts are not made of horn,[11] you know. But I refuse to take your "Bravo!" and your "Lovely!" as the be-all and end-all of excellence. Why? Give that "Lovely!" a thorough sifting: is there anything it does not include? Won't you find Attius' *Iliad*[12] intoxicated with hellebore?[13] And all the romantic ditties dictated by our gorged lords? In a word, won't you find all the stuff written on citron-wood couches? You know how to serve up hot tripe, you know how to give some poor shivering client a worn-out cloak, and then you say, "I love the truth. Tell me the truth about myself." How, actually? Do you really want me to? You're a fool, baldy, your fat paunch sticking out with an overhang of a foot and a half. Lucky Janus,[14] never pummelled from behind by a stork or by waggling hands imitating a donkey's white ears or by a tongue as long as a thirsty Apulian dog's.[15] You, of patrician blood, who have to live without eyes in the back of your heads, turn around and face the backdoor sneer!

[14] The god Janus had faces in front and behind, and therefore could not be made fun of behind his back. Three gestures of mockery follow.

[15] Apulia was a region known for its dryness.

"Quis populi sermo est?" "quis enim nisi carmina
   molli
nunc demum numero fluere, ut per leve severos
65   effundat iunctura unguis. scit tendere versum
non secus ac si oculo rubricam derigat uno.
sive opus in mores, in luxum, in prandia regum
dicere, res grandes nostro dat Musa poetae."
ecce modo heroas sensus adferre docemus
70   nugari solitos Graece, nec ponere lucum
artifices nec rus saturum laudare, ubi corbes
et focus et porci et fumosa Palilia feno,
unde Remus sulcoque terens dentalia, Quinti,
cum trepida ante boves dictatorem induit uxor
75   et tua aratra domum lictor tulit—euge poeta!
est nunc Brisaei quem venosus liber Acci,
sunt quos Pacuviusque et verrucosa moretur
Antiopa "aerumnis cor luctificabile fulta?"
hos pueris monitus patres infundere lippos
80   cum videas, quaerisne unde haec sartago loquendi
venerit in linguas, unde istud dedecus in quo
trossulus exultat tibi per subsellia levis?
nilne pudet capiti non posse pericula cano

69 docemus PGLBob.Sang.: videmus aX$\Phi\Sigma$

---

16 The Palilia (also spelled Parilia) held on April 21st, the anniversary of Rome's foundation, celebrated the guardian goddess of herds and flocks; heaps of hay were burnt as part of the ritual.

17 Lucius Quinctius Cincinnatus was called from his plough to take up the position of Dictator in the crisis of 458 B.C.; see Livy 3.26.   18 The lictor, an official attendant of the magistrates, is here depicted incongruously as a farmworker.

SATIRE 1

I   What does public opinion say?

P   What do you think? That poetry now at last flows with
smooth rhythm, so that critical fingernails glide smoothly
over the joins. The modern poet knows how to make a line
as straight as if he were stretching a plumb line with one
eye closed. Whether his project is to speak against moral-
ity, luxury, or the banquets of lords, the Muse provides
our poet with grand material. Look! We're now teaching
people who used to dabble in Greek doggerel to produce
heroic sentiments, people not skilful enough to depict a
grove or to praise the plentiful countryside, with its bas-
kets, hearth, pigs, and the smoky hay of Pales' festival[16]—
the home of Remus, and yours too, Cincinnatus,[17] polish-
ing your plough beam in the furrow, with your flustered
wife dressing you as Dictator in front of the oxen, and the
lictor[18] carrying home your plough. Bravo, you poet! These
days one person lingers over the varicose tome of Brisaean
Accius[19] and more than one over Pacuvius[20] and his warty
Antiope, "her melancholy heart besieged by troubles."
When you see runny-eyed fathers pouring advice like this
into their sons, need you ask the origin of this stew-up of
language that's got into their tongues, of that outrageous
stuff which puts your young cavaliers in an ecstatic frenzy
along the benches? Doesn't it embarrass you that you can't
defend some grizzled head from threats without wanting

19 I.e. Accius' play *Bacchae*; Brisaeus is an epithet of Diony-
sus/Bacchus.

20 Pacuvius' tragedy *Antiopa*, like Accius's *Bacchae*, devel-
oped a theme from Euripides. The words in quotation marks are
either taken from the play or a parody in archaic language.

pellere quin tepidum hoc optes audire "decenter"?
85 "fur es" ait Pedio. Pedius quid? crimina rasis
librat in antithetis, doctas posuisse figuras
laudatur: "bellum hoc." hoc bellum? an, Romule, ceves?
men moveat quippe et, cantet si naufragus, assem
protulerim? cantas, cum fracta te in trabe pictum
90 ex umero portes? verum nec nocte paratum
plorabit qui me volet incurvasse querela.
"sed numeris decor est et iunctura addita crudis.
cludere sic versum didicit 'Berecyntius Attis'
et 'qui caeruleum dirimebat Nerea delphin,'
95 sic 'costam longo subduximus Appennino.'
'Arma virum,' nonne hoc spumosum et cortice pingui
ut ramale vetus vegrandi subere coctum?"
quidnam igitur tenerum et laxa cervice legendum?
"torva Mimalloneis inplerunt cornua bombis,
100 et raptum vitulo caput ablatura superbo
Bassaris et lyncem Maenas flexura corymbis
euhion ingeminat, reparabilis adsonat echo."
haec fierent si testiculi vena ulla paterni

92–7 *att. interlocutori et* 98–106 *Persio Marcilius, Heinrich*
97 vegrandi *Porphyry, Servius*: praegrandi PaXΦS

---

[21] On this custom of shipwrecked sailors, see 6.29–33n. and
Juv. 14.301–2n.

[22] Nereus = the sea.

[23] These four lines are either a quotation from a contemporary
poet (they are attributed to Nero by the scholiast) or a parody.
They contain a pastiche of Bacchic clichés: Mimallon, Bassaris,
and Maenad are words for Bacchantes, the female worshippers

to hear this lukewarm "Nice!"? "You're a thief," someone says to Pedius. What does Pedius say? He balances the accusations in smooth-shaven antitheses and is praised for composing clever expressions: "That's lovely." "*That*— lovely? Are you wiggling your arse, Romulus? Am I going to be impressed, I'd like to know, and am I going to part with a penny if a shipwreck victim sings a song? Are you singing with a picture of yourself in a shattered ship on your shoulder?[21] The person who wants to bend me with his sorry tale will utter a genuine lament, not one con- cocted overnight.

I   But elegance and smoothness have been added to the raw rhythms of old poetry. That's how "Berecynthian Attis" learned how to end the line, and "The dolphin parting azure Nereus,"[22] and "We stole a rib from the long Apen- nines" too. "Arms and the man!" Isn't this frothy stuff, with a thick crust, like an ancient dried-up branch with swollen bark?

P   Would you try something delicate, then, for reciting with a floppy neck? "Their fierce horns they filled with Mimal- lonian booming, and Bassaris, poised to carry off the head torn from the proud calf, and the Maenad, poised to steer the lynx with ivy clusters, shouts and shouts 'Euhoë,' and reverberating Echo chimes in."[23] Would such things hap- pen if any pulse at all of our fathers' balls still lived in us?

of Bacchus; horns, lynxes, and ivy are associated with Bacchus; Bacchantes traditionally tear apart animals (here a calf); and euhoe is the Bacchic ritual cry (Euhius is a cult title of Bacchus).

viveret in nobis? summa delumbe saliva
105 hoc natat, in labris et in udo est Maenas et Attis
nec pluteum caedit nec demorsos sapit unguis.
  "Sed quid opus teneras mordaci radere vero
auriculas? vide sis ne maiorum tibi forte
limina frigescant: sonat hic de nare canina
110 littera." per me equidem sint omnia protinus alba;
nil moror. euge omnes, omnes bene, mirae eritis res.
hoc iuvat? "hic" inquis "veto quisquam faxit oletum."
pinge duos anguis: "pueri, sacer est locus, extra
meiite." discedo. secuit Lucilius Vrbem,
115 te Lupe, te Muci, et genuinum fregit in illis.
omne vafer vitium ridenti Flaccus amico
tangit et admissus circum praecordia ludit,
callidus excusso populum suspendere naso.
me muttire nefas? nec clam? nec cum scrobe? nusquam?
120 hic tamen infodiam. vidi, vidi ipse, libelle:
auriculas asini quis non habet? hoc ego opertum,
hoc ridere meum, tam nil, nulla tibi vendo
Iliade. audaci quicumque adflate Cratino
iratum Eupolidem praegrandi cum sene palles,
125 aspice et haec, si forte aliquid decoctius audis.

<hr>

107 vero αΧΦΣΣ: verbo PR
121 quis non *codd.*: Mida rex Σ *et vita Persii*

<hr>

24 The snarl is either that of the great man and his household
or that of the aggressive satirist. An allusion to Lucilius 3–4W,
389–90W.

25 A legal type of formula with archaic Latin words.

26 Pictures of snakes were used on notices forbidding the de-
filement of tombs etc.

This effete stuff swims on the saliva, your Maenad and Attis just float on the lips. No bashing the desk here, no taste of bitten fingernails!

I   But what need is there to scrape delicate ears with biting truth? Take care the thresholds of the great don't grow chilly towards you: this is where you'll hear the snarl of a dog's rrrr.[24]

P   Well then, as far as I'm concerned, from now on, everything's fine. I shan't stop you. Bravo, all of you! Well done all, you're marvellous. Will that do? "Defecation prohibited here,"[25] you say. Paint up two snakes:[26] "Lads, this place is off limits—piss outside." I'm off. Lucilius[27] ripped into Rome—you, Lupus, you, Mucius—and broke a molar on them. While his friend is laughing, the rascal Horace touches every fault in him and, once he's got in, he frolics around his heart, clever at dangling the public from his cleaned-out nose. Am I forbidden a mutter? Not even in secret? Not even in a hole? Nowhere? Never mind: I'll dig a hole for it here. I have seen it, yes, have seen it for myself, little book: is there anyone who does not have donkey's ears? This secret, this joke of mine, so insignificant, I'll not sell to you for any *Iliad*. Any of you inspired by bold Cratinus or growing pale at angry Eupolis and the Mighty Old Man,[28] take a look at this too, if you perhaps have an ear for something rather boiled-down. As my reader I want

27 On Lucilius see Juv. 1.20n. Lupus and Mucius were two of Lucilius' targets; cf. Juv. 1.154n.

28 Cratinus, Eupolis, and Aristophanes were the three preeminent authors of Athenian Old Comedy. The three are named at Hor. *Sat.* 1.4.1.

inde vaporata lector mihi ferveat aure,
non hic qui in crepidas Graiorum ludere gestit
sordidus et lusco qui possit dicere "lusce,"
sese aliquem credens Italo quod honore supinus
130   fregerit heminas Arreti aedilis iniquas,
nec qui abaco numeros et secto in pulvere metas
scit risisse vafer, multum gaudere paratus
si cynico barbam petulans nonaria vellat.
his mane edictum, post prandia Callirhoen do.

someone set on fire by those authors with his ear steamed
clean, not the crude man who loves jeering at the sandals
of the Greeks or who can say "One-eye!" to a one-eyed
man, thinking he is Somebody because, stuck up with pro-
vincial importance, as aedile at Arretium he broke up short
measures, not the rascal who knows how to make fun of
sums on the counting board and cones in the furrowed
dust, ready to take huge delight when a cheeky tart tugs a
Cynic's beard. To these I recommend "What's On"[29] in the
morning and *Callirhoe*[30] after lunch.

[29] Lit. "the [praetor's] edict," i.e. an advertisement for a play or
games.

[30] Perhaps the novel *Chaereas and Callirhoe* by Chariton,
which was published not much earlier.

NOTE ON SATIRE 2

Satire 2 maintains the intolerant rejection of contempo-
rary society and its decadent standards from Satire 1. It
is presented as a *genethliakon* or "birthday poem" to a
friend and fellow student of Persius, Plotius Macrinus
(whose name may suggest "Long life"), but becomes a
fierce diatribe on prayer, a standard philosophical and sa-
tirical theme. Persius contrasts the prayers that Macrinus
will offer to his *genius* (his personal god) with those of the
hypocrites who observe proper religious ceremony but
secretly pray for money (1–16). He indignantly suggests
that God is not fooled by this charade (17–30). He then
criticises the foolish prayers of a grandma or superstitious
aunt (31–40) and satirises the illogicality of spending one's
wealth on expensive offerings that are designed to win
greater wealth (41–51). He condemns the use of gold and
other precious substances in temples (52–70). The only ac-
ceptable offering consists of "justice and right blended in
the spirit, the mind pure in its inner depths and a breast
imbued with noble honour" (71–5). This "holier-than-
thou" tone adopted by Persius' persona characterises him
as an intolerant prig, who modulates from friendly advice
into delivering a sermon to the world.

SATIRE 2

Hunc, Macrine, diem numera meliore lapillo,
qui tibi labentis apponit candidus annos.
funde merum genio. non tu prece poscis emaci
quae nisi seductis nequeas committere divis;
5   at bona pars procerum tacita libabit acerra.
haut cuivis promptum est murmurque humilisque
        susurros
tollere de templis et aperto vivere voto.
"mens bona, fama, fides," haec clare et ut audiat hospes;
illa sibi introrsum et sub lingua murmurat: "o si
10   ebulliat patruus, praeclarum funus!" et "o si
sub rastro crepet argenti mihi seria dextro
Hercule! pupillumve utinam, quem proximus heres
inpello, expungam; nam et est scabiosus et acri
bile tumet. Nerio iam tertia conditur uxor."
15   haec sancte ut poscas, Tiberino in gurgite mergis
mane caput bis terque et noctem flumine purgas.
heus age, responde (minimum est quod scire laboro)
de Iove quid sentis? estne ut praeponere cures

    2 apponit aXΦSΣ: apponet PN

64

SATIRE 2

This shining day, which assigns the years as they glide by to
your account—mark it with a special pebble, Macrinus.
Pour undiluted wine to your Guardian Spirit. You at least
do not make requests with a haggling prayer that can only
be entrusted to the gods in confidence, whereas a good
number of our lords will make their libations from a secre-
tive censer. It does not come easy to take one's muttering
and low whispers away from the temples and to make life's
vows open. "Good sense, reputation, credit"—that's what
he says out loud, even for strangers to hear, but this is what
he mutters to himself under his tongue: "Oh, if only uncle
would pop off, I'd give him a splendid funeral!" and "If
only Hercules would favour me and make a pot of silver
chink beneath my hoe!"[1] Or "I wish I could wipe out my
ward—I'm right behind him, the next to inherit. After
all, he suffers from eczema and is swollen with jaundice.
Nerius is already burying his third wife." To make these re-
quests piously, you plunge your head twice and three times
in the morning in Tiber's flow and clean away the night's
thoughts in river water. Hey then, tell me (it's a tiny thing I
strive to know), what is your view of God? Would you care

---

[1] Hercules was the god associated with hidden treasure.

hunc—cuinam? "cuinam?" vis Staio? an—scilicet
    haeres?
20 quis potior iudex puerisve quis aptior orbis?
hoc igitur quo tu Iovis aurem inpellere temptas
dic agedum Staio. "pro Iuppiter, o bone" clamet
"Iuppiter!" at sese non clamet Iuppiter ipse?
ignovisse putas quia, cum tonat, ocius ilex
25 sulpure discutitur sacro quam tuque domusque?
an quia non fibris ovium Ergennaque iubente
triste iaces lucis evitandumque bidental,
idcirco stolidam praebet tibi vellere barbam
Iuppiter? aut quidnam est qua tu mercede deorum
30 emeris auriculas? pulmone et lactibus unctis?
    Ecce avia aut metuens divum matertera cunis
exemit puerum frontemque atque uda labella
infami digito et lustralibus ante salivis
expiat, urentis oculos inhibere perita;
35 tunc manibus quatit et spem macram supplice voto
nunc Licini in campos, nunc Crassi mittit in aedis:
"hunc optet generum rex et regina, puellae
hunc rapiant; quidquid calcaverit hic, rosa fiat."
ast ego nutrici non mando vota. negato,
40 Iuppiter, haec illi, quamvis te albata rogarit.
    Poscis opem nervis corpusque fidele senectae.

[40] rogarit PCLW: rogabit αXMNR

---

[2] An ordinary upright citizen.   [3] The spot where light-
ning struck was declared a *bidental* and consecrated, with the sac-
rifice of sheep, as a shrine to be undisturbed because it was ill-
omened. The custom was associated with the Etruscans, hence
the Etruscan name Ergenna, evidently the priest.

to rank him above—who?—"Who?" How about Staius?[2]
Or would you hesitate at that? Who is a better judge, who a
more suitable guardian for orphan boys? So, go on, tell
Staius exactly how you try to bend God's ear. "God forbid!"
he would cry, "Good God!" But wouldn't God himself cry
"God!"? You think he has forgiven you because, when he
thunders, the holy brimstone shatters the holm oak rather
than you and your household? Or, because you are not ly-
ing in some grove, a dread object to be avoided by order of
Ergenna and sheep's entrails,[3] do you think God is offering
you his stupid beard to tug? And what precisely is the bribe
you use to purchase the ears of the gods? An offering of
lung and greasy guts?

Look—a grandma or superstitious aunt has lifted the
boy from his cradle and first protects his forehead and wet
lips with her wicked finger[4] and magical saliva, an expert at
warding off the withering evil eye.[5] Then she rocks him in
her arms and in earnest prayer launches the scrawny pros-
pect now towards Licinus' estates, now towards Crassus'
palace.[6] "May some king and queen pick him for their son-
in-law, may girls tussle over him. Wherever he treads, may
there be roses." But I entrust no prayers to a nurse. Say no
to her wishes, God, even if she dresses in white to ask you.

You ask for strength for your muscles and a body reli-

[4] The middle finger, which was used for insulting gestures and
was hence the appropriate finger for warding off the evil eye.
[5] Fear of the evil eye led to wearing of amulets (5.31) as well as
anointing with saliva.
[6] Both fabulously rich: Licinus was a freedman of Augustus,
see Juv. 1.109n.; Crassus, the triumvir, had benefitted from Sulla's
proscriptions.

esto age. sed grandes patinae tuccetaque crassa
adnuere his superos vetuere Iovemque morantur.
rem struere exoptas caeso bove Mercuriumque
45 arcessis fibra: "da fortunare Penatis,
da pecus et gregibus fetum." quo, pessime, pacto,
tot tibi cum in flamma iunicum omenta liquescant?
et tamen hic extis et opimo vincere ferto
intendit: "iam crescit ager, iam crescit ovile,
50 iam dabitur, iam iam"—donec deceptus et exspes
nequiquam fundo suspiret nummus in imo.

Si tibi creterras argenti incusaque pingui
auro dona feram, sudes et pectore laevo
excutiat guttas laetari praetrepidum cor.
55 hinc illud subiit, auro sacras quod ovato
perducis facies. "nam fratres inter aenos,
somnia pituita qui purgatissima mittunt,
praecipui sunto sitque illis aurea barba."
aurum vasa Numae Saturniaque inpulit aera
60 Vestalisque urnas et Tuscum fictile mutat.

O curvae in terris animae et caelestium inanis,
quid iuvat hoc, templis nostros inmittere mores
et bona dis ex hac scelerata ducere pulpa?
haec sibi corrupto casiam dissolvit olivo,

45 arcessis CL: accessis α: accersis PXΦ

---

7 God of profit.

8 Presumably bronze statues of gods.

9 I.e. dreams uncorrupted by secretion of bodily humours and
therefore indicators of good health.

10 Numa, the second king of Rome, instructed that all sacred
vessels should be made of pottery.

able in old age. Well, so be it. But your lavish dishes and thick casseroles have forbidden the divinities to assent to these prayers—they get in God's way. You long to heap up your wealth by slaughtering an ox, and you summon Mercury[7] with its liver: "Grant prosperity to my household, grant me herds, and young to my flocks." How, precisely, you scoundrel, when the fat of so many of your heifers is melting in the flame? And still this man strives to get his way with innards and rich sacrificial cakes: "Now my land is increasing, now my sheepfold too, now my wish will be granted, now, now"—until, deluded and despairing, a single coin sighs in vain at the very bottom of his coffers.

Were I to bring you bowls of silver and presents embossed with thick gold, you would break out into a sweat, your heart fluttering with joy and squeezing out drops from your left breast. That's where you got the idea of coating divine likenesses with triumphal gold. "Let those of the bronze brothers,[8] then, be supreme who send us dreams that are most free from catarrh[9] and let them have golden beards." Gold has ousted Numa's crocks[10] and Saturn's bronze,[11] and alters the Vestals' pots and Etruscan earthenware.

O souls bent earthwards and void of celestial thoughts, what help is it to unleash our ways upon the temples and to infer the gods' values from this wicked flesh of ours? It is this flesh that has polluted our olive oil by mixing in casia,[12]

---

[11] In the Saturnian age (the Golden Age: Juv. 6.1n.) vessels were made of bronze.

[12] An exotic spice and perfume.

65 haec Calabrum coxit vitiato murice vellus,
    haec bacam conchae rasisse et stringere venas
    ferventis massae crudo de pulvere iussit.
    peccat et haec, peccat, vitio tamen utitur. at vos
    dicite, pontifices, in sancto quid facit aurum?
70 nempe hoc quod Veneri donatae a virgine pupae.
    quin damus id superis, de magna quod dare lance
    non possit magni Messalae lippa propago?
    conpositum ius fasque animo sanctosque recessus
    mentis et incoctum generoso pectus honesto.
75 haec cedo ut admoveam templis et farre litabo.

this flesh that has misused Tyrian purple for dyeing Cala-
brian fleeces,[13] this flesh that has commanded us to scrape
the pearl from its shell and strip the veins of glowing ore
from the raw dirt. It does wrong, it does wrong, yet it gains
from its weakness. But tell me, you priests, what good is
gold in a sacred place? Exactly as much as the doll[14] given
to Venus by a little girl. So why don't we give the gods what
the runny-eyed descendant of great Messalla[15] cannot give
from his great dish? Justice and right blended in the spirit,
the mind pure in its inner depths and a breast imbued with
noble honour. Let me bring these to the temples, and with
a handful of grits I shall make acceptable sacrifice.

[13] Expensive purple dye, made from shellfish. The finest Ital-
ian wool was from Tarentum, in Calabria.

[14] At puberty girls presented their dolls to Venus, as boys pre-
sented their *bulla* (a pendant) to the Lares.

[15] Possibly Lucius Aurelius Cotta Messalinus, the dissolute
son (Tac. *Ann.* 6.7) of Marcus Valerius Messalla, a great general
and patron in the time of Augustus.

NOTE ON SATIRE 3

In Satire 3 an intolerant young student (resembling the extremist who delivered the diatribe on prayer in Satire 2) has lapsed and is himself on the receiving end of a lecture. The voice delivering the lecture is never identified explicitly; it may be a friend, perhaps a fellow student, or his tutor, or even a superego voice inside his head. The poem is a sustained dialogue between the two.

The opening exchange depicts the student (P) waking late, with a hangover (1–18). In response to his moaning as he sits down to work at his desk, his friend (F) launches into a sermon about the madness of those who will not allow philosophy to help them (19–106), a theme reminiscent of the sermon on madness in Horace, *Satires* 2.3. He criticises the student for his lack of direction and for being content to live a careless, superficial life (19–43). He confesses to having had similar attitudes himself as a boy, but tells the student that he should know better by now (44–57), and asks again if he has any purpose in life or if his life is just "an improvisation" (58–62). Now the friend insists upon the urgency of taking action and thinking about the meaning of life, introducing a series of medical images typifying Persius' use of physical metaphors from Stoicism to convey moral and psychological points (63–76). In response to the imagined mockery of philosophy by a centurion (77–87), the friend imagines a scenario in which a sick man rushes to his doctor in a panic but soon forgets the doctor's advice and returns to his self-indulgent habits (88–106). At this point, the student protests that there is nothing wrong with him (107–9). In reply, the friend drily lists all the weaknesses of his personality that could be cured by philosophy (109–119).

SATIRE 3

Nempe haec adsidue. iam clarum mane fenestras
intrat et angustas extendit lumine rimas.
stertimus, indomitum quod despumare Falernum
sufficiat, quinta dum linea tangitur umbra.
5 "en quid agis? siccas insana canicula messes
iam dudum coquit et patula pecus omne sub ulmo est"
unus ait comitum. verumne? itan? ocius adsit
huc aliquis. nemon? turgescit vitrea bilis:
findor, ut Arcadiae pecuaria rudere credas.
10 iam liber et positis bicolor membrana capillis
inque manus chartae nodosaque venit harundo.
tum querimur crassus calamo quod pendeat umor
nigra sed infusa vanescit sepia lympha,
dilutas querimur geminet quod fistula guttas.
15 "o miser inque dies ultra miser, hucine rerum
venimus? a, cur non potius teneroque columbo
et similis regum pueris pappare minutum

16 a α: at ΧΦ: aut PCMSΣ

---

1 Falernian was a powerful wine from Campania.
2 Lit. "the line is touched by the fifth shadow," referring to a
sundial. It is 11 in the morning.

SATIRE 3

P   I suppose this is now routine. Already the bright morning is coming through the shutters, enlarging the narrow cracks with light. We're snoring enough to make the untamed Falernian[1] stop fizzing, while the shadow reaches the fifth line.[2]

F   "Hey, what are you doing? The mad Dog star[3] has been baking the crops dry for hours now and all the herd's beneath the spreading elm," says one of my mates.

P   Are you sure? Really? Quick, someone come here. No one around? My bottle-green bile is swelling: my head is splitting—you'd think all the herds of Arcadia[4] were braying. Now my book comes to hand, and the two-tone parchment smoothed of hair, some paper and a jointed reed pen. Then we start whining: the liquid hangs from the nib too thickly, but when water's added, the black cuttle ink thins and we whine that the reed keeps globbing together the diluted drops.

F   "You idiot, more idiotic by the day, is this the state we've got to? Oh, why don't you act like a pigeon chick or a little prince instead, and demand your baby food cut up into tiny

---

[3] The rising of the constellation Sirius (Canis Major) in late July began the hot weather called the dog days.

[4] Arcadia was known for its donkeys.

poscis et iratus mammae lallare recusas?"
an tali studeam calamo? "cui verba? quid istas
20 succinis ambages? tibi luditur. effluis amens,
contemnere. sonat vitium, percussa maligne
respondet viridi non cocta fidelia limo.
udum et molle lutum es, nunc nunc properandus et acri
fingendus sine fine rota. sed rure paterno
25 est tibi far modicum, purum et sine labe salinum
(quid metuas?) cultrixque foci secura patella.
hoc satis? an deceat pulmonem rumpere ventis
stemmate quod Tusco ramum millesime ducis
censoremve tuum vel quod trabeate salutas?
30 ad populum phaleras! ego te intus et in cute novi.
non pudet ad morem discincti vivere Nattae.
sed stupet hic vitio et fibris increvit opimum
pingue, caret culpa, nescit quid perdat, et alto
demersus summa rursus non bullit in unda.
35   Magne pater divum, saevos punire tyrannos
haut alia ratione velis, cum dira libido
moverit ingenium ferventi tincta veneno:
virtutem videant intabescantque relicta.
anne magis Siculi gemuerunt aera iuvenci
40 et magis auratis pendens laquearibus ensis
purpureas subter cervices terruit, 'imus,

---

5 The silver saltcellar, like the dish (*patella*, 26), was used
in sacrifice, and its state therefore represented the household's
honour, hence the parenthesis, i.e. "Why worry about your spiri-
tual well-being?"   6 References to P's Etruscan origin and
equestrian status: the *trabea* was a purple garment worn by the
equites on ceremonial occasions such as the ride past (*transvectio*)
the Censor (the emperor) alluded to here.

pieces, and throw a tantrum and refuse to let your mommy sing you to sleep?"

P But how can I work with a pen like this?

F "Who are you fooling? Why do you keep reciting these evasions? It's your move. You're mindlessly draining away —you'll be a laughingstock. When you strike it, the misfired pot with its green clay responds grudgingly: it sounds flawed. You're soft, wet mud—you need to be rushed off right now and shaped non-stop on the rapid wheel. But on your family estate you have a moderate store of grain, a clean and immaculate saltcellar[5] (why worry?), and a carefree salver to worship at your hearth. Is that enough? Or would it suit you to burst your lungs with wind because your branch is the thousandth in a Tuscan pedigree, or because you dress in purple to greet your Censor?[6] Let the mob have your trappings! I know you inside out. You're not embarrassed to live like that dissolute Natta. But he's paralysed with vice, and thick fat has grown over his liver. He has no sense of guilt or of what he's lost. He's sunk so deep that he makes no more bubbles on the surface.

"Great father of the gods, may you punish savage tyrants, when terrible desire dipped in fiery poison has affected their minds, exactly like this: let them see moral excellence and let them pine at abandoning it. What is worse: the sound of the groans from the bronze Sicilian bull[7] and the terrifying sight of the sword hanging from the gilt-panelled ceiling over purpled necks beneath[8]—or a

[7] Made for Phalaris, tyrant of Agrigentum in Sicily, in which his victims were roasted.   [8] The "sword of Damocles," hung by Dionysius I, tyrant of Syracuse, by a single hair above the neck of the courtier Damocles.

imus praecipites' quam si sibi dicat et intus
palleat infelix quod proxima nesciat uxor?
    Saepe oculos, memini, tangebam parvus olivo,
45 grandia si nollem morituri verba Catonis
discere non sano multum laudanda magistro,
quae pater adductis sudans audiret amicis.
iure; etenim id summum, quid dexter senio ferret,
scire erat in voto, damnosa canicula quantum
50 raderet, angustae collo non fallier orcae,
neu quis callidior buxum torquere flagello.
haut tibi inexpertum curvos deprendere mores
quaeque docet sapiens bracatis inlita Medis
porticus, insomnis quibus et detonsa iuventus
55 invigilat siliquis et grandi pasta polenta;
et tibi quae Samios diduxit littera ramos
surgentem dextro monstravit limite collem.
stertis adhuc laxumque caput conpage soluta
oscitat hesternum dissutis undique malis.

45–6 morituri verba catonis | discere αXΦ: morituro verba
catonis dicere L: morituro verba catoni | dicere PΣ
    46 non sano PGLNS: et insano αXCMR
    56 diduxit LWS: deduxit PaXΦS
    57 collem PaX: callem Φ

9 To make it seem as if he were treating sore eyes.
    10 A declamation exercise given to schoolboys: to memorise an
imaginary speech by the younger Cato before he committed sui-
cide in 46 B.C.   11 In playing with *tesserae*, like our dice, the
best throw was three sixes and the worst was three ones (*canis*,
here *canicula*).   12 The second children's game consisted of
throwing nuts or dice into a narrow-necked jar.

man saying to himself, 'I'm falling, I'm falling headlong!'
and turning pale inside, the unlucky man, at something his
wife right beside him does not know?

"Often when I was little, I remember, I used to dab my
eyes with oil,[9] if I didn't want to learn the magnificent
speech of Cato as he faced death,[10] which my lunatic
teacher would heap with praise, while my father listened in
a sweat, with the friends he'd brought along. Fair enough:
the thing I wanted most of all back then was to know what
a lucky treble six would win and how much the losing
dog throw would claw back,[11] how not to be cheated by the
narrow jar's neck,[12] and for no one to whip the whirling
boxwood more deftly than me.[13] You—you're not inexperi-
enced at detecting deviant conduct or at the teachings
of the philosophic portico, bedaubed with Medes in trou-
sers,[14] teachings which the sleepless and close-cropped
youth pore over by night, fed on lentil casserole and gen-
erous helpings of barley porridge. The letter which di-
vides its Samian branches showed its rising hill on the
right path[15] to you, too. You're still snoring and your lolling
head with its joint unhinged is yawning yesterday's yawn,
with your jaws completely unstitched. Is there something

[13] The third game is making a top (made of boxwood) revolve
with a whip.   [14] The *Poikile Stoa* (Painted Portico), which
gave its name to Stoicism. It had a fresco of the battle of Marathon
depicting Persians wearing trousers.

[15] Pythagoras, the philosopher from Samos, represented the
choice which faces a young person as the Greek letter upsilon,
originally written: Ꮍ. After childhood (the stem) a choice must be
made between the difficult path of goodness (the vertical) and the
easy path of vice (the sloping branch to the left).

60 est aliquid quo tendis et in quod derigis arcum?
an passim sequeris corvos testaque lutoque,
securus quo pes ferat, atque ex tempore vivis?
Elleborum frustra, cum iam cutis aegra tumebit,
poscentis videas; venienti occurrite morbo,
65 et quid opus Cratero magnos promittere montis?
discite et, o miseri, causas cognoscite rerum:
quid sumus et quidnam victuri gignimur, ordo
quis datus, aut metae qua mollis flexus et unde,
quis modus argento, quid fas optare, quid asper
70 utile nummus habet, patriae carisque propinquis
quantum elargiri deceat, quem te deus esse
iussit et humana qua parte locatus es in re.
disce nec invideas quod multa fidelia putet
in locuplete penu, defensis pinguibus Vmbris,
75 et piper et pernae, Marsi monumenta clientis,
maenaque quod prima nondum defecerit orca.
Hic aliquis de gente hircosa centurionum
dicat: 'quod sapio satis est mihi. non ego curo
esse quod Arcesilas aerumnosique Solones
80 obstipo capite et figentes lumine terram,
murmura cum secum et rabiosa silentia rodunt
atque exporrecto trutinantur verba labello,
aegroti veteris meditantes somnia: gigni
de nihilo nihilum, in nihilum nil posse reverti.

68 datus PΦS: datur αXMR
78 sapio satis est P: satis est sapio αXΦΣ

---

16 The ancient equivalent of a wild goose chase.
17 Lit. "promise huge mountains." The name Craterus (from
Hor. *Sat.* 2.3.161) denotes any eminent physician.

you're heading for, a target for your bow? Or are you taking pot shots at crows with bricks and clods of mud,[16] not caring where your feet take you? Is your life an improvisation?

"You can see it's useless to ask for hellebore when the sickly skin is already getting bloated. Face the disease at its approach, and what need will you have to promise the earth to Craterus?[17] Learn, you idiotic creatures, discover the rationale of existence: What are we and what sort of life are we born for? What rank is given us at the start? Where and when should we make a smooth turn around the post?[18] What should be the limit to money? What is it right to pray for? What are the uses of new-minted coin? How much should be lavished on your country and your nearest and dearest? What role is assigned you by god and where in the human world have you been stationed? Learn this, and don't be unwilling to learn just because all those pots are going rotten in your richly stocked larder (since your defence of your fat Umbrians), along with the pepper and hams (mementoes of your Marsian client), and because the sprats from the first jar haven't yet run out.

"At this point one of the smelly clan of centurions may say: 'What I know is enough for me. Personally, I have no desire to be like Arcesilas[19] or those troubled Solons with their heads bent, eyes fixed on the ground, while they gnaw their mumbles and rabid silences to themselves and weigh words on their stuck-out lips, repeating the fantasies of some aged invalid: that nothing can come from nothing,

---

[18] Lit. "where the going around of the turning-post is easy and from what point [to make the turn]."

[19] Arcesilas, a philosopher of the 3rd century B.C., believed that nothing can be known.

85   hoc est quod palles? cur quis non prandeat hoc est?'
his populus ridet, multumque torosa iuventus
ingeminat tremulos naso crispante cachinnos.
    'Inspice, nescio quid trepidat mihi pectus et aegris
faucibus exsuperat gravis halitus, inspice sodes'
90   qui dicit medico, iussus requiescere, postquam
tertia conpositas vidit nox currere venas,
de maiore domo modice sitiente lagoena
lenia loturo sibi Surrentina rogabit.
    'heus bone, tu palles.' 'nihil est.' 'videas tamen istuc,
95   quidquid id est. surgit tacite tibi lutea pellis.'
'at tu deterius palles, ne sis mihi tutor.
iam pridem hunc sepeli; tu restas.' 'perge, tacebo.'
turgidus hic epulis atque albo ventre lavatur,
gutture sulpureas lente exhalante mefites.
100   sed tremor inter vina subit calidumque trientem
excutit e manibus, dentes crepuere retecti,
uncta cadunt laxis tunc pulmentaria labris.
hinc tuba, candelae, tandemque beatulus alto
conpositus lecto crassisque lutatus amomis
105   in portam rigidas calces extendit. at illum
hesterni capite induto subiere Quirites."
    Tange, miser, venas et pone in pectore dextram;
nil calet hic. summosque pedes attinge manusque;
non frigent. "visa est si forte pecunia, sive
110   candida vicini subrisit molle puella,
cor tibi rite salit? positum est algente catino

---

20 The language evokes Lucretius' presentation of Epicurean-
ism (*DRN* 1.146–214).

21 A light wine from Sorrento, recommended for invalids.

that nothing can return to nothing.[20] Is this why you're so pale? Is this a reason for missing lunch?' These jibes make the rabble laugh, and with wrinkled nose the muscular youths redouble their quivering cackles.

"'Examine me. I've got strange palpitations in my chest, a sore throat, and my breathing comes hard. Please examine me.' That's what he says to his doctor. He's ordered to take it easy, but when the third night sees his veins running steady, he'll be round at a rich friend's house with a pretty thirsty flagon, asking for mild Sorrentine[21] to drink at the baths. 'Hey, you're looking pale, my friend.' 'It's nothing.' 'Well, you should see to it, whatever it is. Your hide's going puffy and yellow on you.' 'Well, I'm not as pale as you. Don't play the guardian. I buried mine a long time ago, but you're still here.' 'OK, carry on, I'll shut up.' Stuffed from his feast this one goes to bathe, his belly white, his throat emitting long sulphurous stenches. But as he drinks, a fit of shivers comes over him and knocks the hot glass out of his hands, his bared teeth chatter, then the lavish flavourings slide from his slack lips. Then come the trumpet and candles, and finally the dear deceased, laid out on a high bier and plastered thick with perfumed balm, sticks out his stiff heels towards the door. And it's yesterday's new citizens[22] wearing their new hats that carry him out."

P   You idiot, feel my pulse, put your hand on my chest. No fever there. Feel my toes and fingertips. No chill either.

F   "If perhaps you spot some money, or if the dazzling girl next door gives you a seductive smile, does your heart beat steadily? Tough vegetables are served on a chilly plate

---

[22] I.e. the slaves given their freedom and citizenship in the dead man's will. They wear the cap of liberty (*pilleum*), cf. 5.82.

durum holus et populi cribro decussa farina:
temptemus fauces; tenero latet ulcus in ore
putre quod haut deceat plebeia radere beta.
115   alges, cum excussit membris timor albus aristas.
nunc face supposita fervescit sanguis et ira
scintillant oculi, dicisque facisque quod ipse
non sani esse hominis non sanus iuret Orestes."

with flour sifted through the rabble's sieve: let's check your throat. A septic sore is lurking in your tender mouth: you shouldn't chafe it with proletarian beet. You freeze when pale fear stiffens a crop of bristles on your body. And now, when a torch is lit below you, your blood boils and your eyes flash with anger, and you say and do things which even the lunatic Orestes[23] would swear were signs of lunacy."

[23] The archetypal madman. He was driven mad by the Furies when he killed his mother Clytemnestra in revenge for her murder of his father Agamemnon.

NOTE ON SATIRE 4

The theme of this Satire is essentially the ancient maxim from Delphi: "Know Yourself." Persius uses Socrates as the voice of self-knowledge, first in conversation with the young politician Alcibiades, and then in two anecdotes which illustrate people's lack of self-knowledge. Socrates is first imagined addressing his student, Alcibiades, attacking him for his superficiality, lack of knowledge and expertise, and unfitness to hold political power (1–22). After expressing regret that "No one attempts the descent into them selves, no one!" (23–4), Socrates illustrates how we criticise the faults of others but don't see our own, in two vignettes (24–42). In the first, an innocent question about a millionaire elicits a savage attack on his stinginess from a third party (25–32). In the second, a complete stranger launches an unprovoked harangue on the immorality of a person who is innocently sunbathing in the nude (33–41). Socrates concludes that we all try to conceal our weaknesses, whatever they are, by pretending they don't exist (43–50). All this is ammunition for the central, climactic message of the poem (51–2), expressed most memorably in Persius' typically physical and graphic version of the Delphic maxim, "Spit out what isn't you."

SATIRE 4

"Rem populi tractas?" (barbatum haec crede magistrum
dicere, sorbitio tollit quem dira cicutae)
"quo fretus? dic hoc, magni pupille Pericli.
scilicet ingenium et rerum prudentia velox
5 ante pilos venit, dicenda tacendave calles.
ergo ubi commota fervet plebecula bile,
fert animus calidae fecisse silentia turbae
maiestate manus. quid deinde loquere? 'Quirites,
hoc' puta 'non iustum est, illud male, rectius illud.'
10 scis etenim iustum gemina suspendere lance
ancipitis librae, rectum discernis ubi inter
curva subit vel cum fallit pede regula varo,
et potis es nigrum vitio praefigere theta.
quin tu igitur summa nequiquam pelle decorus
15 ante diem blando caudam iactare popello
desinis, Anticyras melior sorbere meracas?
quae tibi summa boni est? uncta vixisse patella
semper et adsiduo curata cuticula sole?

---

1 Socrates.

2 The Athenian statesman Pericles was Alcibiades' guardian.

3 Lit. "theta," the Greek letter standing for death (*thanatos*),
used by judges when passing sentences of death.

SATIRE 4

"Affairs of state—in your hands?" (Imagine the bearded master[1] saying this, the one removed by that fatal gulp of hemlock.) "With what qualifications? Tell me that, ward of great Pericles.[2] Wisdom, I suppose, and knowledge of the world have arrived early, before your whiskers. You are an expert in what must and must not be said. So, when the mob seethes with its anger roused, you feel moved to silence the fevered crowd with an authoritative gesture. What will you say then? 'Citizens of Rome,' imagine, 'this is unjust, that is ill-advised, the third way is more correct.' You undoubtedly know how to weigh justice in the twin dishes of the wavering scales. You can spot a straight line when it passes between curves, even when the rule is deceptive with its bandy feet, and you are competent to stick the black mark[3] onto wrongdoing. So why then, since your pretty looks on the skin's surface are useless, why don't you stop wagging your tail for the flattering rabble before your time, when you'd be better off gulping down undiluted Anticyras?[4] What's your idea of the highest good? To live off rich dishes all the time and pamper your skin with

[4] Towns associated with the production of hellebore, a classic cure for madness.

expecta, haut aliud respondeat haec anus. i nunc,
20 'Dinomaches ego sum' suffla, 'sum candidus.' esto,
dum ne deterius sapiat pannucia Baucis,
cum bene discincto cantaverit ocima vernae.

 Vt nemo in sese temptat descendere, nemo,
sed praecedenti spectatur mantica tergo!
25 quaesieris 'nostin Vettidi praedia?' 'cuius?'
'dives arat Curibus quantum non miluus errat.'
'hunc ais, hunc dis iratis genioque sinistro,
qui, quandoque iugum pertusa ad compita figit,
seriolae veterem metuens deradere limum
30 ingemit "hoc bene sit" tunicatum cum sale mordens
cepe et farratam pueris plaudentibus ollam
pannosam faecem morientis sorbet aceti?'
at si unctus cesses et figas in cute solem,
est prope te ignotus cubito qui tangat et acre
35 despuat: 'hi mores! penemque arcanaque lumbi
runcantem populo marcentis pandere bulbos.
tum, cum maxillis balanatum gausape pectas,
inguinibus quare detonsus gurgulio extat?
quinque palaestritae licet haec plantaria vellant

29 veterem PCLNW: veteris aVXGMR
36 bulbos *Richter*: vulvas *codd.*
38 gurgulio *codd.*: curculio *Hendry*

---

5 Alcibiades' mother was a member of the noble Alcmaeonid family.

6 In Ov. *Met.* 8.624–724 this is the name of an elderly peasant woman; here she is a herb-seller.

7 An allusion to the fable (Phaedrus 4.10) of people criticising other's faults while being unaware of their own.

continual sun? Hang on, you'll get exactly the same reply
from this old woman. Go on now, puff yourself up, 'I'm
Dinomache's son.[5] I'm a dazzler.' Granted; only wrinkled
Baucis[6] has as much sense as you when she expertly touts
her basil to some slob of a slave.

"No one attempts the descent into themselves, no one!
Instead they stare at the knapsack on the back in front of
them![7] Suppose you ask, 'Do you know Vettidius' estates?'
'Whose?' 'That millionaire at Cures whose ploughlands are
more than a kite can fly over.'[8] 'Oh, do you mean him, that
man hated by the gods, with the hostile Guardian Spirit?
When he hangs up his yoke at the perforated crossroads
shrine[9] reluctant to scrape the ancient dirt from his little
jar, he groans, "Let it be all right!" while munching an on-
ion in its jacket with salt. As his slaveboys cheer their pot of
porridge, he gulps down the threadbare dregs of expiring
vinegar.' But if you relax after a massage and focus the sun
on your skin, there will be some stranger right beside you
who nudges you and spits savagely: 'How disgusting!—
Weeding your prick and the recesses of your backside and
exposing your withered nuts[10] to the public! And another
thing, while you comb and perfume the rug on your jaws,
why does your windpipe[11] stick out clean-shaven from
your groin? Even if five wrestling trainers were to pull out

8 A proverbial expression, cf. Juv. 9.54–5n.

9 I.e. on the annual celebration of the Compitalia, held at a
shrine at the crossroads, here described as "perforated," i.e. open
on all sides. The yoke was hung up to symbolise the break from
work.   10 Lit. "onions."

11 The penis is referred to metaphorically. Or possibly it
should be *curculio,* "weevil" (either the bug or its larva).

40 elixasque nates labefactent forcipe adunca,
non tamen ista filix ullo mansuescit aratro.'
    Caedimus inque vicem praebemus crura sagittis.
vivitur hoc pacto, sic novimus. ilia subter
caecum vulnus habes, sed lato balteus auro
45 praetegit. ut mavis, da verba et decipe nervos,
si potes. 'egregium cum me vicinia dicat,
non credam?' viso si palles, inprobe, nummo,
si facis in penem quidquid tibi venit, amarum
si puteal multa cautus vibice flagellas,
50 nequiquam populo bibulas donaveris aures.
respue quod non es; tollat sua munera cerdo.
tecum habita, noris quam sit tibi curta supellex."

52 noris PLNW*Sang*.S: ut noris αVXCGR

these seedlings and make your boiled buttocks shake with their curving clippers, still that bracken of yours won't be tamed by any plough.'

"In turn we shoot and expose our legs to the shots. We live on that basis, that's the way we know. Down in your groin you have a secret wound, but your belt with its wide gold band conceals it. As you like. Cheat and fool your sinews, if you can. 'When the whole neighbourhood tells me I'm wonderful, can't I believe them?' You shameless man, if you go pale at the sight of a coin, if you do whatever comes to prick,[12] if with your securities in place you whip up the horrid Well-head with many weals,[13] it's pointless to offer your thirsty ears to the public. Spit out what isn't you, and let the labourer take back what he gave you. Live on your own, and you'll find out how incomplete your furniture is."

[12] Playing on the usual "whatever comes to mind."

[13] The Well-head was evidently a place in the Forum where moneylenders gathered. Persius refers to the practice of "whipping up" prices or interest rates, keeping them artificially high, hence the "many weals." The investor operates ruthlessly from a position of strength (*cautus*, which in financial contexts refers to secured loans).

NOTE ON SATIRE 5

This, the longest of the poems, draws together many of the themes and characteristics of Persius' satire. It opens in autobiographical mode with a brief interchange between Persius and his tutor and mentor Lucius Annaeus Cornutus (1–29), in which Cornutus responds to Persius' wish for the hundred tongues that poets pray for by reminding him that he has no need of anything but his usual "language of the toga" for his purpose of "scraping sick morals" (14–16). In reply, Persius offers a personal tribute to Cornutus: "I offer you my heart for unfolding, and it is my pleasure to demonstrate to you how much of my soul is yours, Cornutus, dear friend" (21–4). Maintaining the autobiographical presentation, Persius recalls how he learned from Cornutus by spending time with him, and concludes that their lives are in harmony (30–51). Whatever the reality of this relationship, its representation here is closely modelled upon Horace's presentation of his relationship with his father in *Satires* 1.4 and 1.6.

As if to prove his hard-line Stoicism to his tutor in philosophy, Persius then proceeds to incorporate into Satire 5 a substantial sermon on the Stoic theme of freedom, modelled upon Horace, *Satires* 2.7. As an introduction to his speech, Persius remarks upon the variety of human experience and argues for the importance of philosophy (52–72).

After announcing his theme explicitly (73), he distinguishes real freedom from technical, legal freedom (73–82) and then argues that even if we think we are free, we suffer slavery in many forms because we do not understand the nature of true (Stoic) freedom (83–131). To clarify this, Persius supplies extended examples. The first is slavery to Greed (132–41) and the second slavery to Luxury (141–54)—an "alternating enslavement" (154–6). The next example is introduced with the graphic image of the dog trailing from her neck the chain she has broken (157–60): enslavement to Love (161–75). Finally, after a brief glance at Ambition (176–9), Persius attacks the slavery imposed by Superstition (179–88). Throughout this sermon Persius has presented an extreme version of Stoic attitudes. The only corrective appears in the last lines, with the picture of soldiers with their bulging varicose veins mocking the sentiments of the sermon (189–91). Readers are left to form their own view of the balance between these extremes.

SATIRE 5

Vatibus hic mos est, centum sibi poscere voces,
centum ora et linguas optare in carmina centum,
fabula seu maesto ponatur hianda tragoedo,
volnera seu Parthi ducentis ab inguine ferrum.
5 "quorsum haec? aut quantas robusti carminis offas
ingeris, ut par sit centeno gutture niti?
grande locuturi nebulas Helicone legunto,
si quibus aut Procnes aut si quibus olla Thyestae
fervebit saepe insulso cenanda Glyconi.
10 tu neque anhelanti, coquitur dum massa camino,
folle premis ventos nec clauso murmure raucus
nescio quid tecum grave cornicaris inepte
nec scloppo tumidas intendis rumpere buccas.
verba togae sequeris iunctura callidus acri,
15 ore teres modico, pallentis radere mores
doctus et ingenuo culpam defigere ludo.

---

[1] Cf. Hom. *Il.* 2.489 (ten tongues and voices); Virg. *Georg.* 2.43–4 and *Aen.* 6.625–6 (one hundred tongues and voices).

[2] Allusion to Hor. *Sat.* 2.1.15; conflict with the Parthians was a prominent epic theme from Augustus to Nero.

[3] Mount Helicon in Boeotia was associated with the Muses.

[4] Procne cooked her husband Tereus' son in revenge for his

SATIRE 5

This is the way of bards, to demand one hundred voices, to pray for one hundred mouths and one hundred tongues for their songs,[1] whether serving up a tale to be uttered wide-mouthed by the grieving tragic actor or the wounds of a Parthian pulling a weapon from his groin.[2] "Where's all this leading? What enormous lumps of solid song are you heaping up that they need a hundredfold throat to labour over? Let those about to declaim grandiosely gather fogs from Helicon,[3] if there are any who want to boil the pot of Procne or of Thyestes[4] for boring Glyco's[5] frequent feasts. You don't force the wind from your panting bellows while the ore is smelted in the forge, nor do you self-indulgently croak solemn nonsense to yourself, hoarse with pent-up muttering, nor do you strain to burst your swollen cheeks with a pop! You pursue the language of the toga,[6] skilled at the pointed combination, rounded with moderate utterance, clever at scraping sick morals[7] and at nailing fault

raping her sister Philomela. Atreus served up his brother Thyestes' sons to him in their rivalry for power.

[5] A popular tragic actor of the first century A.D.

[6] I.e. common speech; the toga was the regular dress of Roman citizens and comic actors; here it contrasts with the *toga praetexta* associated with tragedy.

[7] Lit. "pallid," suggesting an immoral lifestyle.

hinc trahe quae dicis mensasque relinque Mycenis
cum capite et pedibus plebeiaque prandia noris."
non equidem hoc studeo, pullatis ut mihi nugis
20   pagina turgescat dare pondus idonea fumo.
secrete loquimur. tibi nunc hortante Camena
excutienda damus praecordia, quantaque nostrae
pars tua sit, Cornute, animae, tibi, dulcis amice,
ostendisse iuvat. pulsa, dinoscere cautus
25   quid solidum crepet et pictae tectoria linguae.
hic ego centenas ausim deposcere fauces,
ut quantum mihi te sinuoso in pectore fixi
voce traham pura, totumque hoc verba resignent
quod latet arcana non enarrabile fibra.
30   Cum primum pavido custos mihi purpura cessit
bullaque subcinctis Laribus donata pependit,
cum blandi comites totaque inpune Subura
permisit sparsisse oculos iam candidus umbo,
cumque iter ambiguum est et vitae nescius error
35   diducit trepidas ramosa in compita mentes,
me tibi supposui. teneros tu suscipis annos
Socratico, Cornute, sinu. tum fallere sollers

17 dicis PαGLRS: dices CN: dicas VXW
19 pullatis PαVXΦSΣ: bullatis W
21 secrete Pα: secreti VXΦS
26 fauces PA: voces αVXΦS
36 supposui CNΣ: seposui PαVXΦS

---

8 The colour of mourners' clothes.   9 Camenae were
Roman water deities identified with the Muses.
   10 The *toga praetexta*, bordered with purple, was worn by
freeborn boys until puberty.

with well-bred wit. Draw your talk from here and leave to Mycenae its banquets, heads and feet, and make yourself familiar with ordinary meals." My aim is certainly not to have my page swell with dark-robed nonsense,[8] fit only to give weight to smoke. In privacy we speak. With the encouragement of Camena,[9] I offer you my heart for unfolding, and it is my pleasure to demonstrate to you how much of my soul is yours, Cornutus, dear friend. Tap it: you have the skill to discriminate between what rings solid and the stucco of the painted tongue. At this point I would dare demand a hundredfold throat, to convey in a clear voice how deeply I have fixed you in the windings of my breast, and to have my words unseal all that lies unutterable, deep in my inmost guts.

When first as a timid youth I lost the protective purple[10] and my amulet hung as an offering to the girdled Hearth gods;[11] when my indulgent companions and fresh white folds[12] permitted me to cast my eyes over the whole Subura[13] without risk; at the age when the route is unclear and perplexity ignorant of life splits the agitated mind at the branching crossroads, I put myself in your hands. You adopted[14] my tender years in your Socratic embrace, Cornutus. Then your skilful rule[15] was applied unawares

[11] The pendant (*bulla*), worn by boys as protection against the evil eye, was dedicated at puberty to the household gods (*Lares*), traditionally represented as young men wearing short, girdled tunics.   [12] Of the toga.   [13] The area between the Viminal and Esquiline hills, a busy market area and location of the "red light" district.   [14] The technical term denoting a father's acknowledgement of his child or adoption of another child.

[15] Lit. "measuring rod."

adposita intortos extendit regula mores
et premitur ratione animus vincique laborat
40 artificemque tuo ducit sub pollice voltum.
tecum etenim longos memini consumere soles
et tecum primas epulis decerpere noctes.
unum opus et requiem pariter disponimus ambo
atque verecunda laxamus seria mensa.
45 non equidem hoc dubites, amborum foedere certo
consentire dies et ab uno sidere duci.
nostra vel aequali suspendit tempora Libra
Parca tenax veri, seu nata fidelibus hora
dividit in Geminos concordia fata duorum
50 Saturnumque gravem nostro Iove frangimus una,
nescio quod certe est quod me tibi temperat astrum.
   Mille hominum species et rerum discolor usus;
velle suum cuique est nec voto vivitur uno.
mercibus hic Italis mutat sub sole recenti
55 rugosum piper et pallentis grana cumini,
hic satur inriguo mavult turgescere somno,
hic campo indulget, hunc alea decoquit, ille
in venerem putris; sed cum lapidosa cheragra
fregerit articulos, veteris ramalia fagi,
60 tunc crassos transisse dies lucemque palustrem
et sibi iam seri vitam ingemuere relictam.
at te nocturnis iuvat inpallescere chartis;
cultor enim iuvenum purgatas inseris aures

59 fregerit PΦ: fecerit αVX
61 vitam . . . relictam αVXΦS: vita . . . relicta P

and it straightened out my twisted ways, and my mind was
overcome by reason and strove to surrender and took on its
features, moulded by your thumb. Yes, I remember spend-
ing long days with you and plucking the early evenings for
feasting with you. Together we arrange our work and rest
as one and relax our seriousness at a restrained table. I
wouldn't want you to doubt that the days of us both run in
harmony with a fixed bond and are guided by one star.[16]
Whether Fate holding tight to truth suspends our desti-
nies in the balanced Scales, or whether the hour born for
fidelity divides between the Twins our concordant fates
and we together shatter stern Saturn with our God's fa-
vour,[17] there certainly is some star which fuses me with
you.

There are a thousand types of humankind, and their
experience of life is variegated—they each have their own
desires and no single prayer fits every life. One man ex-
changes wrinkled pepper and seeds of pale cumin for Ital-
ian merchandise under an eastern sun, another prefers to
grow fat, content with sodden sleep, another has a liking
for outdoor exercises; dicing ruins this man, and that man
rots away on sex. But once stony gout has broken their
joints, like the twigs of an old beech tree, then, too late,
they complain that their days gone past were all clogged, a
marshy miasma, and that they have neglected life. But it is
your delight to grow pale over your texts at night, because,
as cultivator of the young, you sow in their cleansed ears

[16] Persius offers an astrological explanation of his close friend-
ship with Cornutus. This passage is imitated from Hor. *Od.*
2.17.17–22.

[17] Saturn was considered a baleful influence and Jupiter (here
"God") a good influence.

fruge Cleanthea. petite hinc, puerique senesque,
65 finem animo certum miserisque viatica canis.
"cras hoc fiet." idem cras fiet. "quid? quasi magnum
nempe diem donas!" sed cum lux altera venit,
iam cras hesternum consumpsimus; ecce aliud cras
egerit hos annos et semper paulum erit ultra.
70 nam quamvis prope te, quamvis temone sub uno
vertentem sese frustra sectabere canthum,
cum rota posterior curras et in axe secundo.
    Libertate opus est. non hac, ut quisque Velina
Publius emeruit, scabiosum tesserula far
75 possidet. heu steriles veri, quibus una Quiritem
vertigo facit! hic Dama est non tresis agaso,
vappa lippus et in tenui farragine mendax.
verterit hunc dominus, momento turbinis exit
Marcus Dama. papae! "Marco spondente recusas
80 credere tu nummos?" "Marco sub iudice palles?"
"Marcus dixit, ita est." "adsigna, Marce, tabellas."
haec mera libertas, hoc nobis pillea donant.
"an quisquam est alius liber, nisi ducere vitam
cui licet ut libuit? licet ut volo vivere, non sum
85 liberior Bruto?" "mendose colligis" inquit
Stoicus hic aurem mordaci lotus aceto,
"hoc relicum accipio, 'licet' illud et 'ut volo' tolle."

66 fiet PCLNS: fiat αVXGW

---

18 Cleanthes was head of the Stoic school at Athens in the 3rd century B.C.   19 Lit. "travel money."   20 Manumitted slaves were eligible for the grain distributions made to citizens in the tribe of their former owner.   21 One form of manumission involved the master turning the slave around.

Cleanthes' corn.[18] Seek from here, both boys and old men, a fixed purpose for your mind and provisions[19] for your miserable white hair. "I will tomorrow." Tomorrow it will be the same story. "What? As if your gift of a day is generous!" But when another day comes, we have already used up yesterday's tomorrow. Look, another tomorrow makes away with these years and will always be just out of reach. That's because in vain you'll chase the tyre in front, although it's turning close to you, beneath the same chassis, since you are running as rear wheel on the second axle.

Freedom is a must. Not that freedom which entitles each Publius, once enrolled in the Veline tribe, to possess a little voucher for mouldy grain.[20] Alas, how barren of truth are those who think one twirl creates a Roman citizen![21] Here is Dama, a worthless lackey, runny-eyed with cheap wine, who'd cheat over a handful of animal feed. Let his master turn him around and with the spinning of a top out comes Marcus Dama. Amazing! "Do you decline to lend your money, with Marcus as guarantor?" "Do you blanch with Marcus as juror?" "Marcus said so, it must be right." "Sign this document, Marcus." This is pure freedom, this is what the cap of liberty[22] gives us. "So is anyone free other than people who can live life as they please? I can live as I like—am I not more free than Brutus?"[23] "Your logic is faulty," says this Stoic, with his ear cleansed by biting vinegar, "I accept the rest, only remove your 'can' and 'as I

---

[22] The hat worn by freedmen as a sign of their status.

[23] Three Bruti represent freedom in Roman history: Lucius Junius Brutus who drove out the kings of Rome, Marcus Brutus the assassin of Julius Caesar, and Decimus Brutus the opponent of Antony.

"vindicta postquam meus a praetore recessi,
cur mihi non liceat, iussit quodcumque voluntas,
90 excepto siquid Masuri rubrica vetabit?"
disce, sed ira cadat naso rugosaque sanna,
dum veteres avias tibi de pulmone revello.
non praetoris erat stultis dare tenuia rerum
officia atque usum rapidae permittere vitae;
95 sambucam citius caloni aptaveris alto.
stat contra ratio et secretam garrit in aurem,
ne liceat facere id quod quis vitiabit agendo.
publica lex hominum naturaque continet hoc fas,
ut teneat vetitos inscitia debilis actus.
100 diluis elleborum, certo conpescere puncto
nescius examen? vetat hoc natura medendi.
navem si poscat sibi peronatus arator
luciferi rudis, exclamet Melicerta perisse
frontem de rebus. tibi recto vivere talo
105 ars dedit et veris speciem dinoscere calles,
ne qua subaerato mendosum tinniat auro?
quaeque sequenda forent quaeque evitanda vicissim,
illa prius creta, mox haec carbone notasti?
es modicus voti, presso lare, dulcis amicis?
110 iam nunc adstringas, iam nunc granaria laxes,

---

[105] veris speciem P: veri speciem N: veri specimen αXΦ

---

[24] At the manumission ceremony.

[25] Masurius Sabinus was an eminent lawyer under Tiberius;
the chapter headings in books of laws were painted red, hence
rubrica.

like'." "Once I have departed from the praetor, made my own master by his wand,[24] why can't I do whatever my inclination dictates, except whatever's forbidden by the red-titled statutes of Masurius?"[25] Learn this lesson, but drop your anger and wrinkled sneer from your nostril, while I tear out the old grandmothers[26] from your lungs. It was never in the praetor's power to impart to fools the subtleties of social duty and to transmit to them how best to exploit life as it races by. You could sooner equip a lanky barrack servant with a harp. Reason stands opposed and jabbers secretly into your ear that no one should be allowed to do what they will make a mess of. Nature and the common law of humankind contain this principle, that feeble ignorance should restrain forbidden actions. Do you mix hellebore, when you don't know how to steady the balance at the precise point? The essence of medicine forbids this. If a thick-booted ploughman, unacquainted with the Morning Star, were to ask for a ship, Melicerta[27] would protest that propriety had disappeared from the world. Has training given you the capacity to live with a straight ankle[28] and do you have the skill to distinguish appearance from truth, so that there is no false jangle from the gold overlaid on copper? What should be pursued and in turn be avoided—have you marked the first category with chalk and the other with charcoal? Are your desires moderate, your household frugal, are you kind to your friends? Can you now close your granaries and now open them up, and

26 The equivalent of "old wives' tales."

27 A sea god associated with the protection of harbours.

28 I.e. on a firm foundation; modelled on Hor. *Ep*. 2.2.205–12.

inque luto fixum possis transcendere nummum
nec gluttu sorbere salivam Mercurialem?
"haec mea sunt, teneo" cum vere dixeris, esto
liberque ac sapiens praetoribus ac Iove dextro.
115 sin tu, cum fueris nostrae paulo ante farinae.
pelliculam veterem retines et fronte politus
astutam vapido servas in pectore volpem,
quae dederam supra relego funemque reduco.
nil tibi concessit ratio; digitum exere, peccas,
120 et quid tam parvum est? sed nullo ture litabis,
haereat in stultis brevis ut semuncia recti.
haec miscere nefas nec, cum sis cetera fossor,
tris tantum ad numeros Satyrum moveare Bathylli.
"liber ego." unde datum hoc sumis, tot subdite rebus?
125 an dominum ignoras nisi quem vindicta relaxat?
"i, puer, et strigiles Crispini ad balnea defer"
si increpuit, "cessas nugator?" servitium acre
te nihil inpellit nec quicquam extrinsecus intrat
quod nervos agitet; sed si intus et in iecore aegro
130 nascuntur domini, qui tu inpunitior exis
atque hic quem ad strigilis scutica et metus egit erilis?
    Mane piger stertis. "surge" inquit Avaritia, "eia
surge." negas. instat. "surge" inquit. "non queo." "surge."
"et quid agam?" "rogat! en saperdas advehe Ponto,

116 politus PVGLN: politas α: polita XCRW
117 in PαX: sub VΦS
123 satyrum αVX: satyri P$\Phi\Sigma$
130 qui *Paris*. 8070, *Bern*. 398: quid αRW: quin PVXΦ

---

29 Mercury was the god of profit.
30 Lit. "meal, flour."

can you step over a coin stuck in the mud and not gulp down Mercury's saliva?[29] When you can truly say, "These things belong to me, these I possess," then be called free and wise with the blessing of the praetors and of God. But if, being just a little while ago of the same batch[30] as us, you retain your old skin and if, though with polished forehead, you keep a crafty fox in your stale breast, I take back what I gave above and pull in my rope. Reason has made no concession to you. Move your finger (and what is so simple?) and you make a mistake. But you will not succeed with any amount of incense in getting a short-weight speck of wisdom to stay put in fools. To mix these things is sacrilege. And, since you are an oaf in other respects, you could not dance the Satyr of Bathyllus[31] as far as the first three steps. "I declare myself free." Where do you get this assumption from, when you are subject to so many influences? Or don't you recognise a master except when the wand releases you from him? "Off you go, slave boy, take Crispinus' scrapers to the baths." If he scolds you, "Still hanging about, you waste of space?" it's certainly not fierce slavery that gets you moving, nothing from the outside enters to jerk your muscles. But if masters are born inside, in your sick liver, how do you emerge unscathed any more than the slave driven to the scrapers by the whip and terror of his master?

In the morning you're snoring lazily. "Get up," says Greed, "come on, get up." You won't. She insists. "Get up," she says. "I can't." "Get up." "What for?" "What a question! Look! Bring herrings from the Black Sea, castor, hemp,

[31] Bathyllus was a comic dancer and choreographer of Augustus' time; cf. Juv. 6.63.

135 castoreum, stuppas, hebenum, tus, lubrica Coa.
     tolle recens primus piper et sitiente camelo.
     verte aliquid; iura." "sed Iuppiter audiet." "eheu,
     baro, regustatum digito terebrare salinum
     contentus perages, si vivere cum Iove tendis."
140 iam pueris pellem succinctus et oenophorum aptas.
     ocius ad navem! nihil obstat quin trabe vasta
     Aegaeum rapias, ni sollers Luxuria ante
     seductum moneat: "quo deinde, insane, ruis, quo?
     quid tibi vis? calido sub pectore mascula bilis
145 intumuit quam non extinxerit urna cicutae.
     tu mare transilias? tibi torta cannabe fulto
     cena sit in transtro Veiientanumque rubellum
     exhalet vapida laesum pice sessilis obba?
     quid petis? ut nummi, quos hic quincunce modesto
150 nutrieras, pergant avidos sudare deunces?
     indulge genio, carpamus dulcia, nostrum est
     quod vivis, cinis et manes et fabula fies,
     vive memor leti, fugit hora, hoc quod loquor inde est."
     en quid agis? duplici in diversum scinderis hamo.
155 huncine an hunc sequeris? subeas alternus oportet
     ancipiti obsequio dominos, alternus oberres.
     nec tu, cum obstiteris semel instantique negaris
     parere imperio, "rupi iam vincula" dicas;

136 et PαVXCRW: e GN: ex L
137 audiet αVXΦ: audiat PLS
150 pergant αXΦ: peragant PRW: stergant V | sudare PΦ: sudore αVXLR

32 Either wines or silks.
33 An inferior type of wine from Etruria.

ebony, incense, glossy Coans.[32] Be first to grab the fresh load of pepper from the camel while it's still thirsty. Do a deal, swear on it." "But God will hear." "For heaven's sake, you fool: if life on good terms with God is your aim, you will have to be content with scraping away with your finger at the saltcellar so often tasted." Now, ready for action, you are saddling the slaves with baggage and bottle. Quick, all aboard! There's nothing stopping you from racing over the Aegean in your enormous bark, unless sly Luxury takes you to one side first to lecture you: "And where are you rushing off to now, you lunatic, where? What are you up to? Even a jug of hemlock couldn't quench the macho bile which has swollen beneath your fevered breast. You?—Leaping over the sea? You?—Having your dinner on the rowers' bench, reclining on a coiled rope, with a pot-bellied mug reeking of reddish Veientan,[33] spoiled by stale pitch? What for? Do you want the coins which you've nurtured here at a modest five per cent[34] to go on to sweat out a greedy eleven? Enjoy yourself,[35] let's grab our pleasures, life is all we have, you'll soon be ashes, a ghost, a tale. Live with death in mind. The hour races by and the time I spend talking is subtracted from it." So what do you do? You are torn apart by a double hook. Do you pursue this, or that? With alternating enslavement, you must by turns submit to your masters, by turns desert them. And, when you have resisted once and refused to obey their insistent commands, you cannot say,

[34] Lit. five-twelfths; in calculations of interest, five-twelfths of a hundredth part per month, i.e. 5% per annum.

[35] Lit. "give your Genius (i.e. appetites) free play."

nam et luctata canis nodum abripit, et tamen illi,
160   cum fugit, a collo trahitur pars longa catenae.
"Dave, cito, hoc credas iubeo, finire dolores
praeteritos meditor" (crudum Chaerestratus unguem
adrodens ait haec). "an siccis dedecus obstem
cognatis? an rem patriam rumore sinistro
165   limen ad obscenum frangam, dum Chrysidis udas
ebrius ante fores extincta cum face canto?"
"euge, puer, sapias, dis depellentibus agnam
percute." "sed censen plorabit, Dave, relicta?"
"nugaris. solea, puer, obiurgabere rubra,
170   ne trepidare velis atque artos rodere casses.
nunc ferus et violens; at, si vocet, haut mora dicas
'quidnam igitur faciam? nec nunc, cum arcessat et ultro
supplicet, accedam?' si totus et integer illinc
exieras, nec nunc." hic hic quod quaerimus, hic est,
175   non in festuca, lictor quam iactat ineptus.
ius habet ille sui palpo, quem ducit hiantem
cretata Ambitio? "vigila et cicer ingere large
rixanti populo, nostra ut Floralia possint
aprici meminisse senes." quid pulchrius? at cum
180   Herodis venere dies unctaque fenestra
dispositae pinguem nebulam vomuere lucernae
portantes violas rubrumque amplexa catinum
cauda natat thynni, tumet alba fidelia vino,

---

36 The young lover in Menander's comedy *Eunuch*, who has fallen in love with the prostitute Chrysis; he is confiding in his slave. Cf. Hor. *Sat*. 2.3.259–71.

37 The *festuca* was the staff used by the lictor in the ceremony of manumission.

"Now I've broken my shackles!" Even when a bitch breaks
the knot after a struggle, as she bolts, a long section of
chain still trails from her neck. "Davus, very soon—I'm ab-
solutely serious—I intend to put my agonies behind me."
Chaerestratus[36] says this, chewing his bleeding fingernail.
"Why should I embarrass my sober relations with my scan-
dalous behaviour? Why should I wreck my inheritance at
that filthy threshold by getting a bad reputation, drunkenly
singing with my torch gone out in front of Chrysis' drip-
ping door?" "Well done, lad. Be wise, slaughter a lamb for
the gods who drive evil away." "But, Davus, do you think
she'll cry if I leave her?" "You're messing about! You'll get a
beating from her red slipper, lad, to stop you struggling
and gnawing at her tight nets. Now you are fierce and vio-
lent, but if she called you, right away you'd say, 'Whatever
shall I do, then? Not go, even now, when she invites me
and positively begs me?' No, if you have got away whole
and in one piece, not even now." Here, here is what we are
looking for, here it is, not in the stick waved by the silly
lictor.[37] That flatterer led along gaping by white-robed
Ambition[38]—is he master of himself? "Go without sleep
and generously lavish chickpeas on the scrabbling mob, so
that old men may reminisce about our Floralia as they
bask." What could be finer? But when the days of Herod[39]
come, and the lamps, wearing violets and arranged along
the greasy window, spew out a fatty fog, when the tail of
tuna fish swims coiling round the red bowl, when the white

[38] Candidates for office wore the white toga. Persius evokes
the activities of canvassing, including treats distributed at public
festivals such as the Floralia.

[39] Likely to be a reference to Jewish religious celebrations.

labra moves tacitus recutitaque sabbata palles.
185　tum nigri lemures ovoque pericula rupto,
　　tum grandes Galli et cum sistro lusca sacerdos
　　incussere deos inflantis corpora, si non
　　praedictum ter mane caput gustaveris ali.
　　　Dixeris haec inter varicosos centuriones,
190　continuo crassum ridet Pulfenius ingens
　　et centum Graecos curto centusse licetur.

pitcher is bulging with wine, you silently move your lips and turn pale at the circumcised sabbath. Then there are black ghouls and the dangers of the broken egg,[40] then there are huge Galli[41] and the one-eyed priestess with her rattle:[42] they hammer into you gods which puff up the body, if you have not taken the prescribed head of garlic three times in the morning.

Talk like this among the centurions with bulging veins and right away huge Pulfenius will give a coarse laugh and bid a clipped one hundred-penny coin for one hundred Greeks.

[40] For an egg to break in the fire was a bad sign.
[41] Eunuch priests of Cybele.
[42] A priestess of Isis.

NOTE ON SATIRE 6

Although the sixth Satire is often said to mark a dramatic change in tone, this view is hard to accept. The poem is presented as an epistle, following in a tradition initiated by Lucilius and developed substantially by Horace. But Persius' withdrawal from Rome to the Ligurian coast does not signify a shift towards contentment. Rather, it is the logical consequence and physical realisation of the isolation proclaimed earlier in the book. His geographical withdrawal is a symbolic expression of independence and detachment from society and its obligations.

The poem starts by indicating that the season is winter and that his addressee, Bassus, is at his Sabine retreat, while Persius himself has left Rome for Liguria (1–11). (This is the lyric poet Caesius Bassus who published Persius' satires after his death.) Persius announces that this location frees him from all kinds of worry (12–17). Then with a contrast between stingy people and lavish people, he declares his own attitude, which lies in between: to enjoy life to the full (18–26). He concedes the necessity to do one's duty by supporting friends in need, even if one's heir complains about the diminution of his inheritance (27–41). At this point, he becomes aggressive towards his heir, taking him to one side and threatening to spend lavishly on the latest public celebration if the heir

doesn't stop complaining, and then hinting that he will find
a beggar to be his heir (42–60). When the heir persists in
objecting to Persius spending his own money, Persius gets
really indignant (61–74). Finally, he tells the heir to go off
and make as much money as he can, since he will obviously
never be satisfied (75–80). This poem, then, epitomises
Persius' independence and self-reliance and, as such, pres-
ents the essence of the aloof, detached persona which he
adopts throughout the book.

SATIRE 6

Admovit iam bruma foco te, Basse, Sabino?
iamne lyra et tetrico vivunt tibi pectine chordae?
mire opifex numeris veterum primordia vocum
atque marem strepitum fidis intendisse Latinae,
5   mox iuvenes agitare iocos et pollice honesto
egregios lusisse senes. mihi nunc Ligus ora
intepet hibernatque meum mare, qua latus ingens
dant scopuli et multa litus se valle receptat.
"Lunai portum, est operae, cognoscite, cives."
10 cor iubet hoc Enni, postquam destertuit esse
Maeonides Quintus pavone ex Pythagoreo.
hic ego securus volgi et quid praeparet auster
infelix pecori, securus et angulus ille
vicini nostro quia pinguior, etsi adeo omnes
15 ditescant orti peioribus, usque recusem
curvus ob id minui senio aut cenare sine uncto

6 egregios . . . senes Φ: egregius . . . senex PaVGL
9 cognoscite aVΦ: cognoscere PΣ

1 In his epic poem *Annals,* Ennius (*praenomen* Quintus) narrates his dream of Homer, who tells him his soul had once been a peacock and was now passing into Ennius, on the Pythagorean be-

SATIRE 6

Has winter already made you move to your Sabine fireside,
Bassus? Are the lyre strings already coming alive for your
stern plectrum? You are a marvellous artist at setting to
rhythm the ancient elements of our speech and inten-
sifying the virile sound of the Latin harp, then again at stir-
ring up youthful jokes and teasing excellent old men with
your respectable thumb. For me now, the Ligurian coast
is providing warmth, and my sea is spending the winter
where the cliffs present a huge flank and the shore retreats
along many valleys. "Get to know the port of Luna, citi-
zens, it's worth your while." That command comes from
Ennius' heart, after he snored off his identity as Quintus
Homer, ex-Pythagorean peacock.[1] Here, I needn't worry
about the mob and the plots of the hostile South Wind
against my herd; I needn't worry because that corner of my
neighbour's field is more fertile than mine, so much so that
even if everyone of inferior origin were growing rich, I
would to the end refuse to become hunched and wasted
by annoyance because of it, or dine without gravy, or sniff

lief of the transmigration of souls. Homer is here denoted by
Maeonides, lit. "the Lydian," a reference to Homer's supposed
origin.

et signum in vapida naso tetigisse lagoena.
discrepet his alius. geminos, horoscope, varo
producis genio: solis natalibus est qui
20   tinguat holus siccum muria vafer in calice empta,
ipse sacrum inrorans patinae piper; hic bona dente
grandia magnanimus peragit puer. utar ego, utar,
nec rhombos ideo libertis ponere lautus
nec tenuis sollers turdarum nosse salivas.
25   messe tenus propria vive et granaria (fas est)
emole. quid metuas? occa et seges altera in herba est.
"at vocat officium, trabe rupta Bruttia saxa
prendit amicus inops remque omnem surdaque vota
condidit Ionio, iacet ipse in litore et una
30   ingentes de puppe dei iamque obvia mergis
costa ratis lacerae." nunc et de caespite vivo
frange aliquid, largire inopi, ne pictus oberret
caerulea in tabula. sed cenam funeris heres
negleget iratus quod rem curtaveris; urnae
35   ossa inodora dabit, seu spirent cinnama surdum
seu ceraso peccent casiae nescire paratus.

23 rombos PCGLNSΣ: scombros αVMRW
24 turdarum PGLNWΣ: turdorum αVCMR
35 inodora PVΦ*Sang*.SΣ: inhonora αΣ

2 The miser uses brine instead of oil as a dressing and even that has to be bought in a small quantity. Pepper was expensive, so he serves it himself to prevent his slaves being too lavish.

3 Gourmands were said to be able to distinguish female birds from male by the flavour.

4 I.e. statues.

the seal on a stale wine bottle. Someone else may take a
different view. You, my horoscope, produce twins with
divergent characters. One man only on birthdays dips his
dry vegetables in brine bought by the cup, the rascal,
sprinkling a dew of sacred pepper over the plate himself.[2]
Another gobbles his way through an enormous fortune,
the great-hearted boy. Me? I prefer to make the most of
things—not so lavish as to serve turbots to my freedmen
nor so sophisticated as to distinguish the subtle flavours of
hen-thrushes.[3] Live to the full extent of your harvest and
mill your granaries completely—you have the right! What
are you afraid of? Harrow again and a second crop is in
leaf. "But duty calls, a shipwrecked friend clings to the
Bruttian rocks, penniless, his entire wealth and his un-
heard prayers sunk in the Ionian Sea. He himself is
stretched out on the shore together with the huge gods
from the stern[4] and already the ribs of his shattered boat
are exposed to the gulls." So now break off a portion of
your green turf[5] and give it to the penniless man, to stop
him wandering around with his picture painted on a sea-
blue placard.[6] But your heir, angry that you are diminish-
ing your wealth, will skimp the funeral banquet. He will
commit your bones to the urn unperfumed, not bothering
to find out if the cinnamon smells dull or if the cassia is
tainted with cherry. "Are you going to diminish your for-

[5] The phrase contains "landed property" (*caespes* = *ager* or
solum) and "capital" (*vivum*, neut. noun).
[6] Shipwreck victims begged for assistance by displaying
graphic pictures of their disaster, cf. 1.89–90.

"tune bona incolumis minuas?" et Bestius urguet
doctores Graios: "ita fit; postquam sapere Vrbi
cum pipere et palmis venit nostrum hoc maris expers,
40 fenisecae crasso vitiarunt unguine pultes."
haec cinere ulterior metuas? at tu, meus heres
quisquis eris, paulum a turba seductior audi.
o bone, num ignoras? missa est a Caesare laurus
insignem ob cladem Germanae pubis et aris
45 frigidus excutitur cinis ac iam postibus arma,
iam chlamydas regum, iam lutea gausapa captis
essedaque ingentesque locat Caesonia Rhenos.
dis igitur genioque ducis centum paria ob res
egregie gestas induco. quis vetat? aude.
50 vae, nisi conives. oleum artocreasque popello
largior. an prohibes? dic clare. "non adeo" inquis
"exossatus ager iuxta est." age, si mihi nulla
iam reliqua ex amitis, patruelis nulla, proneptis
nulla manet patrui, sterilis matertera vixit

51 adeo *a Leid.Voss.13*: audeo PVΦS

---

7 Bestius (Hor. *Ep*. 1.15.37) is the critic of extravagance who
blames everything that is wrong on foreign imports.

8 *Sapere* = both "wisdom" and "taste."

9 I.e. a dispatch announcing his victory and requesting a tri-
umph, *litterae laureatae*.

10 A sarcastic reference to Caligula's campaign in Gaul and on
the Rhine, A.D. 39–40 (Suet. *Cal*. 43–7).

11 Caesonia is Caligula's wife. Local manufacturers are invited
to supply the paraphernalia for the triumphal procession which
would normally come from the booty. The "yellow plush" is either
for blond wigs for the supposed German prisoners or for their
clothing.

tune—and get away with it?" And Bestius[7] blames the
Greek professors: "That's the trouble. Ever since this
emasculated know-how[8] of ours arrived in Rome along
with pepper and dates, the haycutters have spoiled their
porridge with thick oil." Would this criticism make you
afraid, when you're beyond ashes? But you, my heir, who-
ever you are, come a bit further from the crowd and listen.
Haven't you heard, my friend? A laurel[9] has arrived from
Caesar on account of his notable defeat of German man-
power.[10] The cold ashes are being cleared from the altars,
and Caesonia is already announcing contracts for weapons
to decorate doorposts, cloaks of kings, yellow plush for the
prisoners, war chariots, and enormous Rhine paintings.[11]
So I am staging a hundred pairs[12] for the gods and our
leader's Guardian Spirit, on account of his outstanding
achievement. Who'll stop me? Just try it! You'll regret it
if you don't turn a blind eye: I'll treat the rabble to oil,
bread, and meat. Any objections? Speak up! "The field
nearby," you say, "is not so completely cleared of stones."[13]
Well then, if none of my father's sisters is left alive
now, no female cousins on my father's side, if none of my
paternal uncle's great-granddaughters remains, if my

[12] Of gladiators.

[13] A notorious crux. Apparently, the heir refuses to raise his
voice in criticism of Persius' lavish expenditure because of the
crowd's proximity (42): if they know his views, they are likely
to stone him. *Exossatus* lit. = "with the bone(s) removed," so
"cleared of stones." See Lee and Barr, *Satires of Persius*; Bo, *A.
Persi flacci Saturarum Liber*; Harvey, *Commentary on Persius*.

55 deque avia nihilum superest, accedo Bovillas,
  clivumque ad Virbi praesto est mihi Manius heres.
  "progenies terrae?" quaere ex me quis mihi quartus
  sit pater: haut prompte, dicam tamen; adde etiam unum,
  unum etiam: terrae est iam filius et mihi ritu
60 Manius hic generis prope maior avunculus exit.
  qui prior es, cur me in decursu lampada poscis?
      Sum tibi Mercurius; venio deus huc ego ut ille
  pingitur. an renuis? vis tu gaudere relictis?
  "dest aliquid summae." minui mihi, sed tibi totum est
65 quidquid id est. ubi sit, fuge quaerere, quod mihi
          quondam
  legarat Tadius, neu dicta, "pone paterna,
  fenoris accedat merces, hinc exime sumptus,
  quid relicum est?" relicum? nunc nunc inpensius ungue,
  ungue, puer, caules. mihi festa luce coquatur
70 urtica et fissa fumosum sinciput aure,
  ut tuus iste nepos olim satur anseris extis,
  cum morosa vago singultiet inguine vena,
  patriciae inmeiat volvae? mihi trama figurae
  sit reliqua, ast illi tremat omento popa venter?
75 vende animam lucro, mercare atque excute sollers
  omne latus mundi, ne sit praestantior alter

---

14 Bovillae was the first town south of Rome on the *via Appia*.
The *clivus Virbi* was a steep hill on which carriages had to travel
slowly, thus affording ample opportunity for beggars, cf. Juv.
4.116–18n. Manius is proverbially a beggar's name.

15 A proverbial phrase denoting someone with unknown parentage.

mother's sister died without children and no trace survives
from my grandmother, I'm off to Bovillae, and at the hill of
Virbius,[14] right there, is Manius to be my heir. "A son of the
soil?"[15] Ask me who my father was four stages back: I'll tell
you eventually, not right away. Go back one stage more,
one more again: that'll be a son of the soil, and according to
the principles of genealogy, this Manius turns out to be my
great-great-uncle, more or less. You're in front—why do
you demand the torch from me when I'm still running?[16]

I'm your Mercury:[17] I come to you just like the god in
his pictures. Do you say no? Please take what's left and
be grateful. "There's something missing from the total." I
spent a bit on myself, but whatever is left is all yours. Don't
bother asking the whereabouts of the sum that Tadius[18]
bequeathed to me long ago, and don't keep saying, "Write
down your inheritance from your father, add the revenue
of interest, subtract the expenses, what's left?" Left? Come
on, boy, pour the oil on my greens, pour it on more gener-
ously. Do you suppose that I'll have boiled nettles and
smoked pig's cheek split through the ear on holidays, just
so that that wild descendant of yours, stuffed with goose
innards, can some day piss into a patrician cunt when his
pernickety vein sobs in his roving groin? Or that I'll be left
with a threadbare figure, while his priest-belly wobbles
with fat? Sell your soul for profit, haggle and cleverly comb

---

[16] Persius adapts to the theme of inheritance the idea of run-
ners in a relay race passing on the torch of life (Lucr. *DRN* 2.77–9).

[17] God of profit; commonly depicted holding out a moneybag.

[18] Unknown.

Cappadocas rigida pinguis plausisse catasta,
rem duplica. "feci; iam triplex, iam mihi quarto,
iam decies redit in rugam. depunge ubi sistam."
80 inventus, Chrysippe, tui finitor acervi.

every region of the world, to stop anyone beating you at slapping plump Cappadocians on the hard platform,[19] double your wealth. "I have; now it's tripled, now a fourth time, now it's a tenfold increase[20] for me. Make a mark where I'm to stop!" Chrysippus, the man to put a limit to your heap is found![21]

[19] Slaves for sale were slapped to demonstrate their condition. Cappadocia was an important source of slaves.

[20] Lit. "returns into the crease"; Persius puns on "crease."

[21] Chrysippus (c. 280–207 B.C.), head of the Stoic school, posed a notoriously insoluble question: at what point do a number of items become or cease to be a heap?

JUVENAL

NOTE ON SATIRE 1

This is Juvenal's programmatic poem, a statement of his plan, containing a justification of his choice of genre (his "self-defence," *apologia*, and his "refusal" to write epic, *recusatio*) together with an indication of his chosen content, tone, and techniques. In the opening lines of the poem, alternative genres including epic, drama, and elegy are rejected (1–6) along with trite Greek mythology (7–14) in favour of the genre of Lucilius, satire (19–21). The remainder of the poem is presented as a justification for this choice, based first upon a catalogue of the criminals and idiots who supposedly populate the streets of Rome (22–80), and then upon a more detailed portrayal of the particular fault of the misuse of money (81–146). Satire 1, then, establishes the first-person presentation, the angry character of Juvenal's persona, and his indignant tone, so different from the conversational tone of Horace and the compressed, obscure style of Persius. Juvenal borrows from epic its metre, the dactylic hexameter, and its elevated tones, but inserts lowly, mundane words to indicate that satire can replace epic, because epic is remote and irrelevant whereas satire is real and immediate (e.g. 51–62). He also establishes his chosen themes in this poem: horror at the overturning of the status quo and at the corruption and destruction of the central relationship in Roman life, that

of patron and client. In the final section of the poem (14?
71), Juvenal introduces an interlocutor who warns him o
the dangers of satire, to which he responds by asserting hi
right to criticise where criticism is deserved, following
Lucilius' precedent. When he is warned again that this is
risky, he finally appears to capitulate by declaring that he
will attack only the dead, a claim that is both humorous and
patently untrue.

SATIRE 1

Semper ego auditor tantum? numquamne reponam
vexatus totiens rauci Theseide Cordi?
inpune ergo mihi recitaverit ille togatas,
hic elegos? inpune diem consumpserit ingens
5 Telephus aut summi plena iam margine libri
scriptus et in tergo necdum finitus Orestes?
nota magis nulli domus est sua quam mihi lucus
Martis et Aeoliis vicinum rupibus antrum
Vulcani; quid agant venti, quas torqueat umbras
10 Aeacus, unde alius furtivae devehat aurum
pelliculae, quantas iaculetur Monychus ornos,
Frontonis platani convolsaque marmora clamant
semper et adsiduo ruptae lectore columnae.

2 cordi PSΣ: codri RVΦ

---

1 The scene envisaged is a poetry recitation.
2 The poet Cordus is unknown to us; his poem is an epic about
the Athenian hero Theseus.
3 Tragedies. Until the fourth century A.D. the book consisted
of a papyrus roll attached to rods on which it was rolled.
4 Juvenal's criticism of the triteness of contemporary mytho-
logical epic focusses upon the story of the Argonauts, treated by
Valerius Flaccus in the previous generation. The grove of Mars
was where the Golden Fleece was kept in Colchis. The cave of

130

SATIRE 1

Shall I always be stuck in the audience?[1] Never retaliate for being tortured so often by hoarse Cordus' *Song of Theseus*?[2] Let them get away with it, then?—this one reciting to me his Roman comedies and that one his love elegies? Let them get away with wasting my whole day on an enormous *Telephus*, or an *Orestes* written on the back when the margin at the end of the book is already full— and still not finished?[3] No one knows his own house better than I know the grove of Mars and the cave of Vulcan near the Aeolian cliffs.[4] What the winds are up to, which ghosts Aeacus is torturing,[5] the origin of the other guy waltzing off with that filched golden mini-fleece,[6] the size of the ash trees hurled by Monychus[7]—this is the continual shriek from Fronto's plane trees and his tormented marble and the columns shattered by the non-stop reciter.[8] This is

Vulcan was in the Aeolian (mod. Lipari) islands, to the north of Sicily, although Valerius Flaccus locates it on Lemnos.

[5] In epic, the winds stir up storms at sea, e.g. Val. Flacc. *Arg*. 1.608–54. Aeacus is one of the three judges of the dead.

[6] I.e. Jason.   [7] Monychus was a Centaur; the battle of Lapiths and Centaurs was painted on the Argo.

[8] Fronto is a rich man who allows his house and gardens to be used for poetry recitations, possibly the Fronto of Mart. 1.55 and Plin. *Ep*. 2.11.

expectes eadem a summo minimoque poeta.
15 et nos ergo manum ferulae subduximus, et nos
    consilium dedimus Sullae, privatus ut altum
    dormiret. stulta est clementia, cum tot ubique
    vatibus occurras, periturae parcere chartae.
       Cur tamen hoc potius libeat decurrere campo,
20 per quem magnus equos Auruncae flexit alumnus,
    si vacat ac placidi rationem admittitis, edam.
    cum tener uxorem ducat spado, Mevia Tuscum
    figat aprum et nuda teneat venabula mamma,
    patricios omnis opibus cum provocet unus
25 quo tondente gravis iuveni mihi barba sonabat,
    cum pars Niliacae plebis, cum verna Canopi
    Crispinus Tyrias umero revocante lacernas
    ventilet aestivum digitis sudantibus aurum,
    [nec sufferre queat maioris pondera gemmae]
30 difficile est saturam non scribere. nam quis iniquae
    tam patiens Vrbis, tam ferreus, ut teneat se,
    causidici nova cum veniat lectica Mathonis
    plena ipso, post hunc magni delator amici
    et cito rapturus de nobilitate comesa

---

14 *del. Dobree*   29 *del. Nisbet*

---

9 Corporal punishment was regular in Roman schools.

10 A reference to the declamatory exercises used to train schoolboys. The dictator Lucius Cornelius Sulla (138–78 B.C.) was a popular subject of *suasoriae*, set speeches giving advice.

11 Gaius Lucilius (?180 or ?160–102 B.C.), an *eques* born at Suessa Aurunca in Campania, the founder of Roman hexameter satire; here portrayed as an epic hero.

12 Presumably a woman who disgraces herself by participating as an Amazon in a beast-hunt (*venatio*) in the amphitheatre.

exactly what you can expect from the greatest and the least of poets. Well, I too have snatched my hand from under the cane.[9] I too have given Sulla advice, to retire and enjoy a deep sleep.[10] It's a stupid act of mercy, when you run into so many bards everywhere, to spare paper that's bound to be wasted anyway.

Yet why I choose to charge across the same plain where the great protégé of Aurunca steered his chariot,[11] I'll explain, if you have the time and can listen quietly to my reasoning. When a womanly eunuch takes a wife!—when Mevia shoots a Tuscan boar, holding the hunting spears with one breast bared![12]—when the man who made my stiff beard rasp while he shaved me in my youth can single-handedly challenge all the aristocrats with his wealth!—when that remnant of the Nile's trash, that native slave of Canopus, that Crispinus,[13] wafts a gold ring in summer on sweaty fingers while his shoulder hitches up a Tyrian cloak![14]—then it is hard *not* to write satire. After all, who is so tolerant of the injustices of Rome, who is so hardened, that they can contain themselves when along comes the lawyer Matho in his brand new litter, filling it up all by himself?—when behind him comes the man who informed on his powerful friend, the man who will soon grab any scraps left from the carcass of the nobility, the man feared even by

[13] Crispinus, an Egyptian (hence Canopus, a city on the Nile Delta) who rose to equestrian status and high position under Domitian; in Satire 4 he is depicted as a member of Domitian's inner "cabinet of ministers." His cloak of expensive fabric is a sign of decadence.

[14] Line 29: "And cannot endure the weight of a larger gem-stone."

35 quod superest, quem Massa timet, quem munere palpat
    Carus, ut a trepido Thymele summissa Latino;
    cum te summoveant qui testamenta merentur
    noctibus, in caelum quos evehit optima summi
    nunc via processus, vetulae vesica beatae?
40 unciolam Proculeius habet, sed Gillo deuncem,
    partes quisque suas ad mensuram inguinis heres.
    accipiat sane mercedem sanguinis et sic
    palleat ut nudis pressit qui calcibus anguem
    aut Lugudunensem rhetor dicturus ad aram.
45 quid referam quanta siccum iecur ardeat ira,
    cum populum gregibus comitum premit hic spoliator
    pupilli prostantis et hic damnatus inani
    iudicio? quid enim salvis infamia nummis?
    exul ab octava Marius bibit et fruitur dis
50 iratis, at tu victrix, provincia, ploras.
    haec ego non credam Venusina digna lucerna?
    haec ego non agitem? sed quid magis? Heracleas
    aut Diomedeas aut mugitum labyrinthi
    et mare percussum puero fabrumque volantem,
55 cum leno accipiat moechi bona, si capiendi

---

36 ut *Heinrich*: et *codd.*   42–44 *del. Knoche, Helmbold,
post* 36 *Courtney*   46 premit PRΦ: premat VK

---

15 Baebius Massa and Mettius Carus were two notorious in-
formers under Domitian.   16 Latinus was a famous mime
actor and Thymele his leading lady. Carus' attempts at placation
recall a situation from farce.   17 A reference to the flog-
gings, duckings in the river, and other punishments suffered by
the losing contestants in the oratory contests instituted by Calig-
ula at Lyons (Lugdunum) at the altar to Rome and Augustus.

18 Marius Priscus was successfully prosecuted for extortion by

Massa and mollified with gifts by Carus,[15] like Thymele being sent along privately by the terrified Latinus?[16]—when you are shoved out of the way by men who earn legacies by night work, men who are raised to the skies by what is now the royal road to highest advancement—a rich old woman's snatch? Proculeius gets one-twelfth but Gillo eleven-twelfths: each heir gets a share of inheritance to match his performance. Fine, let them take their blood money and turn pale, just like someone who's stepped on a snake with bare feet, or the orator about to give his speech at the altar of Lyons.[17] Why should I describe the immense rage burning in my fevered guts, when the people are intimidated by the herds that follow someone who's defrauded his ward and reduced him to prostitution, and someone else who's been found guilty in a meaningless verdict? After all, what's disgrace, if their money is safe? Marius in exile starts his boozing in the afternoon and savours the anger of the gods, while you, Province, the winner of the case, are in tears.[18] These outrages—can't I think they merit the Venusian lamp?[19] These outrages—can't I have a go at them? What would be better, then?—stories of Heracles or Diomedes or the bellowing in the labyrinth and the sea hit by a boy and the flying workman?[20]—when a pimping husband accepts his wife's

Pliny and Tacitus early in A.D. 100 (Plin. *Ep.* 2.11) and condemned to banishment from Rome and Italy. Cf. 8.120.

[19] Inspired by the satirist Horace, who came from Venusia.

[20] A list of epic themes, including the labours of Hercules, Diomedes' return from the Trojan War, Theseus' killing of the Minotaur in the labyrinth built by Daedalus on Crete, Icarus who fell into the sea when the wax on his wings melted, and his father Daedalus who crafted their wings.

ius nullum uxori, doctus spectare lacunar,
doctus et ad calicem vigilanti stertere naso;
cum fas esse putet curam sperare cohortis
qui bona donavit praesepibus et caret omni
60 maiorum censu, dum pervolat axe citato
Flaminiam puer Automedon? nam lora tenebat
ipse, lacernatae cum se iactaret amicae.
nonne licet medio ceras implere capaces
quadrivio, cum iam sexta cervice feratur
65 hinc atque inde patens ac nuda paene cathedra
et multum referens de Maecenate supino
signator falsi, qui se lautum atque beatum
exiguis tabulis et gemma fecerit uda?
occurrit matrona potens, quae molle Calenum
70 porrectura viro miscet sitiente rubeta
instituitque rudes melior Lucusta propinquas
per famam et populum nigros efferre maritos.
aude aliquid brevibus Gyaris et carcere dignum,
si vis esse aliquid. probitas laudatur et alget;
75 criminibus debent hortos, praetoria, mensas,
argentum vetus et stantem extra pocula caprum.
quem patitur dormire nurus corruptor avarae,

63 licet *Guyet*: libet *codd.*
67 falsi PRV: falsum G: falso Φ
70 rubeta PRV: rubetam Φ

---

[21] Contrary to remarks by commentators, the precise legal
situation here is unclear.

[22] Achilles' charioteer in Homer's *Iliad*.

[23] Maecenas, the renowned patron of the arts (7.94), was also a
byword for effeminacy, cf. 12.38–9.

136

lover's gifts, if she's not entitled to inherit,[21] an expert at watching the ceiling, an expert, too, at snoring over his goblet with a wide-awake nose?—when someone who's lavished his wealth on the stables, who's gone through his entire family fortune, thinks he's entitled to aspire to the command of a cohort, all the while racing his chariot along the Flaminian Way at top speed, a boy Automedon?[22] Yes, really—he was holding the reins himself, while showing off to his girlfriend in the military cloak. Surely I'm allowed to fill a roomy notebook while standing at the crossroads, when an accessory to fraud is carried past on as many as six necks already, exposed to view on this side and that, in his almost naked litter, strongly recalling the languid Maecenas,[23] someone who's turned himself into a wealthy toff with a brief document and a moistened signet ring? Then along comes a powerful lady, who just before offering her husband the mellow Calenian wine[24] will mix in parching toad's poison. A new improved Lucusta,[25] she has taught her simple neighbours to give their blackened husbands a send-off in the face of scandal and crowds alike. If you want to be Somebody, do a daring deed deserving of cramped Gyara[26] and the dungeon. Honesty is praised—and left in the cold. Crimes bring people their pleasure gardens, mansions, dining tables, antique silver plate and goblets with embossed goats. Who can get to sleep for thinking about the man who seduces his greedy

[24] A high quality wine from Campania.

[25] A professional poisoner from Gaul employed by Agrippina to poison Claudius and by Nero to poison Britannicus.

[26] A small island in the Aegean used as a place of banishment.

quem sponsae turpes et praetextatus adulter?
si natura negat, facit indignatio versum
80 qualemcumque potest, quales ego vel Cluvienus.
        Ex quo Deucalion nimbis tollentibus aequor
navigio montem ascendit sortesque poposcit
paulatimque anima caluerunt mollia saxa
et maribus nudas ostendit Pyrrha puellas,
85 quidquid agunt homines, votum, timor, ira, voluptas,
gaudia, discursus, nostri farrago libelli est.
et quando uberior vitiorum copia? quando
maior avaritiae patuit sinus? alea quando
hos animos? neque enim loculis comitantibus itur
90 ad casum tabulae, posita sed luditur arca.
proelia quanta illic dispensatore videbis
armigero! simplexne furor sestertia centum
perdere et horrenti tunicam non reddere servo?
quis totidem erexit villas, quis fercula septem
95 secreto cenavit avus? nunc sportula primo
limine parva sedet turbae rapienda togatae.
ille tamen faciem prius inspicit et trepidat ne
suppositus venias ac falso nomine poscas:
agnitus accipies. iubet a praecone vocari
100 ipsos Troiugenas, nam vexant limen et ipsi

---

27 An amateur poet, unknown to us.

28 An outline of the story of the flood and recreation of human-
kind (cf. Ov. *Met*. 1.253–416): Deucalion and Pyrrha were the two
mortals allowed by the gods to survive; when their boat landed on
Mount Parnassus, Deucalion asked how to restore mankind. The
oracle instructed them to throw stones over their shoulders, re-
creating men and women respectively.

daughter-in-law, about impure brides and teenage adulterers? If talent is lacking, then indignation will inspire my poetry, such as it can, the sort of verses you can expect from me or Cluvienus.[27]

From the time when the rain clouds raised the water level, Deucalion climbed the mountain by ship and asked for an oracle, when gradually the stones grew soft and warm with life, when Pyrrha displayed nude girls to the males,[28] all human activity—prayers, fears, anger, pleasure, joys, hustle and bustle—this is the mishmash of my little book. And when was the supply of vices richer? When did the palm of greed gape open wider? When did gambling arouse such passion? People now come to try their luck at the gaming table not with their wallets but betting from a treasure chest. What massive battles you'll see there, with the croupier acting as armour bearer! Is it not pure madness to lose a hundred thousand sesterces and yet grudge a shirt to a shivering slave? Which of our ancestors built so many country houses or dined in private off seven courses? These days the puny handout[29] sits right on the threshold waiting to be grabbed by a toga-clad mob. But the patron himself takes a nervous look at your face first, in case you've come to make a false claim under someone else's name. Once you're identified, you'll get your money. He tells the herald to summon even the Trojan-born elite[30]—yes, they too besiege the threshold along

[29] Literally "the little basket"; given by wealthy men to their clients as a reward for attendance; formerly food to be carried away in a "basket"; later a payment in money.

[30] The grand old families who claimed descent from the Trojans who accompanied Aeneas to Italy.

nobiscum. "da praetori, da deinde tribuno."
sed libertinus prior est. "prior" inquit "ego adsum.
cur timeam dubitemve locum defendere, quamvis
natus ad Euphraten, molles quod in aure fenestrae
105   arguerint, licet ipse negem? sed quinque tabernae
quadringenta parant. quid confert purpura maior
optandum, si Laurenti custodit in agro
conductas Corvinus ovis, ego possideo plus
Pallante et Licinis?" expectent ergo tribuni,
110   vincant divitiae, sacro ne cedat honori
nuper in hanc urbem pedibus qui venerat albis,
quandoquidem inter nos sanctissima divitiarum
maiestas, etsi funesta Pecunia templo
nondum habitat, nullas nummorum ereximus aras,
115   ut colitur Pax atque Fides, Victoria, Virtus
quaeque salutato crepitat Concordia nido.
sed cum summus honor finito conputet anno,
sportula quid referat, quantum rationibus addat,
quid facient comites quibus hinc toga, calceus hinc est
120   et panis fumusque domi? densissima centum
quadrantes lectica petit, sequiturque maritum
languida vel praegnas et circumducitur uxor.
hic petit absenti nota iam callidus arte
ostendens vacuam et clausam pro coniuge sellam.

114 habitat PRVOTΣ: habitas Φ

---

[31] Equivalent to the property qualification for an *eques*.
[32] Denoting senatorial status.
[33] A cognomen of one of the oldest families.

with the rest of us. "Pay the praetor, then the tribune." But
a freedman is ahead of them. "I was here first," he says.
"Why shouldn't I stand my ground without fear or hesita-
tion, even though I was born on the Euphrates?—a fact
that the womanly windows in my ears would proclaim,
even if I denied it myself. But my five shops give me an
income of four hundred thousand.[31] What more can the
broader purple stripe[32] bestow, if a Corvinus[33] herds
leased sheep on Laurentine land while I own more than
Pallas and people like Licinus?"[34] So let the tribunes wait,
let money rule supreme! The man who's just arrived in our
city with whitened feet[35] shouldn't have to give way to
sacrosanct office! After all, we revere the majesty of riches
more than any god, even though deadly Money does not
yet have a temple to live in and we have not yet set up any
altars to Cash, as we now worship Peace and Loyalty, Vic-
tory, Valour, and Concord who clatters when her nest is
hailed.[36] But when the highest official at the end of the
year computes the income from the handout, the incre-
ment to his accounts, what will the dependants do when
that same handout has to buy their togas and shoes and
bread and smoke at home? Jam-packed litters come seek-
ing the hundred coin handout. Behind her husband trails a
wife who's ill or pregnant, going the rounds. Another man,
an old hand at a familiar trick, claims for his wife in her ab-
sence, pointing in her stead to an empty, curtained sedan

34 Pallas was a freedman of Claudius who amassed a fortune of
phenomenal size. Licinus was a slave of Julius Caesar, freed by
Augustus, who became very rich as procurator of Gaul.
35 A sign of imported slaves.   36 The temple of Con-
cordia at the entrance to the Capitol, used by storks for nesting.

125   "Galla mea est" inquit, "citius dimitte. moraris?
       profer, Galla, caput." "noli vexare, quiescet."
           Ipse dies pulchro distinguitur ordine rerum:
       sportula, deinde forum iurisque peritus Apollo
       atque triumphales, inter quas ausus habere
130   nescio quis titulos Aegyptius atque Arabarches,
       cuius ad effigiem non tantum meiere fas est.
       vestibulis abeunt veteres lassique clientes
       votaque deponunt, quamquam longissima cenae
       spes homini; caulis miseris atque ignis emendus.
135   optima silvarum interea pelagique vorabit
       rex horum vacuisque toris tantum ipse iacebit.
       nam de tot pulchris et latis orbibus et tam
       antiquis una comedunt patrimonia mensa.
       nullus iam parasitus erit. sed quis ferat istas
140   luxuriae sordes? quanta est gula quae sibi totos
       ponit apros, animal propter convivia natum!
       poena tamen praesens, cum tu deponis amictus
       turgidus et crudum pavonem in balnea portas.
       hinc subitae mortes atque intestata senectus.
145   it nova nec tristis per cunctas fabula cenas;
       ducitur iratis plaudendum funus amicis.
           Nil erit ulterius quod nostris moribus addat
       posteritas, eadem facient cupientque minores,
       omne in praecipiti vitium stetit. utere velis,
150   totos pande sinus. dicas hic forsitan "unde
       ingenium par materiae? unde illa priorum
       scribendi quodcumque animo flagrante liberet

           137–8 *del. Ribbeck*   143 crudum VΦ: crudus PRH
           144 intestata Φ: intemptata *Corelli*
           150 dicas VΦ: dices PRO

142

chair. "That's my Galla," he says. "Deal with us quickly. Is there a problem? Galla, stick your head out." "Oh, don't bother her, she'll be resting."

The day itself is marked by a splendid sequence of events: the handout, then the forum with its Apollo, the legal expert, and those triumphal statues, where some Egyptian mogul has had the nerve to set up his titles. At his image it's legitimate to do more than piss. The old and weary clients leave the porches, abandoning their wishes—although the hope of dinner is the one that lasts longest. The poor souls have got to buy their cabbage and firewood. Meanwhile, their lord will be devouring the choicest produce of woodland and sea, reclining alone among the empty couches. The fact is, they consume entire fortunes at a single table chosen from all those splendid, large round tables of such antiquity. Soon there'll be no parasites left! But who can stand such mean extravagance? What a monstrous gullet, that serves itself whole boars, an animal created for parties! The punishment is instant, though, when you take off your cloak and, completely bloated, carry an undigested peacock to the baths. The result: sudden death and intestate old age. The untragic news passes round all the dinner parties and the funeral takes place to the cheers of his angry friends.

Posterity will have nothing to add to our ways: our descendants will do and desire exactly the same. All depravity is standing on the brink of the chasm. Hoist your sails, spread all your canvas. Perhaps you might say now, "Where will you find talent that matches your subject? Where will you find that frankness of past generations for writing

simplicitas?" cuius non audeo dicere nomen?
quid refert dictis ignoscat Mucius an non?
155 "pone Tigillinum, taeda lucebis in illa
qua stantes ardent qui fixo gutture fumant,

* * * * *

et latum media sulcum deducit harena."
qui dedit ergo tribus patruis aconita, vehatur
pensilibus plumis atque illinc despiciat nos?
160 "cum veniet contra, digito compesce labellum:
accusator erit qui verbum dixerit 'hic est.'
securus licet Aenean Rutulumque ferocem
committas, nulli gravis est pertusus Achilles
aut multum quaesitus Hylas urnamque secutus:
165 ense velut stricto quotiens Lucilius ardens
infremuit, rubet auditor cui frigida mens est
criminibus, tacita sudant praecordia culpa.
inde ira et lacrimae. tecum prius ergo voluta
haec animo ante tubas: galeatum sero duelli
170 paenitet." experiar quid concedatur in illos
quorum Flaminia tegitur cinis atque Latina.

post 156 lacuna *Housman*
163 pertusus *Hendry*: percussus Φ

---

37 Publius Mucius Scaevola, an eminent Roman politician attacked by Lucilius; 153–4 may be a quotation from Lucilius.
38 Gaius Ofonius Tigillinus, a favourite of Nero, responsible for punishing the Christians with the torment described in lines 155–7, cf. Tac. *Ann.* 15.44.

whatever their blazing spirits chose?" Is there anyone I don't dare name? What does it matter whether Mucius[37] forgives me or not? "Go ahead, describe Tigillinus,[38] and you'll be ablaze on that pine torch where men stand, burning and smoking with their throats fastened tight * * * ⟨until your corpse⟩ traces a broad furrow straight across the arena." So am I going to let a man who's given aconite[39] to three of his uncles ride by on swaying feather cushions and look down on us from up there? "Yes, and when he comes by, button your lip with your finger: anyone who so much as says 'That's him!' will be treated as an informer. You can pit Aeneas against the fierce Rutulian without fear, and no one's offended by a perforated Achilles or by a Hylas much searched-for when chasing his pitcher.[40] But whenever Lucilius blazes and roars as if with drawn sword,[41] the hearer whose mind is chilled with crime goes red and his heartstrings sweat with silent guilt. Then come rage and tears. So turn all this over in your mind before the trumpets sound. Once you've got your helmet on, it's too late for second thoughts about fighting." Then I'll see what I can get away with saying against the people whose ashes are covered by the Flaminian and the Latin roads.[42]

[39] Poison.

[40] The interruptor refers to three famous epic stories.

[41] Lucilius again appears as an epic warrior: cf. 19–20n.

[42] Since burial within the city of Rome was generally forbidden, the major roads out of Rome were lined with the tombs of people who could afford to erect them.

NOTE ON SATIRE 2

The next poem continues the themes and tone established
in Satire 1. The victims in Satire 2 are men who behave ef-
feminately and who prefer the passive role in same-sex re-
lationships (pathics), an elaboration of the theme of devia-
tions from the "norm" in Satire 1. The attack starts in the
familiar indignant tone, first aimed at hypocritical Stoic
moralists who try to hide their effeminacy (1–35), with
the claim (line 8): "There's no trusting appearances." This
angry condemnation is supplemented by more detached
and ironic comments from a woman Laronia, evidently an
adulteress, who defends her own sex against attacks by the
moralists; this drives the hypocrites away (36–65). Juvenal
then attacks another set of hypocrites, those aristocrats
who make no secret of their proclivities while they pro-
nounce upon morality (65–78). After a graphic image of
contagion spreading from the centre (78–81), the attack
then switches to closet (but not hypocritical) effeminates
and pathics (82–116), then to those who expose their sexu-
ality overtly, by making no secret of getting married and by
entering the gladiatorial arena in a humiliating, shameful
role (117–48). Juvenal closes the poem with a picture of
the disgrace felt by the ghosts of famous, manly Romans in
the Underworld (149–59) and with the phenomenon of
young foreigners being morally corrupted by their visits to
Rome (159–70).

SATIRE 2

Vltra Sauromatas fugere hinc libet et glacialem
Oceanum, quotiens aliquid de moribus audent
qui Curios simulant et Bacchanalia vivunt.
indocti primum, quamquam plena omnia gypso
5   Chrysippi invenias; nam perfectissimus horum,
si quis Aristotelen similem vel Pittacon emit
et iubet archetypos pluteum servare Cleanthas.
frontis nulla fides; quis enim non vicus abundat
tristibus obscenis? castigas turpia, cum sis
10   inter Socraticos notissima fossa cinaedos?
hispida membra quidem et durae per bracchia saetae
promittunt atrocem animum, sed podice levi
caeduntur tumidae medico ridente mariscae.
rarus sermo illis et magna libido tacendi
15   atque supercilio brevior coma. verius ergo
et magis ingenue Peribomius; hunc ego fatis
imputo, qui vultu morbum incessuque fatetur.
horum simplicitas miserabilis, his furor ipse

---

1 To the far north.

2 Manius Curius Dentatus, censor 272 B.C. and representative
of traditional Roman virtue.   3 They display the busts of
Pittacus, one of the famous Seven Sages, the Stoic philosophers
Chrysippus and Cleanthes, and Aristotle.

SATIRE 2

I feel like running away from here beyond the Sarmatians
and the icy Ocean[1] whenever those people who imitate the
Curii[2] but live like Bacchanals have the gall to talk about
morality. Point one: they are ignoramuses, although you'll
find their houses without exception stuffed full of plaster
busts of Chrysippus. This is because the most perfect of
them is the one who has bought a lifelike Aristotle or
Pittacus and who has his shelf display originals of Clean-
thes and company.[3] There's no trusting appearances. After
all, isn't every street packed with grim-looking perverts?
Do you criticise disgusting behaviour when you yourself
are the most notorious digging-hole among Socratic path-
ics? Shaggy limbs and stiff bristles all over your arms
promise a spirit that's fierce, but your arsehole is smooth
when the laughing doctor lances your swollen "figs."[4]
Among that kind, conversation is infrequent: they have a
marked urge for silence and hair well above the eyebrows.
My conclusion? Peribomius behaves more frankly and
honourably than they do.[5] This is a man who admits his dis-
ease in his look and his walk; his behaviour I attribute to
fate. The openness of such people arouses pity and their

---

[4] Piles, thought to be caused by anal intercourse.
[5] A pathic, according to the scholiast.

dat veniam; sed peiores, qui talia verbis
20   Herculis invadunt et de virtute locuti
clunem agitant. "ego te ceventem, Sexte, verebor?"
infamis Varillus ait, "quo deterior te?"
loripedem rectus derideat, Aethiopem albus.
quis tulerit Gracchos de seditione querentes?
25   quis caelum terris non misceat et mare caelo
si fur displiceat Verri, homicida Miloni,
Clodius accuset moechos, Catilina Cethegum,
in tabulam Sullae si dicant discipuli tres?
qualis erat nuper tragico pollutus adulter
30   concubitu, qui tunc leges revocabat amaras
omnibus atque ipsis Veneri Martique timendas,
cum tot abortivis fecundam Iulia vulvam
solveret et patruo similes effunderet offas.
nonne igitur iure ac merito vitia ultima fictos
35   contemnunt Scauros et castigata remordent?
Non tulit ex illis torvum Laronia quendam
clamantem totiens "ubi nunc, lex Iulia, dormis?"

---

6 For the Stoics, Hercules was a model of correct behaviour,
thanks to his Labours.   7 Tiberius Sempronius Gracchus
and his brother Gaius, who provoked civil disturbances, in which
they died.   8 Gaius Verres, infamous governor of the prov-
ince of Sicily in 73–71 B.C., accused by Cicero of corruption and
theft on a massive scale.   9 Titus Annius Milo, tribune of
the plebs who in 52 B.C. murdered Clodius.

10 Publius Clodius Pulcher, tribune of the plebs who in 61 B.C.
was prosecuted for profaning the women-only Bona Dea festival.

11 Lucius Sergius Catilina planned a military coup in 63 B.C.
after failing to become consul by legal means; Gaius Cornelius
Cethegus was one of his fellow conspirators.

12 The "second triumvirate" of Antony, Lepidus, and Octa-

madness itself grants them forgiveness. Much worse are
people who attack such conduct in the words of Hercules[6]
and who swing their bottoms after talking about virtue.
"Shall I be in awe of you, Sextus, when I see you wiggling
your arse?" says the notorious Varillus. "How am I worse
than you?" It should be the man who walks upright who
mocks the man who limps, the white man who mocks the
black. Who could stand the Gracchi[7] moaning about revo-
lution? Who would not confuse sky and land, sea and sky, if
Verres[8] took exception to a thief or Milo[9] to a murderer, if
Clodius[10] accused adulterers and Catiline Cethegus,[11] if
Sulla's three disciples criticised his hit list?[12] Exactly so was
that adulterer[13] of more recent times, defiled by a union
worthy of tragedy, who tried to revive bitter laws to terrify
everyone, even Venus and Mars, at the very moment when
his Julia was unsealing her fertile womb with numerous
abortion-inducers and pouring out lumps which resem-
bled her uncle. Don't you think it's right and justifiable,
then, that the extremes of depravity sneer at bogus
Scaurus-types[14] and bite back when criticised?

Laronia could not stand one of those grim individuals
who kept on shouting, "In whose bed are you now asleep,

vian, of 43 B.C., which followed Sulla's example in proscribing its
enemies.   [13] The emperor Domitian, who had sex with his
niece Julia, thereby committing adultery and incest. She died
when he forced her to undergo an abortion in A.D. 89. In his ca-
pacity as censor, Domitian enforced Augustus' legislation against
adultery. Venus and Mars were caught in the act of adultery by Ve-
nus' husband Vulcan.   [14] Marcus Aemilius Scaurus, consul
in 115 B.C. and censor in 109, with his reputation for integrity and
excellence became a type of upright morality.

atque ita subridens: "felicia tempora, quae te
moribus opponunt. habeat iam Roma pudorem:
40 tertius e caelo cecidit Cato. sed tamen unde
haec emis, hirsuto spirant opobalsama collo
quae tibi? ne pudeat dominum monstrare tabernae.
quod si vexantur leges ac iura, citari
ante omnis debet Scantinia. respice primum
45 et scrutare viros: faciunt peiora, sed illos
defendit numerus iunctaeque umbone phalanges.
magna inter molles concordia. non erit ullum
exemplum in nostro tam detestabile sexu.
Tedia non lambit Cluviam nec Flora Catullam:
50 Hispo subit iuvenes et morbo pallet utroque.
numquid nos agimus causas? civilia iura
novimus? aut ullo strepitu fora vestra movemus?
luctantur paucae, comedunt colyphia paucae.
vos lanam trahitis calathisque peracta refertis
55 vellera, vos tenui praegnantem stamine fusum
Penelope melius, levius torquetis Arachne,

       *   *   *   *   *

horrida quale facit residens in codice paelex.
notum est cur solo tabulas impleverit Hister
liberto, dederit vivus cur multa puellae.

45 peiora *Herwerden*: nam plura OP: qui plura R: hi plura VΦ
post 56 lacuna *Courtney*

---

15 The *lex Iulia de adulteriis coercendis*, enacted by Augustus
in 18 B.C. and revived by Domitian, made a wife's adultery a crimi-
nal act.
16 The two Catones were paragons of Republican morality,
Marcus Porcius Cato (234–149 B.C.), censor in 184, and his great-

Julian law?"[15] and, smiling, this is what she said: "What happy times, that set you up as the enemy of corrupt morality! Let Rome now develop her sense of shame: a third Cato[16] has tumbled from the sky! But, by the way, where did you buy this balsam perfume which wafts from your shaggy neck? Don't be embarrassed to point out the shopowner. But if it's a matter of waking up laws and statutes, it's the Scantinian law[17] which should be summoned before all the rest. Look at men first, subject them to scrutiny. They behave worse, but they've got safety in numbers and in their phalanxes, with shield overlapping shield. The solidarity between effeminates is enormous. You won't find any example so revolting in our sex. Tedia doesn't tongue Cluvia, nor Flora Catulla, but Hispo submits to young men and turns pale from both diseases. We women don't plead cases, do we? Or claim expertise in civil law? Or disturb your courts with an uproar? Few women wrestle, few women consume the meat-rich diet. But you tease the wool and you bring the prepared fleeces back in baskets. You turn the spindle that's pregnant with fine thread better than Penelope, more deftly than Arachne,[18] * * * the sort of task which a dishevelled mistress does as she sits on the block.[19] It's common knowledge why Hister filled his will with his freedman alone, why in his lifetime he made many

grandson of the same name (95–46 B.C.), a Stoic who committed suicide.   [17] The *lex Scantinia*, revived by Domitian, perhaps outlawed sex with young freeborn males.   [18] In Homer's *Odyssey* Penelope's chief occupation is weaving. Arachne produced such a wonderful tapestry that Athene destroyed it in rage and turned her into a spider (Ov. *Met*. 6.1–145).

[19] Another mythological allusion, obscured by the lacuna.

60   dives erit magno quae dormit tertia lecto.
tu nube atque tace: donant arcana cylindros.
de nobis post haec tristis sententia fertur?
dat veniam corvis, vexat censura columbas."
fugerunt trepidi vera ac manifesta canentem
Stoicidae; quid enim falsi Laronia?

65   Sed quid
non facient alii, cum tu multicia sumas,
Cretice, et hanc vestem populo mirante perores
in Proculas et Pollittas? est moecha Fabulla;
damnetur, si vis, etiam Carfinia: talem

70   non sumet damnata togam. "sed Iulius ardet,
aestuo." nudus agas: minus est insania turpis.
en habitum quo te leges ac iura ferentem
vulneribus crudis populus modo victor et illud
montanum positis audiret vulgus aratris.

75   quid non proclames, in corpore iudicis ista
si videas? quaero an deceant multicia testem.
acer et indomitus libertatisque magister,
Cretice, perluces. dedit hanc contagio labem
et dabit in plures, sicut grex totus in agris

80   unius scabie cadit et porrigine porci
uvaque conspecta livorem ducit ab uva.
    Foedius hoc aliquid quandoque audebis amictu;
nemo repente fuit turpissimus. accipient te
paulatim qui longa domi redimicula sumunt

[65] laronia PΦ: latronia KU
[80] porrigine Φ: prurigine PALZ

[20] A woman condemned of adultery adopted the toga worn by the *meretrix* (prostitute).

gifts to his young, still-virgin wife. She who sleeps third in a large bed will be rich. My advice, young woman? Marry and keep quiet: secrets bestow jewels. After all this, is a verdict of 'guilty' passed on us? That's a judgment that acquits the ravens and condemns the doves." As she uttered the obvious truth, the would-be Stoics ran away in a panic. After all, was anything that Laronia said false?

But what will others not do, when you wear gauze, Creticus, and, while the people are staring in amazement at this garment, you deliver an impassioned finale against women like Procula and Pollitta? Fabulla is an adulteress. Imagine even Carfinia found guilty, if you like. But if she is found guilty, she won't put on a toga like that.[20] "But July's blazing—I'm sweltering." Then plead stark naked. Insanity is less disgusting. Just look at the outfit you're wearing for citing laws and statutes, in front of an audience consisting of the populace fresh from victory with their wounds still raw and those famous mountain folk who have just put down their ploughs! Just think how you would protest if you saw those clothes on the person of a judge. I question whether gauze is right even for a witness. You fierce, indomitable champion of liberty, Creticus—you are transparent! This stain is caused by infection and it will spread further, just as the entire herd in the fields dies because of the scab and mange of a single pig, just as a bunch of grapes takes on discoloration from the sight of another bunch.

Some day you will dare something more disgusting than this clothing. No one ever became utterly abominable overnight. Little by little you'll be welcomed by men who in the privacy of their homes wear long bands on their fore-

85   frontibus et toto posuere monilia collo
atque Bonam tenerae placant abdomine porcae
et magno cratere Deam. sed more sinistro
exagitata procul non intrat femina limen:
solis ara deae maribus patet. "ite, profanae,"
90   clamatur, "nullo gemit hic tibicina cornu."
talia secreta coluerunt orgia taeda
Cecropiam soliti Baptae lassare Cotyton.
ille supercilium madida fuligine tinctum
obliqua producit acu pingitque trementis
95   attollens oculos; vitreo bibit ille priapo
reticulumque comis auratum ingentibus implet
caerulea indutus scutulata aut galbina rasa
et per Iunonem domini iurante ministro;
ille tenet speculum, pathici gestamen Othonis,
100   Actoris Aurunci spolium, quo se ille videbat
armatum, cum iam tolli vexilla iuberet.
res memoranda novis annalibus atque recenti
historia, speculum civilis sarcina belli.
nimirum summi ducis est occidere Galbam
105   et curare cutem, [summi constantia civis
Bebriaci campis] solium adfectare Palati
et pressum in faciem digitis extendere panem,

93 tinctum LP: tactum Φ: tectum O
105–6 *del.* summi . . . campis *Nisbet*
106 solium *Vat. Reg. 2029*: spolium PΦ

---

21 A Roman goddess worshipped exclusively by women.
22 A Thracian goddess whose cult was adopted in Athens. Her followers were called Baptae, probably derived from a ritual baptism; the cult was thought to involve transvestism.

heads and have their necks entirely covered with jewellery and who placate the Good Goddess[21] with the udder of a young sow and with a large bowl of wine. But by inversion of the normal custom, women do not cross their threshold and are sent packing: the altar of the goddess is open to males alone. "Get away, you impure women!" is their cry. "No music girl with her horn pipes here." Rites like these were celebrated by torchlight in secret by the Baptae, who used to exhaust Cecropian Cotyto.[22] One of these men has blackened his eyebrows with damp soot and is extending them with a slanting pencil, raising his fluttering eyes as he applies the makeup. Another is drinking from a phallus-shaped glass with his substantial hairdo filling a golden hairnet, dressed in a tartan pattern of different shades of blue or in green satin, and with his slave swearing by his master's Juno.[23] Another holds a mirror, the accoutrement of the pathic Otho,[24] "spoils of Auruncan Actor,"[25] in which he used to admire himself when he'd put on his armour, while giving orders to advance into battle. It's a matter that deserves its mention in recent annals and modern history,[26] that a mirror was part of the kit for civil warfare. It's the mark of the supreme general, I suppose, to slaughter Galba while pampering his skin,[27] to aspire to the Palatine throne while plastering his face with a face mask of dough.

[23] A woman's oath.

[24] Otho (Marcus Salvius Otho) was briefly emperor in A.D. 69 after killing Galba; for the allegation that he was Nero's lover, see cf. Suet. *Otho* 2.2.   [25] An exact quotation from Virg. *Aen*. 12.94, of Turnus' sturdy spear.   [26] Cf. Tac. *Hist*. 1.88.

[27] Lines 105–6: "The courage of the highest citizen on the battlefields of Bebriacum."

quod nec in Assyria pharetrata Sameramis urbe
maesta nec Actiaca fecit Cleopatra carina.
110 hic nullus verbis pudor aut reverentia mensae,
hic †turpis† Cybeles et fracta voce loquendi
libertas et crine senex fanaticus albo
sacrorum antistes, rarum ac memorabile magni
gutturis exemplum conducendusque magister.
115 quid tamen expectant, Phrygio quos tempus erat iam
more supervacuam cultris abrumpere carnem?
    Quadringenta dedit Gracchus sestertia dotem
cornicini, sive hic recto cantaverat aere;
signatae tabulae, dictum "feliciter," ingens
120 cena sedet, gremio iacuit nova nupta mariti.
o proceres, censore opus est an haruspice nobis?
scilicet horreres maioraque monstra putares,
si mulier vitulum vel si bos ederet agnum?
segmenta et longos habitus et flammea sumit
125 arcano qui sacra ferens nutantia loro
sudavit clipeis ancilibus. o pater Vrbis,
unde nefas tantum Latiis pastoribus? unde
haec tetigit, Gradive, tuos urtica nepotes?
traditur ecce viro clarus genere atque opibus vir,

108 urbe V: orbe PΦ
111 †turpis† PVΦ: turpes HT

28 More often spelled Semiramis, a legendary queen of Baby-
lon in Assyria.   29 Cleopatra VII, queen of Egypt, who was
defeated with Antony in the sea battle near Actium in 31 B.C.

30 Cybele was a goddess of Phrygia (Asia Minor) whose cult in
Rome was banned sporadically. Her priests were self-castrated
eunuchs called Galli.

That's something not attempted by quivered Sameramis in her Assyrian city[28] or Cleopatra grieving in her ship at Actium.[29] Here there is no sense of shame in their language, no table manners, here is Cybele's foul * * * and the freedom to speak in an effeminate voice. A crazed white-haired old man is the priest of the rites, a rare and memorable specimen of enormous throat, an expert worth the fee. What are they waiting for? It's already time for them to use their knives to hack away their superfluous flesh in the Phrygian manner.[30]

Gracchus[31] gave a dowry of four hundred thousand sesterces to a trumpeter—or maybe he performed on a horn that was straight. The marriage contract has been witnessed, felicitations offered, a huge company invited to the feast, and the new bride reclines in her husband's lap. O nobles! Is it a censor or a soothsayer that we need? Would you be more horrified, would you think it more monstrous still, if a woman gave birth to a calf or a cow to a lamb? He's wearing the bride's flounces, long dress, and veil—the man who carried the sacred objects swaying from the mystic thong and who sweated under the weight of the sacred shields. O father of Rome,[32] where has it come from, this appalling outrage that afflicts the shepherds of Latium? Where has it come from, this itch that taints your descendants, Gradivus?[33] Look: a man illustrious in family and fortune is handed over in marriage to another man—and

---

[31] This Gracchus (also 8.199–210) is a member of the elite: a Sempronius Gracchus and a Salian priest.

[32] Romulus.

[33] One of the titles of Mars.

130   nec galeam quassas nec terram cuspide pulsas
      nec quereris patri? vade ergo et cede severi
      iugeribus campi, quem neglegis. "officium cras
      primo sole mihi peragendum in valle Quirini."
      "quae causa officii?" "quid quaeris? nubit amicus,
135   nec multos adhibet." liceat modo vivere, fient,
      fient ista palam, cupient et in acta referri.
      interea tormentum ingens nubentibus haeret,
      quod nequeant parere et partu retinere maritos.
      sed melius, quod nil animis in corpora iuris
140   natura indulget: steriles moriuntur, et illis
      turgida non prodest condita pyxide Lyde
      nec prodest agili palmas praebere luperco.
      vicit et hoc monstrum tunicati fuscina Gracchi,
      lustravitque fuga mediam gladiator harenam
145   et Capitolinis generosior et Marcellis
      et Catuli Paulique minoribus et Fabiis et
      omnibus ad podium spectantibus, his licet ipsum
      admoveas cuius tunc munere retia misit.
         Esse aliquid manes et subterranea regna,
150   Cocytum et Stygio ranas in gurgite nigras,
      atque una transire vadum tot milia cumba
      nec pueri credunt, nisi qui nondum aere lavantur.
      sed tu vera puta: Curius quid sentit et ambo

149 aliquid *Burman, Schrader*: aliquos *codd*.

---

34 The Campus Martius (lit. "plain of Mars").

35 The name of the deified Romulus.

36 At the festival of the Lupercalia, young patrician men (*Luperci*) ran naked along the Via Sacra in the Forum, striking people they met with strips of goatskin to promote fertility.

you're not shaking your helmet, or striking the ground
with your spear, or complaining to your father? Off with
you, then—withdraw from the acres of the stern Campus[34]
which you don't care about. "Tomorrow at sunrise I have a
ceremony to attend in the valley of Quirinus."[35] "What's
the occasion?" "Oh, just a friend of mine marrying a man,
and he's invited a few guests." If we are allowed to live just
a little longer, those marriages will take place, they'll take
place openly, they'll even want to be reported in the news.
Meanwhile, the fact that they can't give birth and use their
babies to hang on to their husbands is a huge torment
which these brides cannot escape. But it's better that na-
ture grants their minds no power over their bodies: they
die infertile, and swollen Lyde with her secret medicine
box is no use to them, no more than holding out their
palms to running Lupercus.[36] Yet even this outrage is sur-
passed by Gracchus, wearing a tunic and with a trident in
his hand, who as a gladiator traversed the arena as he ran
away, a man of nobler birth than the Capitolini and Mar-
celli, than the descendants of Catulus and Paulus, than the
Fabii, than all the spectators in the front row, even if you
include the very man who staged that net-throwing show.[37]

The existence of ghosts and the underworld realms and
Cocytus and the black frogs in the whirling Styx and the
idea that all those thousands cross the water in a single
boat[38]—not even boys believe in that, except those not yet
old enough to pay admission at the baths. But suppose all
this were true: what would Curius[39] feel, and both the

[37] The front row is where the senators and imperial family sat.
The man who staged the show is probably the emperor.
[38] The boat is Charon's.   [39] See 2.3n.

Scipiadae, quid Fabricius manesque Camilli?
155   quid Cremerae legio et Cannis consumpta iuventus,
tot bellorum animae, quotiens hinc talis ad illos
umbra venit? cuperent lustrari, si qua darentur
sulpura cum taedis et si foret umida laurus.
illic heu miseri traducimur. arma quidem ultra
160   litora Iuvernae promovimus et modo captas
Orcadas ac minima contentos nocte Britannos,
sed quae nunc populi fiunt victoris in Vrbe
non faciunt illi quos vicimus. "et tamen unus
Armenius Zalaces cunctis narratur ephebis
165   mollior ardenti sese indulsisse tribuno."
aspice quid faciant commercia: venerat obses,
hic fiunt homines. nam si mora longior Vrbem
induerit pueris, non umquam derit amator,
mittentur bracae, cultelli, frena, flagellum.
170   sic praetextatos referunt Artaxata mores.

168 induerit *Nisbet*: †indulsit† *codd*.

Scipios,[40] Fabricius,[41] and Camillus' shade?[42] What about
the legion of Cremera[43] and the fighting youth destroyed
at Cannae,[44] the dead of all those wars, what would they
feel whenever a ghost like this came down to them from
here? They would want to be purified, if they could get
hold of sulphur and torches and moistened laurel. Down
there—the shame of it!—we are paraded in disgrace. I
know that we have advanced our troops beyond the shores
of Juverna[45] and the recently captured Orkneys and the
Britons who are contented with the shortest of nights, but
the people we've defeated don't do the things which go
on in the Rome of the victors. "And yet one Armenian,
Zalaces, who was more effeminate than all other Eastern
lads, is said to have yielded himself to an impassioned tri-
bune." Look at the effects of international relations: he
had come as a hostage, but here we create—human be-
ings! And if such boys put on Roman ways by staying here
longer, they'll never lack a lover and they'll abandon their
trousers, knives, bridles, and whips. That's how they take
teenage Roman morality back in triumph to Artaxata.[46]

[40] Publius Cornelius Scipio Africanus, both elder and youn-
ger: the elder defeated Hannibal at the battle of Zama in 202 B.C.
and the younger conquered Carthage in 146 B.C.

[41] Gaius Fabricius Luscinus, hero of the war with Pyrrhus.

[42] Marcus Furius Camillus captured Veii in 396 B.C. and saved
Rome from the Gauls.

[43] The legion of three hundred Fabii who died heroically
beside the river Cremera in 477 B.C.

[44] Hannibal defeated the Romans at the battle of Cannae in
Apulia in 216 B.C.

[45] Ireland.

[46] The capital of Armenia.

NOTE ON SATIRE 3

Satire 2 began with a wish to flee to the edge of the world, but Juvenal evidently remains in Rome. It is his (perhaps fictional) friend Umbricius who leaves the metropolis. Satire 3, the centrepiece of Book One, relays his long speech explaining his departure. Juvenal sets the scene in the prologue: this is a private conversation with Umbricius immediately prior to his departure, in a grotto near the Porta Capena from where the Via Appia headed south. In the description of the grotto—it is artificial and has been taken over by Jewish beggars—and in his own criticisms of the dangers of city life, Juvenal anticipates themes which Umbricius will develop in his long tirade. Accordingly, Umbricius first complains that he is driven from Rome by those who are dishonest and dishonourable (21–57). Then he complains that true Romans like himself are ousted by foreigners, especially, but not exclusively, Greeks (58–125). And then he deplores the displacement of poor clients like himself by the rich (126–314). The poem finishes with a return to the conversational setting as Umbricius wishes his friend goodbye (315–22).

Juvenal continues from Satire 1 the theme of dysfunctional patron-client relationships by giving Umbricius the perspective of an impoverished Roman client. Umbricius also maintains the indignant tone established in Satires 1 and 2. In his own eyes, he is a paragon of Roman virtue (his name suggests that he is the "ghost" or "shade" of Roman-ness), fleeing an un-Roman Rome and longing for a return of the good old days (312–14). But Juvenal hints that he is, instead, a jealous failure (his name can also be interpreted as "Mr Shady"). He has tried to succeed (e.g. 92–3) but cannot compete and is, consequently, envious of those who can. That perhaps puts his departure in a different light.

SATIRE 3

Quamvis digressu veteris confusus amici
laudo tamen, vacuis quod sedem figere Cumis
destinet atque unum civem donare Sibyllae.
ianua Baiarum est et gratum litus amoeni
5   secessus. ego vel Prochytam praepono Suburae;
nam quid tam miserum, tam solum vidimus, ut non
deterius credas horrere incendia, lapsus
tectorum adsiduos ac mille pericula saevae
Vrbis et Augusto recitantes mense poetas?

       *   *   *   *   *

10   sed dum tota domus raeda componitur una,
11   substitit ad veteres arcus madidamque Capenam.
17   in vallem Egeriae descendimus et speluncas
     dissimiles veris. quanto praesentius esset
     numen aquis, viridi si margine cluderet undas
20   herba nec ingenuum violarent marmora tofum.
12   hic, ubi nocturnae Numa constituebat amicae,

---

4 litus *codd.*: limen *Nisbet*   *post* 9 lacuna *Pearce*
17–20 after 11 *Jahn*: del. *Jacoby*

---

[1] A favourite resort of the Roman elite. Though quiet in comparison with Rome, it was not a ghost town.
[2] The Cumaean Sibyl was the most famous, thanks to Virgil, *Aeneid* 6.   [3] A small, rugged island near Baiae.

SATIRE 3

Although I'm distressed at the departure of my old friend,
all the same I approve of his decision to establish his home
at empty Cumae[1] and to donate a single fellow-citizen to
the Sibyl.[2] It's the gateway to Baiae, a lovely coast, delight-
fully secluded. Personally, I would prefer even Prochyta[3]
to the Subura.[4] After all, have you seen any place so dismal
and lonely that you wouldn't consider it worse to live in
dread of fires, and buildings collapsing continually, and the
thousand other dangers of savage Rome—and poets recit-
ing in the month of August? * * * But while his entire house
was being loaded onto a single waggon, he halted under
the ancient arch of dripping Capena.[5] We walk down into
the vale of Egeria with its artificial grottoes. How much
more real the spirit of the spring would be were the waters
enclosed by a green edge of grass and if marble didn't
profane the native tufa stone. Here, where Numa used to
date his nighttime girlfriend,[6] the grove and shrine of the

---

[4] With its shops and brothels, the Subura was the busiest street
in Rome.   [5] In Rome traffic was heavily restricted during
the day, so Umbricius' possessions have to be carried to the gate
and loaded there.

[6] Numa, the second king of Rome, claimed that his religious
institutions were inspired by meetings with the nymph Egeria
(Livy 1.19.5).

nunc sacri fontis nemus et delubra locantur
Iudaeis, quorum cophinus fenumque supellex;
15 omnis enim populo mercedem pendere iussa est
16 arbor et eiectis mendicat silva Camenis.
21   Hic tunc Vmbricius "quando artibus" inquit "honestis
nullus in Vrbe locus, nulla emolumenta laborum,
res hodie minor est here quam fuit atque †eadem† cras
deteret exiguis aliquid, proponimus illuc
25 ire, fatigatas ubi Daedalus exuit alas.
dum nova canities, dum prima et recta senectus,
dum superest Lachesi quod torqueat et pedibus me
porto meis nullo dextram subeunte bacillo,
cedamus patria. vivant Artorius istic
30 et Catulus, maneant qui nigrum in candida vertunt,
quis facile est aedem conducere, flumina, portus,
siccandam eluviem, portandum ad busta cadaver,
et praebere caput domina venale sub hasta.
quondam hi cornicines et municipalis harenae
35 perpetui comites notaeque per oppida buccae
munera nunc edunt et, verso pollice vulgus
cum iubet, occidunt populariter; inde reversi
conducunt foricas, et cur non omnia? cum sint
quales ex humili magna ad fastigia rerum
40 extollit quotiens voluit Fortuna iocari.
quid Romae faciam? mentiri nescio; librum,

23 †eadem† *codd.*: itidem *Damsté*: ideo *Buecheler*
37 cum RVAU: qum P: quem Φ

---

7 The Roman name for the Muses.
8 Cumae.

sacred spring are rented out to Jews, with their equipment, a hay-lined chest. Why? Every tree has been told to pay its rent to the people, the Camenae[7] have been thrown out, and the grove has now taken up begging.

It was here that Umbricius then spoke: "There's no room in Rome for respectable skills and no reward for hard work. Today my means are less than yesterday, and tomorrow will wear away a bit more from the little that's left. That's why I have resolved to head for the place where Daedalus stripped off his tired wings.[8] While my white hair is still new, while my fresh old age still stands upright, while Lachesis[9] still has something to spin, and while I can walk on my own two feet without the help of a stick in my hand, I must say goodbye to my fatherland. Let Artorius and Catulus[10] live there. Let the men who turn black into white stay on, men who find it easy to take on the contracts for temples, rivers, harbours, for draining floods and transporting corpses to the pyre—men who offer themselves for sale under the spear-sign of ownership.[11] These former horn-players—the permanent followers of country shows, their rounded cheeks a familiar sight through all the towns —now stage gladiatorial shows themselves and kill to please when the city mob demands it with a twist of the thumb. From that, they go back to their contracts for operating the public urinals—and why draw the line at anything? After all, they're the type that Fortune raises up from the gutter to a mighty height whenever she fancies a laugh. What can I do at Rome? I don't know how to tell

[9] One of the three Fates.
[10] Possibly upstarts of the Augustan–Tiberian period.
[11] At a public auction; but J.'s exact meaning is unclear.

si malus est, nequeo laudare et poscere; motus
astrorum ignoro; funus promittere patris
nec volo nec possum; ranarum viscera numquam
45 inspexi; ferre ad nuptam quae mittit adulter,
quae mandat, norunt alii; me nemo ministro
fur erit, atque ideo nulli comes exeo tamquam
mancus et extinctae corpus non utile dextrae.
quis nunc diligitur nisi conscius et cui fervens
50 aestuat occultis animus semperque tacendis?
nil tibi se debere putat, nil conferet umquam,
participem qui te secreti fecit honesti.
carus erit Verri qui Verrem tempore quo vult
accusare potest. tanti tibi non sit opimi
55 omnis harena Tagi quodque in mare volvitur aurum,
ut somno careas ponendaque praemia sumas
tristis et a magno semper timearis amico.

Quae nunc divitibus gens acceptissima nostris
et quos praecipue fugiam, properabo fateri,
60 nec pudor obstabit. non possum ferre, Quirites,
Graecam Vrbem. quamvis quota portio faecis Achaei?
iam pridem Syrus in Tiberim defluxit Orontes
et linguam et mores et cum tibicine chordas
obliquas nec non gentilia tympana secum
65 vexit et ad Circum iussas prostare puellas.
ite, quibus grata est picta lupa barbara mitra.

48 extinctae . . . dextrae *codd.*: extincta . . . dextra *Markland,
Eremita*   54 opimi *Buecheler*: opaci *codd.*

---

[12] Verres is a classic infamous criminal, see 2.26n.

[13] The sands of the river Tagus (mod. Tajo) in Spain and Portugal were thought to contain gold.

lies. I can't praise a book if it's bad and ask for a copy. I'm ignorant of the movements of the stars. I won't and can't predict someone's father's death. I've never examined the entrails of frogs. Taking to the bride her lover's gifts and messages, that's something other people know how to do. No one will be a thief with my help. For that reason, I never get out to the provinces on a governor's staff. It's as if I were crippled, a useless body with a paralysed hand. Is there anyone these days who inspires affection unless he's an accomplice, his mind boiling and seething with secrets that must never be told? If he's made you share some innocent secret, there's nothing he thinks he owes you and there's nothing he'll ever give you. Verres will be fond of the person who can bring an accusation against Verres whenever he likes.[12] Don't prize all the sand of rich Tagus and all the gold that's rolled into the sea[13] so much that you lose sleep and with a long face take bribes that you'll have to give up, a permanent source of fear in your powerful friend.

The race that's now most popular with wealthy Romans —the people I want especially to get away from—I'll name them right away, without any embarrassment. My fellow-citizens,[14] I cannot stand a Greekified Rome. Yet how few of our dregs are Achaeans? The Syrian Orontes has for a long time now been polluting the Tiber, bringing with it its language and customs, its slanting strings along with pipers, its native tom-toms too, and the girls who are told to offer themselves for sale at the Circus. Off you go, if

[14] *Quirites* was the name given to the citizens of Rome when addressed at a public meeting.

rusticus ille tuus sumit trechedipna, Quirine,
et ceromatico fert niceteria collo.
hic alta Sicyone, ast hic Amydone relicta,
70 hic Andro, ille Samo, hic Trallibus aut Alabandis,
Esquilias dictumque petunt a vimine collem,
viscera magnarum domuum dominique futuri.
ingenium velox, audacia perdita, sermo
promptus et Isaeo torrentior. ede quid illum
75 esse velis. quemvis hominem secum attulit ad nos:
grammaticus, rhetor, geometres, pictor, aliptes,
augur, schoenobates, medicus, magus, omnia novit
Graeculus esuriens: in caelum iusseris ibit.
in summa non Maurus erat neque Sarmata nec Thrax
80 qui sumpsit pinnas, mediis sed natus Athenis.
horum ego non fugiam conchylia? me prior ille
signabit fultusque toro meliore recumbet,
advectus Romam quo pruna et cottana vento?
usque adeo nihil est quod nostra infantia caelum
85 hausit Aventini baca nutrita Sabina?
quid quod adulandi gens prudentissima laudat
sermonem indocti, faciem deformis amici,
et longum invalidi collum cervicibus aequat

75 velis *Nisbet*: putes *codd*.   78 iusseris RΦ: miseris PV
82 signabit PRAOZ: signavit VΦ

---

15 I.e. Romulus.

16 Three Greek words which occur in Latin only here.

17 A list of Greek towns and islands.   18 The Esquiline
and Viminal were two of the seven hills of Rome.

19 A rhetorician from north Syria who came to Rome at the
end of the first century A.D.

your taste is a foreign whore in her bright headdress. Ah,
Quirinus,[15] that supposed rustic of yours is putting on his
chaussures grecques and wearing his *médaillons grecs* on
his neck *parfumé à la grecque*.[16] They come—this one
leaving the heights of Sicyon, this other from Amydon, this
one from Andros, that one from Samos, this one from
Tralles or Alabanda[17]—heading for the Esquiline and the
hill named from the willow,[18] to become the innards and
the masters of our great houses. They have quicksilver wit,
shameless presumption, words at the ready, more gushing
than Isaeus.[19] Say what you want him to be. In his own per-
son he has brought anyone you like: school teacher, rheto-
rician, geometrician, painter, masseur, prophet, funam-
bulist, physician, magician—your hungry Greekling has
every talent. Tell him to go to heaven and he will. In short,
it wasn't a Moroccan or a Sarmatian or a Thracian who
sprouted wings, but a man born in the centre of Athens.[20]
I've got to get away from these people in their purple,
haven't I? Is that man going to affix his seal ahead of me
and dine reclining on a couch superior to mine—a man im-
ported to Rome on the wind that brings us damsons and
figs? Does it count for nothing at all, then, that my child-
hood gulped in the Aventine air and was nurtured on the
Sabine berry?[21] Then what do you make of this? They're
the race that's cleverest at flattery. They can praise the ut-
terance of a friend who's illiterate and the looks of a friend
who's ugly. They can liken a weakling's scrawny neck to the

[20] Daedalus.
[21] The olive: the wording evokes the Sabines' reputation for
austerity; to be raised on the Aventine Hill makes Umbricius
quintessentially Roman.

Herculis Antaeum procul a tellure tenentis,
90 miratur vocem angustam, qua deterius nec
ille sonat quo mordetur gallina marito?
haec eadem licet et nobis laudare, sed illis
creditur. an melior cum Thaida sustinet aut cum
uxorem comoedus agit vel Dorida nullo
95 cultam palliolo? [mulier nempe ipsa videtur,
non persona, loqui:] vacua et plana omnia dicas
infra ventriculum et tenui distantia rima.
nec tamen Antiochus nec erit mirabilis illic
aut Stratocles aut cum molli Demetrius Haemo:
100 natio comoeda est. rides, maiore cachinno
concutitur; flet, si lacrimas conspexit amici,
nec dolet; igniculum brumae si tempore poscas,
accipit endromidem; si dixeris 'aestuo,' sudat.
non sumus ergo pares: melior, qui semper et omni
105 nocte dieque potest aliena sumere vultum
a facie, iactare manus laudare paratus,
si bene ructavit, si rectum minxit amicus,
si trulla inverso crepitum dedit aurea fundo.
praeterea sanctum nihil illi et ab inguine tutum,
110 non matrona laris, non filia virgo, nec ipse
sponsus levis adhuc, non filius ante pudicus.

95–6 mulier . . . loqui *del. Jachmann*   103 accipit *codd.*:
arripit *Scholte*   105 aliena PRV: alienum Φ
   109 illi et *Willis: om.* PR: aut Φ: atque U: est nec *or* est et *or* est
vel codd. recc.

---

[22] Hercules achieved victory over Antaeus, an invincible giant
who took his strength from contact with his mother, Earth, by
holding him in the air.

174

muscles of Hercules when he's holding Antaeus far above the earth.[22] They can admire a squeaky voice that sounds as bad as the cock's when he pecks his hen as he mates her. We can offer exactly the same compliments, but it's they who are believed. Is there any comic actor better at playing Thais, or the wife, or Doris without her cloak?[23] You'd say that everything below his little belly was smooth and empty and divided by a thin crack. And yet in Greece, Antiochus won't be a marvel, and neither will Stratocles or Demetrius along with effeminate Haemus:[24] the whole nation is a comic troupe. If you laugh, he is shaken with a louder fit of laughter. If he spots his friend in tears, he weeps, without being sad. If you ask for a bit of warmth in the winter time, he puts on a wrap. If you say, 'I'm hot,' he breaks out in a sweat. So we are not on a par. He's always ahead because, day or night, he can take his expression from someone else's face: he's ready to throw up his hands and cheer if his friend belches nicely or pisses straight or if the golden cup gives a fart when it's turned upside-down.[25] Besides, nothing is sacred to him or safe from his crotch— not the lady of the house, not the virgin daughter, not even her fiancé, still smooth-faced, not the son, uncorrupted till

[23] The three main female roles in Greek and Roman New Comedy: the prostitute (*meretrix*), the wife (*uxor* or *matrona*), and the slave girl (*ancilla*). Lines 95–6: "Without a doubt, it seems as if a real woman is speaking, not just a mask."

[24] Four Greek comic actors working at Rome; Demetrius was famous for his portrayal of older women.

[25] A difficult line. The patron apparently farts at the same time as turning his drinking cup upside down (so Valla).

horum si nihil est, aviam resupinat amici.
[scire volunt secreta domus atque inde timeri.]
et quoniam coepit Graecorum mentio, transi
115   gymnasia atque audi facinus maioris abollae.
Stoicus occidit Baream delator amicum
discipulumque senex ripa nutritus in illa
ad quam Gorgonei delapsa est pinna caballi.
non est Romano cuiquam locus hic, ubi regnat
120   Protogenes aliquis vel Diphilus aut Hermarchus,
qui gentis vitio numquam partitur amicum,
solus habet. nam cum facilem stillavit in aurem
exiguum de naturae patriaeque veneno,
limine summoveor, perierunt tempora longi
125   servitii; nusquam minor est iactura clientis.
     Quod porro officium, ne nobis blandiar, aut quod
pauperis hic meritum, si curet nocte togatus
currere, cum praetor lictorem inpellat et ire
praecipitem iubeat dudum vigilantibus orbis,
130   ne prior Albinam et Modiam collega salutet?
divitis hic servo cludit latus ingenuorum
filius; alter enim quantum in legione tribuni
accipiunt donat Calvinae vel Catienae,
ut semel aut iterum super illam palpitet; at tu,
135   cum tibi vestiti facies scorti placet, haeres
et dubitas alta Chionen deducere sella.

113 *del. Pinzger*

---

26 Possibly a proverb = "of a greater person."

27 Publius Egnatius Celer from Berytus, a Stoic professor who in A.D. 66 gave evidence against his patron and pupil Barea Soranus: Tac. *Ann.* 16.21–33.   28 Tarsus on the banks of the river Cydnus derived its name from the hoof or feather of the

then. If none of these is available, he gets his friend's
grandmother on her back. And since I've started on the
Greeks, leave off the gyms and listen to a crime of a greater
cloak.[26] The elderly Stoic[27] who was raised on that river-
bank where the feather from the Gorgon's nag landed[28]—
he killed his friend and pupil Barea by informing on him.
There's no room for any Roman here in Rome. This is
where some Protogenes or Diphilus or Hermarchus is
king. He never shares a friend—it's his national defect—
but monopolises him. You see, once he's dripped a drop of
the poison which comes naturally to him and his race into
that receptive ear, I am hustled away from the threshold
and my long years of slavery have been wasted. Nowhere is
the ditching of a client more casual.

Besides, not to flatter ourselves, what duty or service is
there left for a poor man here in Rome, even if he takes the
trouble to put on his toga and race along in the dark, only to
find the praetor hurrying his lictor and telling him to go full
speed because the childless have been awake for hours, to
prevent his colleague delivering the morning greeting to
Albina or to Modia first?[29] Here in Rome the son of free-
born parents escorts a rich man's slave, because the slave
can give as much as a military tribune's pay to Calvina or
Catiena, to quiver above her once or twice. But when you
fancy the look of a tart in her dress, you stop and hesitate
about asking Snow White[30] down from her high seat. At

winged horse Pegasus, which sprang from the blood of the Gor-
gon Medusa when Perseus beheaded her. It was a centre for the
study of philosophy   [29] Wealthy childless women.

[30] Chione was a frequent name for prostitutes, contrasting
with the aristocratic lovers Calvina and Catiena.

da testem Romae tam sanctum quam fuit hospes
numinis Idaei, procedat vel Numa vel qui
servavit trepidam flagranti ex aede Minervam:
140   protinus ad censum, de moribus ultima fiet
quaestio. 'quot pascit servos? quot possidet agri
iugera? quam multa magnaque paropside cenat?'
quantum quisque sua nummorum servat in arca,
tantum habet et fidei. iures licet et Samothracum
145   et nostrorum aras, contemnere fulmina pauper
creditur atque deos dis ignoscentibus ipsis.
quid quod materiam praebet causasque iocorum
omnibus hic idem, si foeda et scissa lacerna,
si toga sordidula est et rupta calceus alter
150   pelle patet, vel si consuto volnere crassum
atque recens linum ostendit non una cicatrix?
nil habet infelix paupertas durius in se
quam quod ridiculos homines facit. 'exeat' inquit,
'si pudor est, et de pulvino surgat equestri,
155   cuius res legi non sufficit, et sedeant hic
lenonum pueri quocumque ex fornice nati,
hic plaudat nitidus praeconis filius inter
pinnirapi cultos iuvenes iuvenesque lanistae.'
sic libitum vano, qui nos distinxit, Othoni.

---

31 Publius Cornelius Scipio Nasica, chosen to escort the image
of the goddess Cybele from Mount Ida in Phrygia to Rome in 204
B.C.

32 Numa, the second king of Rome, was famed for his religious
devotion. Lucius Caecilius Metellus as *pontifex maximus* lost his
sight (cf. 6.265) rescuing the image of Minerva (the Palladium)
from the burning temple of Vesta in 241 B.C.

33 Probably a type of gladiator.

Rome, produce a witness as saintly as the man who wel-
comed the Idaean goddess,[31] let Numa step forward, or
the man who rescued a trembling Minerva from the blaz-
ing temple[32]—it's straight to his wealth; his character will
be the last enquiry. 'How many slaves does he keep? How
many acres of farmland does he own? How many and
how lavish are his courses at dinner?' Everyone's credit
matches the amount of coins he keeps in his treasure chest.
Though you swear an oath on the altars of the Samo-
thracian and Roman gods, a poor man is thought to disre-
gard the divine lightning bolts, with the acquiescence of
the gods themselves. Then what do you make of this, that
this same man provides everyone with material and sub-
stance for amusement if his cloak is dirty and torn, if his
toga's rather mucky and one shoe's gaping open where the
leather is split, or if several scars display their coarse new
thread where a gash has been sewn up? There's nothing
harder about unfortunate poverty than the way it makes
people ridiculous. 'If you have any standards,' says some-
one, 'you will please stand up and leave the knights' cush-
ions, if your wealth does not satisfy the legal requirement.
This seating is reserved for the sons of pimps, born in
whatever brothel. Here is where the slick son of the auc-
tioneer will enjoy the show alongside the smart lads of the
crest-snatcher[33] and the trainer.' This is how that fool Otho
decided to categorise us.[34] Here at Rome, has any prospec-

[34] In the theatre the first fourteen rows of seats behind the
orchestra, where the senators sat, were reserved for the *equites*
in accordance with the *lex Roscia theatralis* passed by Lucius
Roscius Otho in 67 B.C., a law revived by Domitian. The property
qualification for equestrian rank was 400,000 sesterces.

160 quis gener hic placuit censu minor atque puellae
sarcinulis inpar? quis pauper scribitur heres?
quando in consilio est aedilibus? agmine facto
debuerant olim tenues migrasse Quirites.
    Haut facile emergunt quorum virtutibus obstat
165 res angusta domi, sed Romae durior illis
conatus: magno hospitium miserabile, magno
servorum ventres, et frugi cenula magno.
fictilibus cenare pudet, quod turpe negabis
translatus subito ad Marsos mensamque Sabellam
170 contentusque illic veneto duroque cucullo.
pars magna Italiae est, si verum admittimus, in qua
nemo togam sumit nisi mortuus. ipsa dierum
festorum herboso colitur si quando theatro
maiestas tandemque redit ad pulpita notum
175 exodium, cum personae pallentis hiatum
in gremio matris formidat rusticus infans,
aequales habitus illic similesque videbis
orchestram et populum; clari velamen honoris
sufficiunt tunicae summis aedilibus albae.
180 hic ultra vires habitus nitor, hic aliquid plus
quam satis est interdum aliena sumitur arca.
commune id vitium est: hic vivimus ambitiosa
paupertate omnes. quid te moror? omnia Romae
cum pretio. quid das, ut Cossum aliquando salutes,
185 ut te respiciat clauso Veiiento labello?

170 veneto *Clausen*: Veneto *Willis*

---

35 A sarcastic reference to her dowry.
36 A *consilium* consisted of assessors who might be consulted
by magistrates, such as aediles.

tive son-in-law ever passed the test if he's inferior in wealth
and no match for the girl's 'baggage'?[35] When is a poor man
ever named as heir? When is he given a seat on the board
by the aediles?[36] Impoverished Roman citizens should
have massed together and marched out long ago.

It's not easy anyway to climb the ladder when cramped
personal resources block your talents, but at Rome the
effort is harder still. Pathetic lodgings cost a lot, slaves'
bellies cost a lot, a meagre supper costs a lot. You're em-
barrassed to dine off earthenware plates, but you'd not call
it disgusting if you were suddenly whisked off to a Marsian
or Sabellan table,[37] happy there with a rough, dark blue
hood.[38] In much of Italy, to tell the truth, no one puts on a
toga unless he's dead. Even at the grand celebration of fes-
tivals in the grassy theatre when the familiar farce has at
last come back to the wooden stage—when baby bumpkin
in his mother's lap cowers in terror at the gaping whitened
mask—even then you'll see everyone dressed the same,
orchestra and populace all alike. White tunics are enough
for the highest aediles as the garb of their glorious office.
Here at Rome the smartness of our clothes is beyond our
means. Here at Rome that little bit extra is sometimes bor-
rowed from someone else's treasure chest. It's a universal
failing: here at Rome we all live in pretentious poverty.
Why say more? At Rome everything comes with a price
tag. What do you pay so you can occasionally say good
morning to Cossus or so Veiento will give you a tight-

[37] Types of primitive frugality, cf. 14.179–88.
[38] This hood was associated with the poor man in comedy.

ille metit barbam, crinem hic deponit amatus;
plena domus libis venalibus: accipe et istud
fermentum tibi habe. praestare tributa clientes
cogimur et cultis augere peculia servis.
190 Quis timet aut timuit gelida Praeneste ruinam
aut positis nemorosa inter iuga Volsiniis aut
simplicibus Gabiis aut proni Tiburis arce?
nos Vrbem colimus tenui tibicine fultam
magna parte sui; nam sic labentibus obstat
195 vilicus et, veteris rimae cum texit hiatum,
securos pendente iubet dormire ruina.
vivendum est illic, ubi nulla incendia, nulli
nocte metus. iam poscit aquam, iam frivola transfert
Vcalegon, tabulata tibi iam tertia fumant:
200 tu nescis; nam si gradibus trepidatur ab imis,
ultimus ardebit quem tegula sola tuetur
a pluvia, molles ubi reddunt ova columbae.
lectus erat Cordo Procula minor, urceoli sex
ornamentum abaci, nec non et parvulus infra
205 centaurus recubans ab eodem marmore Chiron,
iamque vetus Graecos servabat cista libellos
et divina opici rodebant carmina mures.
nil habuit Cordus, quis enim negat? et tamen illud

186 amatus *Guyet, Ruperti*: amati Φ: amatum PRV
203 cordo U: codro VΦ
205 centaurus *Markland*: cantharus et *codd*. | ab eodem *Markland*: sub eodem *codd*.: sub eo de *C.Valesius*: rupto de *Nisbet*
208 cordus U: cordrus V: codrus PRΦ

lipped glance? It's the beard-clipping or hair-dedication of one or other beloved slave:[39] and the house is full of cakes that you have to pay for. 'Take the money and keep your yeast.' We clients are forced to pay taxes and to supplement the savings of well-groomed slaves.

Has anyone now or in the past dreaded collapsing buildings at cool Praeneste or at Volsinii among its wooded hills or at simple Gabii or on the hilltop of sloping Tibur? We inhabit a Rome for the most part supported by thin props. After all, that's how the agent blocks the buildings from falling down. Once he's covered a gaping ancient crack, he tells us to not to worry, as we sleep in a building on the point of collapse. The ideal place to live is without fires and panics in the night. Ucalegon is already shouting 'Fire!' He's already moving out his odds and ends, and the third floor where you live is already smoking. But you don't know anything about it. After all, if the alarm is raised at the bottom of the stairs, the person protected from the rain by only a little roof tile—where the gentle doves produce their eggs—will be the last to burn. Cordus' possessions were: a bed too small for Procula, six small jugs to decorate his sideboard, and, underneath, a little centaur, Chiron, made from the same 'marble,'[40] and a box, by now ancient, which kept his little Greek books safe—and the philistine mice were gnawing the immortal poems. Cordus had nothing, who'd disagree? And yet the wretched man lost that

[39] The slave boys adored by their masters are honoured with ceremonies to mark the first clipping of the beard (cf. 8.166) and the dedication of a lock of hair.   [40] I.e. from earthenware, the same as the jugs. Cordus is not rich enough to own any marble. (This is Markland's interpretation.)

perdidit infelix totum nihil. ultimus autem
210 aerumnae cumulus, quod nudum et frusta rogantem
nemo cibo, nemo hospitio tectoque iuvabit.
si magna Assaraci cecidit domus, horrida mater,
pullati proceres, differt vadimonia praetor.
tum gemimus casus Vrbis, tunc odimus ignem.
215 ardet adhuc, et iam accurrit qui marmora donet,
conferat inpensas; hic nuda et candida signa,
hic aliquid praeclarum Euphranoris et Polycliti
aera, Asianorum vetera ornamenta deorum,
hic libros dabit et forulos mediamque Minervam,
220 hic modium argenti. meliora ac plura reponit
Persicus orborum lautissimus et merito iam
suspectus tamquam ipse suas incenderit aedes.
si potes avelli circensibus, optima Sorae
aut Fabrateriae domus aut Frusinone paratur
225 quanti nunc tenebras unum conducis in annum.
hortulus hic puteusque brevis nec reste movendus
in tenuis plantas facili diffunditur haustu.
vive bidentis amans et culti vilicus horti
unde epulum possis centum dare Pythagoreis.
230 est aliquid, quocumque loco, quocumque recessu,
unius sese dominum fecisse lacertae.

    Plurimus hic aeger moritur vigilando (sed ipsum
languorem peperit cibus inperfectus et haerens

212 Assaraci *Scholte*: asturici PSRVU

218 aera, Asianorum *Housman*: haec asianorum PSRΣ: fae-casianorum *similiave* Φ

---

41 Assaracus was a king of Troy. The mansion belongs to one of the old families who claimed descent from the Trojans.

entire 'nothing.' But the crowning point of his misery is that no one will help him with food or hospitality or shelter when he's naked and begging for scraps. If the grand mansion of Assaracus[41] has been destroyed, then his mother is in mourning and the nobles are in black and the praetor adjourns his hearings. That's when we lament the disasters of Rome and that's when we detest its fires. Before the flames are out, someone's already rushing up to offer marble and contribute building materials. They'll bring gifts: one man some gleaming nude statues, another a masterpiece by Euphranor or bronzes by Polyclitus, antique adornments belonging to the gods of Asia, another books and bookcases and a Minerva centrepiece, and another a heap of silver. Persicus, the richest of the childless, replaces what's gone with more and better things. He's now suspected of setting fire to his own house—and not without reason. If you can tear yourself away from the races, an excellent house at Sora or Fabrateria or Frusino can be bought outright for the annual rent you now pay for your tenement. Here you'll have a little garden, and a well so shallow it doesn't need a rope, for easy water to sprinkle on your tender plants. Live in love with your hoe as the overseer of your vegetable garden, which will enable you to offer a banquet to a hundred Pythagoreans.[42] It's something, wherever you are, however remote, to make yourself the master of a single lizard.

Here at Rome very many invalids die from insomnia, although it's food undigested and clinging to the fevered

---

[42] I.e. vegetarians. Pythagoras' belief in the transmigration of souls led to the ban on the eating of meat.

    ardenti stomacho); nam quae meritoria somnum
235 admittunt? magnis opibus dormitur in Vrbe.
    inde caput morbi. raedarum transitus arto
    vicorum in flexu et stantis convicia mandrae
    eripient somnum Druso vitulisque marinis.
    si vocat officium, turba cedente vehetur
240 dives et ingenti curret super ora Liburna
    atque obiter leget aut scribet vel dormiet intus
    (namque facit somnum clausa lectica fenestra),
    ante tamen veniet: nobis properantibus obstat
    unda prior, magno populus premit agmine lumbos
245 qui sequitur; ferit hic cubito, ferit assere duro
    alter, at hic tignum capiti incutit, ille metretam.
    pinguia crura luto, planta mox undique magna
    calcor, et in digito clavus mihi militis haeret.
    nonne vides quanto celebretur sportula fumo?
250 centum convivae, sequitur sua quemque culina.
    Corbulo vix ferret tot vasa ingentia, tot res
    inpositas capiti, quas recto vertice portat
    servulus infelix et cursu ventilat ignem.
    scinduntur tunicae sartae modo, longa coruscat
255 serraco veniente abies, atque altera pinum
    plaustra vehunt; nutant alte populoque minantur.

---

43 Some traffic was only permitted in the city at night. Drusus is probably Claudius (Tiberius Claudius Drusus), renowned for his profound drowsiness. Seals were thought to experience a deeper sleep than any other animal.

44 The litter is described hyperbolically as a warship.

45 Lit. "with how much smoke the sportula is thronged" [by the crowd around it]. Not exactly the *sportula* of 1.95–126, but a

stomach that induces the malaise in the first place. Which lodgings allow you to rest, after all? You have to be very rich to get sleep in Rome. That's the source of the sickness. The continual traffic of carriages in the narrow twisting streets and the swearing of the drover when his herd has come to a halt would deprive a Drusus or the seals of sleep.[43] If duty calls, the crowd gives way as the rich man is conveyed, racing along above their faces in his huge Liburnian galley,[44] reading or writing on the way or sleeping inside (you know how a litter with its window closed brings on drowsiness). Yet he'll get there first. As I hurry along, the wave ahead gets in the way and the great massed ranks of people behind me crush my kidneys. One pokes me with his elbow, another with a hard pole. This guy bashes my head with a beam, that guy with a wine cask. My legs are caked with mud. Soon I'm trampled by mighty feet from every side and a soldier's hobnail sticks into my toe. Do you see all the smoke that's crowding around the handout?[45] There are a hundred diners and each is followed by his own portable kitchen. Corbulo[46] would have difficulty carrying on his head all those enormous pots and other objects which the wretched little slave transports, keeping his head upright and fanning the flames as he runs. Tunics just recently mended are ripped. A long fir log judders as its waggon gets closer and another cart trundles a whole pine tree. They wobble threateningly way above the crowds.

gathering of men accompanied by slaves with portable cookers, perhaps for the food distributed to members of a *collegium*.

[46] Gnaeus Domitius Corbulo, a general of legendary stature eminent under Claudius and Nero.

187

nam si procubuit qui saxa Ligustica portat
axis et eversum fudit super agmina montem,
quid superest de corporibus? quis membra, quis ossa
260   invenit? obtritum vulgo perit omne cadaver
more animae. domus interea secura patellas
iam lavat et bucca foculum excitat et sonat unctis
striglibus et pleno componit lintea guto.
haec inter pueros varie properantur, at ille
265   iam sedet in ripa taetrumque novicius horret
porthmea nec sperat caenosi gurgitis alnum
infelix nec habet quem porrigat ore trientem.
      Respice nunc alia ac diversa pericula noctis:
quod spatium tectis sublimibus unde cerebrum
270   testa ferit, quotiens rimosa et curta fenestris
vasa cadant, quanto percussum pondere signent
et laedant silicem. possis ignavus haberi
et subiti casus improvidus, ad cenam si
intestatus eas: adeo tot fata, quot illa
275   nocte patent vigiles te praetereunte fenestrae.
ergo optes votumque feras miserabile tecum,
ut sint contentae patulas defundere pelves.
ebrius ac petulans, quia nullum forte cecidit,

259 de AHKTZ: e PRVGO
260 vulgo *Eremita, Knoche, Martyn, Willis*: volgi *codd.*
278 quia *Guyet*: qui *codd.*

---

47 High-quality white or green-veined marble from Luna in
Etruria, formerly Liguria.
48 The strigil was a curved, bladed implement used to scrape
the oil, sweat, and dirt from the skin during bathing.

After all, if the axle that's transporting rocks from Liguria[47] collapses and spills an upturned mountain on top of the masses, what will be left of the bodies? Who will be able to find any limbs or bones? Every corpse, crushed indiscriminately, will disappear, exactly like its soul. Meanwhile the household is oblivious. By this time they are washing the dishes and puffing at the embers with full cheeks, clattering the oily strigils,[48] filling the oil flasks, and arranging the towels. The slave boys bustle around on these different tasks, but their master is already a newcomer sitting on the bank,[49] shuddering at the hideous ferryman. The wretched man has no hopes of a bark across the muddy torrent, because he doesn't have a coin in his mouth to offer.[50]

Now consider the various other dangers of the night. What a long way it is from the high roofs for a tile to hit your skull! How often cracked and leaky pots tumble down from the windows! What a smash when they strike the pavement, marking and damaging it! You could be thought careless and unaware of what can suddenly befall if you go out to dinner without having made your will. As you pass by at night, there are precisely as many causes of death as there are open windows watching you. So make a wish and a pathetic prayer as you go that they'll be content with emptying their shallow basins on you. The drunken thug is in agony from failing, by some chance, to attack anyone.

[49] The bank of one of the rivers in the Underworld, Styx or Cocytus or Acheron. The hideous ferryman is Charon.

[50] It was the custom to place a coin in the mouth of the dead person as the fare for passage across the river of the Underworld.

dat poenas, noctem patitur lugentis amicum
280 Pelidae, cubat in faciem, mox deinde supinus:
[ergo non aliter poterit dormire; quibusdam]
somnum rixa facit. sed quamvis improbus annis
atque mero fervens cavet hunc quem coccina laena
vitari iubet et comitum longissimus ordo,
285 multum praeterea flammarum et aenea lampas.
me, quem luna solet deducere vel breve lumen
candelae, cuius dispenso et tempero filum,
contemnit. miserae cognosce prohoemia rixae,
si rixa est, ubi tu pulsas, ego vapulo tantum.
290 stat contra starique iubet. parere necesse est;
nam quid agas, cum te furiosus cogat et idem
fortior? 'unde venis?' exclamat, 'cuius aceto,
cuius conche tumes? quis tecum sectile porrum
sutor et elixi vervecis labra comedit?
295 nil mihi respondes? aut dic aut accipe calcem.
ede ubi consistas: in qua te quaero proseucha?'
dicere si temptes aliquid tacitusve recedas,
tantumdem est: feriunt pariter, vadimonia deinde
irati faciunt. libertas pauperis haec est:
300 pulsatus rogat et pugnis concisus adorat
ut liceat paucis cum dentibus inde reverti.
nec tamen haec tantum metuas; nam qui spoliet te
non derit clausis domibus postquam omnis ubique
fixa catenatae siluit compago tabernae.
305 interdum et ferro subitus grassator agit rem:

281 del. *Heinecke*
288 prohoemia PRV: praemia Φ

He's going through a night like Pelides[51] had when he was grieving for his friend, lying on his face and now on his back again. It takes a brawl to make him sleep. But however insolent he is, seething with youth and unmixed wine, he keeps clear of the man with the warning signs of scarlet cloak and long retinue of attendants plus plenty of torches and bronze lamps. But me he despises, as I go home escorted usually by the moon or by the short-lived light of a candle—its wick I regulate and tend. Here are the preliminaries to the pathetic brawl, if a brawl it is when you do the beating and I just take it. He stands facing me and tells me to stop. I've no choice but to obey. After all, what can you do when a lunatic forces you, and he's stronger as well? 'Where have you just been?' he yells. 'Whose sour wine and beans have blown you out? Which shoemaker has been eating spring onions and boiled sheep's head with you? Nothing to say? Tell me or you'll get a kicking! Say, where's your pitch? Which synagogue shall I look for you in?' Whether you try to say something or silently retreat, it's all the same. They beat you up just the same and then, still angry, they sue for assault.[52] This is a poor man's freedom: when he's been beaten and treated like a punchbag, he can beg and plead to be allowed to go home with a few teeth left. And this is not all you have to be afraid of. After the houses are locked, when all the shuttering on the shops has been chained and fastened and fallen silent, there'll still be someone who'd rob you. And sometimes a gangster

[51] Achilles, son of Peleus, whose grief at the death of his friend Patroclus is described at Hom. *Il.* 24.10–11.
[52] A *vadimonium* is a guarantee that the defendant will appear in court at a future date.

armato quotiens tutae custode tenentur
et Pomptina palus et Gallinaria pinus,
sic inde huc omnes tamquam ad vivaria currunt.
qua fornace graves, qua non incude catenae?
310 maximus in vinclis ferri modus, ut timeas ne
vomer deficiat, ne marra et sarcula desint.
felices proavorum atavos, felicia dicas
saecula quae quondam sub regibus atque tribunis
viderunt uno contentam carcere Romam.
315   His alias poteram et pluris subnectere causas,
sed iumenta vocant et sol inclinat. eundum est;
nam mihi commota iamdudum mulio virga
adnuit. ergo vale nostri memor, et quotiens te
Roma tuo refici properantem reddet Aquino,
320 me quoque ad Helvinam Cererem vestramque Dianam
converte a Cumis. saturarum ego, ni pudet illas,
auditor gelidos veniam caligatus in agros."

322 auditor PRVF: adiutor Φ

192

will suddenly be at his business with his knife: whenever the Pomptine marsh and Gallinarian forest[53] are safely occupied by an armed patrol, they all race from there into Rome as if to their feeding grounds. Is there a furnace or anvil anywhere that isn't weighed down with the making of chains? Most of our iron is turned into fetters. You should be worried about a shortage of ploughshares and a dearth of mattocks and hoes.[54] Fortunate were our distant ancestors, you'd say, and fortunate those once-upon-a-time generations under the kings and tribunes that saw a Rome satisfied with a single prison.

I could add plenty other reasons to these, but the beasts are calling and the sun is sloping. I must go: the muleteer has been waving to me with his whip for some time. So, goodbye. Don't forget me. And whenever Rome sends you hurrying back to your own Aquinum[55] for a break, invite me too from Cumae to visit Helvius' Ceres and your Diana.[56] I'll come to your cool countryside in my heavy boots and listen to your satires, if they're not embarrassed."

[53] The Pontine marshes were near the coast of Latium between Circeii and Terracina; the Gallinarian forest was in the west of Campania between the river Vulturnus and Cumae. It was difficult to police the bands of gangsters that operated there.

[54] For the cliché that in time of war ploughshares and other agricultural implements are melted down into swords, see Virg. *Georg.* 1.508, Ov. *Fast.* 1.699–700.

[55] A town in Latium on the Via Latina about 75 miles from Rome, often taken (not necessarily correctly) to indicate J.'s birthplace.

[56] A temple of Ceres built by the Helvii, a family prominent in this area. Ceres and Diana were goddesses of the countryside.

NOTE ON SATIRE 4

Though Juvenal commends Umbricius' decision to leave Rome in Satire 3, he himself stays behind. The next person to turn up in Book One is an upstart foreigner, precisely one of the types criticised by Umbricius. Crispinus, who first appeared at 1.26–9, is an Egyptian who has risen to become one of the emperor Domitian's cabinet of advisers (*consilium principis*). The opening lines are an indignant attack on Crispinus for his outrageous lust and riches (1–10). Then Juvenal shifts to "more trivial matters" and tells of his self-indulgence in purchasing an expensive mullet for himself (11–27). Lines 28–33 broaden the scope of the poem by using a comparison between Crispinus and the emperor which indicates that Crispinus is "small fry." Juvenal now pauses and intones an epic invocation of the muse Calliope and her sisters, the Pierides (34–6). But this is no epic narrative. The comments interpolated into the invocation indicate that this is mock-epic, as proved throughout the next section by Juvenal's narrative of the capture of an enormous turbot and its presentation to the emperor Domitian by the fisherman (37–72): epic phrases are mingled with words and ideas alien to epic. At 72 the epic parody takes on the peculiarly epic form of the catalogue, here a catalogue of the advisers summoned to Domitian's *consilium* (72–129). The final section of mock-epic narrative recounts the advice given and the dismissal of the *consilium* (130–49). In the coda, Juvenal expresses the wish that Domitian had always devoted himself to such trivialities (*nugae*) instead of committing murder wantonly (150–4), looking forward from the dramatic setting early in Domitian's reign (see below) to his demise.

With this mock-epic narrative, Juvenal's satire fulfils the possibility voiced in Satire 1 of satire replacing epic. A mock-epic tone is appropriate when an emperor is the object of attack, but it seems clear that Juvenal is engaging in epic parody with a specific target. Statius, an epic poet writing under Domitian, wrote a poem *On the German War* (*De Bello Germanico*) praising Domitian's conduct of the war in 83. The poem (which has not survived) included a catalogue of the emperor's right-hand men; three names which do survive from the catalogue occur in Juvenal's poem. The incorporation of epic parody explains the disjunction between the attack on Crispinus and the attack on Domitian, which begins with the invocation of the Muse at 34–6.

SATIRE 4

Ecce iterum Crispinus, et est mihi saepe vocandus
ad partes, monstrum nulla virtute redemptum
a vitiis, aegrae solaque libidine fortes
deliciae, viduas tantum aspernatus adulter.
5   quid refert igitur, quantis iumenta fatiget
porticibus, quanta nemorum vectetur in umbra,
iugera quot vicina foro, quas emerit aedes?
nemo malus felix, minime corruptor et idem
incestus, cum quo nuper vittata iacebat
10 sanguine adhuc vivo terram subitura sacerdos.
     Sed nunc de factis levioribus. et tamen alter
si fecisset idem caderet sub iudice morum;
nam quod turpe bonis Titio Seiioque decebat
Crispinum. quid agas, cum dira et foedior omni
15 crimine persona est? mullum sex milibus emit,
aequantem sane paribus sestertia libris,

1–36 *del. Ribbeck, Willis*
8 *del. Jahn*

---

[1] See 1.26–8n.

[2] Seduction of a Vestal Virgin was regarded as *incestum*; the
Vestal could be punished by being buried alive.

SATIRE 4

Here's Crispinus[1] again, someone I must often summon to
play his part. He's a monstrosity without a single good
quality to make up for his faults, a feeble dandy, strong
only for lechery, an adulterer who rejects only unpartnered
women. Is it then a matter of any importance, how long are
the colonnades where he tires out his mules, how large are
the shady groves where he is carried along, how numerous
the acres and variety of palaces near the forum that he has
bought? No bad man is happy, least of all a seducer, pol-
luted at that, who recently slept with a priestess in her
headband, who'll go beneath the earth with her blood still
flowing.[2]

But now to more trivial matters. All the same, though, if
another person had done the same thing he would now
stand convicted by the Judge of Morals.[3] Why? Because
what's disgusting in good Titius or Seius[4] was fine behav-
iour for Crispinus. What can you do when the person him-
self is more dreadful and repulsive than any accusation?
He bought a mullet[5] for six thousand—matching thou-
sands and pounds, in fact, as people who amplify the ample

[3] The censor, who regulated expenditure on luxury goods.
[4] Ordinary men.
[5] The red mullet was a symbol of extravagance.

ut perhibent qui de magnis maiora locuntur.
consilium laudo artificis, si munere tanto
praecipuam in tabulis ceram senis abstulit orbi;
20 est ratio ulterior, magnae si misit amicae,
quae vehitur cluso latis specularibus antro.
nil tale expectes: emit sibi. multa videmus
quae miser et frugi non fecit Apicius. hoc tu,
succinctus patria quondam, Crispine, papyro,
25 hoc pretio squamas? potuit fortasse minoris
piscator quam piscis emi; provincia tanti
vendit agros, sed maiores Apulia vendit.
qualis tunc epulas ipsum gluttisse putamus
induperatorem, cum tot sestertia, partem
30 exiguam et modicae sumptam de margine cenae,
purpureus magni ructarit scurra Palati,
iam princeps equitum, magna qui voce solebat
vendere municipes fracta de merce siluros?
    Incipe, Calliope. licet et considere: non est
35 cantandum, res vera agitur. narrate, puellae
Pierides, prosit mihi vos dixisse puellas.
    Cum iam semianimum laceraret Flavius orbem
ultimus et calvo serviret Roma Neroni,
incidit Hadriaci spatium admirabile rhombi
40 ante domum Veneris, quam Dorica sustinet Ancon,

25 squamas *Dorleans*: squamae *codd.*

6 Marcus Gavius Apicius, a wealthy gourmet who lived under
Augustus and Tiberius; his name is attached to a cookbook which
dates from later.   7 The imperial residence.
    8 Not an official title. Crispinus perhaps held the highest position available to an *eques*, the prefecture of the praetorian guard.

put it. I'm impressed by the genius' plan, if by such a splen-
did gift he stole first place in the will of a childless old man
or (an even better ploy) sent it to a grand mistress who
rides in her closed cavern with its wide windows. Don't
expect anything like that. He bought it for himself! We
witness many things that poor mean Apicius[6] didn't do.
Did you, Crispinus—who in the old days were kitted out
for work in your native papyrus clothes—did you pay this
much, this much for scales? The fisherman could perhaps
have been bought for less than his fish. That's the price
of land in the provinces—and Apulia offers better value
still. What kind of banquets are we to think the emperor
himself guzzled at that time, when so many thousand
sesterces—a tiny fraction, a side dish from an ordinary din-
ner—were belched up by the clown-in-purple of the Great
Palace?[7] He's now Leader of the Cavalry,[8] but he used to
sell sprats (his compatriots) from a damaged cargo in a
loud voice.

Commence, Calliope.[9] You may sit down. This is no
poetry recitation. Our theme is the truth. Tell your story,
young girls of Pieria[10]—and may it do me good to call you
"young girls."

Once upon a time, when the last of the Flavians was
mangling a world already half-dead, and Rome was the
slave of a bald Nero,[11] there turned up below the temple of
Venus, which rests upon Doric Ancon,[12] the incredible

[9] The Muse of epic.

[10] The Muses, associated with Pieria near Mount Olympus.

[11] Domitian.

[12] Modern Ancona, on the Adriatic coast, founded from the
Dorian city of Syracuse.

implevitque sinus; neque enim minor haeserat illis
quos operit glacies Maeotica ruptaque tandem
solibus effundit torrentis ad ostia Ponti
desidia tardos et longo frigore pingues.
45   destinat hoc monstrum cumbae linique magister
pontifici summo. quis enim proponere talem
aut emere auderet, cum plena et litora multo
delatore forent? dispersi protinus algae
inquisitores agerent cum remige nudo,
50   non dubitaturi fugitivum dicere piscem
depastumque diu vivaria Caesaris, inde
elapsum veterem ad dominum debere reverti.
si quid Palfurio, si credimus Armillato,
quidquid conspicuum pulchrumque est aequore toto
55   res fisci est, ubicumque natat. donabitur ergo,
ne pereat.
          Iam letifero cedente pruinis
autumno, iam quartanam sperantibus aegris,
stridebat deformis hiems praedamque recentem
servabat; tamen hic properat, velut urgueat Auster.
60   utque lacus suberant, ubi quamquam diruta servat
ignem Troianum et Vestam colit Alba minorem,
obstitit intranti miratrix turba parumper.
ut cessit, facili patuerunt cardine valvae;

---

43 torrentis PSRVΣ: torpentis Φ

---

13 Lake Maeotis = the Sea of Azov, at the northeast corner of
the Black Sea (= Pontus, hence "Pontic flood" here).
14 Domitian, like all emperors, held the office of Pontifex
Maximus for life.
15 Probably informers, possibly jurists.

hulk of an Adriatic turbot. It filled the nets and there it stuck, just as big as the fish concealed by Azov's ice[13] which, when the sun has finally broken up the ice, are poured down to the mouth of the Pontic flood, slow with inertia and bloated from the long cold. This monstrosity is earmarked by the Master of Dingy and Line for the Highest of Priests.[14] After all, who'd dare to put a fish like that on sale or to buy it, when even the beaches are crowded with spies? Right away, the ubiquitous inspectors of the seaweed would be tackling the naked oarsman. Without hesitation they'd claim that the fish was a runaway that had grazed for a long time in Caesar's fishponds and that the escapee should be returned to its former master. If we believe Palfurius or Armillatus,[15] anything in the entire ocean that is rare and fine belongs to the imperial treasury, wherever it swims. So the fish will become a gift, so it won't go to waste.

Now with death-laden autumn giving way to frosts, now with invalids hoping for less frequent fevers,[16] ugly winter was whistling and keeping the catch fresh. All the same, our fisherman was in a hurry, as if the South Wind were at his heels. And when the lakes lay below him, where Alba in ruins still tends the Trojan flame and the lesser Vesta,[17] a gawping crowd blocked his path for a time. As it gave way, the folding doors swung open on easy hinges. The sena-

[16] Fevers were measured by the frequency of their recurrence. A "quartan" fever, i.e. one recurring every third day, was better than a "tertian," which recurred every other day.

[17] Alba Longa, near the Alban Lake, was founded by Aeneas' son Ascanius and housed the flame of Vesta, which the Trojans had brought from Troy. There was a larger temple of Vesta at Rome.

exclusi spectant admissa obsonia patres.
65 itur ad Atriden. tum Picens "accipe" dixit
"privatis maiora focis. genialis agatur
iste dies. propera stomachum laxare sagina
et tua servatum consume in saecula rhombum.
ipse capi voluit." quid apertius? et tamen illi
70 surgebant cristae. nihil est quod credere de se
non possit cum laudatur dis aequa potestas.
sed derat pisci patinae mensura.
                            Vocantur
ergo in consilium proceres, quos oderat ille,
in quorum facie miserae magnaeque sedebat
75 pallor amicitiae. primus clamante Liburno
"currite, iam sedit" rapta properabat abolla
Pegasus, attonitae positus modo vilicus Vrbi,
[anne aliud tum praefecti? quorum optimus atque]
interpres legum sanctissimus omnia, quamvis
80 temporibus diris tractanda putabat inermi
iustitia. venit et Crispi iucunda senectus,
cuius erant mores qualis facundia, mite
ingenium. maria ac terras populosque regenti
quis comes utilior, si clade et peste sub illa
85 saevitiam damnare et honestum adferre liceret
consilium? sed quid violentius aure tyranni,

[78] *del. Heinrich*
[79] quamvis *Hendry:* quamquam VΦΣ: quamque PRK

---

[18] I.e. Agamemnon, an ironic use of a grand Homeric name to
designate the supreme monarch.
[19] Line 78: "After all, what else were prefects at that time? Of
them, the best and . . . "

tors, shut out, watch as the food goes in, right up to King
Atrides.[18] Then the man of Picenum says, "Receive a gift
too big for a private kitchen. Let this be a holiday. Hurry up
and stretch your stomach by stuffing yourself. Eat up a tur-
bot preserved for your glorious epoch. It actually wanted
to be caught." What could be more blatant? All the same,
the emperor's crest was rising. There's nothing that godlike
power can't believe of itself when it's praised. But there
was no plate that measured up to the fish.

So his great advisers are summoned to a meeting—
people he hated, people who showed on their faces the
pallor of that awful, mighty friendship. The first to grab his
cloak and hurry there, while the Liburnian slave was still
shouting, "Get a move on, he is already seated," was Pega-
sus, the man recently appointed as slave manager over an
astonished city of Rome,[19] the most incorruptible of jurists
who thought that however terrible the times, every case
should be handled by justice without a sword.[20] Amiable
old Crispus also arrived, a gentle soul, with a character re-
sembling his eloquence.[21] Who would have been a more
useful companion to the ruler of seas, lands, and peoples,
had he only been allowed, under that plague and disaster,
to condemn his cruelty and offer honourable advice? But
what's more savage than a tyrant's ear? On his whim the

[20] Plotius Pegasus, an eminent jurist and prefect of the city,
whose duty was to keep order with his own court of law and stand-
ing police force. A *vilicus* was the slave who ran his master's house-
hold or estate.

[21] Quintus Vibius Crispus, consul three times and a long-time
survivor of the imperial court.

cum quo de pluviis aut aestibus aut nimboso
vere locuturi fatum pendebat amici?
ille igitur numquam derexit bracchia contra
90 torrentem, nec civis erat qui libera posset
verba animi proferre et vitam inpendere vero.
sic multas hiemes atque octogensima vidit
solstitia, his armis illa quoque tutus in aula.
    Proximus eiusdem properabat Acilius aevi
95 cum iuvene indigno quem mors tam saeva maneret
et domini gladiis tam festinata; sed olim
prodigio par est in nobilitate senectus,
unde fit ut malim fraterculus esse gigantis.
profuit ergo nihil misero quod comminus ursos
100 figebat Numidas Albana nudus harena
venator. quis enim iam non intellegat artes
patricias? quis priscum illud miratur acumen,
Brute, tuum? facile est barbato inponere regi.
    Nec melior vultu quamvis ignobilis ibat
105 Rubrius, offensae veteris reus atque tacendae,
et tamen improbior saturam scribente cinaedo.
Montani quoque venter adest abdomine tardus,
et matutino sudans Crispinus amomo
quantum vix redolent duo funera, saevior illo

---

22 The Acilii: the father may be Manius Acilius Aviola, consul
A.D. 54; the son, Manius Acilius Glabrio, was consul with Trajan in
A.D. 91, but was exiled and executed in 95.

23 A circumlocution for the proverbial *terrae filius*, "son of the
earth," i.e. "a nobody."

24 Lucius Junius Brutus, traditionally the founder of the Ro-
man Republic in 509 B.C., following his expulsion of the kings. He

fate of a friend simply intending to talk about the rain, or the heat, or the showery spring, hangs in the balance. So Crispus never swam against the flood; he was not the kind of patriot who could speak his mind's thoughts freely and risk his life for the truth. That's how he managed to see many winters and his eightieth summer. He was protected by this armour even in that court.

Next to him Acilius was hurrying along, a man of the same age, and with him his young son, who did not deserve the savage death which awaited him so speeded up from his master's swords.[22] (But surviving to old age among the nobility has long been like a miracle. That's why I prefer to be a giant's little brother.[23]) It turned out to do the unfortunate youth no good to appear naked as a hunter in the Alban amphitheatre, spearing Numidian bears close up. After all, is there anyone these days who isn't wise to the tricks of aristocrats? Is there anyone who'd be amazed at that old-time cunning of yours, Brutus?[24] Fooling a bearded king is easy.

Looking just as gloomy in spite of his lowly background came Rubrius, accused of an ancient offence that must not be mentioned, and yet with all the nerve of a pathic writing satire.[25] Montanus' belly too is present, slowed down by his paunch,[26] and Crispinus, dripping with his morning perfume, more overwhelming than a couple of funerals; more

pretended to be "stupid" (*brutus*) to escape the attention of the Tarquin rulers (see Liv. 1.56.7–8).

[25] Rubrius Gallus, a military man and another survivor: during the civil wars of A.D. 68–9 he fought as general for Nero against Galba, for Otho against Vitellius, and for Vespasian.

[26] Possibly Curtius Montanus, a longtime gourmand.

110 Pompeius tenui iugulos aperire susurro,
et qui vulturibus servabat viscera Dacis
Fuscus marmorea meditatus proelia villa,
et cum mortifero prudens Veiiento Catullo,
qui numquam visae flagrabat amore puellae,
115 grande et conspicuum nostro quoque tempore
    monstrum,
[caecus adulator dirusque †a ponte† satelles,]
dignus Aricinos qui mendicaret ad axes
blandaque devexae iactaret basia raedae.
nemo magis rhombum stupuit; nam plurima dixit
120 in laevum conversus, at illi dextra iacebat
belua. sic pugnas Cilicis laudabat et ictus
et pegma et pueros inde ad velaria raptos.
non cedit Veiiento, sed ut fanaticus oestro
percussus, Bellona, tuo divinat et "ingens
125 omen habes" inquit "magni clarique triumphi.
regem aliquem capies, aut de temone Britanno
excidet Arviragus. peregrina est belua: cernis
erectas in terga sudes?" hoc defuit unum
Fabricio, patriam ut rhombi memoraret et annos.

  116 *seclusit Courtney, Willis*
  128 in *codd.*: per *Housman*

---

  27 Possibly one of the Pompeii who had held or were soon to
hold consular office; here an informer.   28 Cornelius
Fuscus, a military man and the second *eques* in the list. He sup-
ported Galba and Vespasian and was appointed praetorian prefect
by Domitian. He was killed by the Dacians in A.D. 86–7.
  29 Aulus Didius Gallus Fabricius Veiiento, *amicus* of Nero,
Domitian, Nerva, and Trajan, and consul three times.

ruthless than him, Pompeius, who could slit throats with a tiny whisper;[27] Fuscus, who was saving his guts for the vultures of Dacia, planning battles in his marble villa;[28] and wary Veiento,[29] along with deadly Catullus, who blazed with passion for a girl he had never seen, a great and remarkable monstrosity even in our age.[30] He should have been a beggar blowing obsequious kisses at the wheels as the carriages come down the hill at Aricia.[31] No one was more impressed by the turbot. You could tell: he made a long speech, turning to the left. The beast, however, lay on his right. That's how he used to praise the Cilician's fighting thrusts[32] and the contraption which whisks boys into the awnings. Veiento won't be outdone. Like a fanatic goaded by your frenzy, Bellona,[33] he breaks into prophecy and says, "This is a mighty omen of a magnificent and glorious triumph. You will take some king prisoner, or else Arviragus will fall from his British chariot pole.[34] The beast is a foreigner: do you see the spikes that bristle up his spine?" The only thing Fabricius failed to mention was the turbot's age and birthplace.

[30] Lucius Valerius Catullus Messalinus, consul twice with Domitian (A.D. 73 and 85), a blind informer with a reputation for cruelty. Line 116: "A blind sycophant, a terrifying courtier from the bridge."

[31] The steep hill into Aricia on the Via Appia made vehicles travel slowly, offering a good opportunity for beggars, cf. Pers. 6.55–6n.

[32] A type of gladiator.

[33] The Roman goddess of war, whose followers were called *fanatici*. Her cult involved noise, ecstasy, and self-mutilation.

[34] Otherwise unknown in classical texts, Arviragus was one of Cymbeline's sons according to Geoffrey of Monmouth (4.16).

130   "Quidnam igitur censes? conciditur?" "absit ab illo
         dedecus hoc" Montanus ait, "testa alta paretur
         quae tenui muro spatiosum colligat orbem.
         debetur magnus patinae subitusque Prometheus.
         argillam atque rotam citius properate, sed ex hoc
135   tempore iam, Caesar, figuli tua castra sequantur."
         vicit digna viro sententia. noverat ille
         luxuriam inperii veterem noctesque Neronis
         iam medias aliamque famem, cum pulmo Falerno
         arderet. nulli maior fuit usus edendi
140   tempestate mea: Circeis nata forent an
         Lucrinum ad stagnum Rutupinove edita fundo
         ostrea callebat primo deprendere morsu,
         et semel aspecti litus dicebat echini.
             Surgitur et misso proceres exire iubentur
145   consilio, quos Albanam dux magnus in arcem
         traxerat attonitos et festinare coactos,
         tamquam de Chattis aliquid torvisque Sygambris
         dicturus, tamquam ex diversis partibus orbis
         anxia praecipiti venisset epistula pinna.
150   Atque utinam his potius nugis tota illa dedisset

141 stagnum *Coleman*: saxum *codd.*
143 semel *codd.*: simul *Pricaeus, Scholte*

"What then is your recommendation? Is it to be cut up?" "Let it be spared that outrage," said Montanus. "A deep platter should be made to contain its ample circumference with a delicate wall. It's a dish that requires a great, instant Prometheus.[35] Quick, hurry up with the clay and wheel! And from this time forth, Caesar, there should be potters among your entourage." His argument, worthy of the man, won the day. He'd known the extravagance of the old imperial court—Nero's midnights and beyond, and that second hunger, when Falernian fires the lungs.[36] No one in my own day had greater skill at eating. He could detect at first bite whether oysters came from Circeii or near the Lucrine lagoon or were produced from the Rutupian seabed.[37] At a glance he would state the native shore of a sea urchin.

All rise, the meeting is over and his great advisers are told to leave. They'd been dragged to his Alban fortress, forced to rush there in bewilderment by their great general, as though to deliver to them a communication about the fierce Chatti and Sygambri,[38] or as though an anxious letter had arrived on express wings from distant regions of the world.

All the same, if only he'd devoted the whole of those

[35] Prometheus is the original potter, from the creation story in which he made humans from clay.

[36] Falernian was a strong wine from Campania.

[37] Oysters were a sign of luxury. They came from Circeii (on the coast south of Rome), the Lucrine lake near Baiae (on the coast of Campania), and Rutupiae (mod. Richborough, on the coast of Kent, England).

[38] German peoples on the empire's frontiers.

tempora saevitiae, claras quibus abstulit Vrbi
inlustresque animas inpune et vindice nullo.
sed periit postquam cerdonibus esse timendus
coeperat: hoc nocuit Lamiarum caede madenti.

savage times to such frivolities, instead of depriving Rome of some noble and glorious souls, getting away with it, with no one to take revenge! But he died as soon as he'd started making the workers afraid of him. He was drenched with the blood of Lamia and his type,[39] but it was this that destroyed him.

[39] The consular Lucius Aelius Plautius Lamia Aelianus, of an aristocratic family, was a victim of Domitian (Suet. *Dom.* 10.2).

NOTE ON SATIRE 5

One of the themes of Satire 4 is the misuse of power and
the complicity of those surrounding the source of power.
Returning to the patron-client relationship, Satire 5 treats
the same theme on a smaller scale than emperor-courtier.
The poem presents the total breakdown of the patron-
client relationship, which was supposed to be based upon
mutual benefits and services. The breakdown is repre-
sented graphically by the two separate menus at the dinner
(24–155), one for the patron and his peers, the other for
the lowly clients. The double menu runs as follows: wine
(24–37), wine cups (37–48), water (49–52), waiters (52–
65), bread (66–79), starters (80–91), seafood dishes (92–
106), the meat and truffles served to the patron but not the
client (114–24), mushrooms (146–8), and apples (149–55).
The description of the two-menu dinner is a vehement
condemnation of the patron for failing to behave like pa-
trons in the "good old days." It is framed by passages in
which Juvenal criticises the lowly client for enduring such
humiliation (1–23 and 156–73) and interrupted by a re-
quest that the patron simply dine with his clients "on equal
terms" (107–13), a plea that falls on deaf ears. The gulf is
too wide for there to be any communication (125–31).

SATIRE 5

Si te propositi nondum pudet atque eadem est mens,
ut bona summa putes aliena vivere quadra,
si potes illa pati quae nec Sarmentus iniquas
Caesaris ad mensas nec vilis Gabba tulisset,
5　quamvis iurato metuam tibi credere testi.
ventre nihil novi frugalius; hoc tamen ipsum
defecisse puta, quod inani sufficit alvo:
nulla crepido vacat? nusquam pons et tegetis pars
dimidia brevior? tantine iniuria cenae?
10　tam ieiuna fames, cum possis honestius illic
et tremere et sordes farris mordere canini?
　　Primo fige loco, quod tu discumbere iussus
mercedem solidam veterum capis officiorum.
fructus amicitiae magnae cibus: imputat hunc rex,
15　et quamvis rarum tamen imputat. ergo duos post
si libuit menses neglectum adhibere clientem,
tertia ne vacuo cessaret culcita lecto,

---

10 cum possis VΦ: cum possit PRFKZ: quin possit *codd.recc.*:
quin poscis? *Lubinus, Graevius*

---

1 Sarmentus and Gabba were *scurrae*, professional buffoons,
associated with Maecenas and Augustus (Caesar). The diners
were ranked according to status.

SATIRE 5

If you are not yet ashamed of your life plan and you persist in your view that the highest good is to live off someone else's crumbs, if you can endure treatment which not even Sarmentus or abject Gabba would have put up with at Caesar's hierarchical tables,[1] I'd hesitate to trust your word, even if you were on oath. I know of nothing less demanding than the belly. Yet, suppose you don't have the little it takes to fill your empty guts, is there no beggar's pitch vacant? Isn't there a bridge or the smaller half of a shared mat anywhere?[2] Is the insult of a dinner worth so much? Is your hunger so famished? Wouldn't it be more dignified to shiver where you are and gnaw filthy bits of dog's bread?

In the first place, get this straight: an invitation to dinner is payment in full for your long-standing services. The reward of Great Friendship is—food. Your Lord enters this as a debt, yes, a debt, however infrequent. So if after two months it's his whim to invite his forgotten client, so the third cushion on some empty couch won't be vacant,[3]

[2] Classic venues for beggars.
[3] The Romans reclined three to a couch.

215

"una simus" ait. votorum summa. quid ultra
quaeris? habet Trebius propter quod rumpere somnum
20 debeat et ligulas dimittere, sollicitus ne
    tota salutatrix iam turba peregerit orbem,
    sideribus dubiis aut illo tempore quo se
    frigida circumagunt pigri serraca Bootae.
        Qualis cena tamen! vinum quod sucida nolit
25 lana pati: de conviva Corybanta videbis.
    iurgia proludunt, sed mox et pocula torques
    saucius et rubra deterges vulnera mappa,
    inter vos quotiens libertorumque cohortem
    pugna Saguntina fervet commissa lagona.
30 ipse capillato diffusum consule potat
    calcataque madet bellis socialibus uva,
    cardiaco numquam cyathum missurus amico.
    cras bibet Albanis aliquid de montibus aut de
    Setinis, cuius patriam titulumque senectus
35 delevit multa veteris fuligine testae,
    quale coronati Thrasea Helvidiusque bibebant
    Brutorum et Cassi natalibus.

31 calcataque . . . uva *Harrison*: calcatamque . . . uvam *codd*. |
madet *Harrison*: tenet *codd*.

---

4 Clients were obliged to visit the houses of their patrons in the
morning to greet them (the *salutatio*).

5 I.e. midnight. This constellation near the North Pole, known
as the Plough or Great Bear (UK) or the Big Dipper (US), moves
slowly, hence its drover Boötes is "sluggish."

6 Trebius' wine is worse than that used for medicinal purposes.

7 Fanatical priests of Cybele.

8 Spanish earthenware.

9 In antiquity.

216

he says, "Let's get together." It's your dream come true!
What more could you ask for? Now Trebius has a good rea-
son for interrupting his sleep and letting his laces fly loose
in his panic that the whole mob of morning visitors has
already completed the round,[4] while the stars are fading,
or even at that hour when the frosty cart of sluggish Boötes
is wheeling round.[5]

But what a dinner! You get wine that fresh wool
wouldn't absorb:[6] you'll see the guests turned into Cory-
bants.[7] Insults open the hostilities, but once you're hit it
won't be long before you're hurling cups too, and mopping
your wounds with a reddened napkin. That's what happens
once battle with the Saguntine crockery[8] starts up and
rages between you guests and the squad of freedmen.
Himself downs a wine bottled when consuls had long hair[9]
and gets drunk on a grape trodden during the Social
Wars,[10] but he'll never send even a spoonful to a friend
who's suffering from indigestion. Tomorrow he'll be drink-
ing something from the hills of Alba or Setia. Old age has
obliterated its origin and label with layers of smoke on the
ancient jar. It's the sort of wine that Thrasea and Helvidius
used to drink, wearing garlands, on the birthdays of Cas-
sius and the Bruti.[11]

[10] The war fought between Rome and her Italian allies (*socii*)
in 91–87 B.C.

[11] Publius Clodius Thrasea Paetus (consul A.D. 56) and his
son-in-law Helvidius Priscus were leaders of the senatorial oppo-
sition to Nero and Vespasian. The Bruti (Marcus Brutus, Decimus
Brutus) and Cassius (Gaius Cassius Longinus) were chief figures
in the assassination of Julius Caesar in 44 B.C.

Ipse capaces
Heliadum crustas et inaequales berullo
Virro tenet phialas: tibi non committitur aurum,
40   vel, si quando datur, custos adfixus ibidem,
qui numeret gemmas, ungues observet acutos.
da veniam: praeclara illi laudatur iaspis.
nam Virro, ut multi, gemmas ad pocula transfert
a digitis, quas in vaginae fronte solebat
45   ponere zelotypo iuvenis praelatus Iarbae.
tu Beneventani sutoris nomen habentem
siccabis calicem nasorum quattuor ac iam
quassatum et rupto poscentem sulpura vitro.
   Si stomachus domini fervet vinoque ciboque,
50   frigidior Geticis petitur decocta pruinis.
non eadem vobis poni modo vina querebar?
vos aliam potatis aquam. tibi pocula cursor
Gaetulus dabit aut nigri manus ossea Mauri
et cui per mediam nolis occurrere noctem,
55   clivosae veheris dum per monumenta Latinae.
flos Asiae ante ipsum, pretio maiore paratus
quam fuit et Tulli census pugnacis et Anci
et, ne te teneam, Romanorum omnia regum
frivola. quod cum ita sit, tu Gaetulum Ganymedem
60   respice, cum sities. nescit tot milibus emptus
pauperibus miscere puer, sed forma, sed aetas

---

12 Aeneas (Virg. *Aen.* 4.36 and 261–2).

13 So-called "Vatinian cups," named after Vatinius (metrically impossible), who was originally a cobbler and then an informer under Nero, had four long spouts resembling his nose.

Virro himself holds capacious goblets encrusted with amber and rough with beryl. His gold isn't entrusted to you, or if it is, a guard is stationed on the spot to count the jewels and keep a watch on your sharp fingernails. Don't blame him: his splendid jasper is much admired. The fact is that Virro, like many people, shifts his jewels from his fingers to his cups—jewels that might have been set on the scabbard-front of the young man who was preferred to jealous Iarbas.[12] But you'll drain a vessel named after the shoemaker at Beneventum[13] with its four nozzles. It's already cracked and looking for sulphur matches in exchange for its broken glass.[14]

If the master's stomach is fevered with food and wine, distilled water cooler than Thracian frosts is ordered. Was I complaining just now that you are not served with the same wines? You drink different water too. And your cup will be handed to you by a Gaetulian footman or the bony hand of a dark Moroccan, a character you'd not want to run into in the middle of the night while being conveyed past the tombs on the hilly Latin Way. Before Himself stands the bloom of Asia, bought for a price higher than the total assets of warrior Tullus and Ancus[15] and, to be brief, the entire bric-a-brac of the kings of Rome. Since that's the case, you must catch the eye of your African Ganymede[16] when you are thirsty. A boy purchased for so many thousands cannot mix drinks for paupers. But of course his good looks and his youth justify his sneer. But when will

[14] Peddlars exchanged broken glass for matches.

[15] The third and fourth kings of Rome, of legendary wealth.

[16] Ganymede was kidnapped by Jupiter to be his cupbearer and lover.

digna supercilio. quando ad te pervenit ille?
quando rogatus adest calidae gelidaeque minister?
quippe indignatur veteri parere clienti
65   quodque aliquid poscas et quod se stante recumbas.
     Maxima quaeque domus servis est plena superbis.
ecce alius quanto porrexit murmure panem
vix fractum, solidae iam mucida frusta farinae,
quae genuinum agitent, non admittentia morsum.
70   sed tener et niveus mollique siligine fictus
servatur domino. dextram cohibere memento;
salva sit artoptae reverentia. finge tamen te
improbulum, superest illic qui ponere cogat:
"vis tu consuetis, audax conviva, canistris
75   impleri panisque tui novisse colorem?"
"scilicet hoc fuerat, propter quod saepe relicta
coniuge per montem adversum gelidasque cucurri
Esquilias, fremeret saeva cum grandine vernus
Iuppiter et multo stillaret paenula nimbo."
80   Aspice quam longo distinguat pectore lancem
quae fertur domino squilla, et quibus undique saepta
asparagis, qua despiciat convivia cauda,
dum venit excelsi manibus sublata ministri.
sed tibi dimidio constrictus cammarus ovo
85   ponitur exigua feralis cena patella.
ipse Venafrano piscem perfundit, at hic qui
pallidus adfertur misero tibi caulis olebit

63 rogatus PRAO: vocatus VΦ   66 *del. Heinrich*
80 distinguat PRV: distendat Φ

your waiter ever get around to you? When will the server of
hot and cold water respond to your request? It's beneath
him, you know, to obey an old client. He resents your ask-
ing for things and your reclining while he's standing.

The greatest houses are always full of arrogant slaves:
here's another. Grumbling audibly, he proffers bread that
is hardly breakable, hunks of solid dough that are already
mouldy, to keep your molars busy without letting you bite.
But for the master is reserved soft snowy-white bread
kneaded from fine flour. Don't forget to control your right
hand: respect for the bread tin must be maintained. Yet
suppose you're feeling rather cheeky, there'll be someone
standing over you to make you put it back: "You imperti-
nent diner! Kindly help yourself from the proper basket
and don't forget the colour of your own bread." "So it was
for this that I so often abandoned my wife and raced up the
Esquiline's freezing climb, while spring-time Jupiter[17] was
raging above with his cruel hail and my cloak was dripping
from the frequent cloudbursts?"

Look at the lobster that's brought to the master: look
how its long breast makes the dish distinctive, how it's
walled on all sides by fine asparagus, how with its tail it
looks down upon the company as it enters, carried on high
by the hands of the tall attendant. But you are served with
crayfish hemmed in by an egg cut in half, a funereal supper
on a tiny plate. Himself drenches his seafood with
Venafran olive oil,[18] but this faded cabbage that's brought
to you—poor you!—will stink of the lamp. The oil pro-

---

[17] As the Italian sky god, "Jupiter" can designate the sky.
[18] Highest quality olive oil, from the border of Latium and
Campania.

lanternam; illud enim vestris datur alveolis quod
canna Micipsarum prora subvexit acuta,
90   propter quod Romae cum Boccare nemo lavatur.
[quod tutos etiam facit a serpentibus atris]
     Mullus erit domini quem misit Corsica vel quem
Tauromenitanae rupes, quando omne peractum est
et iam defecit nostrum mare, dum gula saevit,
95   retibus adsiduis penitus scrutante macello
proxima, nec patimur Tyrrhenum crescere piscem.
instruit ergo focum provincia, sumitur illinc
quod captator emat Laenas, Aurelia vendat.
Virroni muraena datur, quae maxima venit
100 gurgite de Siculo; nam dum se continet Auster,
dum sedet et siccat madidas in carcere pinnas,
contemnunt mediam temeraria lina Charybdim:
vos anguilla manet longae cognata colubrae
aut glaucis sparsus maculis Tiberinus et ipse
105 vernula riparum, pinguis torrente cloaca
et solitus mediae cryptam penetrare Suburae.
     Ipsi pauca velim, facilem si praebeat aurem.
nemo petit modicis quae mittebantur amicis
a Seneca, quae Piso bonus, quae Cotta solebat
110 largiri (namque et titulis et fascibus olim

91 *om.* PRVU, *del. Pulmannus, Willis*
104 glaucis sparsus *Clausen, Willis*: glacie aspersus *codd.*

---

19 I.e. African: Micipsa was the son of Masinissa, king of
Numidia.
20 An African: Boccar is the name of an ancient Mauretanian
king. Line 91: "it even protects them from black snakes."
21 Modern Taormina, Sicily.

vided for your dishes is brought up the Tiber in one of Micipsa's point-nosed reed boats.[19] It's the reason why no one at Rome bathes with Boccar.[20]

The master's mullet will be one sent from Corsica or the Tauromenian cliffs,[21] since our own sea[22] has been totally ransacked to the point of exhaustion, since gluttony rages, the delicatessens raking the nearest waters with nonstop nets—and we don't let the Tyrrhenian fish grow to size. So the provinces stock our kitchens: the provinces are the source of the goods that Laenas the fortune-hunter buys—and Aurelia sells.[23] Virro is served with a lamprey, the biggest that comes from the Sicilian whirlpool.[24] You see, when the South Wind is resting, sitting still in his prison and drying his dripping wings, the nets boldly defy the centre of Charybdis. What's waiting for you is an eel, cousin of the long snake, or a Tiber fish spattered with grey blotches, like you a slave bred on the banks, bloated from the gushing sewer, who knows his way right into the drain under the middle of the Subura.[25]

I'd like a word with Himself, if he'd lend a willing ear. No one asks for the gifts sent to his humble friends by Seneca, the gifts good Piso and Cotta used to dispense.[26] In those days, you know, the glory of giving was prized more

---

[22] *Mare nostrum* usually denotes the Mediterranean, but here the Tyrrhenian Sea.   [23] A wealthy widow: we would expect her to eat the gift herself, not sell it on.   [24] The straits of Messina.   [25] See 3.5n.   [26] Martial names Piso and Seneca as good patrons of the past (12.36.8): Lucius Annaeus Seneca is the famous Stoic philosopher and tutor to Nero; Gaius Calpurnius Piso was the figurehead of the Pisonian conspiracy of A.D. 65; Cotta is probably Cotta Maximus, Ovid's patron.

maior habebatur donandi gloria): solum
poscimus ut cenes civiliter. hoc face et esto,
esto, ut nunc multi, dives tibi, pauper amicis.
　　Anseris ante ipsum magni iecur, anseribus par
115　altilis, et flavi dignus ferro Meleagri
spumat aper. post hunc tradentur tubera, si ver
tunc erit et facient optata tonitrua cenas
maiores. "tibi habe frumentum" Alledius inquit,
"o Libye, disiunge boves, dum tubera mittas."
120　structorem interea, ne qua indignatio desit,
saltantem spectes et chironomunta volanti
cultello, donec peragat dictata magistri
omnia; nec minimo sane discrimine refert
quo gestu lepores et quo gallina secetur.
125　　Duceris planta velut ictus ab Hercule Cacus
et ponere foris, si quid temptaveris umquam
hiscere tamquam habeas tria nomina. quando propinat
Virro tibi sumitve tuis contacta labellis
pocula? quis vestrum temerarius usque adeo, quis
130　perditus, ut dicat regi "bibe"? plurima sunt quae
non audent homines pertusa dicere laena.
quadringenta tibi si quis deus aut similis dis
et melior fatis donaret homuncio, quantus
ex nihilo, quantus fieres Virronis amicus!
135　"da Trebio, pone ad Trebium. vis, frater, ab ipsis

---

[116] spumat PSRA: fumat Φ

---

[27] Meleager killed the Calydonian boar, which was ravaging
the land of Aetolia: see Hom. *Il*. 2.642, Ov. *Met*. 8.270–429.
　　[28] Thunder was thought to make truffles grow larger.
　　[29] See Virg. *Aen*. 8.264–5.

highly than titles and symbols of office. All that we ask is that you dine with us on equal terms. If you do this, then you may, you really may (as many do these days) be lavish to yourself and stingy to your friends.

Before Himself is placed the liver of a huge goose, a fattened fowl the size of a goose and a frothing boar, worthy of blond Meleager's weapon.[27] His next course will be truffles, if it's then spring and the longed-for thunder makes the menu longer.[28] "Libya," says Alledius, "keep your corn to yourself, unyoke your oxen, provided you send us truffles." Meanwhile, to complete your humiliation, you'll watch a carver gyrating and gesticulating with flourishes of his knife, while he performs in full his professor's instructions. Of course, it's a matter of vital importance to carve the hare or chicken with the right gesture.

You'll be dragged by the foot and dumped out of doors like Cacus when Hercules beat him up[29] if you ever attempt to open your mouth as though you had a free man's three names.[30] When will Virro drink your health or take the cup that's been contaminated by your lips? Which of you is so crazy or reckless as to say "Cheers!" to my Lord? There are many things people don't dare say when they have holes in their coats. If some god or mere man, a godlike figure kinder than fate, were to give you an equestrian fortune,[31] you'd turn from a nobody into a great man, into a favoured friend of Virro! "Give some to Trebius! Serve it to Trebius! My brother, would you like a piece from the loin?"

---

[30] Free men had a *praenomen*, *nomen*, and *cognomen*; slaves had only one name.

[31] 400,000 sesterces, the minimum qualification for an *eques*.

ilibus?" o nummi, vobis hunc praestat honorem,
vos estis frater. dominus tamen et domini rex
si vis tum fieri, nullus tibi parvulus aula
luserit Aeneas nec filia dulcior illo.
140 iucundum et carum sterilis facit uxor amicum.
sed tua nunc Mycale pariat licet et pueros tres
in gremium patris fundat semel, ipse loquaci
gaudebit nido, viridem thoraca iubebit
adferri minimasque nuces assemque rogatum,
145 ad mensam quotiens parasitus venerit infans.
    Vilibus ancipites fungi ponentur amicis,
boletus domino, sed quales Claudius edit
ante illum uxoris, post quem nihil amplius edit.
Virro sibi et reliquis Virronibus illa iubebit
150 poma dari, quorum solo pascaris odore,
qualia perpetuus Phaeacum autumnus habebat,
credere quae possis subrepta sororibus Afris:
tu scabie frueris mali, quod in aggere rodit
qui tegitur parma et galea metuensque flagelli
155 discit ab hirsuta iaculum torquere capella.
    Forsitan inpensae Virronem parcere credas.
hoc agit, ut doleas; nam quae comoedia, mimus

---

138 tum *Housman*: tunc PRFO: tu Φ
140 *del*. Jahn   142 semel PR: simul Φ

---

32 Difficult to interpret: perhaps Mycale is a freedwoman with
children who cannot therefore inherit.   33 Green was one
of the chariot teams that raced in the Circus Maximus.

34 An allusion to the story that the emperor Claudius was poi-
soned by his wife Agrippina with his favourite mushroom dish,
Suet. *Cl.* 44.2.

Cash—it's to you he offers this honour, it's you that's his "brother." Yet if you ultimately want to become a lord or overlord, don't have a little Aeneas playing in your hall or a daughter dearer than him. A barren wife makes your friends pleasant and close. But as it is, if your Mycale births and tips three sons into their father's lap in one go, Himself will admire your chattering nest.[32] He'll order green jerseys[33] to be brought for them, along with the tiniest nuts and small coins on request, whenever your baby parasite approaches his table.

The insignificant friends are served fungi of dubious quality. The master gets a mushroom of the kind Claudius ate before the one his wife gave him—after which he ate nothing else.[34] For himself and the other Virros, Virro will order apples whose aroma on its own is a meal: the sort of apples that the everlasting fruit time of the Phaeacians used to produce, apples you could believe had been stolen from the African sisters.[35] Your treat is a scabby apple— like the apple gnawed by the creature dressed up with shield and helmet on the Embankment, that in terror of the whip learns to hurl a javelin from the back of a shaggy she-goat.[36]

You might imagine that Virro is intent on saving money. No—he does it deliberately, to pain you. After all, what

[35] Virro's apples are compared with the produce of Alcinous' ever fertile orchard (Hom. *Od.* 7.114–21) and with the golden apples of the Hesperides (the "African sisters") stolen by Hercules as his final labour.

[36] The Embankment running from the Esquiline to the Colline gate attracted various entertainments, here, a performing monkey.

quis melior plorante gula? ergo omnia fiunt,
si nescis, ut per lacrimas effundere bilem
160   cogaris pressoque diu stridere molari.
tu tibi liber homo et regis conviva videris:
captum te nidore suae putat ille culinae,
nec male coniectat; quis enim tam nudus, ut illum
bis ferat, Etruscum puero si contigit aurum
165   vel nodus tantum et signum de paupere loro?
spes bene cenandi vos decipit. "ecce dabit iam
semesum leporem atque aliquid de clunibus apri,
ad nos iam veniet minor altilis." inde parato
intactoque omnes et stricto pane tacetis.
170   ille sapit, qui te sic utitur. omnia ferre
si potes, et debes. pulsandum vertice raso
praebebis quandoque caput nec dura timebis
flagra pati, his epulis et tali dignus amico.

comedy or farce is better than a whining gut? So, let me tell you, his entire intention is to make you vent your anger in tears and keep you gnashing and grinding your teeth. In your own eyes you are a free man and my Lord's guest. He reckons you're enslaved by the smell of his kitchen—and he's not far wrong. After all, how could anyone who in his childhood wore the Tuscan gold, or at least the symbolic knotted leather thong of the poor man, be so destitute as to put up with Himself more than once?[37] It's the hope of dining well that ensnares you. "Look, any minute now he'll give us a half-eaten hare or a portion from the boar's haunch. Any minute now we'll get a scrappy chicken." So you all wait there in silence, brandishing your bread at the ready, untouched. The man who treats you like this has good taste. If there is nothing you can't put up with, then you deserve it all. Sooner or later, you'll be offering to have your head shaved and slapped, and you won't flinch from a harsh whipping.[38] That's the kind of banquet you deserve, and that's the kind of friend.

[37] The amulet hung around a child's neck was an indication of free status; this was regarded as an Etruscan practice. The affluent used a gold locket, while for poorer people the amulet consisted of a knot in a leather thong.

[38] Trebius will some day turn into a clown with a shaven head who receives blows to the head as part of the entertainment at dinner parties, or will be flogged, a slave's punishment.

NOTE ON SATIRE 6

The focus in the five poems of Book One is upon public life and the foolish, selfish, and criminal acts of, primarily, men. Satire 6, the single poem which constitutes Book Two, provides a counterpoint with its focus upon women as wives. In terms of content, then, Book Two complements Book One. In tone, too: Juvenal's satiric persona is the same angry extremist, with the addition of misogyny to his homophobia, chauvinism, and other bigotries. The poem is unique in surviving Roman satire for its size: including the "Oxford fragment" (34 lines which survive only in a MS held in Oxford) it is almost 700 lines long, on an epic scale.

Satire 6 is not, as has often been said, a blanket rant against women, such as found in earlier classical literature, notably Semonides. Rather, it is a furious dissuasion from marriage, addressed to one Postumus, who evidently ignores Juvenal's advice. The course of the poem reflects his story: he leaves his bachelorhood to marry, and is warned of the consequences—all kinds of humiliation inflicted on him by his wife, especially by her infidelity, culminating in death by poison.

Juvenal opens by describing the ancient times when Chastity still lingered on earth; she departed in disgust at the rise of adultery (1–24). He then asks incredulously if Postumus is intent on getting married and impugns his sanity (25–37). When Postumus points out that a notorious Casanova is also getting married, Juvenal remarks on the absurdity of his looking for a chaste woman (38–59). He then commences his catalogue of Roman wives, which is designed to deter Postumus from marriage. First he depicts the uncontrolled way women behave in the theatres (60–81) and provides an extended vignette of Eppia, the senator's wife who runs away with a gladiator (82–113). Then he gives a salacious picture of the "whore-empress," the emperor Claudius' wife Messalina, trying to satisfy her lust by working in a brothel (114–35). The rich wife buys herself freedom to have lovers (136–41), while the wife who was married for her looks will lord it over her husband, until her beauty fades, at any rate (142–60).

Juvenal then has his misogynistic persona reveal his intolerance (161–83). When presented with a wife who is beautiful, graceful, wealthy, fertile, high-born, and virginal, his response is: "But who can stand a wife who is perfection itself?" (166). He rants against the pride of the perfect wife. He mentions a minor habit that can irritate a husband all the same—excessive use of Greek by a woman (184–99). He goes on to say there is no point in getting married unless you love the woman, then describes the way a wife will lord it over an uxorious husband (200–30). A husband's mother-in-law will aid and abet her daughter in adultery (231–41). Women will participate in lawsuits (242–5) and go in for running, wrestling, and gladiatorial combat (246–67). They will quarrel in bed, turning their guilt about their affairs into tears and defiance (268–85).

Juvenal ponders the source of such monstrous behaviour. He attributes it to "the calamities of long peace" (292) and presents a picture of the effects of Luxury on Roman wives (286–313). This leads easily into his description of the profanation of the all-female Bona Dea ritual, an orgy straight out of male fantasy (314–45). In the Oxford fragment Juvenal condemns the presence of pathics (*cinaedi*, men who take the passive role in same-sex intercourse) in the household, and then reveals that women like having sex with eunuchs (366–78). Even poor women are not immune from such adulterous liaisons and spend all their money on their obsessions with athletes (349–65), while other women fall for musicians (379–97).

But that, says Juvenal, is better than the woman who muscles into male society, a busybody who knows all the latest news and gossip (398–412), or the uncouth wife who whips the neighbours and spews up at her own dinner party (413–33). Worse still is the intellectual woman who embarrasses her husband with her knowledge of history and grammar (434–56). Juvenal reviles the way women beautify themselves for their lovers (457–73), and outlines the typical pattern of a woman's day, starting with her viciousness to her slaves as they prepare her for an assignation with a lover and moving on to the ridiculous measures she takes in her quest for beautification (474–511). He then attacks women's superstitiousness (511–91).

Juvenal next deplores the use of abortion-inducing drugs by rich women, and the practice of secretly adopting abandoned babies into the households of the great (592–609). Then he condemns the use of potions by wives to send their husbands mad and kill their stepsons and even their own children (610–33). Juvenal declares that he is not making any of this up, even though it resembles the stuff of Greek tragedy (634–8). To prove it, he produces a woman who admits to killing her own children: the only

difference is that in Greek tragedy such crimes were com-
mitted out of passion, but now the motive is money (638–
52). The poem finishes with a vision of a Rome populated
by modern Clytemnestras—women who are intent on kill-
ing their husbands (652–61). This is clearly designed as the
clinching argument against getting married. But in the
course of this rant, essentially lacking in structure, Juv-
enal's satiric persona has revealed himself as a misogynist
who would find fault with any wife. This extreme cre-
ation—a truly epic satirist who reaches his climax with a
simile worthy of epic (649–50)—seems to be as far as in-
dignation can go. It is not surprising that Juvenal adopts a
new approach in his next book of Satires.

SATIRE 6

Credo Pudicitiam Saturno rege moratam
in terris visamque diu, cum frigida parvas
praeberet spelunca domos ignemque laremque
et pecus et dominos communi clauderet umbra,
5   silvestrem montana torum cum sterneret uxor
frondibus et culmo vicinarumque ferarum
pellibus, haut similis tibi, Cynthia, nec tibi, cuius
turbavit nitidos extinctus passer ocellos,
sed potanda ferens infantibus ubera magnis
10 et saepe horridior glandem ructante marito.
quippe aliter tunc orbe novo caeloque recenti
vivebant homines, qui rupto robore nati
compositive luto nullos habuere parentes.
multa Pudicitiae veteris vestigia forsan
15 aut aliqua exstiterint et sub Iove, sed Iove nondum
barbato, nondum Graecis iurare paratis
per caput alterius, cum furem nemo timeret
caulibus ac pomis et aperto viveret horto.

---

1 Saturn was the king of the gods before his son Jupiter ousted
him and exiled him to live on earth. His reign on earth, where
he was joined by Chastity (Pudicitia) and Justice (Astraea), was
regarded as the Golden Age.

2 Cynthia was the idol of the love elegist Propertius. A genera-

SATIRE 6

I can believe that Chastity lingered on earth during Saturn's reign[1] and that she was visible for a long time during the era when a chilly cave provided a tiny home, enclosing fire and hearth god and herd and its owners in communal gloom, when a mountain wife made her woodland bed with leaves and straw and the skins of her neighbours, the beasts. She was nothing like *you*, Cynthia, or *you* with your bright eyes marred by the death of your sparrow.[2] Instead she offered her paps for her hefty babies to drain, and she was often more unkempt than her acorn-belching husband. You see, people lived differently then, when the world was new and the sky was young—people who had no parents but were born from split oak or shaped from mud.[3] It's possible that many or at least some traces of ancient Chastity survived under Jupiter too—but that was before Jupiter had got his beard, before the Greeks had taken to swearing by someone else's name, at a time when no one feared that his cabbages or apples would be stolen but people lived with their gardens unwalled. It was afterwards

tion earlier, Catullus had celebrated his love for Lesbia and depicted her distress at the death of her sparrow in Poem 3.

[3] The first humans were said to have been born from rocks and oaks (Virg. *Aen.* 8.314–15) or to have been made from clay by Prometheus.

paulatim deinde ad superos Astraea recessit
20 hac comite, atque duae pariter fugere sorores.
anticum et vetus est alienum, Postume, lectum
concutere atque sacri genium contemnere fulcri.
omne aliud crimen mox ferrea protulit aetas:
viderunt primos argentea saecula moechos.
25   Conventum tamen et pactum et sponsalia nostra
tempestate paras iamque a tonsore magistro
pecteris et digito pignus fortasse dedisti?
certe sanus eras. uxorem, Postume, ducis?
dic qua Tisiphone, quibus exagitere colubris.
30 ferre potes dominam salvis tot restibus ullam,
cum pateant altae caligantesque fenestrae,
cum tibi vicinum se praebeat Aemilius pons?
aut si de multis nullus placet exitus, illud
nonne putas melius, quod tecum pusio dormit,
35 pusio, qui noctu non litigat, exigit a te
nulla iacens illic munuscula, nec queritur quod
et lateri parcas nec quantum iussit anheles.
    "Sed placet Vrsidio lex Iulia. tollere dulcem
cogitat heredem, cariturus turture magno
40 mullorumque iubis et captatore macello."
quid fieri non posse putes, si iungitur ulla
Vrsidio? si moechorum notissimus olim

---

4 The Spirit was the Genius, guardian of the family (*gens*), whose image appeared on the marriage bed.

5 Tisiphone was one of the Furies, who were pictured with snakes in their hair, cf. Virg. *Aen*. 7.329.

6 All ways of committing suicide.

that, little by little, Astraea withdrew to the gods above
with Chastity as her companion. The two sisters ran away
together. It's an ancient and established practice, Postu-
mus, to pound someone else's bed, belittling the Spirit of
the sacred couch.[4] Every other kind of crime came later,
products of the iron age. It was the silver centuries that saw
the first adulterers.

And yet, in our day and age, are you preparing an agree-
ment and contract and wedding vows? Are you already
having your hair combed by a master barber, and have you
perhaps already given her finger your pledge? Well, you
used to be sane, all right. Postumus, are you really getting
married? Tell me what Tisiphone and what snakes are driv-
ing you mad.[5] Can you put up with any woman as your boss
with so many ropes available, when those dizzily high win-
dows are wide open, when the Aemilian bridge offers itself
to you so conveniently?[6] Alternatively, if you don't like any
of these many ways out, don't you think it would be better
to have a boyfriend sleep with you? A boyfriend won't en-
ter into nocturnal disputes, won't demand little presents
from you as he lies there, and won't complain that you're
not exerting yourself or that you're not panting as much as
you're told to.

"But Ursidius approves of the Julian Law.[7] He intends
to raise a darling heir, though he'll be depriving himself of
those large turtle doves and bearded mullets and the for-
tune-hunting meat market." Is anything impossible, do
you suppose, if a woman is marrying Ursidius? If the man
who was once the most notorious of Casanovas, who has so

[7] The Julian Laws, enacted in 18 B.C., promoted marriage and
procreation.

stulta maritali iam porrigit ora capistro,
quem totiens texit periturum cista Latini?
45 quid quod et antiquis uxor de moribus illi
quaeritur? o medici, nimiam pertundite venam.
delicias hominis! Tarpeium limen adora
pronus et auratam Iunoni caede iuvencam,
si tibi contigerit capitis matrona pudici.
50 paucae adeo Cereris vittas contingere dignae,
quarum non timeat pater oscula. necte coronam
postibus et densos per limina tende corymbos.
unus Hiberinae vir sufficit? ocius illud
extorquebis, ut haec oculo contenta sit uno.
55 "magna tamen fama est cuiusdam rure paterno
viventis." vivat Gabiis ut vixit in agro,
vivat Fidenis, et agello cedo paterno.
quis tamen adfirmat nil actum in montibus aut in
speluncis? adeo senuerunt Iuppiter et Mars?
60   Porticibusne tibi monstratur femina voto
digna tuo? cuneis an habent spectacula totis
quod securus ames quodque inde excerpere possis?
chironomon Ledam molli saltante Bathyllo
Tuccia vesicae non imperat, Apula gannit,
65 [sicut in amplexu, subito et miserabile longum.]

44 periturum L, *Guyet, Marshall*: perituri *codd.*
57 cedo *codd.*: credo *De Jonge, Thierfelder*
65 *del. Guyet*

---

8 The famous actor Latinus, evidently in the role of the husband in a farce where the adulterer hides in a chest.

9 An excess of blood was regarded as a sign of madness.

often hidden inside Latinus' closet, in danger of his life,[8] is now inserting his stupid head into the marital halter? That's not all. He's actually looking for a wife of old-fashioned morals. Doctors, lance that swollen vein![9] What a precious creature! If you find a lady who is pure, you should prostrate yourself in worship on the Tarpeian threshold and sacrifice a gilded heifer to Juno.[10] There are so few women fit to touch the fillets of Ceres and whose kisses wouldn't scare their fathers. Tie a garland to your doorposts and stretch the thick ivy clusters all around your threshold.[11] But is one man enough for Hiberina? You'll force her to say first that she'd be happy with one eye. "Yet there's a woman living on her father's country estate who has a high reputation." Well, let her live at Gabii or at Fidenae[12] just as she lived in the countryside—and then I'll grant you that "little farm of her father." But who says that nothing ever happened on the hills or in the caves? Have Jupiter and Mars become so very superannuated?

Can our colonnades show you any woman who matches your wishes? Do our shows with all their tiers contain an object that you could pick out from there and love without anxiety? When sinuous Bathyllus is dancing his pantomimic Leda,[13] Tuccia loses control of her bladder, Apula yelps, and Thymele is all attention. It's then that clodhop-

[10] The Tarpeian shrine was the Capitoline temple of Jupiter, Juno, and Minerva. Juno was the goddess of marriage.

[11] Part of the celebrations for a wedding.

[12] Country towns in Latium.   [13] Evidently a pantomime dancer sharing the name of the favourite of Maecenas. Leda was the mother of Helen, Clytemnestra, Castor, and Pollux by Jupiter, who seduced her in the form of a swan.

attendit Thymele: Thymele tunc rustica discit.
ast aliae, quotiens aulaea recondita cessant,
et vacuo clusoque sonant fora sola theatro,
atque a Plebeiis longe Megalesia, tristes
70 personam thyrsumque tenent et subligar Acci.
Vrbicus exodio risum movet Atellanae
gestibus Autonoes, hunc diligit Aelia pauper.
solvitur his magno comoedi fibula, sunt quae
Chrysogonum cantare vetent, Hispulla tragoedo
75 gaudet: an expectas ut Quintilianus ametur?
accipis uxorem de qua citharoedus Echion
aut Glaphyrus fiat pater Ambrosiusque choraules.
longa per angustos figamus pulpita vicos,
ornentur postes et grandi ianua lauro,
80 ut testudineo tibi, Lentule, conopeo
nobilis Euryalum murmillonem exprimat infans.
　　　Nupta senatori comitata est Eppia ludum
ad Pharon et Nilum famosaque moenia Lagi,
prodigium et mores Vrbis damnante Canopo.
85 inmemor illa domus et coniugis atque sororis
nil patriae indulsit, plorantisque improba natos

84 prodigium *Nisbet*: prodigia *codd.*

---

14 The actress of 1.36, here depicted as learning from Bathyllus' sophistication.　　15 The People's Games (*ludi Plebeii*) took place on November 4th-18th and the *ludi Megalenses* on April 4th-8th. Theatrical entertainments were confined to public holidays.　　16 Atellan farce was a native Italian type of comedy which used improvisation, obscenity, and parody of tragedy. Autone, the mother of Actaeon and sister of Agave and Ino, is a character from tragedy.

ping Thymele learns something.[14] But others, when the
stage curtains have been packed away into retirement,
when the theatre is locked and empty, and the only noise
comes from the courts, and when the People's Games are
past and the Megalesian Games are far away,[15] in their
melancholy mood clutch Accius' mask or wand or tights.
Urbicus in an Atellan farce gets a laugh with his imitation
of Autonoe,[16] and penniless Aelia falls in love with him.
These women pay a lot to get a comic actor's clasp undone.
There are women who stop Chrysogonus from singing.
Hispulla is crazy for a tragic actor. Or would you expect
them to fall for a Quintilian?[17] You're marrying a wife
who'll make the lyre-player Echion or Glaphyrus or the
piper Ambrosius a father. Let's set up the long platforms
along the narrow streets, let's decorate the doorposts and
the doors with abundant laurels, Lentulus, so that your
noble child in his tortoiseshell cradle can remind you of—
Euryalus the gladiator![18]

Eppia, the senator's wife, accompanied a troop of gladi-
ators to Pharos and the Nile and the notorious walls of
Lagus, while Canopus expressed its disapproval of the
monstrous morality of Rome.[19] Oblivious of her home and
husband and sister, she disregarded her fatherland and

[17] Marcus Fabius Quintilianus (A.D. 40–100), the eminent
professor of rhetoric.   [18] Lentulus is a member of the aris-
tocratic Cornelian family but the child he is presented with is
fathered by a *murmillo*, a type of gladiator.

[19] Pharos was the island outside Alexandria, here referred to
as the city of Lagus after the founder of the Greek dynasty of
Egypt. Canopus was a city on the Nile delta which had a reputa-
tion for decadence.

241

utque magis stupeas ludos Paridemque reliquit.
sed quamquam in magnis opibus plumaque paterna
et segmentatis dormisset parvula cunis,
90   contempsit pelagus; famam contempserat olim,
cuius apud molles minima est iactura cathedras.
Tyrrhenos igitur fluctus lateque sonantem
pertulit Ionium constanti pectore, quamvis
mutandum totiens esset mare. iusta pericli
95   si ratio est et honesta, timent pavidoque gelantur
pectore nec tremulis possunt insistere plantis:
fortem animum praestant rebus quas turpiter audent.
si iubeat coniunx, durum est conscendere navem,
tunc sentina gravis, tunc summus vertitur aer:
100   quae moechum sequitur, stomacho valet. illa maritum
convomit, haec inter nautas et prandet et errat
per puppem et duros gaudet tractare rudentis.
qua tamen exarsit forma, qua capta iuventa
Eppia? quid vidit propter quod ludia dici
105   sustinuit? nam Sergiolus iam radere guttur
coeperat et secto requiem sperare lacerto;
praeterea multa in facie deformia, sulcus
attritus galea mediisque in naribus ingens
gibbus et acre malum semper stillantis ocelli.
110   sed gladiator erat. facit hoc illos Hyacinthos;
hoc pueris patriaeque, hoc praetulit illa sorori
atque viro. ferrum est quod amant. hic Sergius idem

---

107 sulcus *Nisbet*: sicut *codd.*: ficus *Buecheler*

---

20 A pantomime actor, cf. 7.87n.

shamelessly deserted her wailing children and, what's
more amazing, Paris[20] and the Games. But although as a
little girl she had slept in great opulence on her family
down in cradles with flounces, she scorned the sea. (Her
reputation she'd scorned a long time ago. That's the tiniest
loss among these luxurious ladies' litters.) And so with
heart undaunted she endured the Tyrrhenian waves and
the Ionian's loud boom, although she had to pass from one
sea to the next so many times. If the reason for the danger
is right and honourable, women are afraid. Their hearts
are frozen with terror and they can't stand on their trem-
bling feet. But they are feisty in matters of daring and dis-
grace. If it's her husband who tells her to, it's hard to board
a ship. That's when the bilge water is sickening, that's when
the sky wheels round and round. But the woman who's ac-
companying her lover has a strong stomach. The other one
pukes all over her husband, but this one takes her food
with the sailors and wanders all over the deck and enjoys
handling the rough ropes. But what were the good looks
and youthfulness that enthralled Eppia and set her on fire?
What did she see in him to make her put up with being
called a gladiator's groupie? After all, her darling Sergius
had already started shaving his throat and with his gashed
arm had hopes of retirement. Besides, his face was really
disfigured: there was a furrow chafed by his helmet, an
enormous lump right on his nose, and the nasty condition
of a constantly weeping eye. But he was a gladiator. That's
what makes them into Hyacinthuses.[21] That's what she
preferred to her sons and her fatherland, to her sister and
her husband. It's the steel that they're in love with. This

[21] A pretty young man of Sparta, loved by Apollo.

accepta rude coepisset Veiiento videri.
    Quid privata domus, quid fecerit Eppia, curas?
115 respice rivales divorum, Claudius audi
116 quae tulerit. dormire virum cum senserat uxor,
119 linquebat comite ancilla non amplius una.
117 sumere nocturnos meretrix Augusta cucullos
118 ausa Palatino et tegetem praeferre cubili.
120 sic nigrum flavo crinem abscondente galero
intravit calidum veteri centone lupanar
et cellam vacuam atque suam; tunc nuda papillis
prostitit auratis titulum mentita Lyciscae
ostenditque tuum, generose Britannice, ventrem.
125 excepit blanda intrantis atque aera poposcit.
[continueque iacens cunctorum absorbuit ictus.]
mox lenone suas iam dimittente puellas
tristis abit, et quod potuit tamen ultima cellam
clausit, adhuc ardens rigidae tentigine volvae,
130 et lassata viris necdum satiata recessit,
obscurisque genis turpis fumoque lucernae
foeda lupanaris tulit ad pulvinar odorem.
[hippomanes carmenque loquar coctumque venenum
privignoque datum? faciunt graviora coactae
135 imperio sexus minimumque libidine peccant.]
    "Optima sed quare Caesennia teste marito?"

119 *ante 117 Schurzfleisch*
120 sic O, *Ribbeck*: sed PRΦ: et FKTUZ   126 om. PRΦ
133–5 *del. Gruppe, Ribbeck*

---

22 Presumably Eppia's husband, possibly the Veiiento of 3.185, 4.113.

same Sergius, if he'd been discharged, would have started to resemble a Veiento.[22]

Are you concerned about what happened in a private household, what Eppia got up to? Then take a look at the rivals of the gods,[23] listen to what Claudius put up with. When his wife[24] realised her husband was asleep, she would leave, with no more than a single maid as her escort. Preferring a mat to her bedroom in the Palace, she had the nerve to put on a nighttime hood, the whore-empress. Like that, with a blonde wig hiding her black hair, she went inside a brothel reeking of ancient blankets to an empty cubicle—her very own. Then she stood there, naked and for sale, with her nipples gilded, under the trade name of "She-Wolf," putting on display the belly you came from, noble-born Britannicus.[25] She welcomed her customers seductively as they came in and asked for their money. Later, when the pimp was already dismissing his girls, she left reluctantly, waiting till the last possible moment to shut her cubicle, still burning with her clitoris inflamed and stiff. She went away, exhausted by the men but not yet satisfied, and, a disgusting creature, with her cheeks filthy, dirty from the smoke of the lamp, she took back to the emperor's couch the stench of the brothel.[26]

"But why does Caesennia's husband swear that she's

[23] A reference to the emperors, deified after their deaths.

[24] Messalina.

[25] The son of Claudius and Messalina.

[26] Lines 133–5: "Shall I mention love potions and spells and poisons brewed and administered to stepsons? When women are driven by the imperative of sex they do worse things. Their crimes of lust are the least important."

bis quingena dedit. tanti vocat ille pudicam,
nec pharetris Veneris macer est aut lampade fervet:
inde faces ardent, veniunt a dote sagittae.
140 libertas emitur. coram licet innuat atque
rescribat: vidua est, locuples quae nupsit avaro.
    "Cur desiderio Bibulae Sertorius ardet?"
si verum excutias, facies non uxor amatur.
tres rugae subeant et se cutis arida laxet,
145 fiant obscuri dentes oculique minores,
"collige sarcinulas" dicet libertus "et exi.
iam gravis es nobis et saepe emungeris. exi
ocius et propera. sicco venit altera naso."
interea calet et regnat poscitque maritum
150 pastores et ovem Canusinam ulmosque Falernas—
quantulum in hoc!—pueros omnes, ergastula tota,
quodque domi non est, sed habet vicinus, ematur.
mense quidem brumae, cum iam mercator Iason
clausus et armatis obstat casa candida nautis,
155 grandia tolluntur crystallina, maxima rursus
murrina, deinde adamas notissimus et Beronices
in digito factus pretiosior. hunc dedit olim
barbarus incestae gestare Agrippa sorori,

158 gestare *Housman*: dedit hunc SΦ: dedit hoc PR*Arov*.
Sang.O

---

27 The Caesennii were an important family. One million sesterces would provide the wealth qualification for entry into the Senate.

28 Canusium in Apulia was famous for its flocks. Falernian wine was one of the best.

the perfect wife?" She brought him a million.[27] For that amount he'll call her faithful. He's not wasting away from Venus' quiver or blazing from her torch. It's the money that sets his flares alight, the arrows come from her dowry. Her freedom is paid for. She can flirt and reply to love letters all she likes in front of her husband. A wealthy woman who marries a greedy man is in effect single.

"Why is Sertorius burning with desire for Bibula?" If you shake out the truth, it's the face he loves, not the wife. The minute she has three wrinkles and her skin gets dry and flabby, her teeth get discoloured and her eyes shrink, his freedman will say to her, "Pack up all your paraphernalia and get out. You're a real nuisance to us now, always wiping your nose. Get out right away, and make it quick. Someone with a dry nose is coming to take your place." Till then, she's in favour and in charge, asking her husband for shepherds, Canusian sheep, Falernian vineyards[28]—such tiny requests!—all his slave boys, all his prison gangs. Anything her neighbour has and she doesn't, must be bought. Then in the month of winter, when Jason the merchant is shut off from view and gleaming booths screen his armed sailors,[29] she'll carry off large crystal vases, the most enormous pieces of agate too, along with a legendary diamond, its value enhanced by Berenice's finger.[30] It was once given by the barbarian Agrippa to his incestuous sister to wear, in

[29] A street market for the sale of figurines was held during December in the Campus Martius; its canvas booths hid the mural depicting Jason and the Argonauts on Agrippa's Colonnade.

[30] Queen Berenice was sister of Agrippa II, King of the Jews, and lived with him for periods of her life.

observant ubi festa mero pede sabbata reges
160 et vetus indulget senibus clementia porcis.
    "Nullane de tantis gregibus tibi digna videtur?"
sit formonsa, decens, dives, fecunda, vetustos
porticibus disponat avos, intactior omni
crinibus effusis bellum dirimente Sabina,
165 rara avis in terris nigroque simillima cycno,
quis feret uxorem cui constant omnia? malo,
malo Venustinam quam te, Cornelia, mater
Gracchorum, si cum magnis virtutibus adfers
grande supercilium et numeras in dote triumphos.
170 tolle tuum, precor, Hannibalem victumque Syphacem
in castris et cum tota Carthagine migra.
"parce, precor, Paean, et tu, dea, pone sagittas;
nil pueri faciunt, ipsam configite matrem"
Amphion clamat, sed Paean contrahit arcum.
175 extulit ergo greges natorum ipsumque parentem,
dum sibi nobilior Latonae gente videtur
atque eadem scrofa Niobe fecundior alba.
quae tanti gravitas, quae forma, ut se tibi semper

---

159 mero Φ: nudo PR*Arov*.O: udo *Nisbet*

---

31 Judaea: a reference to the Jewish sabbath and abstention from pork.   32 After the Sabine women had been seized for marriage by Romulus and the Romans, they intervened between their husbands and fathers to prevent war.

33 Probably a prostitute.   34 Cornelia, mother of Tiberius and Gaius Gracchus, was the daughter of Publius Cornelius Scipio Africanus. During the Second Punic War between Rome and Carthage, her father defeated the Numidian leader Syphax in 203 B.C. and Hannibal at the battle of Zama in 202 B.C.

the place where barefooted kings keep the sabbath as their feast day and their traditional mercy is kind to elderly pigs.[31]

"So is there no woman from all these huge herds who lives up to your requirements?" She can be beautiful, graceful, wealthy, fertile, she can display her ancient ancestors all around her colonnades, she can be more virginal than any of the Sabine women with dishevelled hair who stopped the war[32]—a rare bird on this earth, exactly like a black swan—but who can stand a wife who is perfection itself? I'd rather, much rather, have Venustina[33] than you, Cornelia, mother of the Gracchi, if along with your great virtues you bring a haughty expression and if you count your triumphs as part of your dowry. Take away your Hannibal, please! And your Syphax, defeated in his camp! Out you go, with your Carthage and all![34] "Please show mercy, Healer! Goddess, put down your arrows! The boys are innocent. It's their mother you should shoot!" That's what Amphion shouts, but the Healer draws his bow.[35] That's how Niobe buried her flocks of sons and their father too, for thinking herself more noble than the family of Latona and at the same time more prolific than the white sow of Alba.[36] What comportment and what beauty

[35] Niobe, wife of Amphion, King of Thebes, boasted of her seven sons and seven daughters and thus offended Latona, who sent her two children, Apollo (here called Paean = Healer) and Diana, to shoot the children. Amphion committed suicide and Niobe was turned into a rock.

[36] The white sow with her thirty piglets was the omen that the Trojans had reached the site for the foundation of Alba Longa: see 12.70–4n.

imputet? huius enim rari summique voluptas
180 nulla boni, quotiens animo corrupta superbo
plus aloes quam mellis habet. quis deditus autem
usque adeo est, ut non illam quam laudibus effert
horreat inque diem septenis oderit horis?

Quaedam parva quidem, sed non toleranda maritis.
185 nam quid rancidius quam quod se non putat ulla
formosam nisi quae de Tusca Graecula facta est,
de Sulmonensi mera Cecropis? omnia Graece:
[cum sit turpe magis nostris nescire Latine.]
hoc sermone pavent, hoc iram, gaudia, curas,
190 hoc cuncta effundunt animi secreta. quid ultra?
concumbunt Graece. dones tamen ista puellis,
tune etiam, quam sextus et octogensimus annus
pulsat, adhuc Graece? non est hic sermo pudicus
in vetula. quotiens lascivum intervenit illud
195 ζωὴ καὶ ψυχή, modo sub lodice loquendis
uteris in turba. quod enim non excitet inguen
vox blanda et nequam? digitos habet. ut tamen omnes
subsidant pinnae, dicas haec mollius Haemo
quamquam et Carpophoro, facies tua conputat annos.
200 Si tibi legitimis pactam iunctamque tabellis
non es amaturus, ducendi nulla videtur
causa, nec est quare cenam et mustacea perdas

---

188 *om. Gaybac. II, Ulm., del. Barth*
195 loquendis *Nisbet:* relictis *codd.:* ferendis *Housman*

---

37 A bitter purgative made from the aloe plant.
38 Sulmo was a town in Sabine country. Cecrops was the first king of Athens.

is worth so much if she considers you forever in her debt?
The fact is, there's no pleasure in these rare and exalted ad-
vantages when the woman is spoiled by a pride that con-
tains more aloes[37] than honey. Who, actually, was ever so
devoted that he wouldn't loathe the wife he praises to the
skies and hate her for seven hours of every twelve?

Some faults are minor but too much for husbands to put
up with. After all, what is more nauseating than the fact
that no woman thinks she's beautiful unless she's turned
herself from a Tuscan into a Greeklette, from a woman of
Sulmo into a pure Cecropian woman?[38] Everything is in
Greek. They express their fears and pour out their anger,
their joy, their worries, and all the secrets of their souls in
this language. What else is there? They get laid in Greek.
And though you may allow that in young girls, do you
still use Greek when your eighty-sixth year is knocking on
the door? This language is not decent for an old woman.
Whenever that sexy "Mia vita, mio spirito"[39] pops out, you
are using in public words that should be spoken only be-
neath the blanket. Is there any crotch that's not in fact
aroused by such a seductive and naughty phrase? It has
fingers of its own. But—to flatten all your fine feathers—
though you speak these words more sensuously than Hae-
mus or Carpophorus,[40] your age can be calculated from
your face.

If you are not going to fall in love with the woman who
was promised to you and is joined to you by lawful con-
tract, there seems to be no reason for getting married.
There's no point in wasting the feast and the cakes which

[39] The Latin text has "life and soul" in Greek.
[40] Evidently actors.

labente officio crudis donanda, nec illud
quod prima pro nocte datur, cum lance beata
205   DACICVS et scripto radiat GERMANICVS auro.
si tibi simplicitas uxoria, deditus uni
est animus, summitte caput cervice parata
ferre iugum. nullam invenies quae parcat amanti.
[ardeat ipsa licet, tormentis gaudet amantis
210   et spoliis; igitur longe minus utilis illi
uxor, quisquis erit bonus optandusque maritus.]
nil umquam invita donabis coniuge, vendes
hac obstante nihil, nihil haec si nolet emetur.
haec dabit affectus: ille excludetur amicus
215   iam senior, cuius barbam tua ianua vidit.
testandi cum sit lenonibus atque lanistis
libertas et iuris idem contingat harenae,
non unus tibi rivalis dictabitur heres.
"pone crucem servo." "meruit quo crimine servus
220   supplicium? quis testis adest? quis detulit? audi;
nulla umquam de morte hominis cunctatio longa est."
"o demens, ita servus homo est? nil fecerit, esto:
hoc volo, sic iubeo, sit pro ratione voluntas."
imperat ergo viro. sed mox haec regna relinquit
225   permutatque domos et flammea conterit; inde
avolat et spreti repetens vestigia lecti,
ornatas paulo ante fores, pendentia linquit

209–211 *del. Ribbeck*
214 excludetur *recc.*: excludet U: excludatur PΦ
226 repetens *Markland*: repetit *codd.*

---

41 Titles taken by the emperor Trajan in 102 and 97 respectively which appear on his coins.

have to be given to guests already bloated when the occasion is breaking up, or the present that's offered for the first night, when "Victor in Dacia" and "Victor in Germany," inscribed in gold, glitter on a rich platter.[41] If you're straightforwardly fond of your wife, if your heart is devoted to her alone, then bend your head and be prepared to put your neck beneath the yoke. You'll not find any woman who shows mercy to the man who loves her.[42] You'll never be able to make any gifts if she says no, you'll sell nothing if she objects, and nothing will you buy without her agreement. She'll prescribe your affections for you: that friend of yours, the one whose first beard was witnessed by your door and who's now getting on, will be turned away. Although even pimps and trainers of gladiators have complete freedom when making their wills, although the arena enjoys the same right, your heirs will be dictated to you, including more than one of your rivals. "Crucify that slave." "What crime has he committed to deserve punishment? Who says they witnessed it? Who accused him? Give him a hearing! No hesitation is ever long enough when a person's life is at stake." "You idiot! Is a slave a person? All right, let's accept that he hasn't done anything. But it's my wish and my command. Let my will be reason enough." That's how she orders her husband about. But before long she leaves her kingdom and keeps changing residences, wearing out her bridal veil. Then she flits away again, and returning to her imprint in the bed she'd rejected, leaves behind the doorways which had just been decorated, the drapes hang-

---

[42] Lines 209–11: "Even if she herself is on fire, she enjoys tormenting and fleecing him. So she's much less use as a wife to any man who wants to be a good and desirable husband."

vela domus et adhuc virides in limine ramos.
sic crescit numerus, sic fiunt octo mariti
230 quinque per autumnos, titulo res digna sepulcri.
　　Desperanda tibi salva concordia socru.
illa docet spoliis nudi gaudere mariti,
illa docet missis a corruptore tabellis
nil rude nec simplex rescribere, decipit illa
235 custodes aut aere domat. tum corpore sano
advocat Archigenen onerosaque pallia iactat.
abditus interea latet et secretus adulter,
inpatiensque morae silet et praeputia ducit.
scilicet expectas ut tradat mater honestos
240 atque alios mores quam quos habet? utile porro
filiolam turpi vetulae producere turpem.
　　Nulla fere causa est in qua non femina litem
moverit. accusat Manilia, si rea non est.
conponunt ipsae per se formantque libellos,
245 principium atque locos Celso dictare paratae.
　　Endromidas Tyrias et femineum ceroma
quis nescit, vel quis non vidit vulnera pali,
quem cavat adsiduis rudibus scutoque lacessit
atque omnis implet numeros dignissima prorsus
250 Florali matrona tuba, nisi si quid in illo
pectore plus agitat veraeque paratur harenae?

---

43 A famous Syrian doctor. The mother-in-law's "illness" is a cover for her daughter's love affair.

44 Aulus Cornelius Celsus, a distinguished rhetorician, or one of the jurists called Publius Iuventius Celsus, either father or son.

45 Literally the cloaks worn by athletes after exercise.

ing on the walls and the branches still green over the
threshold. That's how the tally increases. That's how there
come to be eight husbands in five autumns—an achieve-
ment worth recording on her grave.

There's no hope of harmony if your mother-in-law
is alive. She'll train her daughter to enjoy fleecing her
husband bare. She'll train her to reply in no simple or
straightforward way to the letters sent by her seducer.
She'll outwit your chaperons or buy them with a bribe.
Then again, though she's perfectly well, she'll summon
Archigenes and lie there tossing her heavy bedcovers.[43]
Meanwhile her lover lurks concealed, impatiently keeping
quiet while drawing back his foreskin. You don't really ex-
pect a mother to pass on respectable behaviour, so differ-
ent from her own, do you? Besides, it profits the disgusting
old woman to bring up her little daughter to be disgusting.

There's almost no lawsuit where a woman didn't start
the dispute. Manilia will be the prosecutor if she isn't the
defendant. On their own they compose and construct the
documents, and they'll not draw the line at dictating to
Celsus how to open his speech and what points to make.[44]

Everyone knows about the tracksuits in Tyrian purple[45]
and the women's wrestling floors. And everyone's seen the
battered training post, hacked away by her repeated sword
thrusts and bashed by her shield.[46] The lady goes through
all the drill, absolutely qualified for the trumpet at the fes-
tival of Flora.[47] Unless, of course, in her heart she's plan-

[46] She is training to be a gladiator. The *rudis* was the wooden
sword used in practice.

[47] At the Floralia, April 28th–May 3rd, women participated in
such fights, announced as usual by a fanfare.

quem praestare potest mulier galeata pudorem,
quae fugit a sexu? vires amat. haec tamen ipsa
vir nollet fieri; nam quantula nostra voluptas!
255 quale decus, rerum si coniugis auctio fiat,
balteus et manicae et cristae crurisque sinistri
dimidium tegimen! vel si diversa movebit
proelia, tu felix ocreas vendente puella.
hae sunt quae tenui sudant in cyclade, quarum
260 delicias et panniculus bombycinus urit.
aspice quo fremitu monstratos perferat ictus
et quanto galeae curvetur pondere, quanta
poplitibus sedeat quam denso fascia libro,
et ride positis scaphium cum sumitur armis.
265 dicite vos, neptes Lepidi caecive Metelli
Gurgitis aut Fabii, quae ludia sumpserit umquam
hos habitus? quando ad palum gemat uxor Asyli?

    Semper habet lites alternaque iurgia lectus
in quo nupta iacet; minimum dormitur in illo.
270 tum gravis illa viro, tunc orba tigride peior,
cum simulat gemitus occulti conscia facti,
aut odit pueros aut ficta paelice plorat
uberibus semper lacrimis semperque paratis
in statione sua atque expectantibus illam,
275 quo iubeat manare modo. tu credis amorem,

---

48 A Samnite gladiator had only one leg protected.

49 Thracian gladiators wore greaves on both legs.

50 Members of eminent Roman families. For Lepidus, see
8.9n. Metellus lost his sight rescuing a statue of Minerva, cf.
3.138–9n. Quintus Fabius Maximus, nicknamed Gurges ("Maw"),
was a great statesman from the third century B.C.

ning something more and is practising for the real arena.
What sense of modesty can you find in a woman wearing a
helmet, who runs away from—her own gender? It's vio-
lence she likes. All the same, she wouldn't want to be a
man—after all, the pleasure we experience is so little in
comparison! What a fine sight it would be if there were an
auction of your wife's things—her sword belt and her arm
protectors and her crests and the half-size shin guard for
her left leg![48] Or, if it's a different kind of battle that she
fights, you'll be in bliss as your girl sells off her greaves![49]
Yet these are women who break out into a sweat in the
thinnest wrap and whose delicate skin is chafed by the
finest wisp of silk. Hark at her roaring while she drives
home the thrusts she's been taught. Hark at the weight of
the helmet that has her wilting, at the size and the thick-
ness of the bandages that surround her knees—and then
have a laugh when she takes off her armour to pick up the
chamber pot. Tell us, you granddaughters of Lepidus and
blind Metellus and Fabius Maw,[50] what gladiator's woman
ever put on gear like this? When does Asylus' wife grunt at
the training post?[51]

The bed with a bride in it is always full of disputes and
mutual recriminations. Not much sleep there. That's when
she's terrible to her husband, that's when she's worse than a
tigress who's lost her cubs. Guilty about her secret misde-
meanours, she pretends she's upset, detesting your slave
boys or complaining about some made-up mistress. She al-
ways has floods of tears ready at their station, just waiting
for her to tell them exactly how to flow. And then you are

[51] Evidently a gladiator. The name is a slave name.

tu tibi tunc, uruca, places fletumque labellis
exorbes, quae scripta et quot lecture tabellas
si tibi zelotypae retegantur scrinia moechae!
sed iacet in servi complexibus aut equitis. "dic,
280   dic aliquem sodes hic, Quintiliane, colorem."
"haeremus. dic ipsa." "olim convenerat" inquit
"ut faceres tu quod velles, nec non ego possem
indulgere mihi. clames licet et mare caelo
confundas, homo sum." nihil est audacius illis
285   deprensis: iram atque animos a crimine sumunt.
     Vnde haec monstra tamen vel quo de fonte requiris?
praestabat castas humilis fortuna Latinas
quondam, nec vitiis contingi parva sinebant
tecta labor somnique breves et vellere Tusco
290   vexatae duraeque manus ac proximus Vrbi
Hannibal et stantes Collina turre mariti.
nunc patimur longae pacis mala. saevior armis
luxuria incubuit victumque ulciscitur orbem.
nullum crimen abest facinusque libidinis ex quo
295   paupertas Romana perit: huc fluxit et Isthmos
et Sybaris †colles†, huc et Rhodos et Miletos
atque coronatum et petulans madidumque Tarentum.
prima peregrinos obscena pecunia mores

---

276 uruca PSR*Arov*.Σ: curuca Φ
295 huc *Hendry*: hinc *codd*. | et Isthmos *Hendry*: ad ismos Z: ad
istos KU: ad istros Φ: ad indos PR*Arov*.
296 colles *codd.*, *susp. Hendry* | huc *Hendry*: hinc *codd*.

---

52 Lit. "caterpillar."   53 Quintilian (6.75n.) was a barris-
ter as well as a professor of rhetoric.   54 Her "defence" is
that it is human to make mistakes, a proverbial line.

delighted, thinking it's love, you worm,[52] and you kiss away
her tears. But what notes and letters you'd read if you
opened up the writing desk of your jealous adulteress!
Say she's found lying in the arms of a slave—or a knight.
"Quintilian,[53] please, give me one of your lines of defence
for this situation." "I'm stuck. Find one yourself." "We
agreed a long time ago," she says, "that you could do what
you liked and that I could please myself. You can holler all
you like and turn the world upside down, I am human."[54]
There's nothing to match the effrontery of a woman caught
in the act. Her guilt inspires her fury and her defiance.

But where do these monstrosities come from, you're
asking, what's their source? In the old days it was their
lowly position that kept Latin women pure. What kept
the contamination of vice from their tiny homes was hard
work, short sleep, hands chafed and hardened from han-
dling Tuscan fleeces, Hannibal close to Rome, and their
husbands manning the Colline tower.[55] These days, we are
suffering the calamities of long peace. Luxury has settled
down on us, crueller than fighting, avenging the world
we've conquered. From the moment Roman poverty dis-
appeared, no crime or act of lust has been missing: Corinth
and Sybaris and Rhodes and Miletus have poured into
Rome, along with Tarentum, garlanded, insolent and soz-
zled.[56] It was filthy money that first imported foreign ways,

[55] Hannibal reached Rome during 211 B.C., and only heavy
rain prevented a battle with the Roman army, camped between
the Colline and Esquiline Gates (Liv. 26.10).

[56] All Greek cities symbolising decadence. A Roman ambassa-
dor was insulted by the people of Tarentum at a festival there in
281 B.C.

intulit, et turpi fregerunt saecula luxu
300   divitiae molles. quid enim Venus ebria curat?
inguinis et capitis quae sint discrimina nescit,
grandia quae mediis iam noctibus ostrea mordet,
cum perfusa mero spumant unguenta Falerno,
cum bibitur concha, cum iam vertigine tectum
305   ambulat et geminis exsurgit mensa lucernis.
i nunc et dubita qua sorbeat aera sanna
307   Tullia, quid dicat notae collactea Maurae,
308   Maura Pudicitiae veterem cum praeterit aram,
noctibus hic ponunt lecticas, micturiunt hic
310   effigiemque deae longis siphonibus implent
inque vices equitant ac nullo teste moventur.
inde domos abeunt: tu calcas luce reversa
coniugis urinam magnos visurus amicos.
    Nota Bonae secreta Deae, cum tibia lumbos
315   incitat et cornu pariter vinoque feruntur
attonitae crinemque rotant ululantque Priapi
maenades. o quantus tunc illis mentibus ardor
concubitus, quae vox saltante libidine, quantus
ille meri Veneris per crura madentia torrens!

307 *om.* PRA*rov., post* 308 KV*at.Reg.*2029
311 nullo *Hendry*: Luna *codd.*
316 ululantque priapi PSR: ululante priapo Φ: ululantque
"Priape!" *Marzullo*
319 Veneris *Braund cf.* 11.167–70: veteris *codd.*

---

[57] Wine.   [58] The temple of Pudicitia in the Forum
Boarium.   [59] Adopting Hendry's emendation of *Luna* to
nullo, this is a pun on the word *testis*: "with no witness present"
and "with no testicle present."

and effete wealth that corrupted our era with its disgusting decadence. After all, when she's drunk does your Venus care about anything? She doesn't know the difference between head and crotch, the woman who chomps giant oysters when it's already midnight, when the perfumes are foaming after being mixed with undiluted Falernian,[57] when drinking is from a perfume jar, when the ceiling's started going round and round and the table's dancing about with its lamps duplicated. Go on, ask yourself why Tullia sneers as she sniffs the air, and what notorious Maura's "foster-sister" says to her when Maura passes the ancient altar of Chastity.[58] It's here that they halt their litters at night, it's here that they piss and fill the goddess's image with their powerful streams, and take it in turns to ride one another and thrash around with no man present.[59] Then off home they go. When the daylight has returned, you tread in your wife's urine on your way to call on important friends.

Everyone knows the secret rites of the Good Goddess,[60] when the pipe excites the loins and, crazed by horn and wine alike, the maenads of Priapus are carried away, whirling their hair and howling.[61] How their minds are all on fire to get laid then, how they squeal to the dance of their desire, how abundant a torrent of undiluted lust runs over their dripping thighs! Saufeia takes off her garland

---

[60] The Good Goddess (*Bona Dea*) was a Roman fertility goddess worshipped by women, esp. in a ceremony in December, involving abstention from wine and sex.

[61] Priapus was a fertility god, depicted with an erect phallus. He was regarded by the Greeks as the son of Dionysus, hence "maenads."

320 lenonum ancillas posita Saufeia corona
provocat et tollit pendentis praemia coxae,
ipsa Medullinae fluctum crisantis adorat:
palma inter dominas, virtus natalibus aequa.
nil ibi per ludum simulabitur, omnia fient
325 ad verum, quibus incendi iam frigidus aevo
Laomedontiades et Nestoris hirnea possit.
tunc prurigo morae inpatiens, tum femina simplex,
ac pariter toto repetitus clamor ab antro
"iam fas est, admitte viros." dormitat adulter,
330 illa iubet sumpto iuvenem properare cucullo;
si nihil est, servis incurritur; abstuleris spem
servorum, veniet conductus aquarius; hic si
quaeritur et desunt homines, mora nulla per ipsam
quo minus inposito clunem summittat asello.
335 atque utinam ritus veteres aut publica saltem
his intacta malis agerentur sacra; sed omnes
noverunt Mauri atque Indi quae psaltria penem
maiorem quam sunt duo Caesaris Anticatones
illuc, testiculi sibi conscius unde fugit mus,
340 intulerit, ubi velari pictura iubetur
quaecumque alterius sexus imitata figuras.

---

322 fluctum PSRAFΣ: fructum Φ: frictum LO
332 veniet Φ: venit et PR
335 aut *Braund*: et *codd.*

---

62 Medullina was a name of the patrician Furii family. Saufeia
must also be of high status.

63 Priam (the son of Laomedon) and Nestor were the classic
examples of old age. Priam's grand patronymic comes from Virg.
Aen. 8.158.

and issues a challenge to the brothel-keepers' slave girls. She wins the prize for swinging her arse, then she in turn worships Medullina's undulating surges.[62] The contest is between the ladies: their expertise matches their birth. Nothing there will be pretend or imitation. It'll all be done for real. It could create a spark in the son of Laomedon, already chill with age, or in Nestor's swollen scrotum.[63] That's the itch of impatience, that's the moment of pure Woman. The shout's repeated in unison from the entire grotto: "Now's the time! Send in the men!" If her lover's asleep, she'll tell his son to put on his hood and hurry along. If that's no good, there's an assault on the slaves. If there's no prospect of slaves available, they'll pay the water delivery man to come in. If they can't find him and there's a deficit of humans, not a moment passes before she voluntarily offers her arse to be tupped[64] by a donkey. If only our ancient rites, or at least our state ceremonies, were conducted unsullied by such taints. But all the Moors and the Indians know about the "lute girl" who brought a penis larger than both of Caesar's "Anti-Cato" speeches into that place which even a male mouse avoids, all too aware of his balls, the place where any picture portraying the shape of the other sex has to be covered up.[65] And in those old days,

[64] The technical term for putting a male animal to a female animal: *Oxford Latin Dictionary* 8.

[65] A reference to the profanation of the mysteries of the Good Goddess in 62 B.C., when Publius Clodius Pulcher infiltrated the ceremony dressed as a female musician. The ceremony that year was held in the house of Julius Caesar, who would later write two speeches criticising his enemy Cato.

et quis tunc hominum contemptor numinis, aut quis
simpuvium ridere Numae nigrumque catinum
et Vaticano fragiles de monte patellas
345   ausus erat? sed nunc ad quas non Clodius aras?
O1   In quacumque domo vivit luditque professus
obscenum et tremula promittens omnia dextra,
invenies omnis turpes similesque cinaedis.
his violare cibos sacraeque adsistere mensae
O5   permittunt, et vasa iubent frangenda lavari
cum Colocyntha bibit vel cum barbata Chelidon.
purior ergo tuis laribus meliorque lanista,
in cuius numero longe migrare iubetur
psillus ab euhoplo. quid quod nec retia turpi
O10 iunguntur tunicae, nec cella ponit eadem
munimenta umeri †pulsatorisque† tridentem
qui nudus pugnare solet? pars ultima ludi
accipit has animas aliusque in carcere nervos.
sed tibi communem calicem facit uxor et illis

O1–34 *post* 345 *von Winterfeld: post* 365 O
O2 promittens *von Winterfeld*: promittit O
O9 psillus O: psyllus *Postgate*
O9 euhoplo *Eden*: eupholio O
O11 pulsatorisque *ipsa inveni sine auctore*: pulsatamque arma
O: pulsatoremque *Leo*: pulsatorumque *Colin*: pulsantem arma
Harrison

---

[66] Numa, the second king of Rome, was the founder of Roman
religion.   [67] On Clodius, see 6.340–1n.
    [68] *Cinaedus* literally denotes "dancer," evidently an effemi-
nate profession.   [69] The text is obscure and interpretation
difficult. I see these as names appropriate to pathics, with the fem-
inine gender of *barbata* producing a paradox; others have seen

what human being ever scorned divine power? What human being had ever dared to laugh at Numa's earthenware ladles or the black bowls or the brittle dishes from the Vatican hill?[66] But these days, is there any altar without a Clodius?[67]

In any house where a professor of obscenity lives and sports, his fidgety right hand suggesting he stops at nothing, you'll find that everyone is disgusting—no better than pathics.[68] These creatures they allow to pollute the food and to stand close by the sacred table. The crockery which should be smashed once Gourd or bearded Swallow-tail[69] has drunk from it they simply have washed. That makes the gladiator trainer's establishment purer and better than your holy hearth. In his troop Skin is told to keep well away from Loaded.[70] Then there's the fact that the nets aren't kept alongside the tunic of disgrace, and that the shoulder guards and the trident of the gladiator who fights naked are not stored in the same locker.[71] Such souls are relegated to the lowest section of the school and in their prison they have different chains. But your wife has you share a

metaphorical references to oral sex performed on women and men, perhaps with a line missing between O5 and O6.

[70] Another controversial passage. The *psilus* is the light-armed gladiator (Greek, "light-armed soldier"), who may also be depilated. The *euhoplus* (a conjecture) would denote an armoured gladiator, with the possible suggestion that he is also sexually vigorous.

[71] The trainer (*lanista*) stores away the equipment of his troop of gladiators in different places according to status. The text, which is difficult here, seems to rank the professional net fighter (*retiarius*), whose only protection was his trident, net, and shoulder guard, as superior in status to the amateur who wore the tunic.

O15 cum quibus Albanum Surrentinumque recuset
flava ruinosi lupa degustare sepulchri.
horum consiliis nubunt subitaeque recedunt,
his languentem animum reserant et seria vitae,
his clunem atque latus discunt vibrare magistris,
O20 quicquid praeterea scit qui docet. haud tamen illi
semper habenda fides: oculos fuligine pascit
discinctus croceis et reticulatus adulter.
suspectus tibi sit, quanto vox mollior et quo
saepius in teneris haerebit dextera lumbis.
O25 hic erit in lecto fortissimus; exuit illic
personam docili Thais saltata Triphallo.
"quem rides? aliis hunc mimum! sponsio fiat:
purum te contendo virum. contendo: fateris?
an vocat ancillas tortoris pergula? novi
O30 consilia et veteres quaecumque monetis amici,
'pone seram, cohibe.' sed quis custodiet ipsos
custodes, qui nunc lascivae furta puellae
hac mercede silent?" crimen commune tacetur.
prospicit hoc prudens et ab illis incipit uxor.
366 Sunt quas eunuchi inbelles ac mollia semper
oscula delectent et desperatio barbae

O18 reserant *Axelson*: servant O
O22 discinctus *Edwards*: distinctus O
O28 contendo. fateris O: verumne fateris *Morgan, cf. Plaut.*
Truc. 783–4
O31 custodiet *cf.* 347 Φ: custodiat O
366–78 *ante* 349–65 *Braund*

goblet with creatures that the blonde whore from the dilapidated tomb would refuse to join for a drink, even if the wine were from Alba or Surrentum.[72] It's on their advice that women suddenly get married and divorced. It's to them that they confide their depressions and their worries in life. It's from their tuition that they learn how to shimmy their backsides and their hips and whatever else their instructor knows. But he's not always to be trusted. He'll enhance his eyes with soot, his saffron outfit unfastened, a hairnetted adulterer! The more sensuous his voice, the more often his right hand lingers in his smooth crotch, the more suspicious you should be. In bed he'll be supremely virile. There he'll take off his mask, a "Thais" danced by an expert "Triphallus."[73] "Who are you fooling? Keep that masquerade for other people! Let's make a bet: I declare that you are every inch a man. I declare it. Do you admit it? Or do the female slaves get summoned to the torturer's rack? I'm familiar with the advice and all the warnings you, my old friends, offer: 'Bolt the door and keep her in.' But who's going to chaperone the chaperons themselves, when nowadays this is the reward they get for keeping quiet about the naughty girl's affairs." Their complicity guarantees their silence. A clever wife anticipates this and begins with them.

Some women are delighted by un-macho eunuchs with their ever gentle kisses and their unfulfilled beard—and

[72] Fine wines, Alban from Alba Longa, near Rome, and Surrentine from Campania (mod. Sorrento).

[73] The adulterer is pictured as a pantomime actor playing the part of Thais, the mistress of Alexander the Great, who turns out to be like Triphallus, a name of Priapus, in bed.

et quod abortivo non est opus. illa voluptas
summa tamen, quom iam calida matura iuventa
370   inguina traduntur medicis, iam pectine nigro.
ergo expectatos ac iussos crescere primum
testiculos, postquam coeperunt esse bilibres,
tonsoris tantum damno rapit Heliodorus.
373A (mangonum pueros vera ac miserabilis urit
373B debilitas, follisque pudet cicerisque relicti.)
conspicuus longe cunctisque notabilis intrat
375   balnea nec dubie custodem vitis et horti
provocat a domina factus spado. dormiat ille
cum domina, sed tu iam durum, Postume, iamque
378   tondendum eunucho Bromium committere noli.
346   [audio quid veteres olim moneatis amici,
"pone seram, cohibe." sed quis custodiet ipsos
348   custodes? cauta est et ab illis incipit uxor.]
349   Iamque eadem summis pariter minimisque libido,
350   nec melior silicem pedibus quae conterit atrum
quam quae longorum vehitur cervice Syrorum.
ut spectet ludos, conducit Ogulnia vestem,
conducit comites, sellam, cervical, amicas,

---

369 quom *Ribbeck*: quod PRΦ
373AB O, *om.* PΦ, *del.* Buecheler   346–8 *del. Maas*

---

[74] For removal of the testicles. Eunuchs were all sterile but they were not necessarily impotent. Moreover, if they could maintain an erection without ejaculation, this could obviously increase the pleasure they could give.

[75] Heliodorus is a surgeon. The young man he castrates cannot now grow a beard, hence the barber's loss of income.

[76] In contrast with the youth castrated in his teens, these boys

there's no need to use abortion drugs. Yet the height of
their pleasure is when a crotch that's already ripe with the
hot blood of youth and its black quill is taken to visit the
surgeons.[74] So it is that the testicles are allowed to drop
and told to grow first and then, once they make two pounds
in weight, Heliodorus tears them off, to the loss of the bar-
ber and no one else.[75] (But it's a real and pitiable loss that
sears the boys of the slavedealers. They're embarrassed by
the pouch and the chickpea they're left with.[76]) The man
made a eunuch by his mistress catches the eye from far off
and attracts everyone's gaze as he enters the baths: there's
no doubt that he can challenge the guardian of the vine
and the garden.[77] You can let him sleep with his mistress,
Postumus, but don't entrust your Bromius to a eunuch
when he's no longer soft and needs a haircut.[78]

And these days the greatest and least of women alike
experience the same lust. The woman who treads the black
pavement with her bare feet is no better than the woman
conveyed on the shoulders of tall Syrians. To go watch the
games, Ogulnia has to rent a dress, rent attendants, a chair,

---

have had their testes removed before the age of puberty and
therefore have only an empty sack and a tiny childlike penis be-
cause of the lack of testosterone during puberty.

[77] Ithyphallic Priapus.

[78] A long-haired boy favourite named after the god Bacchus.
Because he has reached his late teens and is rough with facial and
body hair, he will have his hair cut and will perhaps be sold and re-
placed with a younger boy. The warning is that the well-endowed
eunuch will damage him if he has (anal) sex with him. Lines 346–
8: "I hear the advice given for ages by you, my old friends: 'Bolt the
door and keep her in.' But who's going to chaperone the chaper-
ons themselves? The wife is clever—that's where she starts."

nutricem et flavam cui det mandata puellam.
355 haec tamen argenti superest quodcumque paterni
levibus athletis et vasa novissima donat.
multis res angusta domi, sed nulla pudorem
paupertatis habet nec se metitur ad illam.
[quem dedit haec posuitque modum. tamen utile quid
sit]
360 prospiciunt aliquando viri, frigusque famemque
formica tandem quidam expavere magistra:
prodiga non sentit pereuntem femina censum.
ac velut exhausta recidivus pullulet arca
nummus et e pleno tollatur semper acervo,
365 non umquam reputat quanti sibi gaudia constent.
379   Si gaudet cantu, nullius fibula durat
380 vocem vendentis praetoribus. organa semper
in manibus, densi radiant testudine tota
sardonyches, crispo numerantur pectine chordae
quo tener Hedymeles operas dedit: hunc tenet, hoc se
solatur gratoque indulget basia plectro.
385 quaedam de numero Lamiarum ac nominis Appi
et farre et vino Ianum Vestamque rogabat,
an Capitolinam deberet Pollio quercum
sperare et fidibus promittere. quid faceret plus

358 illam *Nisbet*: illum *codd.*
359 *del. Nisbet*
365 reputat *recc.*: reputant PRU: repetunt Φ

---

79 I.e. she cannot afford to own these items.
80 Line 359: "The limit which it [Poverty] has given and set.
Yet what is useful . . . "   81 The praetors were the magis-
trates in charge of hiring professional singers for festivals.

a cushion, some woman friends, a nurse, and a blonde girl
to give her orders to.[79] Yet this same woman gives away
whatever's left of her ancestral silver plate, down to the last
vases, to smooth-skinned athletes. Many women are short
of money, but none feels any of the shame of poverty or
matches herself to its limits.[80] Their husbands occasionally
look to the future, and some of them conceive a terror of
cold and hunger, learning the lesson of the ant at long last.
But a spend-spend-spend woman has no awareness of her
failing resources. Just as if the coins were for ever regener-
ating and sprouting up from the exhausted treasure chest
and taken from an ever replenished heap, she gives never a
thought to the cost of her pleasures.

If she enjoys music, no one who sells his voice to the
praetors will hang on to his clasp.[81] She's for ever handling
musical instruments, her thicket of sardonyx rings spark-
ling all over the tortoiseshell lyre, and she strikes the
strings rhythmically with the quivering quill used by ten-
der Hedymeles in his performances.[82] This she hugs, this is
her consolation, and she lavishes kisses upon the beloved
plectrum. A woman from the tally of the Lamiae, with the
name of Appius,[83] kept asking Janus and Vesta with offer-
ings of grain and wine whether Pollio had any chance of
winning the Capitoline crown and of promising victory to
his lyre.[84] Is there anything more she could have done if

[82] The singer's name means "Sweet Melody."
[83] The Aelii Lamiae and the Appii Claudii were two of Rome's
aristocratic families.
[84] A famous harpist and singer. The prize he hopes for is the
crown of oak leaves at the contests in honour of Capitoline Jupiter.

aegrotante viro, medicis quid tristibus erga
390 filiolum? stetit ante aram nec turpe putavit
pro cithara velare caput dictataque verba
pertulit, ut mos est, et aperta palluit agna.
dic mihi nunc, quaeso, dic, antiquissime divom,
respondes his, Iane pater? magna otia caeli;
395 non est, quod video, non est quod agatur apud vos.
haec de comoedis te consulit, illa tragoedum
commendare volet: varicosus fiet haruspex.

   Sed cantet potius quam totam pervolet Vrbem
audax et coetus possit quae ferre virorum
400 cumque paludatis ducibus praesente marito
ipsa loqui recta facie siccisque mamillis.
haec eadem novit quid toto fiat in orbe,
quid Seres, quid Thraces agant, secreta novercae
et pueri, quis amet, quis diripiatur adulter;
405 dicet quis viduam praegnatem fecerit et quo
mense, quibus verbis concumbat quaeque, modis quot.
instantem regi Armenio Parthoque cometen
prima videt, famam rumoresque illa recentis
excipit ad portas, quosdam facit; isse Niphaten
410 in populos magnoque illic cuncta arva teneri
diluvio, nutare urbes, subsidere terras,
quocumque in trivio, cuicumque est obvia, narrat.

   401 siccisque PΦ: strictisque LU

---

85 Part of the ritual at a sacrifice.
86 From so much standing as he reads the entrails.
87 Comets were bad omens, indicating changes of power.

her husband had been sick or if the doctors had been pessimistic about her dear little boy? She stood there in front of the altar, thinking it no disgrace to veil her head[85] for a lyre. She recited the prescribed words in the proper form and went pale when the lamb was opened up. Tell me now, please, father Janus, tell me, most ancient of the gods, do you answer people like her? You must have plenty of leisure in the sky. There's nothing, as far as I can see, nothing to occupy you there. One woman consults you about comic actors, another will want to recommend a tragic actor. The soothsayer will soon get varicose veins![86]

But it's better for her to be musical than to go brazenly racing all over Rome, the sort of woman who can attend men-only meetings and actually converse with the generals in their uniforms in her husband's presence with her face unflinching and her nipples dry. This is the woman who knows everything that's happening throughout the world—what the Chinese and the Thracians are up to, the secrets of the stepmother and the boy, who's in love, and which Casanova they're fighting over. She'll tell you who got the widow pregnant and in which month. She'll tell you the words each woman uses in bed and how many positions she knows. She's the first to see the comet that's bad news for the king of Armenia and Parthia.[87] She picks up the latest tales and rumours at the city gates and she invents some herself. Niphates[88] is on the move, threatening whole populations, and massive flooding has engulfed all the fields, cities are teetering, tracts of land are subsiding—that's what she'll say to anyone she meets at any street corner.

[88] Actually a mountain in Armenia; Juvenal, like Lucan 3.245 and Silius Italicus 13.765, regards it as a river.

Nec tamen id vitium magis intolerabile quam quae
vicinos humiles rapere et concidere loris
415 exsecrata solet. nam si latratibus alti
rumpuntur somni, "fustes huc ocius" inquit
"adferte" atque illis dominum iubet ante feriri,
deinde canem, gravis occursu, taeterrima vultu.
balnea nocte subit, conchas et castra moveri
420 nocte iubet, magno gaudet sudare tumultu,
cum lassata gravi ceciderunt bracchia massa,
callidus et cristae digitos inpressit aliptes
ac summum dominae femur exclamare coegit.
convivae miseri interea somnoque fameque
425 urguentur. tandem illa venit rubicundula, totum
oenophorum sitiens, plena quod tenditur urna
admotum pedibus, de quo sextarius alter
ducitur ante cibum rabidam facturus orexim,
dum redit et loto terram ferit intestino.
430 marmoribus rivi properant, aurata Falernum
pelvis olet; nam sic, tamquam alta in dolia longus
deciderit serpens, bibit et vomit. ergo maritus
nauseat atque oculis bilem substringit opertis.
Illa tamen gravior, quae cum discumbere coepit
435 laudat Vergilium, periturae ignoscit Elissae,
committit vates et comparat, inde Maronem
atque alia parte in trutina suspendit Homerum.

413 quae PR: quod Φ   415 exsecrata *Martyn*: exagitata
Delz: exortata PH: exorata RΦΣ

---

89 Evidently a practice favoured by some athletic types.
90 Wine.
91 Probably a fable.

But no less insufferable is the woman who grabs hold
of her lowly neighbours and lays into them with a whip,
cursing all the while. If her sound sleep is disturbed by a
dog barking, you see, she says, "Quick! Fetch the cudgels
here!" and gives the order that first the owner, then the dog
is to get a thrashing. She's formidable to meet, with an ut-
terly hideous face. It's at night that she goes to the baths,
at night that she gives the command to move camp along
with her perfume jars. She enjoys sweating amidst the din.
When her arms drop to her sides after a workout with
heavy weights, the expert masseur presses his fingers into
her tuft too and forces a shriek from the top of his mistress'
thigh. All this time, her miserable dinner guests are over-
whelmed by sleepiness and hunger. Eventually, she ar-
rives, face flushed and thirsty enough for the whole flagon
of wine which is set at her feet bulging with its full three
gallons. From this she downs two pints before dinner, to
create a raging appetite, until it all comes back up and hits
the ground along with her washed-out insides:[89] streams
are running all over the marble floors and the gilded basin
stinks of Falernian.[90] It's like the long snake that's fallen
into a deep vat,[91] that's exactly how she boozes and spews
up. No wonder her husband feels sick and closes his eyes to
keep down his bile.

But she's much worse, the woman who as soon as she's
taken her place at dinner is praising Virgil and forgiving
Elissa on her deathbed,[92] who pits the poets against one
another and assesses them, weighing in her scales Maro[93]
on this side and Homer on the other. The schoolteachers

---

[92] Dido, queen of Carthage. Virgil describes her tragic death
in *Aeneid* 4.   [93] Publius Vergilius Maro, i.e. Virgil.

cedunt grammatici, vincuntur rhetores, omnis
turba tacet, nec causidicus nec praeco loquetur,
440   altera nec mulier. verborum tanta cadit vis,
tot pariter pelves ac tintinnabula dicas
pulsari. iam nemo tubas, nemo aera fatiget:
443   una laboranti poterit succurrere Lunae.
[inponit finem sapiens et rebus honestis;]
448   non habeat matrona, tibi quae iuncta recumbit,
dicendi genus, aut curvum sermone rotato
450   torqueat enthymema, nec historias sciat omnes,
sed quaedam ex libris et non intellegat. odi
hanc ego quae repetit volvitque Palaemonis artem
servata semper lege et ratione loquendi
ignotosque mihi tenet antiquaria versus.
455   haec curanda viris? opicae castiget amicae
456   verba: soloecismum liceat fecisse marito.
445   nam quae docta nimis cupit et facunda videri
crure tenus medio tunicas succingere debet,
447   caedere Silvano porcum, quadrante lavari.
457   Nil non permittit mulier sibi, turpe putat nil,
cum viridis gemmas collo circumdedit et cum
auribus extentis magnos commisit elenchos.
460   [intolerabilius nihil est quam femina dives.]

      444 *del. Heinrich*
      445–7 *post* 456 *Heinrich*
      455 haec curanda viris? *Postgate*: nec curanda viris *Housman*
      460 *del.* Paldamus

---

    94 It was thought that making a din could drive away the de-
mons who caused eclipses of the moon. Line 444: "Philosophers
say there's a limit even to good things."

give way, the teachers of rhetoric are beaten, the whole
party falls silent, there'll not be a word from any lawyer or
auctioneer—and not even from another woman. Such vig-
orous verbiage pours from her, you'd say it was the sound
of people bashing all their bowls and bells at once. There's
no need now for anyone to wear out the trumpets or the
gongs. On her own she can give assistance to the Moon in
her struggle.[94] Don't let the lady reclining next to you have
her own rhetorical style or brandish phrases before hurl-
ing her rounded syllogism at you. Don't let her know the
whole of history. Let there be a few things in books that she
doesn't even understand. I loathe the woman who is for-
ever referring to Palaemon's *Grammar*[95] and thumbing
through it, observing all the laws and rules of speech, or
who quotes lines I've never heard, a female scholar. Do
men bother about such things? It's the language of her
philistine girlfriend she should be criticising. Husbands
should be allowed their grammatical oddities. The fact of
the matter is that the woman who longs to appear exces-
sively clever and eloquent should hitch up a tunic knee-
high, sacrifice a pig to Silvanus, and pay just a quarter to
enter the baths.[96]

There's nothing a woman doesn't allow herself, nothing
she considers disgusting, once she has put an emerald
choker around her neck and has fastened giant pearls to

[95] The first century schoolteacher Quintus Remmius Palae-
mon wrote a famous grammar book.

[96] All marks of being a man: the *tunica* was male clothing, the
god Silvanus was worshipped by men, and the admittance fee to
the baths was just a *quadrans* for men.

interea foeda aspectu ridendaque multo
pane tumet facies aut pinguia Poppaeana
463   spirat et hinc miseri viscantur labra mariti.
467   tandem aperit vultum et tectoria prima reponit.
incipit agnosci, atque illo lacte fovetur
propter quod secum comites educat asellas
470   exul Hyperboreum si dimittatur ad axem.
464   ad moechum lota veniet cute. quando videri
vult formonsa domi? moechis foliata parantur,
466   his emitur quidquid graciles huc mittitis Indi.
471   sed quae mutatis inducitur atque novatur
tot medicaminibus coctaeque siliginis offas
accipit et madidae, facies dicetur an ulcus?
    Est pretium curae penitus cognoscere toto
475   quid faciant agitentque die. si nocte maritus
aversus iacuit, periit libraria, ponunt
cosmetae tunicas, tarde venisse Liburnus
dicitur et poenas alieni pendere somni
cogitur, hic frangit ferulas, rubet ille flagello,
480   hic scutica; sunt quae tortoribus annua praestent.
verberat atque obiter faciem linit, audit amicas
aut latum pictae vestis considerat aurum
et caedit, longi relegit transversa diurni

464–6 *post* 470 *Ruperti*
469 educat *Housman*: educit *codd.*
464 veniet *Rapheling, Markland*: veniunt *codd.*
471 novatur *Nisbet*: fovetur *codd.*

97 The perfumed face-pack is named after Nero's wife Poppaea.

her elongated ears. Meanwhile her face is a hideous sight, quite ludicrous, all swollen with layers of dough and reeking of rich Poppean creams[97] that get glued to her miserable husband's lips. Eventually she uncovers her face, removing the outer layers of plaster. She starts to be recognisable. She bathes in the milk for which she'd take she-asses in her entourage if she were banished to the Hyperborean region.[98] At her lover's she'll arrive with her skin cleansed. When does she want to look lovely at home? For their lovers they obtain aromatics, for them they buy everything you slender Indians export to us.[99] But when she's coated and freshened up with all those concoctions one after another, and had lumps of hot, moist dough applied, will you call it a face or a sore?

It's worthwhile investigating in detail how they keep themselves occupied during the day. If her husband slept with his back turned last night, the wool-girl[100] has had it, and the hairdressers must remove their tunics, and the Liburnian slave is told he is late and has to pay for someone else's sleep.[101] One breaks the canes, another reddens under the whip, another under the strap. There are women who pay their torturers an annual wage. She lashes them and the whole time daubs her face and listens to her girlfriends or inspects the wide golden stripe on an embroidered dress, and whacks them. She reads over her

[98] A mythical people who lived "beyond the North Wind." The story of the she-asses is told of Poppaea at Plin. *N.H.* 11.238.

[99] Perfumes.

[100] Or perhaps "her secretary."

[101] A Liburnian slave is a litter-bearer.

et caedit, donec lassis caedentibus "exi"
485 intonet horrendum iam cognitione peracta.
praefectura domus Sicula non mitior aula.
nam si constituit solitoque decentius optat
ornari et properat iamque expectatur in hortis
aut apud Isiacae potius sacraria lenae,
490 disponit crinem laceratis ipsa capillis
nuda umeros Psecas infelix nudisque mamillis.
"altior hic quare cincinnus?" taurea punit
continuo flexi crimen facinusque capilli.
quid Psecas admisit? quaenam est hic culpa puellae,
495 si tibi displicuit nasus tuus? altera laevum
extendit pectitque comas et volvit in orbem.
est in consilio materna admotaque lanis
emerita quae cessat acu; sententia prima
huius erit, post hanc aetate atque arte minores
500 censebunt, tamquam famae discrimen agatur
aut animae: tanta est quaerendi cura decoris.
tot premit ordinibus, tot adhuc conpagibus altum
aedificat caput: Andromachen a fronte videbis,
post minor est, credas aliam. cedo si male parvi
505 sortita est lateris spatium breviorque videtur
virgine Pygmaea nullis adiuta coturnis
et levis erecta consurgit ad oscula planta.

504 male *Castiglione*: breve *codd*.

---

102 Her account book is in a format where the roll runs from
top to bottom instead of the normal side-to-side.

103 The tyrants of Sicily, Phalaris of Agrigentum and Diony-
sius I of Syracuse, were bywords for cruelty.

long vertical account book,[102] and whacks them, until the
whackers are exhausted and she booms in a horrible voice
"Off you go!" now that her inquisition is over. The regime
in her house is just as cruel as a Sicilian court.[103] After all, if
she has an assignation and wants to be beautified more
carefully than usual, if she's in a hurry and is already ex-
pected in the park, or rather at the sanctuary of "Madam"
Isis,[104] unlucky Psecas[105] will be arranging her hair with
her own strands torn, with her shoulders and her breasts
stripped bare. "Why is this curl sticking up?" The bullhide
strap is the immediate punishment for the wicked crime of
the twisting ringlet. What has Psecas done wrong? How
can it be your slave girl's fault if you don't like your own
nose? On your left another slave is drawing out and comb-
ing your hair and coiling it into a bun. In her council sits a
slave of her mother's, who was promoted to the wool when
she retired from hairpins after serving her time. Her opin-
ion will be sought first. After her, her inferiors in age and
skill will give their views, as if it were a matter of reputation
or of life itself. That's how much care is given to the quest
for beautification. She weighs down her head with tiers
upon tiers and piles her head high with storeys upon stor-
eys. From the front you'll see an Andromache[106] but from
behind she's smaller. You'd think it was someone else.
Imagine the scenario if by fate's stingy measure she's been
allotted a short flank, and without the help of high-heeled
boots seems shorter than a Pygmy girl and lightly rises up

[104] The temple of Isis was a notorious spot for assignations.

[105] A classic name for a lady's hairdressing slave, from the
Greek for dropping hair oil.

[106] Wife of Hector, said to have been very tall.

281

nulla viri cura interea nec mentio fiet
damnorum. vivit tamquam vicina mariti,
510   hoc solo propior, quod amicos coniugis odit
et servos, gravis est rationibus.
                              Ecce furentis
Bellonae matrisque deum chorus intrat et ingens
semivir, obsceno facies reverenda minori,
mollia qui rapta secuit genitalia testa
515   iam pridem, cui rauca cohors, cui tympana cedunt
plebeia et Phrygia vestitur bucca tiara.
grande sonat metuique iubet Septembris et Austri
adventum, nisi se centum lustraverit ovis
et xerampelinas veteres donaverit ipsi,
520   ut quidquid subiti et magni discriminis instat
in tunicas eat et totum semel expiet annum.
hibernum fracta glacie descendet in amnem,
ter matutino Tiberi mergetur et ipsis
verticibus timidum caput abluet, inde superbi
525   totum regis agrum nuda ac tremibunda cruentis
erepet genibus; si candida iusserit Io,
ibit ad Aegypti finem calidaque petitas
a Meroe portabit aquas, ut spargat in aede
Isidis, antiquo quae proxima surgit ovili.
530   credit enim ipsius dominae se voce moneri.

---

107 Closely associated in cult: on Bellona, see 4.123–4n., and
on Cybele and her eunuch priests, the Galli, see 2.111n.

108 The Campus Martius, which belonged to the Tarquin kings
until the overthrow of Tarquin the Proud in 510 B.C.

on tiptoe to be kissed. All the while, she'll give her husband not a thought. There'll be no mention of the cost. She behaves as if she were her husband's neighbour, more intimate only in that she hates her husband's friends and his slaves, and wrecks his accounts.

Look! In comes the troupe of frenzied Bellona and the Mother of the Gods,[107] along with an enormous eunuch, a face his perverted sidekick must revere. A long time ago now he picked up a shard and cut off his soft genitals. The noisy band and the common drums fall quiet in his presence and his cheeks are clothed in the Phrygian cap. In a booming voice he tells the woman to beware the arrival of September and the southerly winds, unless she purifies herself with a hundred eggs and presents him with her old russet-coloured dresses, to ensure that any serious or unforeseen disaster that's impending disappears into the clothes and atones for the whole year in one go. In the winter time she'll break the ice, step down into the river and submerge herself three times in the morning Tiber, even cleansing her terrified head in those swirling waters. Then, naked and shivering, she'll crawl right across the Proud King's Field[108] on bleeding knees. If white Io tells her to, she'll go to the ends of Egypt and bring back water fetched from sweltering Meroë to sprinkle in Isis' temple, towering next to the ancient sheepfold.[109] You see, she thinks her instructions come from the voice of the Lady herself!

[109] Io was turned into a white heifer and chased by Juno. She visited Egypt and became associated or confused with the goddess Isis. Meroë is further south, a kingdom on the Upper Nile. Isis' temple in the Campus Martius was next to the polling booths (*saepta*) which are here called the "sheepfold."

en animum et mentem cum qua di nocte loquantur!
ergo hic praecipuum summumque meretur honorem
qui grege linigero circumdatus et grege calvo
plangentis populi currit derisor Anubis.
535 ille petit veniam, quotiens non abstinet uxor
concubitu sacris observandisque diebus
magnaque debetur violato poena cadurco.
ut movisse caput visa est argentea serpens,
illius lacrimae meditataque murmura praestant
540 ut veniam culpae non abnuat ansere magno
scilicet et tenui popano corruptus Osiris.
        Cum dedit ille locum, cophino fenoque relicto
arcanam Iudaea tremens mendicat in aurem,
interpres legum Solymarum et magna sacerdos
545 arboris ac summi fida internuntia caeli.
implet et illa manum, sed parcius; aere minuto
qualiacumque voles Iudaei somnia vendunt.
spondet amatorem tenerum vel divitis orbi
testamentum ingens calidae pulmone columbae
550 tractato Armenius vel Commagenus haruspex;
pectora pullorum rimabitur, exta catelli
interdum et pueri; faciet quod deferat ipse.
        Chaldaeis sed maior erit fiducia: quidquid

531 animum *Schotle, Markland*: animam *codd.*
538 ut *Reitzenstein*: et *codd.*
552 ipse *codd.*: ipsa *Markland*

---

110 Anubis, the dog-headed god and guardian of Isis. Here a
priest dressed as Anubis mocks the people for their lamentation
over the "death" of Osiris, the consort of Isis.

There you have the kind of mind and soul that the gods converse with at night! Consequently, the highest, most exceptional honour is awarded to Anubis, who runs along, mocking the wailing populace, surrounded by his creatures in linen garments and with shaved heads.[110] He's the one that asks for a pardon whenever your wife does not refrain from sex on the days which should be kept sacred and a large fine is due for violation of the quilt. When the silver snake has been seen to move its head,[111] it's his tears and his practised mumblings which ensure that Osiris will not refuse to pardon her fault—provided, of course, he's bribed by a fat goose and a slice of sacrificial cake.

No sooner has he gone than a palsied Jewish woman will abandon her hay-lined chest and start begging into her private ear. She's the expounder of the laws of Jerusalem, high priestess of the tree, reliable intermediary of highest heaven.[112] She too gets her hand filled, though with less, because Jews will sell you whatever dreams you like for the tiniest copper coin. Promises of a toy-boy or an enormous bequest from a childless millionaire will be made by a soothsayer from Armenia or Commagene once he's delved into the lung of a dove, still warm. He'll probe the breasts of chickens, the insides of a puppy, and sometimes of a boy too—something he will himself report to the authorities.

But they have even greater faith in the Chaldaeans.[113]

[111] Probably the sacred asp. Snakes were associated with Isis.

[112] Evidently a fortune-teller. The reference to the tree is problematical: see Courtney's note. A word denoting "temple" would make better sense.

[113] Astrologers, highly influential.

dixerit astrologus, credent a fonte relatum
555 Hammonis, quoniam Delphis oracula cessant
et genus humanum damnat caligo futuri.
praecipuus tamen est horum, qui saepius exul.
[cuius amicitia conducendaque tabella
magnus civis obit et formidatus Othoni.]
560 inde fides artis, sonuit si dextera ferro:
[laevaque, si longe castrorum in carcere mansit]
nemo mathematicus genium indemnatus habebit,
sed qui paene perit, cui vix in Cyclada mitti
contigit et parva tandem latuisse Seripho.
565 consulit ictericae lento de funere matris,
ante tamen de te Tanaquil tua, quando sororem
efferat et patruos, an sit victurus adulter
post ipsam; quid enim maius dare numina possunt?
haec tamen ignorat quid sidus triste minetur
570 Saturni, quo laeta Venus se proferat astro,
quis mensis damnis, quae dentur tempora lucro.
illius occursus etiam vitare memento,
in cuius manibus ceu pinguia sucina tritas
cernis ephemeridas, quae nullum consulit et iam
575 consulitur, quae castra viro patriamque petente
non ibit pariter numeris revocata Thrasylli.

558–9 *om.* PFG   561 *del. Willis*
564 latuisse *Schrader*: caruisse *codd.*

---

114 The oracle of Jupiter Ammon in North Africa.
115 The great oracles such as Delphi had fallen into neglect by
this time.
116 Line 561: "and the left hand, if he has languished far away
in a military prison."

286

Whatever the astrologer says they'll believe has come from
Ammon's fountain,[114] now that the oracles at Delphi are si-
lent and the human race is doomed to darkness about the
future.[115] Yet the most important of these is the one that's
been exiled most often. That's the source of their faith in
his skill, if his right hand has clanked with iron.[116] There's
no talent in any astrologer without a criminal record, but
only in the one who nearly died, who just managed to get
sent to a Cycladic island and finally languished on tiny
Seriphus.[117] Your Tanaquil[118] asks for advice about the lin-
gering death of her jaundiced mother—she's already asked
about you!—and about when she'll bury her sister and her
uncles, or whether her lover will outlive her. After all, is
there anything more important that the gods could grant
her? And yet she does not herself understand the threats
from the gloomy planet of Saturn, or the signs under which
Venus has a favourable aspect, which month is destined for
losses, which times are destined for profit. But remember
to avoid ever running into the kind of woman who you'll
see holding in her hands a well thumbed almanac like it
was a clammy ball of amber.[119] She doesn't consult anyone
else, but these days is consulted herself. She will not ac-
company her husband when he heads for camp or for
home if the calculations of Thrasyllus detain her.[120] When

[117] State criminals were banished to small islands such as
Seriphus in the Cyclades.

[118] Wife of the fifth king of Rome, Tarquinius Priscus, and an
expert in divination.

[119] Carried by women for the scent they produced.

[120] The astrologer consulted by the emperor Tiberius.

ad primum lapidem vectari cum placet, hora
sumitur ex libro; si prurit frictus ocelli
angulus, inspecta genesi collyria poscit;
580 aegra licet iaceat, capiendo nulla videtur
aptior hora cibo nisi quam dederit Petosiris.
si mediocris erit, spatium lustrabit utrimque
metarum et sortes ducet frontemque manumque
praebebit vati crebrum poppysma roganti.
585 divitibus responsa dabit Phryx augur et inde

          *   *   *   *   *

conductus, dabit astrorum mundique peritus
atque aliquis senior qui publica fulgura condit.
plebeium in Circo positum est et in aggere fatum.
quae nudis longum ostendit cervicibus aurum
590 consulit ante falas delphinorumque columnas
an saga vendenti nubat caupone relicto.
    Hae tamen et partus subeunt discrimen et omnis
nutricis tolerant fortuna urgente labores,
sed iacet aurato vix ulla puerpera lecto.
595 tantum artes huius, tantum medicamina possunt,
quae steriles facit atque homines in ventre necandos
conducit. gaude, infelix, atque ipse bibendum
porrige quidquid erit; nam si distendere vellet
et vexare uterum pueris salientibus, esses

585 inde PΦΣ: indus *Vat.3192, Vat.3286*
post 585 *lacuna unius versus Housman*
588 *del.* Nisbet   589 nudis *codd.*: nullis *Salmasius*

---

121 An Egyptian astrologer of the second century B.C.
122 The two ends of the racetrack in the Circus Maximus, a
haunt of fortune-tellers.

she decides to drive to the first milestone, she finds the best hour in her book. If the corner of her little eye itches when she rubs it, she asks for ointment only after she's checked her horoscope. If she's ill and lying in bed, no moment seems more right for eating than the one prescribed by Petosiris.[121] If she's less well off, she'll cross the space between the two turning posts[122] and draw the cards that tell her fortune, and offer her forehead and her hand to the seer who asks her to make noisy kisses.[123] Rich women will get their replies from a Phrygian seer, or from someone expensively brought from * * *, or from an expert in the stars and the cosmos, or from the elder who buries lightning strikes for the state.[124] Plebeian destiny is settled in the Circus and the Embankment. The woman displaying a length of gold on her bare neck asks for advice in front of the towers and the dolphin columns[125] about whether to abandon the shopkeeper and marry the cloakseller.

But at least these women undergo the dangers of childbirth and put up with all the work of nursing that their position in life forces on them. By contrast, hardly any woman lies in labour on a gilded bed. So powerful are the skills and drugs of the woman who manufactures sterility and takes contracts to kill humans inside the belly. Celebrate, you poor wretch. Offer your wife whatever she has to drink yourself. After all, if she were prepared to stretch and torture her womb with jumping baby boys, you'd perhaps

[123] Evidently part of the magic.

[124] The priest does this as a form of public purification, cordoning off the place. Cf. Persius 2.27n.

[125] Features of the Circus Maximus.

600 Aethiopis fortasse pater, mox decolor heres
impleret tabulas numquam tibi mane videndus.
　　Transeo suppositos et gaudia votaque saepe
ad spurcos decepta lacus, saepe inde petitos
pontifices, Salios Scaurorum nomina falso
605 corpore laturos. stat Fortuna improba noctu
adridens nudis infantibus: hos fovet ulnis
involvitque sinu, domibus tunc porrigit altis
secretumque sibi mimum parat; hos amat, his se
ingerit utque suos semper producit alumnos.
610 　　Hic magicos adfert cantus, hic Thessala vendit
philtra, quibus valeat mentem vexare mariti
et solea pulsare natis. quod desipis, inde est,
inde animi caligo et magna oblivio rerum
quas modo gessisti. tamen hoc tolerabile, si non
614A [semper aquam portes rimosa ad dolia, semper
614B istud onus subeas ipsis manantibus urnis,
614C quo rabidus nostro Phalarim de rege dedisti.]
615 et furere incipias ut avunculus ille Neronis,
cui totam tremuli frontem Caesonia pulli
infudit. quae non faciet quod principis uxor?
ardebant cuncta et fracta conpage ruebant
non aliter quam si fecisset Iuno maritum
620 insanum. minus ergo nocens erit Agrippinae
boletus, siquidem unius praecordia pressit

606 ulnis *Markland*: omni PFG: omnes Φ
614ABC *om.* PΦ

126 Children abandoned at birth were adopted by families desperate for children, including elite families, such as the Aemilii Scauri, who provided priests such as *pontifices* and *Salii*.

turn out to be father of an Ethiopian. Soon your will would be monopolised by your discoloured heir—whom you'd never want to see in the morning light.

I won't mention spurious children and the joys and prayers so often cheated at the filthy latrines, the high priests and Salian priests so often acquired from there to bear the name of Scaurus in their false persons.[126] There Fortune shamelessly stands at night, smiling on the naked babies. She nurtures them in her arms and gives them a cuddle, then passes them on to exalted houses, preparing a secret farce for herself. These are the children she loves and these she showers with attention, always promoting them as her own special babies.

One man supplies magic incantations and another sells Thessalian potions which enable a wife to confuse her husband's mind and beat him on the buttocks with her sandal. That's the reason you're going mad, that's the reason for the haziness in your head and for your complete amnesia of things you've just done. All the same, that is bearable, provided you don't also start raving like that uncle of Nero, after Caesonia concocted for him the entire forehead of a wobbly foal.[127] Is there any woman who'll hold back from what an emperor's wife has done? The whole world was on fire and collapsing with its fabric in ruins precisely as if Juno had made her husband mad. So Agrippina's mushroom will turn out to be less damaging, seeing that all it did was stop the heart of a single old man and command his

[127] The emperor Caligula was driven mad by his wife Caesonia with an aphrodisiac she had made from *hippomanes*, the membrane on a newborn foal's head.

ille senis tremulumque caput descendere iussit
in caelum et longa manantia labra saliva:
haec poscit ferrum atque ignes, haec potio torquet,
625 haec lacerat mixtos equitum cum sanguine patres.
tanti partus equae, tanti una venefica constat.
    Oderunt natos de paelice; nemo repugnet,
nemo vetet, iam iam privignum occidere fas est.
vos quoque, pupilli, moneo, quibus amplior est res,
630 custodite animas et nulli credite mensae:
livida materno fervent adipata veneno.
mordeat ante aliquis quidquid porrexerit illa
quae peperit, timidus praegustet pocula papas.
    Fingimus haec altum satura sumente coturnum
635 scilicet, et finem egressi legemque priorum
grande Sophocleo carmen bacchamur hiatu,
montibus ignotum Rutulis caeloque Latino?
nos utinam vani! sed clamat Pontia "feci,
confiteor, puerisque meis aconita paravi,
640 quae deprensa patent; facinus tamen ipsa peregi."
tune duos una, saevissima vipera, cena?
tune duos? "septem, si septem forte fuissent."
credamus tragicis quidquid de Colchide torva

      629 quoque *Duff*: ego *codd.*: equo P
      632–3 *om.* PG, *del. Guyet*

shaking head and his lips dripping with strands of saliva to go down to heaven.[128] The other potion, by contrast, insists upon steel and fires, and it tortures and mangles senators and knights in indiscriminate carnage. That was the high price of a mare's offspring, of a single witch.

Wives hate the children born to mistresses. No one would resist, no one would forbid it, because for a long time now it's been lawful to kill a stepson.[129] You fatherless orphans too, who are rather well off, I warn you—watch out for your lives and don't trust a single dish. Those pastries are steaming darkly with maternal poison. Get someone else to taste first anything that's offered to you by the woman who bore you. Get your terrified tutor to drink from the cup before you.

I'm making all this up, am I, letting satire put on tragic high heels? I've exceeded the legal limits of my predecessors and I'm ranting with rotundity worthy of Sophocles a grand song that's new to the Rutulian hills and the Latin sky? If only this were really nonsense! But Pontia[130] declares: "Guilty! I admit it! I gave aconite to my own boys. The murder was discovered and made public. Yet it was I who performed the crime myself." You did away with two at a single meal yourself, did you, cruellest of vipers? Two, yourself? "I'd have done away with seven if there'd happened to be seven." We have to believe what the tragedians say about the savage woman of Colchis and about

---

[128] The mushroom with which Agrippina is said to have poisoned Claudius. The phrase "go down to heaven" may allude to Seneca's satire on Claudius' apotheosis in the *Apocolocyntosis*.

[129] Not legal, but Juvenal implies that it would be condoned.

[130] Martial mentions a poisoner called Pontia, 4.43 and 6.75.

dicitur et Procne; nil contra conor. et illae
645 grandia monstra suis audebant temporibus, sed
non propter nummos. minor admiratio summis
debetur monstris, quotiens facit ira nocentem
hunc sexum et rabie iecur incendente feruntur
praecipites, ut saxa iugis abrupta, quibus mons
650 subtrahitur clivoque latus pendente recedit.
illam ego non tulerim quae conputat et scelus ingens
sana facit. spectant subeuntem fata mariti
Alcestim et, similis si permutatio detur,
morte viri cupiant animam servare catellae.
655 occurrent multae tibi Belides atque Eriphylae
mane, Clytaemestram nullus non vicus habebit.
hoc tantum refert, quod Tyndaris illa bipennem
insulsam et fatuam dextra laevaque tenebat;
at nunc res agitur tenui pulmone rubetae,
660 sed tamen et ferro, si praegustarit Atrides
Pontica ter victi cautus medicamina regis.

647 nocentem Φ: nocentes PGTU

---

131 Medea, princess of Colchis, killed her brother and cut his body into pieces to slow down her father while she was eloping with Jason; she later killed the two children she had with Jason after he deserted her. Procne killed her son and served up his body to her husband Tereus as revenge for his raping her sister Philomela.

132 Alcestis volunteered to die on behalf of her husband Admetus, king of Thessaly.

133 Belus was the father of Danaus, father of the fifty Danaids who, with one exception, killed their husbands on their wedding night.

Procne.[131] I won't attempt to dispute it. Those women too dared monstrosities enormous for their own times—but not because of money. Those heights of monstrosity elicit less amazement when it's anger that makes the female sex into criminals—when with frenzy inflaming their guts, they're swept along out of control like rocks torn from crags where the mountain beneath them caves in and its face recedes from the overhanging slope. The woman I cannot stand is the one who calculatingly commits an enormous crime in full command of her senses. They watch Alcestis endure her husband's death[132] and, if a similar swap were offered to them, they'd happily see their husbands die to save their puppy's life. Every morning you'll run into a granddaughter of Belus[133] and an Eriphyle many times over.[134] There's no street without its Clytemnestra. The only difference is this. The daughter of Tyndareus[135] wielded a stupid and clumsy double-headed axe with both her hands, but these days the matter is accomplished with the tiny lung of a toad. Yet she'll use steel too, if her Atrides[136] has taken the cautionary measure of dosing himself with the Pontic antidotes of the three times conquered king.[137]

[134] Eriphyle accepted a bribe to persuade her husband Amphiaraus to participate in the attack of the "Seven Against Thebes" even though it would be fatal to him.

[135] Clytemnestra, the adulterous wife of Agamemnon, king of Mycenae, who killed her husband on his return from Troy.

[136] Agamemnon.

[137] Mithridates VI, king of Pontus, defeated by Pompey after three Roman campaigns against him. His long life was said to be due to his self-immunisation against poison.

NOTE ON SATIRE 7

The opening of Satire 7, the first poem of Book Three, marks a new departure for Juvenal: there are no angry questions or marks of indignation. This is a new, calmer persona who is even capable of optimism—for a moment —concerning the prospects for poets of patronage by the emperor (1–21), even if the usual pessimism of satire then takes over. In contrast with his optimism regarding imperial support, Juvenal is in no doubt that other patrons will do anything to avoid supporting poets (22–97). At this point, he moves on to the prospects for patronage and payment of other writers and intellectuals. Writers of history fare no better than poets (98–105). Advocates (*causidici*, that is, those who exercise their rhetorical skills in court) find that the rewards are thin (106–49) and so do the teachers of rhetoric (*rhetores*, 150–215), and schoolteachers (*grammatici*, 216–43). Yet this is not a simple lament on behalf of unappreciated clients. At the same time, by undermining the value of their skills and expertise, Juvenal hints that these intellectuals may not deserve patronage. The poem revisits the treatment of clients by patrons in Book One, but with a world-weary, ironic detachment which deplores but accepts the conduct of both parties. The clear structure of the poem enhances the impression that Juvenal has created a new, more controlled form of satire: not only is each section clearly announced but the topics are borrowed, in reverse order, from Suetonius' contemporary work *De Viris Illustribus* ("On Famous Men").

SATIRE 7

Et spes et ratio studiorum in Caesare tantum;
solus enim tristes hac tempestate Camenas
respexit, cum iam celebres notique poetae
balneolum Gabiis, Romae conducere furnos
5   temptarent, nec foedum alii nec turpe putarent
praecones fieri, cum desertis Aganippes
vallibus esuriens migraret in atria Clio.
nam si Pieria quadrans tibi nullus in umbra
ostendatur, ames nomen victumque Machaerae
10   et vendas potius commissa quod auctio vendit
stantibus, oenophorum, tripedes, armaria, cistas,
Alcithoen Pacci, Thebas et Terea Fausti.
hoc satius quam si dicas sub iudice "vidi"
quod non vidisti; faciant equites Asiani,
15   [quamquam et Cappadoces faciant equitesque Bithyni]
altera quos nudo traducit gallica talo.
nemo tamen studiis indignum ferre laborem

15 *del. Guyet, Pinzger*

---

1 The emperor, possibly Trajan (98–117), probably Hadrian (117–38).   2 The Roman name for the Muses.
3 One of the Muses.   4 A spring on Mount Helicon in Boeotia, one of the places associated with the Muses.

SATIRE 7

The hopes and incentives of literature depend upon
Caesar[1] alone. He's the only one these days to have given a
second glance to the despondent Camenae.[2] This is a time
when distinguished and well-known poets have already
been applying for the lease on a bathhouse at Gabii or a
bakehouse at Rome, when others haven't considered it
horrid or disgraceful to become public announcers, when
in her hunger Clio[3] has deserted the vales of Aganippe[4]
and moved into the salesrooms. The fact is that if you're
offered not a penny in the Pierian grove,[5] you'd better
like the name and lifestyle of Machaera[6] and sell to the by-
standers the items offered in the battle of the salesroom—
the winejars, three-legged tables, bookcases, trunks, Pac-
cius' *Alcithoe,* and Faustus' *Thebes* and *Tereus*.[7] That
(after all) is better than declaring in front of a judge "I saw
it" when you didn't. Leave that to the knights from Asia,
the ones betrayed when one of their slippers shows a bare
ankle.[8] Yet from now on, no one will have to submit to

[5] Pieria near Mount Olympus was the birthplace of the Muses.

[6] Evidently an auctioneer.

[7] Tragedies, otherwise unknown.

[8] Their slippers reveal the mark of the fetters, indicating that
they arrived as slaves.

cogetur posthac, nectit quicumque canoris
eloquium vocale modis laurumque momordit.
20   hoc agite, o iuvenes. circumspicit et stimulat vos
materiamque sibi ducis indulgentia quaerit.
    Si qua aliunde putas rerum expectanda tuarum
praesidia atque ideo croceae membrana tabellae
impletur, lignorum aliquid posce ocius et quae
25   componis dona Veneris, Telesine, marito,
aut clude et positos tinea pertunde libellos.
frange miser calamum vigilataque proelia dele,
qui facis in parva sublimia carmina cella,
ut dignus venias hederis et imagine macra.
30   spes nulla ulterior; didicit iam dives avarus
tantum admirari, tantum laudare disertos,
ut pueri Iunonis avem. sed defluit aetas
et pelagi patiens et cassidis atque ligonis.
taedia tunc subeunt animos, tunc seque suamque
35   Terpsichoren odit facunda et nuda senectus.
    Accipe nunc artes ne quid tibi conferat iste
quem colis et Musarum et Apollinis aede relicta.
ipse facit versus atque uni cedit Homero
propter mille annos, tu si dulcedine famae
40   succensus recites, maculosas commodat aedes.
haec longe ferrata domus servire iubetur
in qua sollicitas imitatur ianua porcas.
scit dare libertos extrema in parte sedentis

22 expectanda Φ: spectanda P: speranda *Housman*

39 tu *Hermann*: et P: at GVat. 3288: ac U: aut Φ

40 maculosas *Heinrich*: maculosos F: maculonus Φ: maculonis PG

42 porcas *Jessen*: portas *codd*.

drudgery that's beneath his writing—that applies to any-one who weaves the voice's eloquence in harmonious metres, anyone who has chomped on laurel. To work, young men! Our leader's generosity is looking around and urging you on in search of suitable material.

If you're looking to get support for your fortunes from anywhere else, and if that makes you fill up the parchment of your yellow page, you'd better get some firewood right away, Telesinus, and offer your compositions to Venus' husband,[9] or else lock away your booklets in the store and let them be pierced by worms. Break your pen and wipe out those battles you spent all night over, you poor thing, writing sublime poetry in your tiny attic, just to win an ivy crown and a scrawny statue. There's nothing else to hope for. Miserly rich men long ago learned how to offer only admiration and only praise (nothing more) to intellectuals, like boys when they see Juno's bird.[10] But your years, which could have faced the sea and the helmet and the spade, have flowed away. That's when boredom creeps into the mind, that's when old age, eloquent but poverty-stricken, hates itself and its Muse.

Let me tell you the ruses adopted by the patron you cul-tivate, abandoning the temple of Apollo and the Muses, so he doesn't have to give you anything. He himself writes verses and yields only to Homer, on account of his thou-sand years' seniority. If you give a recitation, fired by the sweetness of fame, he lends you a squalid house. This dis-tant, barricaded building with doors that make the sound of squealing sows he'll require to be put at your disposal. He knows how to position his freedmen on the seats at the

---

[9] Vulcan, the god of fire.   [10] The peacock.

ordinis et magnas comitum disponere voces;
45 nemo dabit regum quanti subsellia constant
et quae conducto pendent anabathra tigillo
quaeque reportandis posita est orchestra cathedris.
nos tamen hoc agimus tenuique in pulvere sulcos
ducimus et litus sterili versamus aratro.
50 nam si discedas, laqueo tenet ambitioso
[consuetudo mali tenet insanabile multos]
scribendi cacoethes et aegro in corde senescit.
      Sed vatem egregium, cui non sit publica vena,
qui nihil expositum soleat deducere, nec qui
55 communi feriat carmen triviale moneta,
hunc, qualem nequeo monstrare et sentio tantum,
anxietate carens animus facit, omnis acerbi
inpatiens, cupidus silvarum aptusque bibendis
fontibus Aonidum. neque enim cantare sub antro
60 Pierio thyrsumque potest contingere maesta
paupertas atque aeris inops, quo nocte dieque
corpus eget: satur est cum dicit Horatius "euhoe."
quis locus ingenio, nisi cum se carmine solo
vexant et dominis Cirrhae Nysaeque feruntur
65 pectora vestra duas non admittentia curas?
magnae mentis opus nec de lodice paranda
attonitae currus et equos faciesque deorum
aspicere et qualis Rutulum confundat Erinys.
nam si Vergilio puer et tolerabile desset

50–1 laqueo . . . mali *del. Housman*
50 ambitioso *Braund*: ambitiosi *codd*: ambitiosum *Jahn*
51 *om.* L, *del. Jahn*
60 maesta PAL: sana GHKTUΣ: saeva FOZ

ends of rows and how to distribute his retinue with their loud voices. But none of these lords will give you the price of the benches or of the tiers of seats on their hired beams or of the front rows with the chairs that have to be returned afterwards. Yet we keep at it, tracing furrows in the thin dust and turning over the seashore with our barren ploughs. The fact is that if you try to give it up, the itch for writing holds you in its ambitious noose[11] and endures into old age in your sickly heart.

But the outstanding bard—the one with no common vein of talent, the one who generally spins nothing trite, the one who coins no ordinary song from the public mint, the likes of whom I cannot point out, but can only imagine—he is the product of a mind free from worry and without bitterness, a mind that longs for the woods and is fit to drink the springs of the Muses. Unhappy poverty, you see, cannot sing inside the Pierian cavern or grasp the thyrsus: it lacks the cash which the body needs, night and day. Horace was full when he spoke the Bacchic cry "Evoë!" What room is there for genius? None, unless your hearts have only a single focus, and torment themselves with poetry alone, swept away by the lords of Cirrha and Nysa.[12] A great soul, not one perplexed about buying a blanket, is needed for visions of chariots and horses and the gods' faces and the kind of Fury that drove the Rutulian crazy.[13] After all, if Virgil hadn't had a slave boy and decent lodg-

[11] Line 51: "A bad habit, it has an incurable hold on many people."

[12] Apollo and Bacchus, referred to by places associated with them, Cirrha near Delphi and Nysa, perhaps in Asia.

[13] Turnus in Virg. *Aen*. 7. 445–66.

70   hospitium, caderent omnes a crinibus hydri,
      surda nihil gemeret grave bucina. poscimus ut sit
      non minor antiquo Rubrenus Lappa coturno,
      cuius et alveolos et laenam pignerat Atreus?
      non habet infelix Numitor quod mittat amico,
75   Quintillae quod donet habet, nec defuit illi
      unde emeret multa pascendum carne leonem
      iam domitum; constat leviori belua sumptu
      nimirum et capiunt plus intestina poetae.
      contentus fama iaceat Lucanus in hortis
80   marmoreis, at Serrano tenuique Saleiio
      gloria quantalibet quid erit, si gloria tantum est?
      curritur ad vocem iucundam et carmen amicae
      Thebaidos, laetam cum fecit Statius Vrbem
      promisitque diem: tanta dulcedine captos
85   adficit ille animos tantaque libidine volgi
      auditur. sed cum fregit subsellia versu
      esurit, intactam Paridi nisi vendit Agaven.
      ille et militiae multis largitur honorem,
      semenstri vatum digitos circumligat auro.
90   quod non dant proceres, dabit histrio. tu Camerinos
      et Baream, tu nobilium magna atria curas?
      praefectos Pelopea facit, Philomela tribunos.

      88 largitur PΦ*Arov*.: largitus G*Vat. 3286*

---

    14 An unknown tragedian.
    15 A selfish rich man and his mistress.
    16 Marcus Annaeus Lucanus, author of the epic *Civil War*.
    17 Serranus and Saleius Bassus were both epic poets.
    18 Publius Papinius Statius was the author of the epic poems
Thebaid and *Achilleid* (unfinished), occasional display poetry

ings, all the snakes would have fallen from the Fury's hair
and no terrifying blast would have sounded from her silent
war trumpet. Can we expect Rubrenus Lappa[14] to be as
great as the ancient tragedians when his *Atreus* has to be
pawned for his dishes and cloak? Numitor is too poor to
send a present to his client, though he has a gift for Quin-
tilla,[15] and he was rich enough to purchase a lion (already
tamed) which eats large quantities of meat. I suppose a
beast costs less and a poet's guts hold more. Lucan[16] may
recline in his gardens of marble, happy with his fame, but
what will even enormous glory do for Serranus and starv-
ing Saleius,[17] if it's glory and nothing else? When Statius
has made Rome happy by fixing a day, everyone rushes
to hear his gorgeous voice and the poetry of his darling
Thebaid.[18] Their hearts are captivated by the sheer lus-
ciousness he inspires and the crowd listens in sheer ec-
stasy. But when he's broken the benches with his poetry,
he'll go hungry unless he sells his virgin *Agave* to Paris.[19]
He's the one who generously hands out positions in the
army and puts the gold ring on the fingers of bards after
just six months.[20] A dancer gives what the great men won't.
Do you frequent the grand halls of the aristocracy, the
Camerini and Barea?[21] It's *Pelopea* that appoints prefects

(*Silvae*), and pantomime librettoes such as *Agave* mentioned be-
low.   [19] A famous pantomime actor, a favourite of Domitian
until his execution in 83.

[20] Six months' service as an officer (*tribunus*) was the quali-
fication for equestrian status, marked by a gold ring. Emperors
from Claudius on made such appointments; Juvenal implies that
Paris can influence such appointments.

[21] Aristocrats.

haut tamen invideas vati quem pulpita pascunt.
quis tibi Maecenas, quis nunc erit aut Proculeius
95   aut Fabius, quis Cotta iterum, quis Lentulus alter?
tum par ingenio pretium, tunc utile multis
pallere et vinum toto nescire Decembri.
     Vester porro labor fecundior, historiarum
scriptores? perit hic plus temporis atque olei plus.
100 nullo quippe modo millensima pagina surgit
omnibus et crescit multa damnosa papyro;
sic ingens rerum numerus iubet atque operum lex.
quae tamen inde seges? terrae quis fructus apertae?
quis dabit historico quantum daret acta legenti?
105 "sed genus ignavum, quod lecto gaudet et umbra."
     Dic igitur quid causidicis civilia praestent
officia et magno comites in fasce libelli.
ipsi magna sonant, sed tum cum creditor audit
praecipue, vel si tetigit latus acrior illo
110 qui venit ad dubium grandi cum codice nomen.
tunc inmensa cavi spirant mendacia folles
conspuiturque sinus; veram deprendere messem
si libet, hinc centum patrimonia causidicorum,
parte alia solum russati pone Lacertae.

93 *del. Markland*

---

22 Pantomime plays on themes of rape and incest in which
Paris might have starred.
23 Patrons of poets and writers from the period of the late Re-
public and early Empire. Maecenas was the patron of Virgil and
Horace; Fabius and Cotta supported Ovid.

and *Philomela* tribunes.[22] But don't go envying bards fed by the stage. Who these days will behave like a Maecenas, a Proculeius, or a Fabius? Who'll be a second Cotta or another Lentulus?[23] In those days rewards matched genius. In those days many found it worth their while to turn pale and go without wine for the whole of December.[24]

You writers of history, is your hard work more profitable, then? This is an activity on which more time and midnight oil is wasted. There is universally no limit, and that's a fact, as the thousandth page rises and grows, bankrupting you with all that papyrus. That's governed by the huge quantity of facts and the laws of the genre. Yet what is the crop from that activity? What is the fruit of that earth you have ploughed? Who will give a historian the same fee as a newsreader? "But they're lazy types, relishing their loungers in the shade."

Then tell me what advocates earn from their services in the courts and from the huge bundle of briefs that keep them company. They talk big anyway, but especially when a creditor is listening, or if someone more urgent still nudges them in the side, arriving with a large account book to claim that dodgy debt. That's when their capacious bellows exhale immense lies and they cover their chests with spit.[25] If you'd like to discover their real harvest, you can put on one side the wealth of a hundred advocates and on the other just that of red-jacketed Lizard.[26] The leaders

[24] The Saturnalia, a time of festivity.
[25] Possibly a reference to the practice of spitting into one's chest to avert retribution for boasting.
[26] Lizard was one of the charioteers who raced for the Red faction in the Circus Maximus.

115 consedere duces, surgis tu pallidus Aiax
dicturus dubia pro libertate bubulco
iudice. rumpe miser tensum iecur, ut tibi lasso
figantur virides, scalarum gloria, palmae.
quod vocis pretium? siccus petasunculus et vas
120 pelamydum aut veteres, Maurorum epimenia, bulbi
aut vinum Tiberi devectum, quinque lagonae,
si quater egisti. si contigit aureus unus,
inde cadunt partes ex foedere pragmaticorum.
"Aemilio dabitur quantum licet, at melius nos
125 egimus." huius enim stat currus aeneus, alti
quadriiuges in vestibulis, atque ipse feroci
bellatore sedens curvatum hastile minatur
eminus et statua meditatur proelia lusca.
sic Pedo conturbat, Matho deficit, exitus hic est
130 Tongilii, magno cum rhinocerote lavari
qui solet et vexat lutulenta balnea turba
perque forum iuvenes longo premit assere Maedos
133 empturus pueros, argentum, murrina, villas;
135 et tamen est illis hoc utile. purpura vendit
136 causidicum, vendunt amethystina; convenit illi
137 et strepitu et facie maioris vivere census,
134 spondet enim Tyrio stlattaria purpura filo.
138 sed finem inpensae non servat prodiga Roma.

124 at *Ruperti, Cramer*: et *codd.*
134 *post* 137 *Courtney*
135 *om.* U, *del. Knoche*
136 illi P*Arov. Mico Sang.*: illis Φ

are seated and you stand up, a pale Ajax,[27] to make a case
for your client's contested liberty in front of a yokel judge.
Strain and burst your liver, you poor thing, so that in your
exhaustion you can pin up green palm leaves to decorate
your staircase. What reward does your voice get? A tiny
shoulder of dried-up ham and a jar of little tunnies, or an-
cient onions (a month's rations for a Moroccan), or wine
brought down the Tiber, five flasks, if you have taken on
four cases. If you come by one gold piece, some of that dis-
appears according to the contract made with the solicitors.
"Though we did a better job in court, Aemilius can name
his fee." The reason is that in his entrance hall there stands
a chariot made of bronze with four tall horses, and the
man himself[28] sits on a fierce charger, threatening from up
there with his drooping spear, a one-eyed statue rehears-
ing battles. That's what brings Pedo to bankruptcy and
Matho to failure. This too will be the end for Tongilius,
who always bathes with his large flask of rhinocerus horn
and disturbs the baths with his dirty mob, weighing down
his strong Maedian bearers with his long litter poles on his
way through the forum to buy slave boys, silver plate, agate
vases or country houses. And yet this display works. His
purple and violet clothes are an advocate's advertisement.
It pays him to live with a bustle and show beyond his real
income. His exotic purple with its Tyrian thread acts as a
guarantee, you see. But extravagant Rome sets no limits to
expenditure.

[27] Parody of the dispute over the armour of Achilles between
Ajax and Ulysses at the opening of Ovid, *Metamorphoses* 13.

[28] Aemilius' ancestor who celebrated the triumph commemo-
rated by the statue.

Fidimus eloquio? Ciceroni nemo ducentos
140 nunc dederit nummos, nisi fulserit anulus ingens.
respicit haec primum qui litigat, an tibi servi
octo, decem comites, an post te sella, togati
ante pedes. ideo conducta Paulus agebat
sardonyche, atque ideo pluris quam Gallus agebat,
145 quam Basilus. rara in tenui facundia panno.
quando licet Basilo flentem producere matrem?
quis bene dicentem Basilum ferat? accipiat te
Gallia vel potius nutricula causidicorum
Africa, si placuit mercedem ponere linguae.
150 Declamare doces? o ferrea pectora Vetti,
cum perimit saevos classis numerosa tyrannos.
nam quaecumque sedens modo legerat, haec eadem
     stans
perferet atque eadem cantabit versibus isdem.
occidit miseros crambe repetita magistros.
155 quis color et quod sit causae genus atque ubi summa
quaestio, quae veniant diversa parte sagittae,
nosse volunt omnes, mercedem solvere nemo.
"mercedem appellas? quid enim scio?" "culpa docentis
scilicet arguitur, quod laevae parte mamillae
160 nil salit Arcadico iuveni, cuius mihi sexta
quaque die miserum dirus caput Hannibal implet,

139 fidimus eloquio PG*Arov.*: ut redeant veteres Φ
149 ponere P*Arov.*: inponere Φ*Ant.*: poscere *Buecheler,
Markland*   151 cum *codd.*: cui *Jahn*

---

29 Marcus Tullius Cicero (106–43 B.C.), the most famous ora-
tor of Republican Rome.
30 There were schools of rhetoric in Gaul and Africa, which af-

Do we put our faith in eloquence? There's no one these days who will give Cicero[29] two hundred, unless there's a huge ring flashing on his hand. The first thing a litigant looks for is whether you have a household of eight slaves and an escort of ten clients, a litter to follow you, and citizens to walk in front. That's the reason why Paulus conducted cases with a sardonyx ring he'd hired, and that's the reason why he earned a higher fee than Gallus or Basilus. Eloquence in thin rags is a rare phenomenon. When is Basilus allowed to bring on a mother in mourning? Who would put up with Basilus however well he spoke? Make Gaul your destination or, better, Africa, the nanny of advocates,[30] if you've made the decision to earn a living with your tongue.

Do you teach rhetoric? Vettius must have a heart of steel, when his crowded class slays "The Cruel Tyrant."[31] You know how it is: what they've just read sitting down each in turn will repeat standing up, chanting the same things in the same lines. All that rehashed cabbage kills the poor teachers. Everyone wants to know the arguments and the types of cases and the crucial points and the shots that will be fired from the other side, but no one is prepared to pay. "You ask me to pay? But what have I learned?" "I suppose it's the fault of the teacher, then, that our Arcadian teenager[32] feels nothing throb in the left side of his breast when he fills my poor head every five days with his 'Hanni-

ter Juvenal's time produced some of Rome's most distinguished orators.

[31] A standard classroom topic.

[32] I.e. a dunce: Arcadia was regarded as the most backward area of Greece.

quidquid id est de quo deliberat, an petat Vrbem
a Cannis, an post nimbos et fulmina cautus
circumagat madidas a tempestate cohortes.
165 quantum vis stipulare et protinus accipe: quid do
ut totiens illum pater audiat?" haec alii sex
vel plures uno conclamant ore sophistae
et veras agitant lites raptore relicto;
fusa venena silent, malus ingratusque maritus
170 et quae iam veteres sanant mortaria caecos.
ergo sibi dabit ipse rudem, si nostra movebunt
consilia, et vitae diversum iter ingredietur
ad pugnam qui rhetorica descendit ab umbra,
summula ne pereat qua vilis tessera venit
175 frumenti; quippe haec merces lautissima. tempta
Chrysogonus quanti doceat vel Pollio quanti
lautorum pueros, artem scindes Theodori.
    Balnea sescentis et pluris porticus in qua
gestetur dominus quotiens pluit. anne serenum
180 expectet spargatve luto iumenta recenti?
hic potius, namque hic mundae nitet ungula mulae.
parte alia longis Numidarum fulta columnis
surgat et algentem rapiat cenatio solem.
quanticumque domus, veniet qui fercula docte
185 conponit, veniet qui pulmentaria condit.

180 spargatve *Heinrich, Markland*: spargatque *codd.*

---

33 Another set topic in rhetoric classes.

34 After his victory at Cannae in 216 B.C. Hannibal could have conquered the Romans by an immediate march on Rome, but was stopped by a storm.

bal the Terrible'?[33] It hardly matters what the debate is:
whether to head for Rome from Cannae, or whether after
the rain and thunder he should exercise caution and make
his troops turn around though they're still wet from the
storm?[34] State your price and you'll get it on the spot: what
would I give for his father to hear him as often as I have?"
That's what six or more other professors yell with one voice
as they abandon "The Rapist" to engage in real lawsuits.
"The Administering of Poison" goes silent and so does
"The Wicked, Ungrateful Husband" and "The Cures for
Chronic Blindness."[35] So this is the advice I have for any-
one who comes down from the grove of rhetoric to fight for
the tiny fee which buys his cheap corn coupon (after all,
that's the most lavish reward he can expect). If he'll follow
my advice, he'll take early retirement and enter a different
path of life. Find out the fees that Chrysogonus and Pollio
receive for teaching music to the sons of the wealthy and
you'll tear up Theodorus' *Handbook of Rhetoric*.[36]

The master's baths cost him six hundred thousand and
his colonnade, for driving on rainy days, even more. Or
would you want him to wait for a clear sky or to spatter his
animals with fresh mud? It's much better here, where his
mule stays clean with gleaming hooves. Elsewhere, he'll
have a diningroom constructed, resting on tall columns of
Numidian marble, to catch the winter sunshine. However
much the house costs, someone will come to arrange the
dishes expertly and to spice the food. Among all this ex-

[35] Further topics which might be set by professors of rhetoric.
Seneca the Elder's *Controversiae* provide other examples.

[36] Theodorus was a famous rhetorician from Gadara who
taught Tiberius.

hos inter sumptus sestertia Quintiliano,
ut multum, duo sufficient: res nulla minoris
constabit patri quam filius. "unde igitur tot
Quintilianus habet saltus?" exempla novorum
190 fatorum transi. felix et pulcher et acer,
felix et [sapiens et nobilis et generosus
adpositam] nigrae lunam subtexit alutae,
felix orator quoque maximus et iaculator
et, nisi perfrixit, cantat bene. distat enim quae
195 sidera te excipiant modo primos incipientem
edere vagitus et adhuc a matre rubentem.
si Fortuna volet, fies de rhetore consul;
si volet haec eadem, fiet de consule rhetor.
Ventidius quid enim? quid Tullius? anne aliud quam
200 sidus et occulti miranda potentia fati?
servis regna dabunt, captivis fata triumphum.
felix ille tamen corvo quoque rarior albo.
paenituit multos vanae sterilisque cathedrae,
sicut Tharsimachi probat exitus atque Secundi
205 Carrinatis; et hunc inopem vidistis, Athenae,
nil praeter gelidas ausae conferre cicutas.
di maiorum umbris tenuem et sine pondere terram

191–2 sapiens . . . adpositam *del. Reeve*
192 *del. Jahn, Scholte*
194 et nisi *Courtney*: et ni *Weidner*: et si *codd.*: etsi *Eden*

---

[37] The famous professor of rhetoric.

[38] The crescent-shaped ivory sewn to the shoe was a sign of patrician or senatorial status. Lines 191–2: "Wise and noble and well-born and [sews] the affixed . . . "

[39] Juvenal here reworks Horace's description of the wise man

pense, two thousand sesterces will be enough—a fortune
—for Quintilian.[37] No item will cost a father less than
his son. "So how come Quintilian owns so many estates?"
Don't go into freak cases of good fortune. The lucky man is
handsome and energetic. And the lucky man sews the cres-
cent to his black shoe.[38] The lucky man is also the greatest
orator and javelin-thrower and a marvellous singer, unless
he has caught a cold.[39] You see, it makes a huge difference
what star sign greets you as you start emitting your first
yells, still red from your mother's womb. If Fortune wants,
she'll turn you from teacher into consul. And if she wants,
she'll turn you from consul into teacher. Just think of Ven-
tidius[40] and Tullius.[41] Are they cases of anything more than
the stars and the astonishing power of mysterious destiny?
It's destiny that bestows kingdoms upon slaves and tri-
umphs upon prisoners-of-war. But that lucky man is even
more rare than a white crow. Many have regretted their
empty and fruitless Chairs of Rhetoric, as the death of
Thrasymachus proves and that of Carrinas Secundus:
Athens, you saw his poverty too and you dared offer him
nothing but chilly hemlock.[42] May the gods make the earth
on our ancestors' shades soft and light, may they have

(*sapiens*) from *Ep*. 1.1.106–8, substituting the lucky man for sar-
castic effect.

[40] Publius Ventidius Bassus arrived in Rome as a prisoner in
89 B.C. but attained the position of consul in 43, and in 38 cele-
brated a triumph over the Parthians (see line 201).

[41] Servius Tullius, the sixth king of Rome, was the son of a
slavewoman.　　　　　　　[42] Both were rhetoricians, apparently
associated with Athens, who according to the scholiast committed
suicide. Secundus was banished by Caligula.

spirantisque crocos et in urna perpetuum ver,
qui praeceptorem sancti voluere parentis
210 esse loco. metuens virgae iam grandis Achilles
cantabat patriis in montibus et cui non tunc
eliceret risum citharoedi cauda magistri;
sed Rufum atque alios caedit sua quemque iuventus,
Rufum, quem totiens Ciceronem Allobroga dixit.
215   Quis gremio Celadi doctique Palaemonis adfert
quantum grammaticus meruit labor? et tamen ex hoc,
quodcumque est (minus est autem quam rhetoris aera),
discipuli custos praemordet acoenonoetus
et qui dispensat frangit sibi. cede, Palaemon,
220 et patere inde aliquid decrescere, non aliter quam
institor hibernae tegetis niveique cadurci,
dummodo non pereat mediae quod noctis ab hora
sedisti, qua nemo faber, qua nemo sederet
qui solet obliquo lanam deducere ferro,
225 dummodo non pereat totidem olfecisse lucernas
quot stabant pueri, cum totus decolor esset
Flaccus et haereret nigro fuligo Maroni.
rara tamen merces quae cognitione tribuni
non egeat. sed vos saevas inponite leges,
230 ut praeceptori verborum regula constet,
ut legat historias, auctores noverit omnes
tamquam ungues digitosque suos, ut forte rogatus,

224 solet *Scholte*: docet *codd.*

---

43 Achilles was educated by the centaur Chiron, half-man,
half-horse.
44 Rufus is not otherwise known. His students call him a
"backwoods Cicero."

316

blooming crocuses and everlasting springtime in the urn. They thought that the teacher should have the role of a revered parent. When Achilles (already grown) was taking music lessons in his native hills, he was fearful of the cane and wouldn't mock the tail of his lyre-playing teacher.[43] But these days Rufus and the rest are beaten by their young students—yes, the Rufus they so often styled "the Gallic Cicero."[44]

When do Celadus and clever Palaemon pocket the reward a schoolteacher deserves?[45] Yet even from that, whatever it amounts to (and it's less than the pay of a rhetoric teacher), the pupil's philistine attendant nibbles off a bit for himself, and the cashier too takes a chunk. Give in, Palaemon, let yourself be beaten down, like a peddlar haggling over a winter mat or a white quilt. Just make sure that you get something for sitting from midnight onwards in a place where no blacksmith would sit and no one used to carding wool with their slanting steel comb. Just make sure that you get something for breathing the stink of as many lamps as there are boys, while your Horace gets totally discoloured and the soot sticks to your blackened Virgil. But it's rare to get your fee without a tribune's investigation. Yet you parents, you lay down savage laws for the teacher: that he should be precise in his use of grammar, that he should be familiar with the history books and should know all the authors like his own fingers and nails. If he's asked a ran-

---

[45] Celadus (not otherwise known) and Palaemon are examples of *grammatici*, teachers at the school below the school of rhetoric. Quintus Remmius Palaemon, author of a famous *Grammar*, taught Persius and Quintilian.

dum petit aut thermas aut Phoebi balnea, dicat
nutricem Anchisae, nomen patriamque novercae
235 Anchemoli, dicat quot Acestes vixerit annis,
quot Siculi Phrygibus vini donaverit urnas.
exigite ut mores teneros ceu pollice ducat,
ut si quis cera voltum facit; exigite ut sit
et pater ipsius coetus, ne turpia ludant,
240 ne faciant vicibus. non est leve tot puerorum
observare manus oculosque in fine trementis.
"haec" inquit "cura," sed cum se verterit annus,
accipe, victori populus quod postulat, aurum.

236 siculi PGL: siculis U: siculus Φ

dom question while he's heading for the hot baths or for Phoebus' spa,[46] he must be able to identify Anchises' nurse and to state the name and birthplace of the stepmother of Anchemolus and how long Acestes lived and how many jars of Sicilian wine he gave to the Trojans.[47] Require that the teacher shape their tender characters as if he were moulding a face from wax with his thumb. Require that he take the father's role in that scrum, ensuring that they don't play dirty games and don't take turns with one another. It is no light thing to keep a watch on all those boys with their hands and eyes quivering till they come. "That's your job," says the father, but at the turnaround of the year, you get the same gold as the crowd demands for their winning fighter.[48]

[46] A private bathing house owned by a freedman called Phoebus.

[47] All these questions relate to the *Aeneid*, but not all can be answered from the text of Virgil.

[48] A victorious gladiator might win four or five gold coins for a single success.

NOTE ON SATIRE 8

This poem, the centrepiece of Book Three, is essentially a persuasion addressed to an aristocratic-sounding man, Ponticus, to rely on his own worth and achievements, or rather, a dissuasion from relying on his inheritance, his blue blood, and the achievements of his ancestors. Though Ponticus is not known, his name suggests a descendant of a general who had achieved military success in the Pontic (Black Sea) region. Juvenal poses the central question immediately: "What's the use of pedigrees?" (1). The theme is a commonplace, but Juvenal's treatment unusual: he walks through an imaginary aristocratic atrium, pointing out the contradictions between high ancestry and corrupt morality (1–38), asserting that "the one and only nobility is personal excellence" (20). He then turns to Rubellius Blandus, who is puffed up with self-importance, and demands from him personal rather than inherited excellence (39–70). Returning to Ponticus, he repeats his warning and spells out the kind of conduct he would find acceptable (71–86). He imagines Ponticus as the governor of a wealthy province. He advises him to restrain both his own greed (87–126) and that of his entourage (127–41). Juvenal then shifts to another scandal—the consul Lateranus disgracing himself and his ancestors by driving his chariot himself and frequenting low diners, without incurring criticism from his peers (142–82). He attacks the aristocrats who expose themselves to humiliation by going on stage or participating in gladiatorial combat (183–210). His crowning example of disgrace is the emperor Nero (211–30). After a few more negative examples, the poem draws to a close with a catalogue of people of humble origins who behaved more courageously and patriotically than the aristocrats (231–68). Finally, Juvenal produces the clinching argument in a wonderful *reductio ad absurdum*: there is no point in relying on pedigrees because everyone is ultimately descended from the herdsmen and the criminals in Romulus' asylum (269–75). This new Juvenal is clearly a nihilist with an acute sense of humour.

SATIRE 8

Stemmata quid faciunt? quid prodest, Pontice, longo
sanguine censeri, pictos ostendere vultus
maiorum et stantis in curribus Aemilianos
et Curios iam dimidios umeroque minorem
5   Corvinum et Galbam auriculis nasoque carentem,
quis fructus generis tabula iactare capaci
censorem posse ac multa contingere virga
fumosos equitum cum dictatore magistros,
si coram Lepidis male vivitur? effigies quo
10   tot bellatorum, si luditur alea pernox
ante Numantinos, si dormire incipis ortu
Luciferi, quo signa duces et castra movebant?
cur Allobrogicis et magna gaudeat ara

6–8 *del. Guyet, Jachmann* | 7 *om.* Φ

7 censorem *Harrison*: corvinum P: fabricium Φ: pontifices
Housman | posse ac *Withof, Housman*: posthac P: post haec GK

8 fumosos PFG: famosos Φ

1 Mention of Aemiliani evokes Publius Cornelius Scipio
Aemilianus (185–129 B.C.), one of the central figures in Roman
politics, military affairs, and culture during the second century.
The Curii were an ancient patrician family which included
Manius Curius Dentatus, conqueror of Pyrrhus (275 B.C.).
Marcus Valerius Corvinus received his name from his single com-

SATIRE 8

What's the use of pedigrees? What's the advantage, Ponticus, of being valued by the length of your bloodline, of displaying the painted portraits of ancestors, Aemiliani standing tall in their chariots, Curii now in halves, a Corvinus minus his shoulders, and a Galba missing his ears and nose?[1] What's to be gained from being able to boast a Censor in your enormous family chart and to make connections through many branches with smoke-grimed Masters of the Cavalry along with a Dictator,[2] if, under the noses of the Lepidi,[3] the life you live is rotten? What's the point of all those statues of warriors, if you gamble the night away in front of Numantini,[4] if you don't go to sleep until Lucifer rises, the moment when those generals started advancing their standards and camps? Why should a Fabius born in

bat with a Gaul (349 B.C.) in which he was helped by a crow (*corvus*). The emperor Galba, from the *gens Sulpicia*, claimed he was descended from Jupiter and Pasiphae.

[2] In the Republic a Dictator was appointed in emergencies; his second in command was called Master of the Cavalry.

[3] An eminent family in the late Republic, part of the *gens Aemilia*, including the consul of 79 B.C. and the triumvir with Antony and Octavian.

[4] Numantinus was the name conferred on Scipio Aemilianus (see 8.3n.) after his capture of Numantia in Spain (133 B.C.).

natus in Herculeo Fabius lare, si cupidus, si
15 vanus et Euganea quantumvis mollior agna,
si tenerum attritus Catinensi pumice lumbum
squalentis traducit avos emptorque veneni
frangenda miseram funestat imagine gentem?
tota licet veteres exorment undique cerae
20 atria, nobilitas sola est atque unica virtus.
Paulus vel Cossus vel Drusus moribus esto,
hos ante effigies maiorum pone tuorum,
praecedant ipsas illi te consule virgas.
prima mihi debes animi bona. sanctus haberi
25 iustitiaeque tenax factis dictisque mereris?
agnosco procerem; salve Gaetulice, seu tu
Silanus: quocumque alto de sanguine rarus
civis et egregius patriae contingis ovanti,
exclamare libet populus quod clamat Osiri
30 invento. quis enim generosum dixerit hunc qui
indignus genere et praeclaro nomine tantum
insignis? nanum cuiusdam Atlanta vocamus,

17 traducit PSAGUΣ: producit FHLOZ
27 alto *Richards*: alio PΦ

5 The ancient family of Fabii claimed descent from Hercules;
famous members included Quintus Fabius Maximus who took
the name Allobrogicus after he defeated the Gallic tribe of the
Allobroges (121 B.C.). The Great Altar of Hercules stood in the
cattle market at Rome.

6 Sheep from this area of Venetia were valued for their fine
wool. The name is chosen because it echoes the Greek word
εὐγένεια, "noble birth."

7 From Mount Etna.

Hercules' house take delight in Allobrogici and the Great Altar[5] if he's greedy and silly and even soppier than a Euganean lamb,[6] if he disgraces his unkempt ancestors by having his groin rubbed smooth by Catanian pumice,[7] and if his dealing in poison pollutes his wretched clan with his statue that ought to be shattered? Though you adorn your entire atrium with ancient wax portraits in every direction, the one and only nobility is personal excellence. So, be a Paulus or a Cossus or a Drusus[8]—in morality. Rate that ahead of your ancestors' statues, let that go ahead of the rods of office when you're consul. Your first debt to me is quality of soul. Do you deserve a reputation as an upright champion of justice in word and action? Then I acknowledge a true noble. Welcome, Gaetulicus, or you, Silanus:[9] whatever your exalted blood, if you benefit your rejoicing fatherland as a rare and outstanding citizen, I want to cheer like the people do when Osiris has been found.[10] After all, who'd use the label "thoroughbred" of a person unworthy of his breeding and who was distinguished by his glorious name and nothing else? It's our practice to call

[8] Lucius Aemilius Paulus Macedonicus defeated Perseus of Macedon at the battle of Pydna (168 B.C.). Gnaeus Cornelius Lentulus Cossus received the title Gaetulicus for his victory over the Gaetuli in North Africa (A.D. 6). Nero Claudius Drusus (38–9 B.C.) fought with his brother, the future emperor Tiberius, in Germany.

[9] For the name Gaetulicus, see 8.21n. The Iunii Silani were a family prominent in the early principate.

[10] In Egyptian cult, the discovery and resurrection of the murdered Osiris was marked by the shout, "We have found him! We rejoice!" (Sen. Apoc. 13.4).

Aethiopem Cycnum, pravam extortamque puellam
Europen; canibus pigris scabieque vetusta
35 levibus et siccae lambentibus ora lucernae
nomen erit Pardus, Tigris, Leo, si quid adhuc est
quod fremat in terris violentius. ergo cavebis
et metues ne tu sic Creticus aut Camerinus.
    His ego quem monui? tecum mihi sermo, Rubelli
40 Blande. tumes alto Drusorum stemmate, tamquam
feceris ipse aliquid propter quod nobilis esses,
ut te conciperet quae sanguine fulget Iuli,
non quae ventoso conducta sub aggere texit.
"vos humiles" inquis "volgi pars ultima nostri,
45 quorum nemo queat patriam monstrare parentis,
ast ego Cecropides." vivas et originis huius
gaudia longa feras. tamen ima plebe Quiritem
facundum invenies, solet hic defendere causas
nobilis indocti; veniet de pube togata
50 qui iuris nodos et legum aenigmata solvat;
hinc petit Euphraten iuvenis domitique Batavi
custodes aquilas armis industrius. at tu

33 pravam ΦP: parvam ALO
49 pube *Housman*: plebe PSAGLU: gente F

11 Quintus Caecilius Metellus (consul 69 B.C.) received the
name Creticus for his conquest of Crete (68–7 B.C.). The Ca-
merini were a branch of the ancient *gens Sulpicia*.
12 Evidently a son of Julia who in A.D. 33 married Rubellius
Blandus. If so, this unknown son was the brother of Rubellius
Plautus (Tac. *Ann.* 13.19). Julia was the daughter of Tiberius' son
Drusus Caesar, hence *Drusorum*. Henderson raises the possibil-

someone's dwarf "Atlas," his Ethiopian slave "Swan," and his bent and deformed girl "Miss Europe." Lazy dogs bald with chronic mange who lick the edge of a lamp dry will get the name "Leopard" or "Tiger" or "Leo," or whatever in the world has a fiercer roar. So you'd better be careful and watch out that you aren't a Creticus or a Camerinus on the same principle.[11]

Who is it I've been warning like this? It's you I'm talking to, Rubellius Blandus.[12] You are swollen with the exalted pedigree of the Drusi, as if you yourself had done something to make you noble, as if it was down to you that your mother was resplendent with Julian blood instead of being a hired weaver[13] underneath the windy Embankment. "You're proles," you say, "the dregs of the Roman people. Not one of you can name his father's country. But I am descended from Cecrops."[14] Lucky you! I wish you long-lasting joy in your ancestry! But in the lowest rabble, you'll come across a Roman who is eloquent, who will take on defence cases for the uneducated nobleman. From this toga-wearing company will emerge a man who can undo legal knots and riddles of regulations. From here comes the energetic young soldier headed for the Euphrates and for the eagles guarding the defeated Batavi.[15] But you—you're

ity that Rubellius Blandus is a fictitious rhetorical figure (*Figuring Out Roman Nobility*, Exeter 1997, pp. 92–3).

[13] The equivalent modern insult is "washerwoman."

[14] I.e. indigenous Roman nobility: the pompous nobleman uses the Greek term *Cecropides* (descendant of Cecrops, the originary king of Athens) metaphorically.

[15] A reference to two frontier regions of the Roman empire, in the east and the west (the Batavi lived by the Rhine).

nil nisi Cecropides truncoque simillimus Hermae.
nullo quippe alio vincis discrimine quam quod
55   illi marmoreum caput est, tua vivit imago.
      Dic mihi, Teucrorum proles, animalia muta
quis generosa putet nisi fortia? nempe volucrem
sic laudamus equum, facili cui plurima palma
fervet et exultat rauco victoria Circo;
60   nobilis hic, quocumque venit de gramine, cuius
clara fuga ante alios et primus in aequore pulvis.
sed venale pecus Coryphaei posteritas et
Hirpini, si rara iugo Victoria sedit.
nil ibi maiorum respectus, gratia nulla
65   umbrarum; dominos pretiis mutare iubentur
exiguis, trito et ducunt epiraedia collo
segnipedes dignique molam versare nepotes.
ergo ut miremur te, non tua, privum aliquid da
quod possim titulis incidere praeter honores
70   quos illis damus ac dedimus, quibus omnia debes.
      Haec satis ad iuvenem quem nobis fama superbum
tradit et inflatum plenumque Nerone propinquo.
rarus enim ferme sensus communis in illa
fortuna. sed te censeri laude tuorum,
75   Pontice, noluerim sic ut nihil ipse futurae
laudis agas. miserum est aliorum incumbere famae,

---

66 trito et *Goth.2.52, Laur.34.34*: et trito P*Sang*: trito AGU:
tritoque Φ   68 privum *Salmasius*: primum *codd.*

---

16 Herms were statues of the god Hermes which stood outside
Athenian houses. A mutilated Herm lacked nose and phallus.
17 Mock-epic. Cf. *Troiugenas* at 1.100 and *Troiades* at Persius
1.4n.

nothing but "descended from Cecrops," the spitting image of a mutilated Herm.[16] In fact, you have the advantage in only one respect: his head is made of marble but your image is alive.

Tell me, o descendant of Trojans:[17] in the case of dumb animals, who would think them "thoroughbred" unless they are strong? That's the reason we praise the speedy racehorse: his countless wins—first place comes easily—bring a seething, riotous reception in the hoarse Circus. The "noble" horse is the one which, whatever his pasture, speeds clear of the rest and which has the leading dust cloud on the flat. By contrast, the ones sired by Coryphaeus and Hirpinus[18] are "livestock for sale," if it's but rarely that victory lands on their harness. There is no respect for ancestors there, no regard for their ghosts. Slow-footed descendants, fit for nothing except to turn the millstone, are made to swap owners for minimal prices and pull carts with their worn necks. So, if I'm to be impressed by you and not your heritage, offer me something personal, something I can inscribe in your record of achievement, apart from those titles which we gave (and continue to give) to those men to whom you owe everything.

I've said enough to the young man who, so tradition reports, was proud and pompous and full of his close connection with Nero. It's pretty rare that you'll find considerateness in people of that class. But I wouldn't want you, Ponticus, to be valued for the praise given to your family and to do nothing yourself to earn praise in the future. It's terrible to rely on the reputation of other people. There's a

---

[18] Famous successful horses in chariot teams.

ne conlapsa ruant subductis tecta columnis:
stratus humi palmes viduas desiderat ulmos.
esto bonus miles, tutor bonus, arbiter idem
80 integer. ambiguae si quando citabere testis
incertaeque rei, Phalaris licet imperet ut sis
falsus et admoto dictet periuria tauro,
summum crede nefas animam praeferre pudori
et propter vitam vivendi perdere causas.
85 dignus morte perit, cenet licet ostrea centum
Gaurana et Cosmi toto mergatur aeno.
    Expectata diu tandem provincia cum te
rectorem accipiet, pone irae frena modumque,
pone et avaritiae, miserere inopum sociorum:
90 ossa vides regum vacuis exucta medullis.
respice quid moneant leges, quid curia mandet,
praemia quanta bonos maneant, quam fulmine iusto
et Capito et Tutor ruerint damnante senatu,
piratae Cilicum. sed quid damnatio confert?
95 praeconem, Chaerippe, tuis circumspice pannis,
cum Pansa eripiat quidquid tibi Natta reliquit,
iamque tace; furor est post omnia perdere naulum.
    Non idem gemitus olim neque vulnus erat par
damnorum sociis florentibus et modo victis.

90 regum Φ: rerum PFGHU
93 tutor ΦΣ: numitor PS*Mico*

---

19 A Sicilian tyrant famous for torturing his victims in a bull made of bronze.

20 Oysters from the Lucrine lake, a special delicacy. Cosmus was a famous perfume-producer.   21 The wealthy client-kings of the East whose kingdoms became Roman provinces.

risk of the roof collapsing in ruins when the columns are removed. When it's trailing on the ground, the vine-shoot misses the elm it was married to. Be a good soldier, a good guardian, an incorruptible judge, too. If you're summoned as a witness in some tricky, murky case, even if Phalaris[19] commands you to commit perjury and dictates his lies with his Torture-Bull close by, think it the worst evil to put survival ahead of honour and for sake of life to lose the reasons for living. The person who deserves death is already dead, even though he eats a hundred Gauran oysters for dinner and bathes in a bronze tubful of Cosmus' perfume.[20]

When you finally enter your long-awaited province as its Governor, bridle and limit your anger and your greed, too, have some sympathy for the impoverished provincials. What you see are the bones of the kings[21] sucked dry, with their marrows empty. Keep an eye on the provisions of the laws, the Senate's instructions, the enormous rewards which await good governors, the entirely justified thunderbolt of senatorial condemnation which caused the destruction of Capito and Tutor, for plundering the Cilicians.[22] But what good came from that condemnation? Look around for someone to auction off your rags, Chaerippus, seeing that Pansa is stealing everything that Natta left you, and then shut up! On top of it all, you'd be mad to lose your fare.

In the old days, when the provincials were still flourishing and just recently defeated, they didn't groan like this, and the pain of their losses wasn't the same. In those

[22] Capito was condemned for extortion in Cilicia; Tutor is unknown to us. The Cilicians were famed as robbers, so this is a paradox.

100 plena domus tunc omnis, et ingens stabat acervos
   nummorum, Spartana chlamys, conchylia Coa,
   et cum Parrhasii tabulis signisque Myronis
   Phidiacum vivebat ebur, nec non Polycliti
   multus ubique labor, rarae sine Mentore mensae.
105 inde Dolabella †atque hinc† Antonius, inde
   sacrilegus Verres referebant navibus altis
   occulta spolia et plures de pace triumphos.
   nunc sociis iuga pauca boum, grex parvus equarum,
   et pater armenti capto eripietur agello,
110 ipsi deinde Lares, si quod spectabile signum.
   [si quis in aedicula deus unicus; haec etenim sunt
   pro summis, nam sunt haec maxima. despicias tu]
   forsitan inbellis Rhodios unctamque Corinthon
   despicias. merito quid resinata iuventus
115 cruraque totius facient tibi levia gentis?
   horrida vitanda est Hispania, Gallicus axis
   Illyricumque latus; parce et messoribus illis
   qui saturant Vrbem Circo scenaeque vacantem;
   quanta autem inde feres tam dirae praemia culpae,
120 cum tenuis nuper Marius discinxerit Afros?
   curandum in primis ne magna iniuria fiat

105 Dolabella Φ: Dolabellae *Ruperti*: dolo bellans *Eden* |
⟨audax⟩ Antonius *Knoche*: ⟨rapax⟩ Antonius *Nisbet*: ⟨astuque⟩
Antonius *Eden*: praedoque Antonius *Braund* | hinc atque hinc
Weidner   111–12 *del. Manso*

---

23 The top Greek artists of the fifth and fourth centuries B.C.
Phidias' "ivories" are statues in ivory and gold; Mentor was a
silversmith.   24 Two infamous provincial governors con-
demned of extortion in the late Republic.

days, their houses were bulging: there were huge piles of money, purple Spartan wraps and Coan silks, paintings by Parrhasius and statues by Myron along with ivories by Phidias—very lifelike—with works of Polyclitus everywhere and hardly a table without a piece by Mentor.[23] From there, Dolabella, * * * Antonius,[24] from there that villain Verres[25] kept bringing home secret loot in their tall ships—more triumphs in peacetime than in war. These days, when a little farmstead is seized, the provincials have only a few yoke of oxen and a tiny herd of mares, but these will be kidnapped, even the stallion of the herd, along with the household gods themselves, if there are any decent statues.[26] You may perhaps despise the unsoldierly Rhodians and perfumed Corinth—and quite rightly so: what harm will you suffer from a whole race of smooth-skinned young men with depilated legs? It's hairy Spain you need to avoid, and the Gallic region, and the Illyrian coast. Keep clear, too, of those harvesters[27] who glut Rome, when she is at leisure for the races and the stage shows. But anyway, how big are the rewards that you'll get from such a horrendous crime, seeing that Marius[28] recently stripped the impoverished Africans bare? The most important thing is not to give deep offence to people who

[25] Attacked by Cicero for his depredations as propraetor of Sicily, 73–70 B.C.

[26] Lines 111–12: "if there is a single god left in his little shrine. That's because these make up the top choice, these are now the maximum available."

[27] Africans: huge quantities of grain were imported from Africa to Rome, hence "glut."

[28] Cf. 1.49n.

fortibus et miseris. tollas licet omne quod usquam est
auri atque argenti, scutum gladiumque relinques.
[et iaculum et galeam; spoliatis arma supersunt.]
125 quod modo proposui, non est sententia, verum est;
credite me vobis folium recitare Sibyllae.
   Si tibi sancta cohors comitum, si nemo tribunal
vendit acersecomes, si nullum in coniuge crimen
nec per conventus et cuncta per oppida curvis
130 unguibus ire parat nummos raptura Celaeno,
tum licet a Pico numeres genus, altaque si te
nomina delectant omnem Titanida pugnam
inter maiores ipsumque Promethea ponas.
[de quocumque voles proavom tibi sumito libro.]
135 quod si praecipitem rapit ambitio atque libido,
si frangis virgas sociorum in sanguine, si te
delectant hebetes lasso lictore secures,
incipit ipsorum contra te stare parentum
nobilitas claramque facem praeferre pudendis.
140 omne animi vitium tanto conspectius in se
crimen habet, quanto maior qui peccat habetur.
   Quo mihi te solitum falsas signare tabellas
in templis quae fecit avus statuamque parentis
ante triumphalem? quo, si nocturnus adulter
145 tempora Santonico velas adoperta cucullo?
praeter maiorum cineres atque ossa volucri
carpento rapitur pinguis Lateranus et ipse,

123–4 scutum . . . galeam *del. Hermann*
124 *del. Lachmann*   134 *del. Ribbeck*

---

29 A female prophet whose predictions were written on palm
leaves.   30 A Harpy.

are brave as well as unhappy. Although you remove every last piece of their gold and silver, you'll still leave them shield and sword. What I've just set down is no rhetorical cliché—it's the truth. Believe me, I'm reciting to you a Leaf of the Sibyl.[29]

If your diplomatic entourage behaves honourably, if no long-haired lad sells your verdicts, if your wife is above reproach, not poised to race through the district courts and every town snatching loot with curving talons like Celaeno,[30] then I'll let you count your breeding from Picus,[31] and, if it's exalted names that please you, I'll let you include the entire Titan battle line and Prometheus himself among your ancestors.[32] But if you are whirled along by ambition and lust, if you break your lashes in provincials' blood, if you get a kick out of blunted axes and exhausted lictors,[33] then the nobility of your ancestors themselves starts to work against you and to hold a bright torch over things you should be ashamed of. Every fault of character lays itself open to criticism—and the higher the wrongdoer's status, the more glaring the criticism.

What good is it to me that you make a habit of sealing forged wills in the temples built by your grandfather and in front of your father's triumphal statue? Or if you creep out for adulterous liaisons at night with your head covered by a Gallic hood? Fat Lateranus[34] hurtles past the ashes and

---

[31] Lit. "Woodpecker," an early mythical king of Latium.

[32] Line 134: "Take your great-grand-daddy from whatever book you like."   [33] Attendants of magistrates such as provincial governors; here the lictors serve as executioners.

[34] Perhaps Plautius Lateranus, consul designate in A.D. 65 under Nero.

ipse rotam adstringit sufflamine mulio consul,
nocte quidem, sed Luna videt, sed sidera testes
150 intendunt oculos. finitum tempus honoris
cum fuerit, clara Lateranus luce flagellum
sumet et occursum numquam trepidabit amici
iam senis ac virga prior adnuet atque maniplos
solvet et infundet iumentis hordea lassis.
155 interea, dum lanatas robumque iuvencum
more Numae caedit, Iovis ante altaria iurat
solam Eponam et facies olida ad praesepia pictas.
sed cum pervigiles placet instaurare popinas,
obvius adsiduo Syrophoenix udus amomo
160 currit, Idymaeae Syrophoenix incola portae,
hospitis adfectu dominum regemque salutat,
et cum venali Cyane succincta lagona.

Defensor culpae dicet mihi "fecimus et nos
haec iuvenes." esto, desisti nempe nec ultra
165 fovisti errorem. breve sit quod turpiter audes,
quaedam cum prima resecentur crimina barba.
indulge veniam pueris: Lateranus ad illos
thermarum calices inscriptaque lintea vadit
maturus bello, Armeniae Syriaeque tuendis
170 finibus et Rheno atque Histro. [praestare Neronem

148 sufflamine mulio GU*Sang.*: sufflamine multo *Laur.34.40*:
multo sufflamine P   159 adsiduo *codd.*: Assyrio *Dorleans* |
udus Φ: unctus A   161 salutat PΦ: salutans *Leo*
170 finibus *Markland*: amnibus *codd.*
170–1 praestare . . . aetas *del. Nisbet*

35 The goddess of muleteers.

bones of his ancestors in his speeding vehicle and person-
ally, personally, applies the brake to the wheel—a mule-
teer consul! Granted, he does this at night—but the Moon
sees it, and the stars are witnesses, watching intently.
When his period of office is completed, Lateranus will pick
up his whip in broad daylight. He'll never worry about
meeting a now elderly friend—in fact, he'll greet him first
with his lash. He'll even undo the bales of hay and shake
out the barley for his tired animals. In the meantime,
though he sacrifices woolly ewes and ruddy oxen according
to Numa's rite, at Jupiter's altar he swears only by Epona[35]
and the pictures painted on the stinking stables. Then
when he decides to renew his all-night ritual in the diner,
the Syrian Jew runs to meet him, the Syrian Jew, inhabitant
of the Idymaean Gate,[36] dripping with nonstop perfume,
greeting him with a host's welcome as "My master" and
"My lord," accompanied by Cyane,[37] with her skirt hitched
up and her bottle for sale.

Someone will defend his behaviour, saying to me, "We
too behaved like that when we were young." That's as
may be, but you surely stopped, and didn't foster the mis-
take any further. Disgraceful derring-do ought not to last
long: there are some faults which should be trimmed with
your first beard. Make allowances for boys: but Lateranus
headed for those bathhouse wine cups and painted awn-
ings when he was old enough for war, for defending the
boundaries of Armenia and Syria, the Rhine and the Dan-

[36] Probably a scornful way of referring to the Porta Capena
with its Jewish enclave.

[37] A prostitute; lit. "Dark Blue" (of her eyes).

securum valet haec aetas.] mitte Ostia, Caesar,
mitte, sed in magna legatum quaere popina.
invenies aliquo cum percussore iacentem,
permixtum nautis et furibus ac fugitivis,
175   inter carnifices et fabros sandapilarum
et resupinati cessantia tympana galli.
aequa ibi libertas, communia pocula, lectus
non alius cuiquam, nec mensa remotior ulli.
quid facias talem sortitus, Pontice, servum?
180   nempe in Lucanos aut Tusca ergastula mittas.
at vos, Troiugenae, vobis ignoscitis et quae
turpia cerdoni Volesos Brutumque decebunt.
    Quid si numquam adeo foedis adeoque pudendis
utimur exemplis, ut non peiora supersint?
185   consumptis opibus vocem, Damasippe, locasti
sipario, clamosum ageres ut Phasma Catulli.
Laureolum velox etiam bene Lentulus egit,
iudice me dignus vera cruce. nec tamen ipsi
ignoscas populo; populi frons durior huius,
190   qui sedet et spectat triscurria patriciorum,
planipedes audit Fabios, ridere potest qui
Mamercorum alapas. quanti sua verbera vendant
quid refert? vendunt nullo cogente Nerone,

192 verbera *Courtney*: funera PAU

---

38 Lines 170–1: "His is the perfect age for giving Nero security."   39 A *gallus* was a eunuch priest of Cybele.

40 Estates where slaves were worked in chain gangs and kept in prisons.

41 Names of old Republican families.

42 Not known. The name Damasippus appears among the

ube.[38] Despatch your lieutenant to Ostia, Caesar, but first look for him in a huge—diner. You'll find him reclining next to some hit man, mingling with sailors and thieves and runaway slaves, among executioners and coffin-makers and the now silent tom-toms of a priest sprawled flat on his back.[39] There, it's "freedom" for all alike, shared cups. There, no one gets a separate couch or a table set apart. What would you do, Ponticus, if you happened to have a slave like that? You would surely send him off to Lucania or the Etruscan chain gangs.[40] But you of Trojan blood, you forgive yourselves. Behaviour that would disgrace a labourer is fine for a Volesus and a Brutus.[41]

The cases we cite are revolting and disgusting—but what if there are always worse to come? When you'd squandered all your money, Damasippus,[42] you hired out your voice to the stage, to act the noisy "Ghost" by Catullus.[43] Nifty Lentulus[44] took the part of Laureolus and did it rather well: in my opinion, he deserved a real cross.[45] And don't you go excusing the populace. It has a hardened gaze, this populace that can sit and watch the tri-fooleries of aristocrats, listen to barefoot Fabii,[46] and laugh at slapstick by Mamerci.[47] The price they sell their beatings for—what does it matter? They sell themselves without any Nero forcing them, and they have no hesitation in selling, even

Iunii and Licinii. It is also the name of the bankrupt in Horace *Sat.* 2.3.   [43] A Neronian mime writer.

[44] A member of the aristocratic *gens Cornelia.*

[45] A play about the life and execution by crucifixion of the bandit Laureolus.   [46] Mime actors wore no shoes. On the Fabii see 8.14n.   [47] Members of the *gens Aemilia*, which traced its ancestry back to Mamercus, son of King Numa.

nec dubitant celsi praetoris vendere ludis.
195   finge tamen gladios inde atque hinc pulpita poni:
quid satius? mortem sic quisquam exhorruit, ut sit
zelotypus Thymeles, stupidi collega Corinthi?
res haut mira tamen citharoedo principe mimus
nobilis. haec ultra quid erit nisi ludus? et illic
200   dedecus Vrbis habes, nec murmillonis in armis
nec clipeo Gracchum pugnantem aut falce supina;
damnat enim talis habitus [sed damnat et odit,
nec galea faciem abscondit]: movet ecce tridentem.
postquam vibrata pendentia retia dextra
205   nequiquam effudit, nudum ad spectacula voltum
erigit et tota fugit agnoscendus harena.
credamus tunicae, de faucibus aurea cum se
porrigat et longo iactetur spira galero.
ergo ignominiam graviorem pertulit omni
210   volnere cum Graccho iussus pugnare secutor.
    Libera si dentur populo suffragia, quis tam
perditus ut dubitet Senecam praeferre Neroni,
cuius supplicio non debuit una parari
simia nec serpens unus nec culleus unus?

195 poni P: pone Φ
202 *del. Guyet*
202–3 sed . . . abscondit *del. Hermann*
204 vibrata *codd.*: librata *Courtney*

---

48 The names of actors.
49 Nero.
50 This noble appears not as a heavy-armed gladiator—a
murmillo or a *Thraex* or a *secutor* ("chaser," below), with body

340

at the shows put on by the praetor on high. Yet imagine this choice: on one side violent death, on the other the stage. Which is better? Was there anyone so terrified of death that he'd prefer to be Thymele's jealous husband or the straight man to the clown Corinthus?[48] Yet when an emperor plays the lyre,[49] a noble mime actor is not such an amazing thing. Beyond this, what is there except the gladiatorial school? And that's where you've got the disgrace of Rome: a Gracchus fighting, but not in a murmillo's gear, and not with shield or curving blade. He rejects that sort of get-up, you see: look, he's brandishing a trident.[50] Once he has poised his right hand and cast the trailing net without success, he raises his bare face to the spectators and runs off, highly recognisable, all through the arena. There is no mistaking his tunic, stretched out golden from his throat, and the twisted cord bobbing from his tall hat.[51] And so the chaser told to fight against Gracchus suffered a loss of face more serious than any wound.

If the people were given a free vote, who would be so depraved as to hesitate about choosing Seneca over Nero?[52] For his punishment more than a single monkey and a single snake and a single sack needed to be pro-

---

armour, shield, and sword—but as a net-thrower (*retiarius*) with minimal gear: a tunic and net, trident, and dagger for weapons. The less the concealment, the lower the status of gladiators.

[51] The outfit of a Salian priest. For Gracchus, see 2.117n.

[52] In the Pisonian conspiracy against Nero, there was talk of making Seneca emperor. See Tac. *Ann.* 15.48–74.

215 par Agamemnonidae crimen, sed causa facit rem
dissimilem. quippe ille deis auctoribus ultor
patris erat caesi media inter pocula, sed nec
Electrae iugulo se polluit aut Spartani
sanguine coniugii, nullis aconita propinquis
220 miscuit, in scena numquam cantavit Oresten,
Troica non scripsit. quid enim Verginius armis
debuit ulcisci magis aut cum Vindice Galba?
[quod Nero tam saeva crudaque tyrannide fecit]
haec opera atque hae sunt generosi principis artes,
225 gaudentis foedo peregrina ad pulpita cantu
prostitui Graiaeque apium meruisse coronae.
maiorum effigies habeant insignia vocis,
ante pedes Domiti longum tu pone Thyestae
syrma vel Antigones aut personam Melanippes,
230 et de marmoreo citharam suspende colosso.
    Quid, Catilina, tuis natalibus atque Cethegi
inveniet quisquam sublimius? arma tamen vos
nocturna et flammas domibus templisque parastis,

220 Oresten *Weidner*: Orestes *codd.*   223 *del. Knoche*
225 cantu PGU: saltu Φ
229 aut *Hermann*: seu *Vat.3192, Vat.3286*: tu Φ
233 parastis Φ: paratis P

---

53 The traditional punishment for a murderer of close rela-
tions was to be sewn up in a sack with parricidal animals and
thrown into the sea. Nero allegedly murdered his mother and
several other relatives and wives.
    54 Orestes, who killed his mother Clytemnestra to avenge his
father's murder.   55 Whereas Nero killed his sister Antonia
and his wife Octavia, tried to poison his mother Agrippina, and did
poison Britannicus and his aunt Domitia.

vided.[53] His crime was that of Agamemnon's son,[54] but
motive makes his case different. The fact is, Orestes, on
the authority of the gods, was avenging his father, who'd
been slaughtered at a banquet. But he did not pollute him-
self with Electra's jugular or his Spartan wife's blood, he
didn't prepare poison for any relations,[55] he never went on
stage to sing the part of Orestes,[56] he never wrote an epic
Troy.[57] Is there anything that more deserved vengeance by
Verginius with his armies, or by Galba and his ally Vin-
dex?[58] These were the achievements and these the skills of
our highborn emperor, who enjoyed prostituting himself
on foreign stages with his horrid singing, and winning
Greek parsley crowns. Let your ancestors' statues have
the prizes won by your voice. Go on, put your long gown
of Thyestes in front of Domitius' feet, or your mask of
Antigone or Melanippe,[59] and hang your lyre on your
colossus made of marble.

What ancestry more exalted than yours, Catiline, or
that of Cethegus can be found?[60] Yet you plotted to attack
homes and temples at night and set them on fire, like the

---

[56] For Nero's performances as Orestes, see Suet. *Ner.* 21.3,
Dio 63.9.4.   [57] Line 223: "Of all that Nero did in his tyranny
so cruel and savage."

[58] Three key rebels against Nero: Julius Vindex, governor
of part of Gaul, led a revolt against Nero and was a supporter
of Galba, who became the next emperor; Verginius Rufus sup-
pressed the revolt of Vindex but acquiesced in Nero's fall and
Galba's assumption of power.

[59] References to Nero's acting, wearing the long robe and
mask of tragic actors. Domitius is his father, Gnaeus Domitius
and/or a more distant ancestor.

[60] See 2.27n.

ut bracatorum pueri Senonumque minores,
235   ausi quod liceat tunica punire molesta.
sed vigilat consul vexillaque vestra coercet.
hic novus Arpinas, ignobilis et modo Romae
municipalis eques, galeatum ponit ubique
praesidium attonitis et in omni monte laborat.
240   tantum igitur muros intra toga contulit illi
nominis ac tituli, quantum sibi Leucade, quantum
Thessaliae campis Octavius abstulit udo
caedibus adsiduis gladio; sed Roma parentem,
Roma patrem patriae Ciceronem libera dixit.
245   Arpinas alius Volscorum in monte solebat
poscere mercedes alieno lassus aratro;
nodosam post haec frangebat vertice vitem,
si lentus pigra muniret castra dolabra.
hic tamen et Cimbros et summa pericula rerum
250   excipit et solus trepidantem protegit Vrbem,
atque ideo, postquam ad cumulos stragemque volabant
qui numquam attigerant maiora cadavera corvi,
nobilis ornatur lauro collega secunda.

241 sibi *Jahn*: in PSGU: non Φ: unda *Weidner*: vix *Hermann*,
Ribbeck: ima *Eden*
251 cumulos *Nisbet*: Cimbros *codd.*

---

61 The Senones were Gauls who sacked Rome in 390 B.C. The
Narbonese Gauls wore trousers, *bracae.*
62 An inflammable coating made of pitch used on people who
were burnt alive.
63 Cicero was from Arpinum, a town (*municipium*) east of
Rome, and was the first of his family to enter the Senate, hence the
technical term "new man."

sons of trousered Gauls and descendants of the Senones,[61]
committing an outrage which could lawfully be punished
by the "uncomfortable shirt."[62] But the consul[63] is alert: he
halts your banners. He—a "new man" from Arpinum, of
humble origin, a municipal knight new to Rome—posts
helmeted troops all around to protect the terrified people
and is busy on every hill. So without stepping outside the
walls, his peacetime toga brought him as much titled dis-
tinction as Octavius grabbed for himself at Leucas and on
the fields of Thessaly with his sword wet from nonstop
slaughter.[64] The difference is that Rome was still free when
she called Cicero the Parent and Father of his Native
Land. In the Volscian hills, the other man from Arpinum
used to work for a wage, labouring behind someone else's
plough.[65] Later on, he got the centurion's lumpy staff
broken on his head if he was lazy in digging the camp's
defences with a sluggish pick. Yet it's he that takes on the
Cimbri[66] in a national emergency, he alone that protects a
trembling Rome. And that's why, when the ravens flew
down to feast on the slaughtered heaps (and they had
never fastened on corpses that were bigger), his nobly
born fellow consul[67] is honoured with the second-place

---

[64] The future emperor Augustus, here referred to belittlingly
as Octavius (not Octavian), won major battles at Actium in 31 B.C.
(here referred to as Leucas, an island nearby) and at Philippi in 42
B.C. (here conflated with Thessaly).

[65] Gaius Marius (157–86 B.C.), who in his early days worked
for hire and served as a private soldier.

[66] Marius defeated the Cimbri and Teutones in battles in 102
and 101 B.C.

[67] Quintus Lutatius Catulus, who was eclipsed by Marius in
the celebration of the triumph.

plebeiae Deciorum animae, plebeia fuerunt
255 nomina; pro totis legionibus hi tamen et pro
omnibus auxiliis atque omni pube Latina
sufficiunt dis infernis Terraeque parenti.
[pluris enim Decii quam quae servantur ab illis.]
ancilla natus trabeam et diadema Quirini
260 et fascis meruit, regum ultimus ille bonorum.
prodita laxabant portarum claustra tyrannis
exulibus iuvenes ipsius consulis et quos
magnum aliquid dubia pro libertate deceret,
quod miraretur cum Coclite Mucius et quae
265 imperii finis Tiberinum virgo natavit.
occulta ad patres produxit crimina servus
matronis lugendus; at illos verbera iustis
adficiunt poenis et legum prima securis.
  Malo pater tibi sit Thersites, dummodo tu sis
270 Aeacidae similis Volcaniaque arma capessas,
quam te Thersitae similem producat Achilles.
et tamen, ut longe repetas longeque revolvas
nomen, ab infami gentem deducis asylo;
maiorum primus, quisquis fuit ille, tuorum
275 aut pastor fuit aut illud quod dicere nolo.

258 *del. Markland, Dobree*

---

68 Publius Decius Mus, father and son, who both offered
themselves in the ceremony called *devotio*, committing them-
selves and the enemy to death, in battles in 340 and 295 B.C. re-
spectively.   69 Line 258: "the Decii were worth more than
everything they saved."
    70 Romulus.   71 Servius Tullius, the sixth king of Rome.
    72 Three stories from the early Republic when Lars Porsenna
was trying to restore the monarchy. Gaius Mucius put his right

laurel. Plebeian were the souls of the Decii,[68] plebeian too
their names. Yet they are enough for the gods below and
for Mother Earth in place of all the legions and all the al-
lies and all the youth of Latium.[69] A man born of a slave girl
won the robes and crown and rods of Quirinus[70]—he was
the last of our good kings.[71] The traitors who were plan-
ning to undo the bolts of the gates to the exiled tyrants
were the sons of the consul himself, precisely the people
who should have been doing something impressive for
shaky liberty, something to be admired by Mucius or
Cocles or the girl who swam the Tiber, the empire's bound-
ary.[72] It was a slave who revealed the secret plot to the
senators, and for this he deserved to be mourned by the
Roman matrons, while those traitors got their just rewards:
flogging and the first legally sanctioned axe.

I'd prefer that your father were Thersites, provided
you behaved like the grandson of Aeacus and brandished
the weapons made by Vulcan, rather than that Achilles
fathered you to behave like Thersites.[73] And after all, al-
though you trace your name far back and unroll it far back,
you derive your family from the notorious refuge:[74] the
first of your ancestors, whoever he was, was either a herds-
man or something I'd rather not mention.

hand in the fire to demonstrate his courage to Porsenna; Horatius
Cocles defended the bridge across the Tiber against Porsenna un-
til it could be destroyed; and Cloelia was a hostage who escaped
from Porsenna by swimming across the Tiber.

[73] Aeacus was Achilles' grandfather. Thersites, who spoke out
against Agamemnon in the *Iliad*, combines low birth and low
behaviour.

[74] Often called the "asylum"; to increase the population of
Rome, Romulus opened the doors even to slaves and criminals
seeking refuge.

NOTE ON SATIRE 9

Here Juvenal returns to the theme of patron and client for the last time, in the final poem of Book Three. The client in this poem is Naevolus ("Mr Warty"), a man who has interpreted his duties rather broadly to include satisfying the patron's desire to be penetrated in anal intercourse, having sex with the patron's wife at the patron's request, and fathering the patron's children. The poem is unique because it is the only one of Juvenal's Satires in dialogue form. It starts with Juvenal asking Naevolus why he is looking so miserable and unkempt (1–26). In his reply Naevolus attacks the stinginess of his former patron and reveals that the man is a pathic (27–46). Juvenal expresses surprise at Naevolus' lack of success, given that he always used to consider himself attractive (46–7), which provokes another vehement and indignant outburst from Naevolus, in which he reveals that he saved his patron's marriage by sleeping with his wife and fathered two children for him (48–90). Juvenal offers sympathy heavily laden with irony (90–1), at which point Naevolus panics and tries to swear Juvenal to secrecy (92–101). In reply Juvenal says that rich men can never have secrets (102–23). Naevolus asks for some more specific advice (124–9), and in reply Juvenal reassures him that he will find another pathic patron and advises him to keep using his aphrodisiac (130–4). Naevolus gloomily rejects this advice, lists his minimum needs in life, and then complains that Fortune always turns a deaf ear to his prayers (135–50). This final treatment of the patron-client relationship shows both patron and client in an unpleasant light. The indignant but selfish, amoral, and unscrupulous Naevolus is shown to be ridiculous by his own self-revelations and by his interlocutor's ironic remarks.

SATIRE 9

Scire velim quare totiens mihi, Naevole, tristis
occurras fronte obducta ceu Marsya victus.
quid tibi cum vultu, qualem deprensus habebat
Ravola dum Rhodopes uda terit inguina barba?
5 [nos colaphum incutimus lambenti crustula servo.]
non erit hac facie miserabilior Crepereius
Pollio, qui triplicem usuram praestare paratus
circumit et fatuos non invenit. unde repente
tot rugae? certe modico contentus agebas
10 vernam equitem, conviva ioco mordente facetus
et salibus vehemens intra pomeria natis.
omnia nunc contra: vultus gravis, horrida siccae
silva comae, nullus tota nitor in cute, qualem
Bruttia praestabat calidi tibi fascia visci,
15 sed fruticante pilo neglecta et squalida crura.
quid macies aegri veteris, quem tempore longo
torret quarta dies olimque domestica febris?

5 *del. Guyet, Pinzger, Markland*

---

1 Marsyas the satyr challenged Apollo to a musical contest. He
lost and was then flayed alive. There was a statue of him in the
Forum.

2 Line 5: "We give a beating to the slave who licks the pastries."

SATIRE 9

Naevolus, I'd like to know why I so often run into you looking gloomy with an overcast scowl like the beaten Marsyas.[1] What are you doing with a face like Ravola's when he was caught rubbing Rhodope's crotch with his wet beard?[2] I can't imagine a more miserable face on Crepereius Pollio,[3] who goes around offering triple the interest rate and cannot find anyone foolish enough to take him up. Where have all those wrinkles suddenly come from? It's a fact that you used to be happy with nothing much, playing the homebred knight, an elegant dinner guest with biting humour and forceful witticisms bred within the city limits. Now everything's the reverse. Your face is grim, your unoiled hair a bristling forest, your skin has completely lost that glossiness which you used to get from strips soaked with hot Bruttian pitch[4]—instead, your legs are neglected and dirty with sprouting hair. Why this emaciation, like a chronic invalid's, tormented for ages by a fever that comes every third day and that long ago became a member of the household? We can detect the tortures of

[3] A rich man reduced to begging at 11.43.
[4] Pitch from the pine forests at Bruttium, in the toe of Italy, was used as a depilatory.

deprendas animi tormenta latentis in aegro
corpore, deprendas et gaudia; sumit utrumque
20   inde habitum facies. igitur flexisse videris
propositum et vitae contrarius ire priori.
nuper enim, ut repeto, fanum Isidis et Ganymedem
Pacis et advectae secreta Palatia matris
et Cererem (nam quo non prostat femina templo?)
25   notior Aufidio moechus celebrare solebas,
quodque taces, ipsos etiam inclinare maritos.
   "Vtile et hoc multis vitae genus, at mihi nullum
inde operae pretium. pingues aliquando lacernas
[munimenta togae, duri crassique coloris]
30   et male percussas textoris pectine Galli
accipimus, tenue argentum venaeque secundae.
fata regunt homines, fatum est et partibus illis
quas sinus abscondit. nam si tibi sidera cessant,
nil faciet longi mensura incognita nervi,
35   quamvis te nudum spumanti Virro labello
viderit et blandae adsidue densaeque tabellae
sollicitent, αὐτὸς γὰρ ἐφέλκεται ἄνδρα κίναιδος.
quod tamen ulterius monstrum quam mollis avarus?
'haec tribui, deinde illa dedi, mox plura tulisti.'
40   computat et cevet. ponatur calculus, adsint
cum tabula pueri; numera sestertia quinque

29 *del. Ribbeck*

---

5 A list of temples that were regular places for adulterous assignations. The worship of Cybele, the Great Mother, involved initiation into the mysteries, hence "secret." The festival of Ceres involved abstinence from sex by the female celebrants, hence the parenthetical question.

the soul as it lies deep in the sick body, and we can detect its delights, too. From there the face derives both moods. So you've apparently changed your life plan and you're going the way opposite to your past. After all, it's not so long ago, as I recall, that you were often to be found at the shrine of Isis and at the Ganymede in the temple of Peace and at the secret Palace of the imported Mother and at Ceres[5] (is there, then, any temple where women don't prostitute themselves?), a lover more notorious than Aufidius,[6] and (something you keep quiet about) laying their husbands too.

"Many people find even this way of life profitable, but I get no reward for my efforts. From time to time I get a coarse overcloak[7] loosely made by a Gallic weaver's comb, or some thin silver plate of inferior quality. It's fate that rules humans—even the parts hidden under our clothes have their fate. You see, if the stars abandon you, nothing will be achieved by the unprecedented length of your long cock, though Virro[8] with drooling lips has seen you in the nude and his many coaxing love letters assail you nonstop. 'For the man can't help being attracted by the—pathic.'[9] Yet what monstrosity is worse than a stingy pervert? 'I paid you this, then I gave you that, and later you got still more.' He computes it while wiggling his arse. All right, let's get out the calculator and the slave boys with their records:

[6] A notorious playboy, cf. Mart. 5.61.10.

[7] Line 29: "to protect my toga, of a harsh and rough quality."

[8] Virro, the name of the sadistic patron in Satire 5, here seems to represent any mean patron.

[9] A parody of Hom. *Od.* 16.294 and 19.13, in which the last word σίδηρος, "steel," is replaced by "pathic."

omnibus in rebus, numerentur deinde labores.
an facile et pronum est agere intra viscera penem
legitimum atque illic hesternae occurrere cenae?
45 servus erit minus ille miser qui foderit agrum
quam dominum."
                        Sed tu sane tenerum et puerum te
et pulchrum et dignum cyatho caeloque putabas.
    "Vos humili adseculae, vos indulgebitis umquam
cultori? iam nec morbo donare paratis?
50 en cui tu viridem umbellam, cui sucina mittas
grandia, natalis quotiens redit aut madidum ver
incipit et strata positus longaque cathedra
munera femineis tractat secreta kalendis.
dic, passer, cui tot montis, tot praedia servas
55 Apula, tot milvos intra tua pascua lassas?
te Trifolinus ager fecundis vitibus implet
suspectumque iugum Cumis et Gaurus inanis,
nam quis plura linit victuro dolia musto?
quantum erat exhausti lumbos donare clientis
60 iugeribus paucis! melius, dic, rusticus infans
cum matre et casulis et conlusore catello
cymbala pulsantis legatum fiet amici?
'improbus es cum poscis' ait. sed pensio clamat

46–7 *locutori alteri assignavi*   48–9 *del. Ribbeck*
49 paratis *Braund*: parati *codd.*
55 lassas GU: lassos PSΦΣ
60 melius, dic, *Castiglione*: meliusne hic PΦ: melius nec hic
AL: melius nunc *Housman*

---

10 I.e. as pretty as Ganymede, Jupiter's cupbearer.

count five thousand paid in total and then let's count up my exertions. Or is it easy and straightforward to drive a penis worthy of the name into your guts and there meet yesterday's dinner? The slave who ploughs the soil will have an easier life than the one who ploughs his master."

But I thought you used to consider yourself a soft, pretty boy, good enough for the heavenly cup?[10]

"Will you rich men ever gratify your lowly hanger-on or your follower? Are you unwilling to spend money even on your sickness now? There's your recipient of a green parasol and large amber balls when his birthday comes round or rainy spring begins and, lounging on his soft chaise longue, he fondles his secret Ladies' Day presents.[11] Tell me, you little love bird, for whom are you keeping all those hills and farms in Apulia that tire out all those kites within your pastureland?[12] The productive vines from your Trifoline land, or the ridge which overlooks Cuma, or hollow Gaurus keep you well supplied[13]—after all, is there anyone who seals more vats of vintages that will keep for years? Would it be a big deal to make a gift of a few acres to your exhausted client's loins? Tell me, is it better that your rustic child, along with his mother and toy houses and puppy playmate, becomes a bequest to your friend who clashes the cymbals?[14] 'It's impertinent of you to beg,' he says. But my rent shouts, 'Beg!' and my slave boy makes

[11] The Matronalia on March 1 was when women received gifts from their husbands.

[12] A proverbial expression denoting a huge distance, because birds of prey like the kite are strong fliers.

[13] All places in the Bay of Naples area.   [14] The patron's friend is a eunuch priest of the goddess Cybele.

'posce,' sed appellat puer unicus ut Polyphemi
65   lata acies per quam sollers evasit Vlixes.
     alter emendus erit, namque hic non sufficit, ambo
     pascendi. quid agam bruma spirante? quid, oro,
     quid dicam scapulis puerorum aquilone Decembri
     et pedibus? 'durate atque expectate cicadas'?
70   Verum, ut dissimules, ut mittas cetera, quanto
     metiris pretio quod, ni tibi deditus essem
     devotusque cliens, uxor tua virgo maneret?
     scis certe quibus ista modis, quam saepe rogaris
     et quae pollicitus. fugientem nempe puellam
75   amplexu rapui; tabulas quoque ruperat et iam
     signabat; tota vix hoc ego nocte redemi
     te plorante foris. testis mihi lectulus et tu,
     ad quem pervenit lecti sonus et dominae vox.
     instabile ac dirimi coeptum et iam paene solutum
80   coniugium in multis domibus servavit adulter.
     quo te circumagas? quae prima aut ultima ponas?
     nullum ergo meritum est, ingrate ac perfide, nullum
     quod tibi filiolus, quod filia nascitur ex me?
     tollis enim et libris actorum spargere gaudes
85   argumenta viri. foribus suspende coronas:
     iam pater es, dedimus quod famae opponere possis.

74 nempe *Housman*: saepe *codd.*
76 signabat *codd.*: migrabat *Highet*
83 quod *Schurzfleisch, Ruperti*: vel *codd.*

15 The Cyclops Polyphemus had a single eye which Ulysses
blinded in order to escape from the cave in which he and his crew
were held captive (Hom. *Od.* 9).

his demands, as single as the broad eye of Polyphemus—clever Ulysses' means of escape.[15] I'll have to buy another, since this one isn't enough, and both will have to be fed. What'll I do when winter starts blowing? What'll I say, please, to the boys' shoulder blades and feet in December's northerly gales? 'Hang on and wait for the cicadas'?[16]

"But though you ignore and disregard my other services, how do you value the fact that if I had not been your devoted and obedient client, your wife would still be a virgin? You know very well indeed how often you asked for that favour—the different ways you wheedled and the promises you made. Your bride was actually walking out on you when I grabbed her and embraced her. She'd even destroyed the contract and was already in the process of making a new arrangement. I spent the whole night on it and only just managed to retrieve the situation, with you sobbing outside the door. My witness is the couch—and you—you could surely hear the sound of the bed and its mistress' voice. There are many households where a lover has saved a marriage that's shaky and starting to fall apart and already more or less dissolved. Which way can you turn? What are your priorities? Is it no service, no service at all, you ungrateful cheat, that your little son or your daughter is my child? After all, you acknowledge them as your own and you're delighted to splash all over the newspapers the proofs of your virility. Hang the garlands over your doors: now you're a daddy—and it's me who's given

[16] Cicadas are a sign of summer. Naevolus' words are a parody of Aeneas' encouragement to his crew at Virg. *Aen.* 1.207 *durate et vosmet rebus servate secundis.*

iura parentis habes, propter me scriberis heres,
legatum omne capis nec non et dulce caducum.
commoda praeterea iungentur multa caducis,
si numerum, si tres implevero."

90   Iusta doloris,
Naevole, causa tui; contra tamen ille quid adfert?

   "Neglegit atque alium bipedem sibi quaerit asellum.
haec soli commissa tibi celare memento
et tacitus nostras intra te fige querelas;
95 nam res mortifera est inimicus pumice levis.
qui modo secretum commiserat, ardet et odit,
tamquam prodiderim quidquid scio. sumere ferrum,
fuste aperire caput, candelam adponere valvis
non dubitat. [nec contemnas aut despicias quod
100 his opibus] numquam cara est annona veneni.
ergo occulta teges ut curia Martis Athenis."

   O Corydon, Corydon, secretum divitis ullum
esse putas? servi ut taceant, iumenta loquentur
et canis et postes et marmora. claude fenestras,

99–100 nec . . . opibus *del.* Ribbeck

---

17 Roman law (the Augustan *leges Iulia* and *Papia Poppaea*) rewarded parenthood and penalised celibacy and childlessness; for example, a childless heir forfeited half of any bequest made to him (line 88), and a parent might pick up these "windfalls" (*caduca*).

18 A father of three legitimate children gained extra privileges under the *ius trium liberorum*.

19 A reference to the proverbially huge size of the donkey's penis, as well as to the burdens Naevolus has borne while a client.

you something to contradict the gossip. Because of me you possess the privileges of a parent,[17] and you can be mentioned in people's wills, you can receive bequests intact, and some nice unexpected gifts too. What's more, many benefits will come along with those gifts if I make up the number to the full three."[18]

You have a perfectly justifiable case for feeling resentful, Naevolus. But what does he say in reply?

"He takes no notice. He's looking out for another two-legged donkey.[19]—Make sure you keep these confidences of mine absolutely to yourself. Keep quiet, and lock my complaints away inside you. An enemy kept smooth by pumice[20] is deadly. The man who's just shared his secret with me is blazing with hatred, as if I'd betrayed everything I know. He'll have no hesitation in using a knife or breaking my head open with a cosh or lighting a candle at my door. And[21] the cost of poison is never high. So please keep my secrets hidden, like the Council of Mars at Athens."[22]

O Corydon, Corydon![23] Do you think a rich man can ever have a secret? Even if his slaves keep quiet, his horses will talk and so will his dog and his doorposts and his marble floors. Close the shutters, put curtains across the

---

[20] Depilation is presented as a mark of effeminates in satire.

[21] Lines 99–100: "you shouldn't disregard or belittle the fact that, for wealth like his."

[22] The Areopagus, which judged homicide cases, was proverbial for the secrecy of its deliberations.

[23] A play on Virg. *Ecl.* 2.69, *a Corydon, Corydon, quae te dementia cepit?* where Corydon tries to shake off his unrequited love for the arrogant boy Alexis.

105 vela tegant rimas, iunge ostia, tolle lucernam,
    e medio fac eant omnes, prope nemo recumbat;
    quod tamen ad cantum galli facit ille secundi,
    proximus ante diem caupo sciet, audiet et quae
    finxerunt pariter libarius, archimagiri,
110 carptores. quod enim dubitant componere crimen
    in dominos, quotiens rumoribus ulciscuntur
    baltea? nec derit qui te per compita quaerat
    nolentem et miseram vinosus inebriet aurem.
    illos ergo roges quidquid paulo ante petebas
115 a nobis, taceant illi. sed prodere malunt
    arcanum quam subrepti potare Falerni
    pro populo faciens quantum Saufeia bibebat.
    vivendum recte est, cum propter plurima, tum ex his
    [idcirco ut possis linguam contemnere servi]
120 praecipue causis, ut linguas mancipiorum
    contemnas; nam lingua mali pars pessima servi.
    [deterior tamen hic qui liber non erit illis
    quorum animas et farre suo custodit et aere.]
       "Vtile consilium modo, sed commune, dedisti.
125 nunc mihi quid suades post damnum temporis et spes
    deceptas? festinat enim decurrere velox
    flosculus, angustae miseraeque brevissima vitae
    portio; dum bibimus, dum serta, unguenta, puellas
    poscimus, obrepit non intellecta senectus."

105 tolle lucernam *Nisbet*: tollite lumen PAKOTZ: tollito lu-
men GHU   106 face eant *Haupt*: taceant P: clament Φ
    118–23 *del. Ribbeck*
    118 recte est PA: recte Φ | tum ex his *Kenney*: tunc est PA:
tunc GU: tunc his Φ   119 *post* 123 Φ, *om. Vat.Ottob. 2885,
Vat.Pal.1700*: *del. Pithoeus, Pinzger*
    122–3 *del. Pinzger*

chinks, fasten the doors, turn out the light, make everyone leave, don't let anyone sleep close by—all the same, what the master does at the second cock-crow will be known to the nearest shopkeeper before dawn, along with all the fictions of the pastry cook, the head chefs, and the carvers. After all, is there any allegation they refrain from concocting against their masters? Rumours are their revenge for getting belted. And there'll always be someone who'll seek you out at the crossroads, even if you don't want to hear, who'll drench your poor ear with his drunken story. So it's them you need to ask what you were wanting of me a little while ago, to keep quiet. But they actually like betraying secrets better than drinking stolen Falernian wine in the quantities that Saufeia used to down when she was carrying out a public sacrifice.[24] There are lots of reasons for living a proper life, but[25] especially this, that you get to ignore the tongues of your slaves. The tongue, in fact, is the very worst part of a bad slave.[26]

"The advice you've just given me is sound, but too general. What do you suggest I do right now, after all my wasted time and cheated hopes? The fleeting blossom, you know, the briefest part of our limited and unhappy life, is speeding to an end. While we drink and call for garlands and perfumes and girls, old age is creeping up, undetected."

[24] See 6.320n.

[25] Line 119: "for that reason, so you can ignore the tongue of your slave."

[26] Lines 122–3: "Yet worse still is the situation of the man who cannot be free from those he keeps alive with his bread and cash."

130 Ne trepida, numquam pathicus tibi derit amicus
  stantibus et salvis his collibus; undique ad illos
  conveniunt et carpentis et navibus omnes
  qui digito scalpunt uno caput. altera maior
  spes superest [tu tantum erucis inprime dentem]

     * * * * *

134A gratus eris: tu tantum erucis inprime dentem.
 135 "Haec exempla para felicibus; at mea Clotho
  et Lachesis gaudent, si pascitur inguine venter.
  o parvi nostrique Lares, quos ture minuto
  aut farre et tenui soleo exorare corona,
  quando ego figam aliquid quo sit mihi tuta senectus
140 a tegete et baculo? viginti milia fenus
  pigneribus positis, argenti vascula puri,
  sed quae Fabricius censor notet, et duo fortes
  de grege Moesorum, qui me cervice locata
  securum iubeant clamoso insistere Circo;
145 sit mihi praeterea curvus caelator, et alter
  qui multas facies pingit cito; sufficiunt haec.
  quando ego pauper ero? votum miserabile, nec spes
  his saltem; nam cum pro me Fortuna vocatur,
  adfixit ceras illa de nave petitas
150 quae Siculos cantus effugit remige surdo."

   132 conveniunt Φ: convenient PAΣ
   134 tu tantum erucis inprime dentem PΦ: turbae, properat
quae crescere, molli *Housman*   *post* 134 lacuna *nonnullorum*
versuum Ribbeck   134A *exstat* PA, *om.* Φ

---

  27 For the Romans, a classic sign of an effeminate.
  28 Lacuna after 134 with the sense: "get into the good books of
rich old women, like X, Y, and Z."

Don't worry, you'll never be without a pathic patron as long as these hills stay standing. From all over the world they come here in their carriages and ships, everyone who scratches his head with one finger.[27] There's one other prospect which is even better: * * * .[28] You'll be most welcome. Just keep on chewing that love salad.[29]

"Keep those examples of yours for the lucky ones. My Clotho and Lachesis[30] are pleased if my cock can feed my belly. Ah, my own tiny Hearth Gods (I always make my requests with a few grains of incense or meal and a simple garland), when will I ever make a catch that will save my old age from the beggar's mat and stick? All I want is an income of twenty thousand from secure investments, some silver cups, plain, but the sort that would be banned by the censor Fabricius,[31] and two hefty bodyguards from the Moesian gang to enable me to take my place safely in my hired litter at the noisy racecourse. In addition, I'd like an engraver, stooped by his work, and an artist who can do multiple portraits in moments. That's enough. But when will I even be poor? It's a feeble prayer, with little hope of success. The trouble is that when Fortune is summoned on my behalf, she has already plugged her ears with wax fetched from the ship which escaped from the songs of Sicily thanks to its deaf crew."[32]

---

[29] The green vegetable arugula was and still is regarded as an aphrodisiac.   [30] Two of the three Fates.

[31] Gaius Fabricius Luscinus, censor in 275 B.C., strictly enforced the rules on the permitted amount of silver plate.

[32] Ulysses gave his crew earplugs so that they would not be bewitched by the Sirens' song as they sailed past Sicily (Hom. *Od.* 12).

NOTE ON SATIRE 10

This poem, which opens Book Four, is presented as a kind of didactic "sermon," reminiscent of Horace's diatribe satires (*Satires* 1.1–3) and his "sermons" of second-hand philosophers (*Satires* 2.3, 4, and 7). The theme of Satire 10 is the objects and folly of prayer, and it is perhaps best known by the title of Samuel Johnson's imitation, *The Vanity of Human Wishes*. The poem is clearly structured with sections on power (56–113), eloquence (114–32), military success (133–87), long life (188–288), and beauty (289–345). These follow an introduction (1–53) which first raises the central question "What is rational about our fears and desires?" (4–5) and then suggests the dangers of asking for wealth in particular. After establishing a new persona based on the philosopher Democritus, who laughed at everything he saw people do (28–53), Juvenal asks: "So what are the pointless and damaging things that people ask for? What are the right reasons for covering the knees of the gods with wax?" (54–5) In each of the sections that follows, he exposes the "fog of confusion" with which people surround themselves and at the end gently mocks the entire process of prayer (346–53). He adds a list of positive suggestions of the best objects of prayer (356–62). But the irreverence of the description of the act of prayer (354–5)— "Yet, to actually give you something to ask for and some

reason to offer the guts and sacred little sausages of a shin-
ing white piglet at the little shrines," the prelude to the line
which is probably the best-known quotation from Juvenal,
"you should pray for a sound mind in a sound body" (*mens
sana in corpore sano* 356)—together with the wry tone of
the ending (363–6), with its suggestion that people make
things worse for themselves, both detract from the serious-
ness of the advice.

SATIRE 10

Omnibus in terris, quae sunt a Gadibus usque
Auroram et Gangen, pauci dinoscere possunt
vera bona atque illis multum diversa, remota
erroris nebula. quid enim ratione timemus
5 aut cupimus? quid tam dextro pede concipis ut te
conatus non paeniteat votique peracti?
evertere domos totas optantibus ipsis
di faciles. nocitura toga, nocitura petuntur
militia; torrens dicendi copia multis
10 et sua mortifera est facundia; viribus ille
confisus periit admirandisque lacertis;
sed pluris nimia congesta pecunia cura
strangulat et cuncta exuperans patrimonia census
quanto delphinis ballaena Britannica maior.
15 temporibus diris igitur iussuque Neronis
Longinum et magnos Senecae praedivitis hortos
claudit et egregias Lateranorum obsidet aedes
tota cohors: rarus venit in cenacula miles.
pauca licet portes argenti vascula puri

---

1 The wrestler Milo of Croton.

SATIRE 10

In all the lands extending from Cadiz as far as Ganges
and the Dawn, there are few people who can remove the
fog of confusion and distinguish real benefits from their
opposite. After all, what is rational about our fears and
desires? When you begin a project, how often is your prog-
ress so good that you don't regret the effort or the ac-
complishment of your wish? Entire households have been
wrecked by gods actually complying with their occupants'
own prayers. In peacetime and in war, people ask for things
that will do them damage. To many people, their torrential
flood of speech and their own eloquence is fatal. In one
case, a man died from relying on his strength and awe-
inspiring muscles.[1] More people still are suffocated by
money accumulated with too much care, by wealth that
goes beyond all other fortunes—as huge as the British
whale compared with dolphins. That explains why, in those
times of terror, on Nero's orders, an entire cohort sur-
rounded Longinus[2] and the vast gardens belonging to Sen-
eca the millionaire, and besieged the splendid house of the
Laterani. Rarely does a soldier enter a garret. Though
you're carrying only a few cups of plain silver when you set

[2] Gaius Cassius Longinus was a lawyer exiled in A.D. 65 after
the Pisonian conspiracy.

367

20   nocte iter ingressus, gladium contumque timebis
et mota ad lunam trepidabis harundinis umbra:
cantabit vacuus coram latrone viator.
prima fere vota et cunctis notissima templis
divitiae, crescant ut opes, ut maxima toto
25   nostra sit arca foro. sed nulla aconita bibuntur
fictilibus; tunc illa time cum pocula sumes
gemmata et lato Setinum ardebit in auro.
      Iamne igitur laudas quod de sapientibus alter
ridebat, quotiens a limine moverat unum
30   protuleratque pedem, flebat contrarius alter?
sed facilis cuivis rigidi censura cachinni:
mirandum est unde illi oculis suffecerit umor.
perpetuo risu pulmonem agitare solebat
Democritus, quamquam non essent urbibus illis
35   praetextae, trabeae, fasces, lectica, tribunal.
quid si vidisset praetorem curribus altis
extantem et medii sublimem pulvere Circi
in tunica Iovis et pictae Sarrana ferentem
ex umeris aulaea togae magnaeque coronae
40   tantum orbem, quanto cervix non sufficit ulla?
quippe tenet sudans hanc publicus et, sibi †consul†
ne placeat, curru servus portatur eodem.
da nunc et volucrem, sceptro quae surgit eburno,

       30 alter Φ: auctor PAGU
       32 illi *Braund*: ille *codd*.
       41 consul *codd*.: praeses *Courtney*

---

    3 Two philosophers, Democritus (born c. 460 B.C. in Thrace)
and the Presocratic Heraclitus of Ephesus (sixth century B.C.).

out on a journey at night, you'll be terrified of swords and
sticks, and you'll panic at the twitch of a reed's shadow in
the moonlight. A traveller who is empty-handed can sing
in the mugger's face. Prayer no. 1, so very familiar in all
the temples, is usually for money: "Let my wealth grow!"
"Let my treasure chest be the biggest in the whole forum!"
But you won't drink poison from earthenware. That you
only need fear when you are handed a goblet studded with
jewels, and when Setian wine glows in your golden bowl.

So now do you approve the two philosophers? One of
them would laugh whenever he stretched and stirred one
foot from his threshold, while his opposite number would
cry.[3] But anyone can easily condemn with a sardonic laugh;
what is amazing is where all the liquid flooding his eyes
came from. Democritus' sides shook with nonstop laugh-
ter, even though the cities of his day didn't have togas with
purple edges, and togas with purple stripes, and rods of of-
fice, and litters, and daises. What if he'd seen our praetor
standing conspicuously up there in his tall chariot, in the
thick of the Circus dust, wearing the tunic of Jupiter, with
the Tyrian hangings of an embroidered toga falling from
his shoulders and a huge crown so big around that no neck
is strong enough for it?[4] In fact, a public slave holds it,
sweating profusely, and—so the president doesn't get too
pleased with himself—he rides in the same vehicle. Throw
in the bird that soars from his ivory sceptre, the horn-play-

Juvenal is inspired by Seneca's contrast between them at *Tranq.
An.* 15.2. Democritus is depicted as the laughing philosopher at
Hor. *Ep.* 2.1.194.

[4] The occasion is the procession at the Ludi Romani, over
which the urban praetor presided.

illinc cornicines, hinc praecedentia longi
45 agminis officia et niveos ad frena Quirites,
defossa in loculos quos sportula fecit amicos.
tum quoque materiam risus invenit ad omnis
occursus hominum, cuius prudentia monstrat
summos posse viros et magna exempla daturos
50 vervecum in patria crassoque sub aere nasci.
ridebat curas nec non et gaudia volgi,
interdum et lacrimas, cum Fortunae ipse minaci
mandaret laqueum mediumque ostenderet unguem.
Ergo supervacua aut quae perniciosa petuntur?
55 propter quae fas est genua incerare deorum?
Quosdam praecipitat subiecta potentia magnae
invidiae, mergit longa atque insignis honorum
pagina. descendunt statuae restemque secuntur,
ipsas deinde rotas bigarum inpacta securis
60 caedit et inmeritis franguntur crura caballis.
iam strident ignes, iam follibus atque caminis
ardet adoratum populo caput et crepat ingens
Seianus, deinde ex facie toto orbe secunda
fiunt urceoli, pelves, sartago, matellae.
65 pone domi laurus, duc in Capitolia magnum
cretatumque bovem: Seianus ducitur unco
spectandus, gaudent omnes. "quae labra, quis illi
vultus erat! numquam, si quid mihi credis, amavi

---

5 Abdera in Thrace had a reputation for stupidity, despite being the birthplace of Democritus and Protagoras.

6 An obscene gesture then as now.

7 Wax tablets with requests written on them were placed on the knees of gods' statues.

ers there, here the escort in long lines walking ahead of him and the snowy white citizens at his bridle, transformed into friends by the handouts buried inside their purses. Democritus in his time, too, found things to laugh at in every encounter with people. His shrewdness demonstrates that men of excellence, who will make great role models, can be born in a dense climate in a country of morons.[5] He would laugh at the anxieties of the mob and at their delights, too, and sometimes at their tears, while to Fortune's threats he himself would say, "Go throttle yourself!" and show his middle finger at her.[6]

So what are the pointless and damaging things that people ask for? What are the right reasons for covering the knees of the gods with wax?[7]

Some people are toppled by their power, object of great envy, some are sunk by their long and glorious roll of honours. Down their statues come, dragged by a rope, then even the chariot's wheels are smashed and slashed by the axe, and the legs of the innocent nags are shattered. Now the flames are hissing, now that head idolised by the people is glowing from the bellows and furnace: huge Sejanus is crackling.[8] Then the face that was number two in the whole world is turned into little jugs, basins, frying pans, and chamber pots. Hang your homes with laurel, drag a huge bull, whitened with chalk, up to the Capitol! Sejanus is being dragged by a hook—a sight worth seeing. Everyone's celebrating. "Look at his lips! Look at his face! Take it from me, I never liked the man." "But what was the

[8] Lucius Aelius Sejanus, the praetorian prefect who virtually ran the empire for Tiberius, especially after his retirement to Capri. His ambition led to his execution in A.D. 31.

hunc hominem." "sed quo cecidit sub crimine? quisnam
70   delator quibus indicibus, quo teste probavit?"
"nil horum; verbosa et grandis epistula venit
a Capreis." "bene habet, nil plus interrogo." sed quid
turba Remi? sequitur fortunam, ut semper, et odit
damnatos. idem populus, si Nortia Tusco
75   favisset, si oppressa foret secura senectus
principis, hac ipsa Seianum diceret hora
Augustum. iam pridem, ex quo suffragia nulli
vendimus, effudit curas; nam qui dabat olim
imperium, fasces, legiones, omnia, nunc se
80   continet atque duas tantum res anxius optat,
panem et circenses. "perituros audio multos."
"nil dubium, magna est fornacula." "pallidulus mi
Bruttidius meus ad Martis fuit obvius aram;
quam timeo, victus ne poenas exigat Aiax
85   ut male defensus. curramus praecipites et,
dum iacet in ripa, calcemus Caesaris hostem.
sed videant servi, ne quis neget et pavidum in ius
cervice obstricta dominum trahat." hi sermones
tunc de Seiano, secreta haec murmura volgi.

85 ut male defensus Φ: a male defensis *Hendry*

---

9 Ordinary Romans; Remus was Romulus' brother.

10 Nortia was the Etruscan goddess of Fortune; Sejanus was
from Volsinii in Etruria.   11 Tiberius transferred elections
of magistrates from the people to the Senate in A.D. 14.

12 I.e. corn doles and the chariot races at the Circus Maximus.

13 The orator Bruttidius Niger was evidently an accuser of vic-
tims of Sejanus and after Sejanus' fall was therefore at risk from
reprisals by Tiberius.

charge that brought him down? Who informed on him?
What was the evidence and the witnesses that were used to
prove the case?" "Nothing like that. An enormous, wordy
letter came from Capri." "All right, no more questions."
But what of Remus' mob?[9] They are followers of Fortune,
as always, and hate those who are condemned. This same
crowd, if Nortia had supported her Etruscan,[10] if the aged
emperor had been smothered off his guard, would be hail-
ing Sejanus as Augustus within minutes. It's way back that
they discarded their responsibilities—since the time we
stopped selling our votes.[11] The proof? The people that
once used to bestow military commands, high office, le-
gions, everything, now limits itself. It has an obsessive de-
sire for two things only—bread and circuses.[12] "I hear
many are to die." "No doubt about it. The furnace is huge."
"My friend Bruttidius looked rather pale when I met him
at the altar of Mars.[13] I'm terribly frightened that 'defeated
Ajax' will take reprisals for being badly defended.[14] Let's
get a move on and trample on Caesar's enemy while he's ly-
ing on the riverbank. But make sure our slaves see us, so
they can't deny it and drag their terrified master to court
with a noose around his neck." Those were their remarks
about Sejanus at that time, those were the secret whispers
of the mob.

[14] "Defeated Ajax" is an oblique reference to Tiberius: Ajax
tried to kill the umpires after they awarded the arms of Achilles
to his rival Ulysses, but in a fit of madness killed the domestic
animals instead. According to Suetonius (61–2), Tiberius' cruelty
increased after Sejanus' death.

90　　Visne salutari sicut Seianus, habere
　　　tantundem atque illi summas donare curules,
　　　illum exercitibus praeponere, tutor haberi
　　　principis angusta Caprearum in rupe sedentis
　　　cum grege Chaldaeo? vis certe pila, cohortis,
95　　egregios equites et castra domestica; quidni
　　　haec cupias? et qui nolunt occidere quemquam
　　　posse volunt. sed quae praeclara et prospera tanti,
　　　ut rebus laetis par sit mensura malorum?
　　　huius qui trahitur praetextam sumere mavis
100　 an Fidenarum Gabiorumque esse potestas
　　　et de mensura ius dicere, vasa minora
　　　frangere pannosus vacuis aedilis Vlubris?
　　　ergo quid optandum foret ignorasse fateris
　　　Seianum? nam qui nimios optabat honores
105　 et nimias poscebat opes, numerosa parabat
　　　excelsae turris tabulata, unde altior esset
　　　casus et inpulsae praeceps inmane ruinae.
　　　quid Crassos, quid Pompeios evertit et illum,
　　　ad sua qui domitos deduxit flagra Quirites?
110　 summus nempe locus nulla non arte petitus
　　　magnaque numinibus vota exaudita malignis.
　　　ad generum Cereris sine caede ac sanguine pauci
　　　descendunt reges et sicca morte tyranni.
　　　　　Eloquium ac famam Demosthenis aut Ciceronis
115　 incipit optare et totis quinquatribus optat

112 sanguine GU: vulnere PΦ

---

15 Astrologers.
16 All small, depopulated towns in Latium.

374

Do you wish to be greeted like Sejanus? To be as rich? To dispense the seats of highest office to some, and to appoint others to army commands? To be seen as the emperor's guardian as he sits on the narrow rock of Capri with his herd of Chaldaeans?[15] I'm sure you'd like his javelins and cohorts and excellent cavalry and personal barracks. Why shouldn't you? Even people with no desire to kill like to have the power to do so. But what prestige and prosperity is worth having, if success is matched by an equal measure of disasters? Would you prefer to wear the purple-edged toga of the man you see being dragged along, to being "the boss" at Fidenae or Gabii, to laying down the law over weights and measures, to smashing short vessels as aedile-in-rags at deserted Ulubrae?[16] So will you admit that Sejanus didn't know what to ask for? Let me explain: he kept asking for more and more honours and demanding more and more wealth. In so doing, he was building a high-rise multistorey tower, and from there the fall would be greater and the collapse of the toppled ruin terrible. What was it that demolished the Crassi, the Pompeys, and the man who tamed the citizens of Rome and brought them under his lash?[17] Nothing else but the top position, sought by every trick in the book. Nothing else but ambitious prayers granted by malicious gods. Few kings go down to Ceres' son-in-law[18] without slaughter and carnage, few tyrants avoid a bloodless death.

The eloquence and reputation of Demosthenes or Cicero is what boys keep on praying for throughout the spring

[17] Caesar, who with Pompey and Crassus made up the so-called First Triumvirate.

[18] Pluto, king of the Underworld.

quisquis adhuc uno parcam colit asse Minervam,
quem sequitur custos angustae vernula capsae.
eloquio sed uterque perit orator, utrumque
largus et exundans leto dedit ingenii fons.
120 ingenio manus est et cervix caesa, nec umquam
sanguine causidici maduerunt rostra pusilli.
"o fortunatam natam me consule Romam":
Antoni gladios potuit contemnere si sic
omnia dixisset. ridenda poemata malo
125 quam te, conspicuae divina Philippica famae,
volveris a prima quae proxima. saevus et illum
exitus eripuit, quem mirabantur Athenae
torquentem et pleni moderantem frena theatri.
dis ille adversis genitus fatoque sinistro,
130 quem pater ardentis massae fuligine lippus
a carbone et forcipibus gladiosque paranti
incude et luteo Volcano ad rhetora misit.
  Bellorum exuviae, truncis adfixa tropaeis
lorica et fracta de casside buccula pendens
135 et curtum temone iugum victaeque triremis
aplustre et summa tristis captivos in arce

128 torquentem *Markland*: torrentem *codd.*
136 summa . . . arce *Braund*: summo . . . arcu *codd.*

---

19 The feast of Minerva, the goddess of learning, March 19th-23rd, was kept as a holiday by teachers.
20 Cicero's opposition to Antony culminated in his death in 43 B.C., after which his head and hands were fixed to the platform where he had so often delivered speeches.
21 An inept line from Cicero's poem *De consulatu suo* ("On His Own Consulship").

holidays, every boy who goes to school accompanied by a house slave to guard his narrow satchel and who still worships thrifty Minerva with a single tiny coin.[19] But it was because of their eloquence that both orators died. It was the abundant, overflowing gush of talent that sent both to their deaths. It was talent that had its hands and neck severed.[20] The rostrum was never drenched in the blood of a feeble advocate. "O Rome, you are fortunate, born in my consulate."[21] He could have laughed at Antony's swords if everything he said had been like this. I rank his ridiculous verses above you, immortal *Philippic*, next to the first on the roll, with your distinguished reputation.[22] A harsh death snatched him away, too, the object of Athens' admiration when he was twisting and controlling the reins of her packed assembly.[23] He was born with the gods against him and a malignant fate, and was sent off by his father to the professor of rhetoric, away from the coal and tongs and sword-manufacturing anvil and filthy Vulcan, eyes running from the soot of the glowing ore.[24]

The trophies of war—the breastplate fastened to a bare tree trunk, a cheekpiece hanging from a shattered helmet, a chariot's yoke missing its pole, a stern ornament from a defeated warship, a dejected prisoner at the citadel's

[22] Cicero's speeches against Antony were called *Philippics*, a title taken from Demosthenes' speeches against Philip. The second *Philippic* was widely admired.

[23] After his speeches against Philip of Macedon, Demosthenes poisoned himself in 322 B.C. to avoid capture by the Macedonians.

[24] Demosthenes' father was a wealthy businessman who owned a sword factory.

humanis maiora bonis creduntur. ad hoc se
Romanus Graiusque et barbarus induperator
erexit, causas discriminis atque laboris
140 inde habuit: tanto maior famae sitis est quam
virtutis. quis enim virtutem amplectitur ipsam,
praemia si tollas? patriam tamen obruit olim
gloria paucorum et laudis titulique cupido
haesuri saxis cinerum custodibus, ad quae
145 discutienda valent sterilis mala robora fici,
quandoquidem data sunt ipsis quoque fata sepulcris.
　　Expende Hannibalem: quot libras in duce summo
invenies? hic est quem non capit Africa Mauro
percussa oceano Niloque admota tepenti
150 rursus ad Aethiopum populos aliosque elephantos.
additur imperiis Hispania, Pyrenaeum
transilit. opposuit natura Alpemque nivemque:
diducit scopulos et montem rumpit aceto.
iam tenet Italiam, tamen ultra pergere tendit.
155 "acti" inquit "nihil est, nisi Poeno milite portas
frangimus et media vexillum pono Subura."
o qualis facies et quali digna tabella,
cum Gaetula ducem portaret belua luscum!
exitus ergo quis est? o gloria! vincitur idem

150 aliosque Φ: altosque PA

25 The great Carthaginian general who occupied Italy for six-
teen years during the Second Punic War (late third century B.C.).
26 Pliny seems to distinguish three different provenances (and
perhaps kinds) of elephants (*N.H.* 8.32): Africa, Ethiopia, and
India.

height—these are considered glories more than human.
It is for these that the commander, Roman or Greek or
foreign, exerts himself. These give him the incentive for
his danger and hard work. That's how much more intense
is the thirst for fame than for goodness. After all, who em-
braces goodness for itself, if you remove its rewards? Yet
there have been times when a country has been sunk by
the ambition of a few, by their lust for renown and for an
inscription to cling to the stones that guard their ashes,
stones that can be split open by the evil strength of the bar-
ren fig tree, seeing that even graves have been allotted
their own lifespan.

Put Hannibal in the scales:[25] how much will you find
the greatest general weighs? This is the man too big for
Africa—a country pounded by the Moroccan ocean and
stretching to the warm Nile down to the tribes of the Ethi-
opians and different elephants.[26] Spain increases his em-
pire and he vaults the Pyrenees. Nature throws the Alps
and snow in his path: he splits the rocks and bursts through
the mountain with vinegar.[27] Already he has Italy, yet he
aims to advance further still. "I have achieved nothing," he
says, "unless our Carthaginian army shatters the city gates,
unless I plant my banner right in the Subura." What a
sight! And what a cartoon it would've made—the one-eyed
general riding on his Gaetulian beast![28] So how does it
end? O glory! This same man is defeated[29] and he sits, a

[27] See Livy 21.37.

[28] An African elephant from Mauretania.

[29] Line 160: "of course. He beats a speedy retreat into exile
[and] there [he sits], an important and."

160 [nempe et in exilium praeceps fugit atque ibi magnus]
mirandusque cliens sedet ad praetoria regis,
donec Bithyno libeat vigilare tyranno.
finem animae, quae res humanas miscuit olim,
non gladii, non saxa dabunt nec tela, sed ille
165 Cannarum vindex et tanti sanguinis ultor
anulus. i, demens, et saevas curre per Alpes
ut pueris placeas et declamatio fias.
    Vnus Pellaeo iuveni non sufficit orbis,
aestuat infelix angusto limite mundi
170 ut Gyarae clausus scopulis parvaque Seripho;
cum tamen a figulis munitam intraverit urbem,
sarcophago contentus erit. mors sola fatetur
quantula sint hominum corpuscula. creditur olim
velificatus Athos et quidquid Graecia mendax
175 audet in historia, constratum classibus †isdem†
suppositumque rotis solidum mare; credimus altos
defecisse amnes epotaque flumina Medo
prandente et madidis cantat quae Sostratus alis.
ille tamen qualis rediit Salamine relicta,
180 in Corum atque Eurum solitus saevire flagellis

160 *del. Nisbet*   175 isdem P: idem AFG

---

30 After his defeat at Zama in 202 B.C., Hannibal left Carthage
in 193 for the court of Prusias of Bithynia; he committed suicide
some ten years later.

31 His poison was kept in a signet ring. This is fitting revenge:
after Hannibal's victory over Rome at Cannae in 216 B.C. he sent
home rings taken from the Roman dead.

32 Alexander the Great (356–323 B.C.), born in Pella, Macedo-
nia, who conquered the Greek world and Asia as far as India.

conspicuous dependant, at the king's mansion, waiting until his Bithynian majesty chooses to wake.[30] That life once caused havoc for humanity, but its end will come not from swords or rocks or missiles. No, it will be that famous avenger of Cannae, retaliating for all the bloodshed—a little ring.[31] Off you go, you maniac, zoom through the hostile Alps—to entertain schoolboys and to be put into their speeches.

One world is not enough for the young man from Pella.[32] In discontent he seethes at the narrow limits of the universe as if confined on the rocks of Gyara or tiny Seriphus.[33] But once he's entered the city that's fortified by potters, his coffin will be big enough.[34] It's only death that reveals the minuscule size of human bodies. The stories of Mount Athos once taking sail and all the other lies that Greece dares tell as history are believed—of the sea being paved by the fleets and made into a solid ground for wheels.[35] We believe the stories of deep rivers running dry and streams being drunk up by the Medes at lunch—and all the songs recited by Sostratus with his armpits drenched.[36] Yet in what state did he come back from abandoning Salamis?[37] He'd made a habit of venting his barbaric rage by lashing the winds Corus and Eurus, who'd

[33] Small islands used for imprisonment.

[34] He died in Babylon, a city built of bricks.

[35] Stories about Xerxes, king of Persia, told by Herodotus (7.21–37): on his expedition against Greece in 480 B.C., he crossed the Hellespont on a bridge made of ships and sailed through a canal across the isthmus of Athos. Medes = Persians.

[36] An unknown poet.   [37] Xerxes, defeated at the battle of Salamis near Athens in 480 B.C.

barbarus, Aeolio numquam hoc in carcere passos,
ipsum conpedibus qui vinxerat Ennosigaeum
(mitius id sane. quid? non et stigmate dignum
credidit? huic quisquam vellet servire deorum?)—
185   sed qualis rediit? nempe una nave, cruentis
fluctibus ac tarda per densa cadavera prora.
has totiens optata exegit gloria poenas.
    "Da spatium vitae, multos da, Iuppiter, annos."
[hoc recto voltu, solum hoc et pallidus optas.]
190   sed quam continuis et quantis longa senectus
plena malis! deformem et taetrum ante omnia vultum
dissimilemque sui, deformem pro cute pellem
pendentisque genas et talis aspice rugas
quales, umbriferos ubi pandit Thabraca saltus,
195   in vetula scalpit iam mater simia bucca.
plurima sunt iuvenum discrimina, pulchrior ille
hoc atque ille alio, multum hic robustior illo:
una senum facies, cum voce trementia membra
et iam leve caput madidique infantia nasi;
200   frangendus misero gingiva panis inermi.
usque adeo gravis uxori natisque sibique,
ut captatori moveat fastidia Cosso.
non eadem vini atque cibi torpente palato
gaudia; nam coitus iam longa oblivio, vel si
205   coneris, iacet exiguus cum ramice nervus
et, quamvis tota palpetur nocte, iacebit.
anne aliud sperare potest haec inguinis aegri

183 quid? *Weber*: quod *codd.*
189 *del. Guyet, Markland*
197 ille Φ: *om.* PO
207 aliud *Hendry*: aliquid *codd.*

382

never experienced anything like it in their Aeolian prison. He'd thrown the Earth-Shaker himself[38] into chains. (That was rather lenient. Why? Didn't he think he deserved being branded too? Which of the gods would choose to be this man's slave?) But what state was he in? In a single ship, as you know, with the waves bloodstained and the prow slowly proceeding through the jammed corpses. Such so often is the price of prayers for glory.

"Give me a long life, Jupiter, give me many years."[39] But just think of the many, never ending disadvantages an extended old age is full of! Take a look at its face, first of all—ugly and hideous and unrecognisable—and the ugly hide in place of skin and the drooping jowls and the wrinkles. The mother ape scratches wrinkles like those on her aged cheek in the extensive shady groves of Thabraca.[40] There are so many differences between young men: he is better looking than him and he than another, he is much more sturdy than him. But old men all look the same: voice and body trembling alike, head now quite smooth, a baby's dripping nose. The pathetic creature has to munch his bread with weaponless gums. He's so disgusting to his wife and kids and to himself that he makes even Cossus the fortune-hunter feel sick. The delights of food and wine are no longer the same as his palate grows numb, and as for sex—it's now just a distant memory, or if you try to rouse him, his stringy little prick lies limp with its enlarged vein and will stay limp though you coax it all night long. Or is there anything else these sickly white-haired genitals can hope for?

---

[38] Neptune.   [39] Line 189: "This is the only thing you pray for when you're feeling assertive or you're pale with anxiety."

[40] On the coast of Numidia, North Africa, mod. Tabarka.

canities? quid quod merito suspecta libido est
quae venerem adfectat sine viribus?

                       Aspice partis
210   nunc damnum alterius. nam quae cantante voluptas,
sit licet eximius, citharoedo sive Seleuco
et quibus aurata mos est fulgere lacerna?
quid refert, magni sedeat qua parte theatri
qui vix cornicines exaudiet atque tubarum
215   concentus? clamore opus est ut sentiat auris
quem dicat venisse puer, quot nuntiet horas.
praeterea minimus gelido iam in corpore sanguis
febre calet sola, circumsilit agmine facto
morborum omne genus, quorum si nomina quaeras,
220   promptius expediam quot amaverit Oppia moechos,
quot Themison aegros autumno occiderit uno,
quot Basilus socios, quot circumscripserit Hirrus
pupillos, quot larga viros exorbeat uno
Maura die, quot discipulos inclinet Hamillus;
225   percurram citius quot villas possideat nunc
quo tondente gravis iuveni mihi barba sonabat.
ille umero, hic lumbis, hic coxa debilis; ambos
perdidit ille oculos et luscis invidet; huius
pallida labra cibum accipiunt digitis alienis,
230   ipse ad conspectum cenae diducere rictum
suetus hiat tantum ceu pullus hirundinis, ad quem
ore volat pleno mater ieiuna. sed omni
membrorum damno maior dementia, quae nec

223 larga *Hendry*: longa *codd.*
233 maior *codd.*: peior *Guyet* | quae *codd.*: qua *Scholte*

---

41 I.e. oral sex.

Then there's the fact that lust that attempts sex without the strength is (quite rightly) suspect.[41]

Now take a look at the loss of another faculty. For example: what pleasure is there in music, even though the singer is superlative, or in Seleucus the lyre-player,[42] or the pipers in the glittering golden cloaks? What difference does it make where he sits in the huge theatre if he can hardly hear the horn-players or the fanfare of trumpets? The slave boy has to shout to make his ear hear his visitor's name or what time it is. Besides, the little blood in his already icy body warms up only with fever. All types of disease dance around him in a troop. If you ask their names, I could sooner state the number of Oppia's lovers, of Themison's patients murdered in a single autumn, of the partners swindled by Basilus and the wards swindled by Hirrus, the number of men sucked off by generous Maura in a single day, the number of pupils laid by Hamillus.[43] I could more rapidly run through the number of villas now owned by the man who made my stiff beard rasp when he shaved me as a young man. One is crippled in his shoulder, another in the groin, another in the hip. The loss of both eyes makes this man jealous of one-eyed men. That man takes food in his bloodless lips from someone else's fingers. He used to split his jaws wide at the sight of dinner but now just gapes like a swallow's chick when his fasting mother flies to him with her mouth full. But worse than any physical decline is the dementia. It doesn't remember the

[42] Unknown.

[43] It is difficult to connect these names with specific individuals. Themison is the name of a physician of the first century B.C.

nomina servorum nec voltum agnoscit amici
235   cum quo praeterita cenavit nocte, nec illos
quos genuit, quos eduxit. nam codice saevo
heredes vetat esse suos, bona tota feruntur
ad Phialen; tantum artificis valet halitus oris,
quod steterat multis in carcere fornicis annis.
240   Vt vigeant sensus animi, ducenda tamen sunt
funera natorum, rogus aspiciendus amatae
coniugis et fratris plenaeque sororibus urnae.
haec data poena diu viventibus, ut renovata
semper clade domus multis in luctibus inque
245   perpetuo maerore et nigra veste senescant.
rex Pylius, magno si quicquam credis Homero,
exemplum vitae fuit a cornice secundae.
felix nimirum, qui tot per saecula mortem
distulit atque suos iam dextra conputat annos,
250   quique novum totiens mustum bibit. oro parumper
attendas quantum de legibus ipse queratur
fatorum et nimio de stamine, cum videt acris
Antilochi barbam ardentem, cum quaerit ab omni
quisquis adest socio cur haec in tempora duret,
255   quod facinus dignum tam longo admiserit aevo.
haec eadem Peleus, raptum cum luget Achillem,
atque alius, cui fas Ithacum lugere natantem.
incolumi Troia Priamus venisset ad umbras
Assaraci magnis sollemnibus, Hectore funus
260   portante ac reliquis fratrum cervicibus inter

---

44 Nestor, who ruled over three generations. The crow was
thought to live for nine generations.
45 The "right hand" (*dextra*) was used to count hundreds and
thousands.

names of slaves or recognise the face of a friend who dined
with him the previous evening or the children he fathered
and raised himself. You see, in a cruel will, he keeps his
own children from becoming his heirs and leaves every-
thing to Phiale. That's the power of the breath of her skilful
mouth, which was for sale for many years in the brothel's
den.

Although his mental powers are still alert, yet he'll have
to lead the funerals of his sons and gaze at the pyre of his
beloved wife or brother and urns that contain his sisters.
This is the price of long life—to grow old with domestic di-
saster continually renewed, with grief after grief, perma-
nent mourning, and black clothing. The king of Pylos, if
you believe great Homer at all, was an example of survival
second only to the crow.[44] And of course he was happy. He
put off death for so many generations, counted his years by
the hundreds,[45] and so often drank the new vintage. Pay at-
tention, please, for a moment to the complaints he himself
voices about the decrees of fate and his overlong thread of
life at the sight of his spirited Antilochus' beard on fire,[46]
questioning every companion present as to why he has sur-
vived to see this day and what crime he has committed to
deserve such a long lifespan. This was exactly what Peleus
said when he mourned the loss of Achilles. So, too, the
other father who rightly mourned his floating Ithacan.[47]
Priam would have joined the shade of Assaracus[48] with
grand ceremonial—while Troy was still standing, his body
conveyed by Hector and the other brothers' shoulders,

[46] Nestor's son, killed at Troy before he had started to shave.
[47] Laertes, the father of Odysseus, who mistakenly mourned
his son too soon.   [48] Son of Tros, the founder of Troy.

Iliadum lacrimas, ut primos edere planctus
Cassandra inciperet scissaque Polyxena palla,
si foret extinctus diverso tempore, quo non
coeperat audaces Paris aedificare carinas.
265 longa dies igitur quid contulit? omnia vidit
eversa et flammis Asiam ferroque cadentem.
tunc miles tremulus posita tulit arma tiara
et ruit ante aram summi Iovis ut vetulus bos,
qui domini cultris tenue et miserabile collum
270 praebet ab ingrato iam fastiditus aratro.
exitus illi utcumque hominis, sed torva canino
latravit rictu quae post hunc vixerat uxor.
    Festino ad nostros et regem transeo Ponti
et Croesum, quem vox iusti facunda Solonis
275 respicere ad longae iussit spatia ultima vitae.
exilium et carcer Minturnarumque paludes
et mendicatus victa Carthagine panis
hinc causas habuere; quid illo cive tulisset
natura in terris, quid Roma beatius umquam,
280 si circumducto captivorum agmine et omni
bellorum pompa animam exhalasset opimam,
cum de Teutonico vellet descendere curru?
provida Pompeio dederat Campania febres

271 illi *Willis*: ille *codd*.

---

49 Hector, Cassandra, and Polyxena were all children of Priam. So too was Paris, who caused the Trojan War by abducting Helen.

50 Hecuba, Priam's wife, was taken prisoner by the Greeks. She was supposedly later transformed into a dog.

51 Mithridates, king of Pontus (see 6.661n.), was a classic example of long life. For the meeting between the lawgiver Solon

accompanied by the tears of the Trojan women, with the first cries of lamentation initiated by Cassandra and Polyxena, her cloak torn—if he had died at a different time, before Paris had begun to construct his daring ships.[49] What advantages, then, did his long life bring? He saw everything wrecked and Asia collapsing by fire and sword. Then a doddering soldier, he removed his crown, took up his weapons, and fell in front of the altar of highest Jupiter, like a decrepit ox, now rejected by the ungrateful plough, that offers its pitiful, scrawny neck to its master's knives. His end, at any rate, was the end of a human being. In contrast, the wife that survived him opened her bitch's jaws and barked fiercely.[50]

I pass over the King of Pontus and Croesus, who was told by the eloquent voice of Solon the Just to take a good look at the final portions of a long life, and turn rapidly to Roman examples.[51] This was the cause of exile, prison, Minturnine marshes, and begging for bread in defeated Carthage.[52] Is there anything more wonderful that nature or Rome could have ever given the world than that citizen—had he breathed out his triumphal soul after the procession of the line of prisoners and all the parade of war, when he was on the point of stepping down from his Teutonic chariot?[53] Campania, foreseeing the future, had granted to Pompey the fevers he should have longed for,

and Croesus, king of Lydia, in which Solon advised against using the label "fortunate" until a person was dead, see Herodotus 1.32.

[52] Events towards the end of the life of Gaius Marius (157–86 B.C.).

[53] Marius celebrated a victory over the Teutones.

optandas, sed multae urbes et publica vota
285 vicerunt; igitur Fortuna ipsius et Vrbis
servatum victo caput abstulit. hoc cruciatu
Lentulus, hac poena caruit ceciditque Cethegus
integer et iacuit Catilina cadavere toto.
  Formam optat modico pueris, maiore puellis
290 murmure, cum Veneris fanum videt, anxia mater
usque ad delicias votorum. "cur tamen" inquit
"corripias? pulchra gaudet Latona Diana."
sed vetat optari faciem Lucretia qualem
ipsa habuit, cuperet Rutilae Verginia gibbum
295 accipere osque suum Rutilae dare. filius autem
corporis egregii miseros trepidosque parentes
semper habet: rara est adeo concordia formae
atque pudicitiae. sanctos licet horrida mores
tradiderit domus ac veteres imitata Sabinos,
300 praeterea castum ingenium voltumque modesto
sanguine ferventem tribuat natura benigna
larga manu (quid enim puero conferre potest plus
custode et cura natura potentior omni?),
non licet esse viro. nam prodiga corruptoris
305 improbitas ipsos audet temptare parentes:
tanta in muneribus fiducia. nullus ephebum
deformem saeva castravit in arce tyrannus,

295 osque *Weidner*: atque PΦ

---

54 Pompey survived a serious illness at Naples in Campania in
50 B.C., but in 48 he was killed and decapitated in Egypt after
losing the battle of Pharsalus.
55 Lentulus and Cethegus, collaborators in Catiline's conspir-
acy in 63 B.C., died in prison, while Catiline fell on the battlefield.

but the public prayers of many cities prevailed.[54] The result was that, after his defeat, Fortune, his own and Rome's, severed the head which she had saved. This was a mangling, this was a punishment that Lentulus avoided; Cethegus died unmutilated and Catiline lay dead with his corpse intact.[55]

Good looks—that's what the anxious mother prays for when she sees the shrine of Venus, in a quiet whisper for her sons but more loudly for her daughters, going to the most extravagant of prayers. "Yet why do you criticise me?" she says. "Latona rejoices in her Diana's beauty." But Lucretia stops me praying for looks like hers.[56] Verginia would love to have Rutila's hump and to give Rutila her face.[57] Yes, and a son with a superlative body always makes his parents miserable and nervous, since beauty so rarely coincides with purity. Though his house has a tradition of rustic, pure morality, copying the ancient Sabines, and though kind Nature endows him generously with an innocent disposition and a face that glows with modest blushes —after all, what more can a boy receive from Nature, who is more powerful than any guardian and vigilance?—he is not permitted to take the male role.[58] The reason? The lavish unscrupulousness of the seducer, which brazenly tempts even the parents. So much confidence they have in their bribes. No ugly adolescent has ever been castrated by

[56] Lucretia was raped by Sextus Tarquinius, son of the last of the seven kings of Rome, and committed suicide afterwards: see Livy 1.57–8.   [57] Verginia was killed by her father rather than let Appius Claudius have her (Livy 3.44–51). Nothing is known of the hunchback Rutila.

[58] In sexual intercourse.

nec praetextatum rapuit Nero loripedem nec
strumosum atque utero pariter gibboque tumentem.
310 I nunc et iuvenis specie laetare tui, quem
maiora expectant discrimina. fiet adulter
publicus et poenas metuet quascumque mariti
irati reddent, nec erit felicior astro
Martis, ut in laqueos numquam incidat. exigit autem
315 interdum ille dolor plus quam lex ulla dolori
concessit: necat hic ferro, secat ille cruentis
verberibus, quosdam moechos et mugilis intrat.
sed tuus Endymion dilectae fiet adulter
matronae. mox cum dederit Servilia nummos
320 fiet et illius quam non amat, exuet omnem
corporis ornatum; quid enim ulla negaverit udis
inguinibus, sive est haec Oppia sive Catulla?
[deterior totos habet illic femina mores.]
"sed casto quid forma nocet?" quid profuit immo
325 Hippolyto grave propositum, quid Bellerophonti?
[erubuit nempe haec ceu fastidita repulso]
nec Stheneboea minus quam Cressa excanduit, et se
concussere ambae. mulier saevissima tunc est

313 irati PHT: lex irae *Housman*: ex ira *Clausen* | reddent *Harrison*: debent *debet* P
323 *del. Markland, Heinrich*
326 *del. Knoche* | nempe haec PΦ: certe FLOZ

59 The net set to catch the lovers Aphrodite (Venus) and Ares (Mars) by her husband Hephaestus (Vulcan): Hom. *Od*. 8.266–369. 60 The penalties for adultery included provision for the death of the male adulterer only if he was a slave, ex-slave, or condemned criminal.

a tyrant in his barbaric castle. No teenager with a limp or scrofula or bulging belly and hump was ever raped by Nero.

Go on, then, take pride in your lad's good looks—there are greater dangers that await him. He'll become a notorious Casanova, fearing whatever punishment furious husbands exact. His star won't turn out any luckier than that of Mars at never falling into the net.[59] Yet sometimes their resentment goes beyond what any law allows.[60] Death by the sword, savage slicing with lashes, even buggery with a mullet —that's the fate of some adulterers. But your Endymion will become the lover of a married woman he has fallen for.[61] Soon, when Servilia has given him her money, he'll become the lover of a woman he's not in love with and strip her of all her personal jewellery. (After all, you can't expect any woman to say no to her juicy crotch, if she's an Oppia or a Catulla.[62]) "But if he's pure, what harm can beauty do him?" On the contrary, what good did it do to Hippolytus or to Bellerophon to have an austere lifestyle?[63] The rejected Stheneboea flared up just as much as the Cretan— and both women lashed themselves to rage. Woman is most savage when her hatred is goaded by a sense of

[61] Endymion was the beautiful young man with whom Selene, the Moon, fell in love.

[62] At 220 Oppia is said to have many lovers; similarly the beautiful Catulla in Martial (8.53). Line 323: "That's the centre of morality in the worse kind of woman."   [63] Both were accused of rape by older women after resisting seduction. Hippolytus rejected his Cretan stepmother Phaedra and Bellerophon his hostess Stheneboea. Line 326: "What happened was that the one woman blushed like a woman scorned, and."

cum stimulos odio pudor admovet. elige quidnam
330 suadendum esse putes cui nubere Caesaris uxor
destinat. optimus hic et formonsissimus idem
gentis patriciae rapitur miser extinguendus
Messalinae oculis; dudum sedet illa parato
flammeolo Tyriusque palam genialis in hortis
335 sternitur et ritu decies centena dabuntur
antiquo, veniet cum signatoribus auspex.
[haec tu secreta et paucis commissa putabas?]
non nisi legitime volt nubere. quid placeat dic.
ni parere velis, pereundum erit ante lucernas;
340 si scelus admittas, dabitur mora parvula, dum res
nota Vrbi et populo contingat principis aurem.
[dedecus ille domus sciet ultimus. interea tu]
obsequere imperio, si tanti vita dierum
paucorum. quidquid levius meliusque putaris,
345 praebenda est gladio pulchra haec et candida cervix.
  Nil ergo optabunt homines? si consilium vis,
permittes ipsis expendere numinibus quid
conveniat nobis rebusque sit utile nostris;
nam pro iucundis aptissima quaeque dabunt di.
350 carior est illis homo quam sibi. nos animorum
inpulsu caeco vanaque cupidine ducti
coniugium petimus partumque uxoris, at illis

337 *del. Markland, forte e satura 9*   342 *del. Nisbet*
351 caeco *Leo*: et caeca *codd.* | vanaque *Housman*: magnaque
codd.

shame. Select the advice you think should be given to the
man Caesar's wife plans to marry. He's the finest and most
handsome of the patrician race, but he's swept towards a
pitiful snuffing-out by Messalina's eyes.[64] She's been sitting
there waiting for a while now, with her bridal veil ready
and a purple marriage couch set up in the gardens in full
view. Following the ancient custom, a dowry of a million
will be paid, and the augur and witnesses will be there.[65]
She will not get married unless it's done lawfully. What's
your decision? If you are not prepared to obey her, you'll
die before the lamps are lit. If you go through with the
crime, there'll be the briefest delay, until the matter that's
known to Rome and the people reaches the emperor's
ear.[66] Comply with her command, if a few days of life are
worth it. Whichever you decide is easier and better, you'll
have no choice but to offer your lovely white neck for exe-
cution.

So is there nothing for people to pray for? If you want
my advice, you'll let the gods themselves estimate what
will suit us and benefit our circumstances: you see, the
gods will bestow gifts that are the most appropriate rather
than nice. They care more about people than people do
themselves. While we are led by our blind emotional im-
pulses and by empty desire to seek marriage and children
from a wife, it is the gods who know who our boys will be

[64] In A.D. 48 Claudius' wife Messalina celebrated her "mar-
riage" to the handsome C. Silius while her husband was away (see
Tac. *Ann.* 11.26–38).   [65] Line 337: "Did you imagine that
this affair was a secret, shared with just a few?"

[66] Line 342: "He'll be the last to hear about the scandal in his
own home. In the meantime."

notum qui pueri qualisque futura sit uxor.
ut tamen et poscas aliquid voveasque sacellis
355   exta et candiduli divina tomacula porci,
orandum est ut sit mens sana in corpore sano.
fortem posce animum mortis terrore carentem,
qui spatium vitae extremum inter munera ponat
naturae, qui ferre queat quoscumque labores,
360   nesciat irasci, cupiat nihil et potiores
Herculis aerumnas credat saevosque dolores
et venere et cenis et pluma Sardanapalli.
monstro quod ipse tibi possis dare; semita certe
tranquillae per virtutem patet unica vitae.
365   nullum numen habes, si sit prudentia: nos te,
nos facimus, Fortuna, deam caeloque locamus.

355 tomacula FZ: tumacula P: thymatula GU
356 del. Reeve
359 dolores GU: labores PSΦSang.
365–6 del. Guyet, cf. 14.315–16

and what kind of wife she'll be. Yet, to actually give you something to ask for and some reason to offer the guts and little sacred sausages of a shining white piglet at the little shrines, you should pray for a sound mind in a sound body. Ask for a heart that is courageous, with no fear of death, that reckons long life among the least of Nature's gifts, that can put up with any anguish, that is unfamiliar with anger, that longs for nothing, that prefers the troubles and gruelling Labours of Hercules to the sex and feasts and downy cushions of Sardanapallus.[67] I'm showing you something you can give yourself. There is no doubt that the only path to a peaceful life lies through goodness. Fortune, you'd have no power, if we were sensible: it's we who make you a goddess, it's we who give you a place in the sky.

[67] The last king of Assyria, associated with luxury, the antithesis of the hero Hercules, whose Twelve Labours made him a saint-like figure.

NOTE ON SATIRE 11

The next poem in Book Four opens with a contradiction between two extremes of behaviour, like Horace *Satires* 1.1–3, and emphasises the importance of self-knowledge, recalling Horace's stress upon the "mean" in those and other poems (1 55). With the question "Do I practise what I preach?" (56) Juvenal introduces the theme of self-consistency and shifts into an epistolary style. The remainder of the poem is an invitation to dinner, reminiscent of Horace's dinner invitation poem, *Epistles* I.5, addressed to someone called Persicus, a name that conjures up luxurious and exotic tastes (56–63). Juvenal outlines the food that will be served (64–89), the decor of the diningroom (90–135), the slaves who will serve at table (136–61), and the entertainments the guests will enjoy (162–82), all liberally spiced with antitheses designed to underline the moral value of the dinner here proposed. Juvenal concludes by inviting his addressee to leave behind his worries and give himself a holiday (183–208) with this country feast he proposes in the middle of the city—a paradox. The tone seems much more genial, but the satiric sting may reside in the addressee's name, because if Persicus is accustomed to dining lavishly, this invitation may be construed as a reproach.

SATIRE 11

Atticus eximie si cenat, lautus habetur,
si Rutilus, demens. quid enim maiore cachinno
excipitur volgi quam pauper Apicius? omnis
convictus, thermae, stationes, omne theatrum
5   de Rutilo. nam dum valida ac iuvenalia membra
sufficiunt galeae dumque ardent sanguine, fertur
non cogente quidem sed nec prohibente tribuno
scripturus leges et regia verba lanistae.
multos porro vides, quos saepe elusus ad ipsum
10 creditor introitum solet expectare macelli,
et quibus in solo vivendi causa palato est.
egregius cenat meliusque miserrimus horum
et cito casurus iam perlucente ruina.
interea gustus elementa per omnia quaerit
15 numquam animo pretiis obstantibus; interius si
attendas, magis illa iuvant quae pluris ementur.
ergo haut difficile est perituram arcessere summam

14 quaerit *Markland*: quaerunt *codd*.

---

[1] Tiberius Claudius Atticus, an immensely rich contemporary
of Juvenal.   [2] Apicius: see 4.23n.

[3] The oath of service to the trainer of gladiators involved train-
ees committing themselves "body and soul" (Petr. *Sat*. 117).

SATIRE 11

If Atticus[1] dines lavishly, he's considered elegant. If Rutilus does so, he's considered crazy. After all, what gets a greater laugh from the crowd than an impoverished Apicius?[2] Rutilus is the talk of every dinner party, every bathhouse, every piazza, every theatre. The reason? They say that, while his limbs are hot-blooded and strong and young enough for the soldier's helmet, he's about to sign up to the rules and royal decrees of the gladiator-trainer[3]— and with no compulsion from the tribune, but no prohibition either.[4] You can see many like him, of course. Their only reason for living lies in gourmandise. Their creditors, to whom they've often given the slip, always lie in wait for them at the entrance to the meat market. The one with the choicest and richest dinner is the most doomed, facing imminent disaster, with the cracks in his façade already letting in the light. Meanwhile he probes air, land, and sea for relishes, and price is no obstacle at all to his enthusiasm. If you look closely, they get more pleasure from the more expensive purchases! So it's not hard for them to raise funds that will soon run out by pawning silver dishes

[4] A free man who entered gladiatorial school had to inform one of the tribunes.

lancibus oppositis vel matris imagine fracta,
et quadringentis nummis condire gulosum
20   fictile; sic veniunt ad miscellanea ludi.
refert ergo quis haec eadem paret; in Rutilo nam
luxuria est, in Ventidio laudabile nomen
sumptus et a censu famam trahit. illum ego iure
despiciam, qui scit quanto sublimior Atlas
25   omnibus in Libya sit montibus, hic tamen idem
ignorat quantum ferrata distet ab arca
sacculus. e caelo descendit γνῶθι σεαυτόν
figendum et memori tractandum pectore, sive
coniugium quaeras vel sacri in parte senatus
30   esse velis; neque enim loricam poscit Achillis
Thersites, in qua se traducebat Vlixes.
ancipitem seu tu magno discrimine causam
protegere adfectas, te consule, dic tibi qui sis,
orator vehemens an Curtius et Matho buccae.
35   noscenda est mensura sui spectandaque rebus
in summis minimisque, etiam cum piscis emetur,
ne mullum cupias, cum sit tibi gobio tantum
in loculis. quis enim te deficiente crumina
et crescente gula manet exitus, aere paterno
40   ac rebus mersis in ventrem fenoris atque
argenti gravis et pecorum agrorumque capacem?
talibus a dominis post cuncta novissimus exit

23 sumptus *Heinrich*: sumit *codd*.
37 ne PSAFGU*Sang.*: nec Φ

---

5 Some rich man.
6 The saying inscribed on Apollo's temple at Delphi.

or by melting down mother's statue. It's not hard for them
to flavour their gourmet's earthenware at a cost of four
hundred thousand. That's how they come to the hash of the
gladiatorial school. Consequently, a lot depends on who
provides the feast. In the case of Rutilus it's called extrava-
gance, but in Ventidius' case[5] expense gives him a credit-
able reputation and he derives esteem from his wealth. I'd
be absolutely right to despise the person who knows how
much higher Atlas is than all the mountains of Libya but
who has no idea about the difference between a little
money bag and a treasure chest reinforced with iron. The
saying "Know Yourself" comes from heaven.[6] It should be
fixed and pondered in the unforgetting heart, whether
you're looking for a wife or aiming for a place in the sa-
cred Senate. Just think: Thersites doesn't demand Achilles'
breastplate—the one Ulysses made such a fool of himself
in.[7] If you aspire to defend a difficult case of great impor-
tance, ask yourself the question, tell yourself what you
are—a powerful orator, or a windbag like Curtius and
Matho? You must know your own measure and keep it in
sight in matters great and small, even in the business of
buying fish. The danger is that you'll want mullet when all
you have in your money box is goby. After all, what end
awaits you as your wallet fails and your appetite grows,
when you have sunk your paternal inheritance and prop-
erty in your belly, which swallows investment income and
heavy silver plate and herds and estates? In the case of
lords like these, the last thing to go is the little ring[8]—and

---

[7] Ulysses won the competition for Achilles' weapons (Ov. *Met.*
13.1–383); Juvenal suggests that they were not a good fit.

[8] Denoting equestrian status.

anulus, et digito mendicat Pollio nudo.
non praematuri cineres nec funus acerbum
45   luxuriae sed morte magis metuenda senectus.
hi plerumque gradus: conducta pecunia Romae
et coram dominis consumitur; inde, ubi paulum
nescio quid superest, [et pallet fenoris auctor,
qui vertere solum] Baias et ad ostrea currunt.
50   cedere namque foro iam non est deterius quam
Esquilias a ferventi migrare Subura.
ille dolor solus patriam fugientibus, illa
maestitia est, caruisse anno circensibus uno.
sanguinis in facie non haeret gutta, morantur
55   pauci ridiculum et fugientem ex Vrbe Pudorem.
     Experiere hodie numquid pulcherrima dictu,
Persice, non praestem vita et moribus et re,
si laudem siliquas occultus ganeo, pultes
coram aliis dictem puero sed in aure placentas.
60   nam cum sis conviva mihi promissus, habebis
Evandrum, venies Tirynthius aut minor illo
hospes, et ipse tamen contingens sanguine caelum.
[alter aquis, alter flammis ad sidera missus]
     Fercula nunc audi nullis ornata macellis.
65   de Tiburtino veniet pinguissimus agro
haedulus et toto grege mollior, inscius herbae

48–9 et pallet . . . solum *del. Nisbet*
57 vita Φ: vitae P: tibi vita *Nisbet*   63 *del. Heinrich*

---

9 Lines 48–9: "and the creditor is getting worried, they've already gone into voluntary exile."
10 A resort in the Bay of Naples favoured by the Roman elite; oysters were a delicacy cultivated in the nearby Lucrine Lake.

Pollio goes begging with his finger bare. It is not a prema-
ture demise or an early funeral that should strike dread
into the extravagant—worse than death is old age. The
usual stages are these. Money is borrowed at Rome and
squandered right in front of the lenders. Then, when some
tiny amount is left,[9] they're racing off to Baiae and its oys-
ters.[10] These days, you know, it's no worse to be declared
bankrupt than to move to the Esquiline from the seething
Subura.[11] The only grief, the only regret these fugitives ex-
perience is missing the Circus races for a year. Not a drop
of blood lingers in their faces: Shame is mocked and, as she
rushes out of Rome, there are few who detain her.

You'll find out today, Persicus, whether or not I live up
to this wonderful talk in actuality, in lifestyle and behav-
iour—if I sing the praises of beans while being a glutton at
heart, if I ask my slave for polenta in public but whisper
"pastries" in his ear. You see, since you have agreed to
come as my guest, I'll be your own Evander and you'll be
the hero of Tiryns, or that lesser guest who all the same
includes heaven in his ancestry.[12]

Now listen to my courses, ungarnished by products
from the market. From my Tiburtine farm will come a
little kid, plumpest and tenderest of the herd. He's unac-

[11] Housing on the Esquiline was expensive.

[12] King Evander received as his guests on the Palatine first
Hercules, born at Tiryns near Argos, and later Aeneas (Virg. Aen.
8.359–69), here described humorously as "that lesser guest." Both
had divine ancestry (Hercules' father was Jupiter; Aeneas' mother
was Venus) and both were deified, Aeneas after drowning in the
river Numicius and Hercules on a pyre on Mount Oeta. Line 63:
"One was delivered to the stars by water, the other by fire."

necdum ausus virgas humilis mordere salicti,
qui plus lactis habet quam sanguinis, et montani
asparagi, posito quos legit vilica fuso.
70 grandia praeterea tortoque calentia feno
ova adsunt ipsis cum matribus, et servatae
parte anni quales fuerant in vitibus uvae,
Signinum Syriumque pirum, de corbibus isdem
aemula Picenis et odoris mala recentis
75 nec metuenda tibi, siccatum frigore postquam
autumnum et crudi posuere pericula suci.
haec olim nostri iam luxuriosa senatus
cena fuit. Curius parvo quae legerat horto
ipse focis brevibus ponebat holuscula, quae nunc
80 squalidus in magna fastidit conpede fossor,
qui meminit calidae sapiat quid volva popinae.
sicci terga suis rara pendentia crate
moris erat quondam festis servare diebus
et natalicium cognatis ponere lardum
85 accedente nova, si quam dabat hostia, carne.
cognatorum aliquis titulo ter consulis atque
castrorum imperiis et dictatoris honore
functus ad has epulas solito maturius ibat
erectum domito referens a monte ligonem.
90   Cum tremerent autem Fabios durumque Catonem
et Scauros et Fabricium, rigidique severos
censoris mores etiam collega timeret,
nemo inter curas et seria duxit habendum

---

13 See 2.3n; he was once found cooking a turnip himself (Plin.
N.H. 19.87).

14 Slaves were often punished by hard labour in gangs of ditch-
diggers.

quainted with pasture and hasn't yet been bold enough
to nibble the low willow shoots—there's more milk than
blood in him. With the kid, there'll be wild asparagus,
picked by my foreman's wife after she's finished her spin-
ning. There'll also be large eggs, still warm in wisps of hay,
along with their own mother hens, and grapes kept for half
the year, just as fresh as they were on the vine, Signian and
Syrian pears, and in the same baskets fresh-smelling ap-
ples as good as those from Picenum—and no worry: their
autumn juice has been dessicated by the frost and they've
shed their dangerous unripeness. This would already have
been a luxurious feast long ago, even for our Senate. With
his own hands Curius[13] used to cook on his modest hearth
the humble vegetables he'd picked in his own garden.
These days, a filthy ditchdigger in his huge shackles[14]
would turn up his nose at such vegetables, all the while
reminiscing about the taste of tripe in the steaming diner.
In those times, it was their custom to keep a back of dried
pork hanging from the wide-barred rack for festivals, and
to serve their relatives a birthday treat of bacon along with
fresh meat, if a sacrificial offering made it available. A rela-
tive who'd held the title of consul three times, who'd com-
manded armies and who'd held office as Dictator,[15] would
hurry back to such a feast earlier than usual, carrying his
spade on his shoulder from the mountainside he'd tamed.

Back when people quaked at the Fabii and at stern Cato
and at the Scauri and Fabricius, and when the strict cen-
sor's rigid morality scared even his colleague,[16] no one
thought it a matter of serious concern what kind of tortoise

15 See 8.8n.
16 Exemplars of Republican morality.

qualis in Oceani fluctu testudo nataret,
95   clarum Troiugenis factura et nobile fulcrum;
sed nudo latere et parvis frons aerea lectis
vite coronati caput ostendebat aselli,
ad quod lascivi ludebant ruris alumni.
[tales ergo cibi qualis domus atque supellex.]
100 tunc rudis et Graias mirari nescius artes
urbibus eversis praedarum in parte reperta
magnorum artificum frangebat pocula miles,
ut phaleris gauderet equus caelataque cassis
Romuleae simulacra ferae mansuescere iussae
105 imperii fato, geminos sub rupe Quirinos
ac nudam effigiem clipeo venientis et hasta
pendentisque dei perituro ostenderet hosti.
ponebant igitur Tusco farrata catino:
argenti quod erat solis fulgebat in armis.
110 omnia tunc quibus invideas, si lividulus sis.
templorum quoque maiestas praesentior, et vox
nocte fere media tacitamque audita per Vrbem
litore ab Oceani Gallis venientibus et dis
officium vatis peragentibus. his monuit nos,
115 hanc rebus Latiis curam praestare solebat
fictilis et nullo violatus Iuppiter auro.
illa domi natas nostraque ex arbore mensas
tempora viderunt; hos lignum stabat ad usus,

97 vite *Hennin*: vile *codd.*

99 *del. Markland, Heinrich*

106 in [*ante* clipeo] *H.Valesius suppl.* | venientis PG*Sang.*Σ:
ful***entis U: fulgentis Φ

112 tacitamque *Nisbet*: mediamque *codd.*

swimming in Ocean's waves would make a splendid and il-
lustrious headrest for our Trojan-born elite. Instead, their
couches were modest with undecorated sides, the bronze
front displaying a donkey's head garlanded with a vine—
and around this the naughty country children would play.[17]
In those days a soldier was a simple man with no apprecia-
tion of Greek art. If there were goblets made by great
craftsmen in his share of the booty from a sacked city, he
would break them up, just so his horse could delight in
trappings and his helmet be embossed with images for his
enemy to see at the moment of death: Romulus' beast
commanded by order of fate to grow tame, or the twin
Quirini under the rock, or the image of the god swooping
down stripped of shield and spear.[18] No surprise, then, that
they would serve their porridge in Tuscan bowls. What
silver they had, they kept to make their armour gleam. All
this you might envy them—if you are of an envious disposi-
tion! And another thing, the power of the temples was
more tangible then. When the Gauls were advancing from
the Ocean's shore, a voice was heard around the middle of
the night through silent Rome—the gods were acting as
prophets.[19] That was Jupiter's warning to us, that was the
protection he would offer to Latium when he was made of
earthenware and not spoiled by gold. Those times saw
tables that were homegrown, made from our own trees.
That was the reason for the timber stacked up, if the East

---

[17] Line 99: "Their food matched their homes and furniture."
[18] The images on the helmet are of the wolf that suckled
Romulus and Remus, the twins themselves, and their father, the
god Mars, on his way to visit Rhea Silvia.
[19] The Gallic invasion of 391 B.C.: see Livy 5.32.6.

annosam si forte nucem deiecerat Eurus.
120   At nunc divitibus cenandi nulla voluptas,
nil rhombus, nil damma sapit, putere videntur
unguenta atque rosae, latos nisi sustinet orbis
grande ebur et magno sublimis pardus hiatu
dentibus ex illis quos mittit porta Syenes
125 et Mauri celeres et Mauro obscurior Indus,
et quos deposuit Nabataeo belua saltu
iam nimios capitique graves. hinc surgit orexis,
hinc stomacho vires; nam pes argenteus illis,
anulus in digito quod ferreus. ergo superbum
130 convivam caveo, qui me sibi comparat et res
despicit exiguas. adeo nulla uncia nobis
est eboris, nec tessellae nec calculus ex hac
materia, quin ipsa manubria cultellorum
ossea. non tamen his ulla umquam obsonia fiunt
135 rancidula aut ideo peior gallina secatur.
      Sed nec structor erit cui cedere debeat omnis
pergula, discipulus Trypheri doctoris, apud quem
sumine cum magno lepus atque aper et pygargus
et Scythicae volucres et phoenicopterus ingens
140 et Gaetulus oryx hebeti lautissima ferro
caeditur et tota sonat ulmea cena Subura.
nec frustum capreae subducere nec latus Afrae
novit avis noster, tirunculus ac rudis omni

---

20 Juvenal envisages three sources of ivory: imports via Aswan
(mod. Egypt), on the southern frontier of the Roman empire;
Mauretania (Morocco); and India (cf. Plin. *N.H.* 8.32). There
were no elephants in Nabataea (mod. Jordan), but this was a trade
route from India.

Wind had happened to blow down an ancient walnut tree.

But these days, the rich get no pleasure from dining, the turbot and venison have no taste, the fragrances and roses seem rotten, unless the enormous round tabletop rests on a massive piece of ivory, a rampant snarling leopard made from tusks imported from the gate of Syene and the speedy Moors and from the Indian who is darker still, the tusks dropped by the beast in the Nabataean grove when they've become too large and heavy for its head.[20] This is the source of rising appetite, this gives the stomach strength. To these people, a table leg made of silver is the equivalent of an iron ring on their finger.[21] That's why I avoid the snobbish guest who compares me with himself and looks down on my meagre resources. You know, I don't have an ounce of ivory—no dice or counting-stones made of the stuff—and even the handles of my knives are bone. But they never make the meals I serve rotten, and the chicken I carve isn't any the worse for that reason.

And I won't have a carver who is revered by the whole carving school, a pupil of Professor Trypherus.[22] At his studio, they use blunt steel to slice hare along with huge sow's udder, boar, and gazelle, pheasants and enormous flamingo and Gaetulian antelope, really lavish fare: the elmwood feast resounds through the whole Subura. And my little table slave hasn't learned how to filch a hunk of venison or a slice of guinea fowl. He's a raw recruit, un-

[21] The iron ring was worn by plebeians, whereas senators and *equites* wore a gold ring.

[22] His name means "Dainty" or "Luxurious."

tempore et exiguae furtis inbutus ofellae.
145 plebeios calices et paucis assibus emptos
porriget incultus puer atque a frigore tutus,
non Phryx aut Lycius, non a mangone petitus
quisquam erit et magno: cum posces, posce Latine.
idem habitus cunctis, tonsi rectique capilli
150 atque hodie tantum propter convivia pexi.
pastoris duri hic filius, ille bubulci.
suspirat longo non visam tempore matrem
et casulam et notos tristis desiderat haedos
ingenui voltus puer ingenuique pudoris,
155 qualis esse decet quos ardens purpura vestit,
nec pupillares defert in balnea raucus
testiculos, nec vellendas iam praebuit alas,
crassa nec opposito pavidus tegit inguina guto.
hic tibi vina dabit diffusa in montibus illis
160 a quibus ipse venit, quorum sub vertice lusit.
[namque una atque eadem est vini patria atque ministri.]
    Forsitan expectes ut Gaditana canoro
incipiant prurire choro plausuque probatae
ad terram tremulo descendant clune puellae.
165 (spectant hoc nuptae iuxta recubante marito
quod pudeat narrare aliquem praesentibus ipsis.)
inritamentum veneris languentis et acres
ramitis urticae; [maior tamen ista voluptas

144 furtis Φ: frustis P
147–8 non . . . magno *del. Guyet*   148 et Φ: in PSFGU
    161 *del. Markland*   165–6 PA: *post* 160 FLZ: *om.* GKTU:
del. Pinzger   168 ramitis *Housman cf. Juv. 10.205:* divitis
codd.   168–9 maior . . . sexus *del. Jachmann*

tutored all his days, and initiated only in the theft of tiny meatballs. Ordinary cups, bought for a few coins, will be handed round by a slave boy not dressed elaborately but wrapped up warmly, not a Phrygian or a Lycian got from the dealer at great expense. When you want something, ask for it in Latin. All my slaves are dressed alike, their hair is cut short and straight, and it's only been combed today because of the party. This one's the son of a tough shepherd, that one's a cattleman's son. He sighs for the mother he hasn't seen in ages, and pines for his little cottage and the young goats he knew so well. There is a noble decency in the boy's face and behaviour, the kind that suits lads clothed in glowing purple.[23] His voice hasn't broken, he doesn't cart his teenage testicles into the baths, he hasn't yet presented his armpits to be plucked bare, and he doesn't nervously shield his thick penis behind an oil flask.[24] The wine this boy will serve you was bottled in the same mountains as he comes from—he's played beneath their peaks.

Perhaps you're expecting Spanish floor shows to get aroused with their vibrant dancing, the girls shimmying to the floor, wiggling their bottoms to appreciative applause. (It's a sight watched by young wives, reclining next to their husbands, though you'd be embarrassed to describe it in their presence.) It provokes jaded desire and sharply goads the swollen cock vein.[25] Its tension rises more and more

[23] The *toga praetexta* with its purple stripe worn by boys who were freeborn.

[24] Some slave boys had their testicles removed to increase development of the penis.

[25] Lines 168–9: "Yet greater is that pleasure experienced by the other sex."

413

alterius sexus] magis ille extenditur, et mox
170   auribus atque oculis concepta urina movetur.
non capit has nugas humilis domus. audiat ille
testarum crepitus cum verbis, nudum olido stans
fornice mancipium quibus abstinet, ille fruatur
vocibus obscenis omnique libidinis arte,
175   qui Lacedaemonium pytismate lubricat orbem;
[namque ibi fortunae veniam damus. alea turpis,
turpe et adulterium mediocribus: haec eadem illi
omnia cum faciunt, hilares nitidique vocantur.]
nostra dabunt alios hodie convivia ludos:
180   conditor Iliados cantabitur atque Maronis
altisoni dubiam facientia carmina palmam.
quid refert, tales versus qua voce legantur?
     Sed nunc dilatis averte negotia curis
et gratam requiem dona tibi, quando licebit
185   per totum cessare diem. non fenoris ulla
mentio nec, prima si luce egressa reverti
nocte solet, tacito bilem tibi contrahat uxor
umida suspectis referens multicia rugis
vexatasque comas et voltum auremque calentem.
190   protinus ante meum quidquid dolet exue limen,
pone domum et servos et quidquid frangitur illis
aut perit, ingratos ante omnia pone sodalis.

176–8 *del. Ribbeck*

---

26 Wine is tasted and spat onto the floor, which is made of
Laconian or Spartan marble, perhaps the favoured green marble

and the next thing is that the sights and sounds make the pent-up liquid flow. You won't find frivolities like that in my humble home. The cracking sound of castanets along with words too obscene for the naked slave standing for sale in the stinking brothel, enjoyment of disgusting language and all the pornographic arts—they are for the man who lubricates his patterned floor of Spartan marble with his spat wine.[26] My party today will offer other forms of entertainment. We'll have a recitation from the author of the *Iliad* and from the poems of sublime Maro[27] which challenge Homer's supremacy. With poetry like this, it hardly matters how it's read.[28]

But now adjourn your worries, put business matters aside, and treat yourself to a pleasant break, as you'll be free to relax for the entire day. There'll be no mention of interest due, and don't let your wife intensify your silent rage if she makes a habit of going out at dawn and coming back at night with her gauze dress damp and suspiciously wrinkled, her hair dishevelled, and her face and ears flushed. Strip off anything that annoys you right in front of my doorstep. Leave behind your household and your slaves and whatever they've broken or lost. Most of all, leave behind the ingratitude of your friends. Meanwhile,

from the Eurotas Valley. For marble floors as a sign of luxury, cf. Sen. *Ep.* 16.8. Lines 176–8: "In this respect, you see, we make allowances to the wealthy. For ordinary people, gambling is disgraceful, so too is adultery. But when *they* do precisely the same, they're called stylish and full of fun."

[27] Virgil.

[28] The household does not include a professional reciter of poetry.

interea Megalesiacae spectacula mappae
Idaeum sollemne colunt, similisque triumpho
195   praeda caballorum praetor sedet ac, mihi pace
inmensae nimiaeque licet si dicere plebis,
totam hodie Romam Circus capit, et fragor aurem
percutit, eventum viridis quo colligo panni.
nam si deficeret, maestam attonitamque videres
200   hanc Vrbem veluti Cannarum in pulvere victis
consulibus. spectent iuvenes, quos clamor et audax
sponsio, quos cultae decet adsedisse puellae:
nostra bibat vernum contracta cuticula solem
effugiatque togam. iam nunc in balnea salva
205   fronte licet vadas, quamquam solida hora supersit
ad sextam. facere hoc non possis quinque diebus
continuis, quia sunt talis quoque taedia vitae
magna: voluptates commendat rarior usus.

the tiers of spectators are celebrating the Idaean ritual of the Megalesian flag[29] and the praetor is sitting there as if in a triumph, the prey of the nags,[30] and, if I may say so without offending the populace too huge to count, today the whole of Rome is inside the Circus. The shouting is ear-shattering—and this tells me that the Green jackets have won.[31] If they'd lost, you know, you'd see this Rome of ours dumbstruck and in mourning, as when the consuls were defeated in the dust of Cannae.[32] The races are a fine sight for our young men, who are fit for the noise and bold betting, with a chic young woman at their side; my wrinkled skin would rather drink in the spring sunshine and escape the toga. You can head for the baths at once with a clear conscience, although there's still a full hour till midday.[33] This is something you'd not be able to do for five days in a row, because even this kind of life is enormously tedious. Pleasures are enhanced by rare indulgence.

[29] The Megalesia was held on April 4th–10th in honour of Cybele, the Great (Greek: $\mu\epsilon\gamma\acute{\alpha}\lambda\eta$) Mother Goddess, whose cult originated in Asia Minor, associated with Mount Ida. The flag was the starting signal for the races.

[30] The praetor in charge of the games had to finance the teams that competed in the races.

[31] The four Circus "factions" were the Greens, the Blues, the Reds, and the Whites. The Greens dominated during the early empire.

[32] Hannibal inflicted a crushing defeat on the Romans at the battle of Cannae in 216 B.C.

[33] The "sixth hour" was noon; bathing generally took place in mid-afternoon (the eighth hour).

NOTE ON SATIRE 12

The final poem in Book Four also has an addressee with a significant name. In the first part of the poem (1–16) Juvenal describes to Corvinus a sacrifice he is offering for the safe return of his friend Catullus from near ship-wreck. This leads him into a lengthy mock-epic narrative of Catullus' danger and his escape from the storm (17–82). Juvenal then returns to the opening context of his sacrifice (83–92), and reassures Corvinus that he is not sacrificing because he is after Catullus' money (93–8). The remainder of the poem is a condemnation of legacy-hunters (a frequent theme of Horace, e.g. *Satires* 2.5). The final section of the poem may initially appear to have little connection with the first part. But the realisation that friendship is the central theme—true friendship, as shown by Juvenal in his celebration of his friend's survival, and false friendship, as shown by the legacy-hunters—gives the poem shape and coherence. Moreover, if the addressee is himself a legacy-hunter, as his name ("raven," a carrion-eating bird) seems to suggest, this makes even better sense of the themes and structure of the poem.

SATIRE 12

Natali, Corvine, die mihi dulcior haec lux,
qua festus promissa deis animalia caespes
expectat. niveam reginae ducimus agnam,
par vellus dabitur pugnanti Gorgone Maura;   ·
sed procul extensum petulans quatit hostia funem
Tarpeio servata Iovi frontemque coruscat,
quippe ferox vitulus templis maturus et arae
spargendusque mero, quem iam pudet ubera matris
ducere, qui vexat nascenti robora cornu.
si res ampla domi similisque adfectibus esset,
pinguior Hispulla traheretur taurus et ipsa
mole piger, nec finitima nutritus in herba,
laeta sed ostendens Clitumni pascua sanguis;
et grandi cervix iret ferienda ministro
ob reditum trepidantis adhuc horrendaque passi
nuper et incolumem sese mirantis amici.
nam praeter pelagi casus et fulminis ictus

14 et grandi cervix iret *Housman*: iret et grandi cervix PAΣ: iret
et a grandi cervix Φ   17 fulminis PSAΣ: fulguris Φ

1 Juno.
2 Minerva, whose breastplate (aegis) displayed the head of
Medusa, the Gorgon killed by Perseus in Mauretania.

SATIRE 12

Today is sweeter to me than my own birthday, Corvinus.
It's the day when the rejoicing altar turf waits for the ani-
mals I've promised to the gods. For the queen of the gods[1]
we are bringing a snow-white lamb. An identical fleece
will be offered to the goddess who fights armed with her
Moroccan Gorgon.[2] But the victim reserved for Tarpeian
Jupiter[3] is playfully tugging and shaking the lengthy rope
and tossing his head. He's a spirited calf, you see, the right
age for temple and altar, ready for sprinkling with unmixed
wine. He's now embarrassed to pull at his mother's teats
and he butts the oak trees with his budding horns. If my
personal resources were ample, as ample as my feelings, a
bull fatter than Hispulla would be dragged along, his very
bulk making him slow, not one raised on local pastures, but
with his blood attesting the fertile fields of Clitumnus,[4] and
his neck would advance for the blow from the tall atten-
dant. This is for the return of my friend, still shaking from
his recent ordeal and amazed that he survived. The rea-
son? Besides the dangers of the sea, he even escaped the

[3] The third Capitoline deity: the Tarpeian rock was at the
southern end of the Capitoline Hill.
[4] A small river in Umbria. The region's white cattle were
prized as sacrificial victims.

evasit. densae caelum abscondere tenebrae
nube una subitusque antemnas inpulit ignis.
20　cum se quisque illo percussum crederet et mox
attonitus nullum conferri posse putaret
naufragium velis ardentibus, omnia fiunt
talia, tam graviter, si quando poetica surgit
tempestas genus ecce aliud discriminis! audi
25　et miserere iterum, quamquam sint cetera sortis
eiusdem pars, dira quidem sed cognita multis
et quam votiva testantur fana tabella
plurima: pictores quis nescit ab Iside pasci?
accidit et nostro similis fortuna Catullo.
30　　Cum plenus fluctu medius foret alveus et iam,
alternum puppis latus evertentibus undis,
arbori incertae nullam prudentia cani
rectoris conferret opem, decidere iactu
coepit cum ventis, imitatus castora, qui se
35　eunuchum ipse facit cupiens evadere damno
testiculi: adeo medicatum intellegit inguen.
"fundite quae mea sunt" dicebat "cuncta" Catullus,
praecipitare volens etiam pulcherrima, vestem
purpuream teneris quoque Maecenatibus aptam,
40　atque alias quarum generosi graminis ipsum
infecit natura pecus, sed et egregius fons
viribus occultis et Baeticus adiuvat aer.
ille nec argentum dubitabat mittere, lances

32 arbori *Lachmann*: arboris *codd.* | incertae PO: incerta F:
incerto Φ: incerti A*Vat. 2810*
33 conferret *Lachmann*: cum ferret Φ

lightning strokes. Thick darkness hid the sky with a single mass of cloud, and a flash of fire struck the yardarms. When every man thought he'd been hit and in his terror quickly decided that no shipwreck could be compared with sails on fire—it all happens like this, just as appalling, whenever a poetic storm blows up—then, look! a different kind of danger. Listen and pity him a second time. The rest is, admittedly, part of the same experience, terrible without doubt, but familiar to many, as all those shrines with their votive tablets indicate. Everyone knows that painters make their bread and butter from Isis.[5] That's the kind of fate that my friend Catullus met.

When the hold was half-full of water, with the waves already rocking the stern this way and that, and the white-haired helmsman's skill could not stabilise the wavering mast, he began to do a deal with the winds by jettison, in imitation of the beaver who makes himself a eunuch in his wish to escape through the loss of a testicle. That's how well he understands the drugs in his groin.[6] "Ditch my things," Catullus kept saying, "the whole lot!" He was willing to throw overboard even his finest possessions: purple clothes fit even for delicate Maecenases,[7] and other fabrics from flocks actually dyed by the nature of superior grass, with additional assistance from the excellent water with its hidden properties and from the climate of Baetica.[8] He had no hesitation about jettisoning silver plate, dishes

[5] Sailors who survived disaster at sea thanked the goddess Isis for her help by offering votive tablets which they paid artists to paint. [6] The drug is *castoreum*. [7] The renowned patron of the arts was a byword for effeminacy.

[8] A region of southern Spain with rivers rich in gold.

Parthenio factas, urnae cratera capacem
45 et dignum sitiente Pholo vel coniuge Fusci;
adde et bascaudas et mille escaria, multum
caelati, biberat quo callidus emptor Olynthi.
sed quis nunc alius, qua mundi parte quis audet
argento praeferre caput rebusque salutem?
50 [non propter vitam faciunt patrimonia quidam,
sed vitio caeci propter patrimonia vivunt.]
  Iactatur rerum utilium pars maxima, sed nec
damna levant. tunc adversis urguentibus illuc
reccidit ut malum ferro summitteret, ac se
55 explicat angustum: discriminis ultima, quando
praesidia adferimus navem factura minorem.
i nunc et ventis animam committe dolato
confisus ligno, digitis a morte remotus
quattuor aut septem, si sit latissima, taedae;
60 mox cum reticulis et pane et ventre lagonae
accipe sumendas in tempestate secures.
sed postquam iacuit planum mare, tempora postquam
prospera vectoris fatumque valentius Euro
et pelago, postquam Parcae meliora benigna
65 pensa manu ducunt hilares et staminis albi
lanificae, modica nec multum fortior aura
ventus adest, inopi miserabilis arte cucurrit
vestibus extentis et, quod superaverat unum,
velo prora suo. iam deficientibus Austris
70 spes vitae cum sole redit. tum gratus Iulo

50–1 *del. Bentley*
54 reccidit AFLUZ: recidit PSGO: decidit HKT

424

made for Parthenius,[9] a three-gallon mixing bowl big
enough for thirsty Pholus[10] or even for Fuscus' wife,[11] plus
baskets and a thousand plates and many engraved goblets
from which the canny purchaser of Olynthus[12] had drunk.
Who else is there, anywhere in the world, who would have
the nerve to prefer his life to his money, his survival to his
property?

Most of the useful articles have gone overboard, but not
even these losses bring any relief. Then under pressure of
adversity he resorted to lowering the mast with steel. And
so he gets himself out of his corner: that's the ultimate
in danger, when the remedy we supply makes the ship
smaller. Off you go then, entrust your life to the winds, re-
lying on a sawn plank, four fingers of pinewood away from
death, or seven, if it's extra thick. Just remember in fu-
ture that along with your nets of bread and round-bellied
flagons you'll need axes—for use in a storm. But once the
sea lay flat, once the passenger's conditions improved and
his destiny turned out more powerful than wind and ocean,
once the Fates were working better stints with generous
hands and cheerfully spinning threads of white wool, and
once there sprang up a wind not much stronger than a
slight breeze, the pitiable ship ran on with its skill impover-
ished, using clothes spread out along with its own sail, the
only one left. Now that the South Winds were subsiding,
hope of life returned along with the sun. Then into view

---

[9] Domitian's chamberlain. Famous ownership increased the
value of objets d'art.　　　[10] A centaur who entertained Hercu-
les with a huge mixing bowl.　　　[11] Unknown.

[12] Philip II of Macedon who took the Greek city of Olynthus
by bribery.

atque novercali sedes praelata Lavino
conspicitur sublimis apex, cui candida nomen
scrofa dedit, laetis Phrygibus mirabile sumen,
et numquam visis triginta clara mamillis.
75 tandem intrat positas inclusa per aequora moles
Tyrrhenamque pharon porrectaque bracchia rursum
quae pelago occurrunt medio longeque relinquunt
Italiam; non sic veteres mirabere portus
quos natura dedit. sed trunca puppe magister
80 interiora petit, Baianae pervia cumbae,
tuti stagna sinus, gaudent ubi vertice raso
garrula securi narrare pericula nautae.
    Ite igitur, pueri, linguis animisque faventes
sertaque delubris et farra inponite cultris
85 ac mollis ornate focos glebamque virentem.
iam sequar et sacro, quod praestat, rite peracto
inde domum repetam, graciles ubi parva coronas
accipiunt fragili simulacra nitentia cera.
hic nostrum placabo Iovem Laribusque paternis
90 tura dabo atque omnis violae iactabo colores.
cuncta nitent, longos erexit ianua ramos
et matutinis operatur festa lucernis.
    Neu suspecta tibi sint haec, Corvine, Catullus,
pro cuius reditu tot pono altaria, parvos

---

78 veteres *Nisbet*: igitur *codd.*

---

13 Iulus, son of the Trojan (here "Phrygian") Aeneas, left the
city of Lavinium, named after his stepmother Lavinia, and
founded a new city on Mount Alba (lit. "white"), which he named
after the white sow found there, in accordance with prophecy
(Virg. *Aen*. 8.42–8).

came the elevated peak which Iulus loved, the spot he preferred to his stepmother's Lavinium.[13] This is the peak that got its name from the white sow, whose udder stunned the delighted Phrygians, famous for her thirty teats, a sight never seen before. Finally it enters the breakwaters built out through the water they enclose, and passes the Tuscan lighthouse and the arms which stretch back out and meet in mid-sea, leaving Italy far behind.[14] You'll not be so impressed by ancient harbours created by nature. To resume, with his crippled ship the captain heads for the inner basin in the sheltered bay, which a Baian boat[15] could cross, where the sailors, with their heads shaved,[16] enjoy telling in safety the long-winded stories of their dangers.

Off you go, then, boys! With tongues and minds well-behaved, put garlands on the shrines and grain on the knives, and decorate the soft hearths and green turf. I'll be right behind you, and once I've performed the major rite properly I'll come back home. There the little images, gleaming with fragile wax, are receiving their slender crowns. Here I shall propitiate my own Jupiter, offering incense to my paternal house gods and scattering the multi-coloured pansies. Everything is gleaming. The door has put up its long branches and joins in the festive celebration with its morning lamps.

And so you'll not be suspicious about all this, Corvinus, the Catullus whose return I mark by setting up all these al-

[14] The Portus Augusti, built by Claudius a little north of Ostia, Rome's port, now silted up.

[15] A light pleasure boat.

[16] In fulfilment of religious vows made during the storm.

95   tres habet heredes. libet expectare quis aegram
      et claudentem oculos gallinam inpendat amico
      tam sterili; verum haec nimia est inpensa, coturnix
      nulla umquam pro patre cadet. sentire calorem
      si coepit locuples Gallitta et Pacius orbi,
100   legitime fixis vestitur tota libellis
      porticus, existunt qui promittant hecatomben,
      quatenus hic non sunt nec venales elephanti,
      nec Latio aut usquam sub nostro sidere talis
      belua concipitur, sed furva gente petita
105   arboribus Rutulis et Turni pascitur agro,
      Caesaris armentum nulli servire paratum
      privato, siquidem Tyrio parere solebant
      Hannibali et nostris ducibus regique Molosso
      horum maiores ac dorso ferre cohortis,
110   partem aliquam belli, et euntem in proelia turrem.
      nulla igitur mora per Novium, mora nulla per Histrum
      Pacuvium, quin illud ebur ducatur ad aras
      et cadat ante Lares Gallittae victima sola
      tantis digna deis et captatoribus horum.
115   alter enim, si concedas, mactare vovebit
      de grege servorum magna ut pulcherrima quaeque
      corpora, vel pueris et frontibus ancillarum
      inponet vittas et, si qua est nubilis illi

110 turrem PGU: turbam Φ: turmam A*Vat. 2810*
116 ut P: et Φ

428

tars has three little heirs. I'd happily wait to see who'd pay
for a sickly chicken, just closing its eyes, for so unprofitable
a friend. In fact, a hen is too much expense. No one ever
kills even a quail for a man with children. If wealthy and
childless Gallitta and Pacius have a hint of fever, the entire
colonnade is clothed in petitions stuck up in the proper
way. There are people who will promise a hundred oxen—
not elephants, seeing that here there are none, not even for
cash. Such a beast doesn't breed in Latium or anywhere in
our climate. It's grazing in Rutulian forests and the land
of Turnus, for sure, but brought from the dark nation, a
herd that belongs to Caesar.[17] They are not prepared to be
the slave of any private individual, since their ancestors
were used to obeying Tyrian Hannibal and Roman gener-
als and the Molossian king.[18] They carried cohorts on their
backs—quite a proportion of the forces—and towers ad-
vancing into battle. No delay, in that case, for Novius,
no delay for Pacuvius Hister[19] before taking that ivory to
the altars and felling it in front of Gallitta's house gods,
the only victim good enough for such divinities and their
fortune-hunters. The latter, you know, if you were to let
him, will promise to slaughter from his herd of slaves the
tallest bodies (since these are the best-looking). He'll put
sacrificial bands on his slave boys or slave girls' foreheads,

[17] The emperor's elephants were kept in Latium in the former
territory of Turnus and the Rutulians.   [18] Elephants were
used in battle during the third century B.C. by Pyrrhus, king of
Epirus (including the Molossians), and by Hannibal of Carthage
(which was colonised from Tyre). The Romans first used them in
the war against Philip V of Macedon in 200 B.C.

[19] Fortune-hunters.

Iphigenia domi, dabit hanc altaribus, etsi
120 non sperat tragicae furtiva piacula cervae.
laudo meum civem, nec comparo testamento
mille rates; nam si Libitinam evaserit aeger,
delebit tabulas inclusus carcere nassae
post meritum sane mirandum atque omnia soli
125 forsan Pacuvio breviter dabit, ille superbus
incedet victis rivalibus. ergo vides quam
grande operae pretium faciat iugulata Mycenis.
vivat Pacuvius quaeso vel Nestora totum,
possideat quantum rapuit Nero, montibus aurum
130 exaequet, nec amet quemquam nec ametur ab ullo.

and if he has an Iphigeneia of marrying age at home he'll offer her too on the altar, though without any hope of the secret atonement of the deer in tragedy.[20] Good for my fellow Roman!—a thousand ships are nothing compared with a will. The reason? If the invalid escapes from Libitina,[21] he'll destroy his will, caught in the fisherman's trap after some utterly amazing kindness by Pacuvius, and in a few words he'll perhaps leave everything to him as sole heir.[22] Then he will lord it over his beaten rivals. So you see how very worthwhile it was to murder that girl from Mycenae.[23] Long live Pacuvius! May he live as long even as Nestor, I pray. May he own as much as Nero stole. May he make mountains of gold. And may he love no one at all—and may no one love him.

[20] Iphigeneia was sacrificed to Diana by her father Agamemnon so that the Greek fleet could sail for Troy. In one version of the story by Euripides, she was saved by the substitution of a deer.

[21] Goddess of funerals.

[22] Legacy-hunters were represented as fisherman, e.g. Hor. *Sat.* 2.5.44.

[23] Iphigeneia, Agamemnon's daughter, here = a daughter.

NOTE ON SATIRE 13

The opening poem in Book Five is a consolation addressed
to Calvinus for his being defrauded of a small sum of
money, as the opening reveals (1–18). Actually, it is a
mock-consolation, an ironically trivial version of the stan-
dard Roman rhetorical and literary form in the event of
bereavement, since Juvenal shows precious little sympathy
towards his addressee. Juvenal starts by expressing amaze-
ment at Calvinus' reaction, which he considers excessive
and unrealistic in this day and age, when perjury is not the
exception but the rule (19–70). After trying to set Cal-
vinus' loss in perspective (71–4), he demonstrates how eas-
ily perjurers swear their false oaths (75–85), and imagines
their self-justifications (86–105) and further acts of bra-
zenness (106–11), while the victim is scolding the gods for
their inaction (112–19). At this point, Juvenal commences
his consolation proper by permitting Calvinus to grieve if
his loss is unparalleled (120–34). But the parade of similar
and worse cases in court suggests that his experience is un-
remarkable (135–73). At this point Calvinus bursts in with
an angry question: "Is the perjurer and his irreligious fraud
going to get away without punishment?" (174–5) In re-
sponse, Juvenal offers many arguments designed to re-
move his desire for revenge: that it is petty (175–92) and

that a guilty conscience is punishment in itself, whether the crime is merely planned (192–210) or actually carried out (210–49). He closes by promising that Calvinus will eventually have his satisfaction.

SATIRE 13

Exemplo quodcumque malo committitur, ipsi
displicet auctori. prima est haec ultio, quod se
iudice nemo nocens absolvitur, improba quamvis
gratia fallaci praetoris vicerit urna.
5 quid sentire putas homines, Calvine, recenti
de scelere et fidei violatae crimine? sed nec
tam tenuis census tibi contigit, ut mediocris
iacturae te mergat onus, nec rara videmus
quae pateris: casus multis hic cognitus ac iam
10 tritus et e medio fortunae ductus acervo.
ponamus nimios gemitus. flagrantior aequo
non debet dolor esse viri nec volnere maior.
tu quamvis levium minimam exiguamque malorum
particulam vix ferre potes spumantibus ardens
15 visceribus, sacrum tibi quod non reddat amicus
depositum. stupet haec qui iam post terga reliquit
sexaginta annos Fonteio consule natus?
an nihil in melius tot rerum proficis usu?

1–4 *del. Reeve, post* 195 *Richards*

---

1 Praetors served as judges in some of the Roman courts.
Cheating could occur in the selection of judges and in the casting
of their votes in the voting urn.

434

SATIRE 13

Whenever a bad example is set, it doesn't make the perpetrator feel good. This is the first vengeance: no one who is guilty is acquitted by his own verdict, even though the praetor's corrupt favour may have won the case with a rigged vote.[1] Calvinus, what do you think people feel about this recent crime and about the charge of trust betrayed? Yet it's not as if you're a man of such slender means that the burden of a moderate loss will sink you. And your experience is something we see happen all too often. This is a case of bad luck familiar to many people. By now it's banal, plucked at random from fortune's heap. Let's end this excessive grieving. A man's resentment shouldn't rage more fiercely than is reasonable, or exceed his injury. You can hardly put up with the tiniest, most minuscule crumb of misery, however trivial. You're blazing, with your guts in a ferment, because a friend won't give back the money you entrusted to him.[2] Can this surprise someone who was born in the year that Fonteius was consul,[3] who's got sixty years behind him? Have you gained no benefit whatsoever from all your experience of the world?

[2] Lit. a "sacred" or "untouchable" deposit.
[3] There were consuls of this name in A.D. 58, 59, and 67.

Magna quidem sacris quae dat praecepta libellis
20   victrix fortunae sapientia, ducimus autem
hos quoque felices, qui ferre incommoda vitae
nec iactare iugum vita didicere magistra.
quae tam fausta dies, ut cesset prodere furtum,
perfidiam, fraudes atque omni ex crimine lucrum
25   quaesitum et partos gladio vel pyxide nummos?
rari quippe boni: numera, vix sunt totidem quot
Thebarum portae vel divitis ostia Nili.
nona aetas agitur peioraque saecula ferri
temporibus, quorum sceleri non invenit ipsa
30   nomen et a nullo posuit natura metallo.
nos hominum divomque fidem clamore ciemus
quanto Faesidium laudat vocalis agentem
sportula? dic, senior bulla dignissime, nescis
quas habeat veneres aliena pecunia? nescis
35   quem tua simplicitas risum vulgo moveat, cum
exigis a quoquam ne peieret et putet altis
esse aliquod numen templis araeque rubenti?
quondam hoc indigenae vivebant more, priusquam
sumeret agrestem posito diademate falcem
40   Saturnus fugiens, tunc cum virguncula Iuno
et privatus adhuc Idaeis Iuppiter antris;
nulla super nubes convivia caelicolarum

23 fausta *Markland*: festa *codd.* | furtum *Nisbet*: furem *codd.*
26 numera PU^2: numerum FLUZ: innumerum G: numero
AHKOT: numeres *Schurzfleisch*
28 nona Φ: non FK: nunc P
36 altis *Courtney*: ullis *codd.*

Great, for sure, is the advice that Philosophy, conquer-
or of fortune, gives in her sacred books. Yet we consider
happy, too, people who've learned from life's teachings to
put up with the unpleasant things in life and not to resist
the yoke. What day is so auspicious that it doesn't produce
cases of theft, betrayal, and fraud, profit gained by every
kind of crime, and money acquired by the blade or poison
box? Good people are rare. Count them: they are hardly as
many as the gates of Thebes or the mouths of the rich
Nile.[4] We are living in the ninth age, an era worse than the
age of iron. Nature herself can find no name for its wicked-
ness and has no metal to label it.[5] What are we doing, in-
voking the assistance of mortals and immortals with a noise
that matches Faesidius' vocal entourage cheering him as
he pleads?[6] Tell me, old man (though you deserve a boy's
locket),[7] don't you know the attractions of money that
doesn't belong to you? Don't you know how your foolish-
ness provokes the mob to laugh when you demand from
anyone that he keep his oath and believe that divinity exists
in the high temples or the reddening altar? Once upon a
time, the aborigines lived like that, before Saturn dropped
his crown and picked up the rustic sickle as he ran away.[8] In
those days, Juno was still a little girl and Jupiter lived as an
ordinary guy in the caves of Ida. There were no banquets
of the celestials above the clouds, no Trojan boy, no beauti-

---

[4] Seven.   [5] The decline of humanity was represented as
the ages of gold, silver, bronze, and iron in Hesiod's *Works and
Days*; Juvenal takes this further.   [6] His entourage evidently
consisted of clients who hope to receive a handout (*sportula*).

[7] Worn by young boys, for protection.

[8] Saturn ruled the gods until Jupiter ousted him.

nec puer Iliacus formonsa nec Herculis uxor
ad cyathos et iam saccato nectare tergens
45 bracchia Volcanus Liparaea nigra taberna;
prandebat sibi quisque deus nec turba deorum
talis ut est hodie, contentaque sidera paucis
numinibus miserum urguebant Atlanta minori
pondere; nondum imi sortitus triste profundi
50 imperium Sicula torvos cum coniuge Pluton,
nec rota nec Furiae nec saxum aut volturis atri
poena, sed infernis hilares sine regibus umbrae.
improbitas illo fuit admirabilis aevo,
credebant quo grande nefas et morte piandum
55 si iuvenis vetulo non adsurrexerat et si
barbato cuicumque puer, licet ipse videret
plura domi fraga et maiores glandis acervos;
tam venerabile erat praecedere quattuor annis
primaque par adeo sacrae lanugo senectae.
60 nunc si depositum non infitietur amicus,
si reddat veterem cum tota aerugine follem,
prodigiosa fides et Tuscis digna libellis
quaeque coronata lustrari debeat agna.
egregium sanctumque virum si cerno, bimembri
65 hoc monstrum puero et miranti sub aratro

44 saccato *Schurzfleisch, Willis*: siccato *codd.*
49 imi *Housman*: aliquis Φ
54 quo P: quod Φ: quom *Knoche*
65 miranti Φ: mirantis G: mirandis PA

---

9 The Trojan boy is Ganymede, abducted by Jupiter to be
his cupbearer. Hebe, daughter of Jupiter and Juno, became the

ful wife of Hercules in charge of the cups, no Vulcan wiping clean his arms, blackened from his Liparean workshop, once the nectar was strained.[9] Each god lunched alone, and the crowd of gods wasn't as it is today. The stars were content with just a few divinities and weighed down on poor Atlas with lighter pressure.[10] Not yet had grim Pluto drawn as his allocation the gloomy kingdom of the abyss along with his Sicilian wife.[11] There was no wheel yet, or Furies, or rock, or vengeance of the black vulture.[12] Instead, with no rulers of the Underworld, the ghosts were cheerful. At that time, wickedness provoked astonishment. They considered it a major outrage, punishable by death, if a young man didn't stand up for an older man, or a boy for anyone with a beard, even if he saw more strawberries and bigger heaps of acorns in his own home. That's how much respect came from four years' seniority. That's how the first fuzz was the equivalent of sacred old age. But these days, if a friend does not renege upon your financial arrangement, if he returns to you your ancient purse with all its rust, it's a stupendous act of loyalty which calls for a consultation of the Etruscan books[13] and atonement with the sacrifice of a garlanded lamb. If I get a glimpse of an outstanding, honest man, I rank this prodigy with a mutant baby, or the

deified Hercules' wife, pouring nectar for the gods. Vulcan's cave was in the Aeolian (mod. Lipari) islands.   [10] Atlas carried the heavens on his shoulders.   [11] Proserpina, daughter of Ceres, whom Pluto abducted from Sicily.

[12] Some of the classic tortures in the Underworld: the wheel of Ixion, the rock of Sisyphus, the liver of Tityos attacked by vultures.

[13] The books of Etruscan soothsayers (see 2.121) were consulted for the interpretation of portents.

piscibus inventis et fetae comparo mulae,
sollicitus, tamquam lapides effuderit imber
examenque apium longa consederit uva
culmine delubri, tamquam in mare fluxerit amnis
70 gurgitibus miris et lactis vertice torrens.
    Intercepta decem quereris sestertia fraude
sacrilega? quid si bis centum perdidit alter
hoc arcana modo, maiorem tertius illa
summam, quam patulae vix ceperat angulus arcae?
75 tam facile et pronum est superos contemnere testes,
si mortalis idem nemo sciat. aspice quanta
voce neget, quae sit ficti constantia voltus.
per Solis radios Tarpeiaque fulmina iurat
et Martis frameam et Cirrhaei spicula vatis,
80 per calamos venatricis pharetramque puellae
perque tuum, pater Aegaei Neptune, tridentem,
addit et Herculeos arcus hastamque Minervae,
quidquid habent telorum armamentaria caeli.
si vero et pater est, "comedam" inquit flebile "nati
85 sinciput elixi Pharioque madentis aceto."
    Sunt in fortunae qui casibus omnia ponant
et nullo credant mundum rectore moveri
natura volvente vices et lucis et anni,
atque ideo intrepidi quaecumque altaria tangunt.
90 [est alius metuens ne crimen poena sequatur.]
hic putat esse deos et peierat, atque ita secum:
"decernat quodcumque volet de corpore nostro

90 *del. Jahn*

discovery of fish beneath a surprised plough, or a pregnant mule. I am as alarmed as if it had rained stones, or a swarm of bees had settled in a long cluster on the roof of a shrine, or as if a river had gushed a flood of milk with amazing eddies into the sea.

Ten thousand sesterces have been diverted in an act of sacrilegious fraud—that's your complaint? What if a secret deposit of two hundred thousand has been lost by someone else in the same way? Or someone else again a still greater sum than that, almost too much for the corner of his capacious treasure chest? It's so easy and straightforward to ignore the divine witnesses, if there's no mortal in the know. See how loud he is in his denials! See the composure of his shamming face! He swears by the rays of the Sun and the Tarpeian thunderbolts[14] and the lance of Mars and the arrows of the prophet of Cirrha,[15] by the shafts and quiver of the virgin huntress, and by your trident, Neptune, father of the Aegean. He throws in the bow of Hercules and the spear of Minerva—all the weapons in the celestial armoury. And if he's also a father, he says with a tear, "May I boil my son and eat his head, dripping with Egyptian vinegar!"

There are people who attribute everything to accidents of fortune. They believe that the universe operates without any guide and that nature rolls along the changes of the days and years, and for that reason they'll touch any altar you like without flinching. Another believes in the existence of the gods but still commits perjury, reasoning with himself like this, "Let Isis do whatever she likes with my

---

[14] Jupiter's temple on the Capitoline Hill was near the Tarpeian rock.   [15] Apollo: Cirrha was near Delphi.

Isis et irato feriat mea lumina sistro,
dummodo vel caecus teneam quos abnego nummos.
95 et pthisis et vomicae putres et dimidium crus
sunt tanti. pauper locupletem optare podagram
nec dubitet Ladas, si non eget Anticyra nec
Archigene; quid enim velocis gloria plantae
praestat et esuriens Pisaeae ramus olivae?
100 ut sit magna, tamen certe lenta ira deorum est.
[si curant igitur cunctos punire nocentes]
quando ad me venient? sed et exorabile numen
fortasse experiar; solet his ignoscere. multi
committunt eadem diverso crimina fato:
105 ille crucem sceleris pretium tulit, hic diadema."
sic animum dirae trepidum formidine culpae
confirmat, tunc te sacra ad delubra vocantem
praecedit, trahere immo ultro ac vexare paratus.
nam cum magna malae superest audacia causae,
110 creditur a multis fiducia. mimum agit ille,
urbani qualem fugitivus scurra Catulli:
tu miser exclamas, ut Stentora vincere possis,
vel potius quantum Gradivus Homericus, "audis,
Iuppiter, haec nec labra moves, cum mittere vocem
115 debueris vel marmoreus vel aeneus? aut cur
in carbone tuo charta pia tura soluta
ponimus et sectum vituli iecur albaque porci

101 *del. Nisbet*

---

16 An Olympic runner.   17 Anticyra was the source of
hellebore, a cure for madness: Pers. 4.16n. Archigenes was a fa-
mous Syrian doctor.   18 Pisa was the town near Olympia
where the Olympic games were held.

body, let her blast my eyes with her angry rattle, so long as I can keep the money I've denied receiving, even if I lose my sight. Tuberculosis and putrid abscesses and an amputated leg are worth it. If Ladas[16] were poor, he should have no hesitation in praying for the rich man's gout, unless he were in need of Anticyra or Archigenes.[17] After all, what does the glory of swiftfootedness bring, or the hungry branch of the Pisaean olive?[18] Great though it is, the anger of the gods is, all the same, really slow.[19] When will they get round to me? And I may even find that the deity is bid-dable, inclined to forgiveness in these cases. The same crimes are committed by many people, but with differing outcomes. That guy got crucified as the reward for his vil-lainy, but this guy got crowned." When his heart is shaking with terror at his dreadful guilt, that's how he steadies him-self. Then, when you summon him to the sacred shrine, he gets there before you and is quite prepared to drag you there himself and to go on the offensive. After all, a bad case backed up by huge effrontery makes this confidence very convincing. He's acting out a farce, just like clever Catullus' runaway clown,[20] while you're roaring, you poor thing, enough to outdo Stentor,[21] or, rather, as loud as Mars in Homer,[22] "Jupiter, do you hear this without moving your lips? You really should have spoken out, whether you're made of marble or of bronze. Why else do we unwrap our pious incense to put it on your glowing charcoal? Or our slices of calf liver, or the white fat from a pig? As I see it,

[19] Line 101: "So if it's their job to punish everyone that's guilty." [20] A Neronian mime-writer.
[21] A herald at Hom. *Il.* 5.785–6. [22] At Hom. *Il.* 5.859–61 Ares/Mars roars as loud as nine or ten thousand men.

omenta? ut video, nullum discrimen habendum est
effigies inter vestras statuamque Vagelli."
120   Accipe quae contra valeat solacia ferre
et qui nec Cynicos nec Stoica dogmata legit
a Cynicis tunica distantia, non Epicurum
suspicit exigui laetum plantaribus horti.
curentur dubii medicis maioribus aegri:
125 tu venam vel discipulo committe Philippi.
si nullum in terris tam detestabile factum
ostendis, taceo, nec pugnis caedere pectus
te veto nec plana faciem contundere palma,
quandoquidem accepto claudenda est ianua damno,
130 et maiore domus gemitu, maiore tumultu
planguntur nummi quam funera; nemo dolorem
fingit in hoc casu, vestem diducere summam
contentus, vexare oculos umore coacto:
ploratur lacrimis amissa pecunia veris.
135   Sed si cuncta vides simili fora plena querela,
si deciens lectis diversa parte tabellis
vana supervacui dicunt chirographa ligni,
arguit ipsorum quos littera gemmaque princeps
sardonychum, loculis quae custoditur eburnis,
140 ten, o delicias, extra communia censes
ponendum? quid? tu gallinae filius albae,
nos viles pulli nati infelicibus ovis?

123 suspicit PFGU: suscipit Φ
132 diducere PHKOT: deducere Φ
137 *cf.* 16.41   141 quid? *Heinrich*: quia *codd.*

23 The declaimer mentioned at 16.23. The significance of his
statue is not clear.

there's no distinction between your images and a statue of Vagellius."[23]

On the other hand, here's a consolation that even an ordinary person can offer—someone who's not read the Cynics or the doctrines of the Stoics (the same as the Cynics except for their shirts), who's not admired Epicurus, happy with the plants in his tiny garden.[24] Patients in a difficult condition need to be looked after by expert doctors, but you can entrust your pulse even to one of Philippus' students.[25] If in the whole world there's no crime you can point to as loathsome as this, I'll shut up. I won't tell you not to thump your chest with your fists or bash your face with the flat of your hand. After all, when a loss has been sustained, you have to close your doors. Cash is lamented with louder groaning and wailing all through the household than a death. In such a situation no one feigns his pain or draws the line at ripping the edge of his clothes and distressing his eyes with water that's forced out. The loss of money is mourned with real tears.

But if you see all the courts busy with similar complaints—if after a contract has been read ten times by their opponents people declare the signature false and the entire document worthless, although they are convicted by their own handwriting and by their gemstone, a prince of sardonyx kept in an ivory case—do you, you precious creature, think that you should be reckoned as extraordinary? What? Are you the son of a white hen and we the common chicks hatched from cursed eggs? Your experience is run

[24] The Cynics believed in living naturally, e.g. dispensing with clothing. Epicurus established his philosophical school in a garden at Athens.   [25] An unknown doctor.

rem pateris modicam et mediocri bile ferendam,
si flectas oculos maiora ad crimina. confer
145 conductum latronem, incendia sulpure coepta
atque dolo, primos cum ianua colligit ignes;
confer et hos, veteris qui tollunt grandia templi
pocula adorandae robiginis et populorum
dona vel antiquo positas a rege coronas;
150 haec ibi si non sunt, minor exstat sacrilegus qui
radat inaurati femur Herculis et faciem ipsam
Neptuni, qui bratteolam de Castore ducat;
[an dubitet solitus totum conflare Tonantem?]
confer et artifices mercatoremque veneni
155 et deducendum corio bovis in mare, cum quo
clauditur adversis innoxia simia fatis.
haec quota pars scelerum, quae custos Gallicus Vrbis
usque a lucifero donec lux occidat audit?
humani generis mores tibi nosse volenti
160 sufficit una domus; paucos consume dies et
dicere te miserum, postquam illinc veneris, aude.
quis tumidum guttur miratur in Alpibus aut quis
in Meroe crasso maiorem infante mamillam?
caerula quis stupuit Germani lumina, flavam
165 caesariem et madido torquentem cornua cirro?
[nempe quod haec illis natura est omnibus una.]
ad subitas Thracum volucres nubemque sonoram
Pygmaeus parvis currit bellator in armis,
mox inpar hosti raptusque per aera curvis
170 unguibus a saeva fertur grue. si videas hoc

153 *del. J. D. Lewis*
164 germani *codd.*: Germanus *Willis*
166 *del. Markland, Pinzger*

446

of the mill. It calls for middling rage, if you take a look at
more serious crimes. Compare the hired hit man, or the
fires deliberately started with matches, when the front
door catches the first flames. Compare the people who
filch from an ancient temple large chalices of venerable
rust, gifts of nations, or crowns dedicated by some king
long ago. If no such items are there, a minor vandal will
emerge to scrape the thigh of a gilded Hercules or even the
face of a Neptune or strip the gold leaf from a Castor. And
compare the manufacturer and supplier of poison, and the
man who should be thrown into the sea in an ox skin, along
with the innocent, ill-fated ape that's enclosed with him.[26]
This is only a tiny proportion of the crimes that Gallicus,[27]
guardian of Rome, hears continuously from the morning
star until the sun sets! If you want to understand the
behaviour of humankind, a single courthouse is enough.
Spend a few days there and then dare to call yourself
unlucky, after you've come away. Is there anyone who is
amazed at a swollen throat in the Alps,[28] or at a breast big-
ger than its fat baby in Meroë?[29] Whoever gawped at a
German's blue eyes and yellow hair twisting into points
with its greasy curls? A Pygmy warrior in his tiny armour
races towards the raucous cloud of Thracian birds that's
suddenly appeared and in a moment he's been grabbed by
a savage crane and carried off through the air in its curved

[26] The punishment for parricides: see 8.213–14n.

[27] Gaius Rutilius Gallicus, City Prefect under Domitian.

[28] Goitre, a swollen thyroid gland, a condition common in the
Alps.

[29] A district of Ethiopia on the Nile.

gentibus in nostris, risu quatiare; sed illic
[quamquam eadem adsidue spectentur proelia, ridet]
nemo, ubi tota cohors pede non est altior uno.
  "Nullane peiuri capitis fraudisque nefandae
175 poena erit?" abreptum crede hunc graviore catena
protinus et nostro (quid plus velit ira?) necari
arbitrio: manet illa tamen iactura, nec umquam
depositum tibi sospes erit, sed corpore trunco
invidiosa dabit missus solacia sanguis.
180 "at vindicta bonum vita iucundius ipsa."
nempe hoc indocti, quorum praecordia nullis
interdum aut levibus videas flagrantia causis.
[quantulacumque adeo est occasio sufficit irae.]
Chrysippus non dicet idem nec mite Thaletis
185 ingenium dulcique senex vicinus Hymetto,
qui partem acceptae saeva inter vincla cicutae
accusatori nollet dare. [plurima felix
paulatim vitia atque errores exuit, omnes
prima docens rectum, sapientia.] quippe minuti
190 semper et infirmi est animi exiguique voluptas
ultio. continuo sic collige, quod vindicta
nemo magis gaudet quam femina. cur tamen hos tu
evasisse putes, quos diri conscia facti
mens habet attonitos et surdo verbere caedit

172 del. Ruperti | quando Jacobs: quanquam codd.
179 missus Wakefield: minimus codd.: nimium Vianello: socius
Courtney   183 del. Heinrich
187-9 plurima . . . sapientia del. Guyet

talons, no match for his enemy.[30] If you saw this among our own people, you'd shake with laughter. But there,[31] where the entire army is no taller than one foot, no one laughs.

"Is the perjurer and his irreligious fraud going to get away without punishment?" Imagine that he'd been taken away in the heaviest chains immediately and executed at our discretion—what more could anger want? All the same, your loss remains. That sum of money will never be restored to you, and the blood that's been shed from that headless corpse will give you a consolation that brings with it hatred. "But vengeance is good, sweeter than life itself." That's what the uneducated say. Their innards you can sometimes see blazing for the slightest reason, or for no reason at all. That's not what Chrysippus[32] will say, or gentle-minded Thales,[33] or the old man who lived near sweet Hymettus, the one who would never have given his accuser a drop of the hemlock he received while he was in cruel custody.[34] The fact is that vengeance is invariably the pleasure of a petty, weak, and tiny mind. You can gather this straightaway from the fact that no one revels in vengeance more than a woman. Yet why should you think that people have got away with it, when guilty awareness of their terrible deeds keeps them paralysed and thrashes them with its

[30] There were stories and pictures of the battles between the cranes that flew south from Thrace and the Pygmies of Ethiopia, e.g. Hom. *Il.* 3.3–6.　　[31] Line 172: "Although such battles are witnessed day after day, [no one] laughs."

[32] Second founder of the Stoic school in the third century B.C.

[33] Thales of Miletus (7th-6th century B.C.), one of the Seven Sages and a founder of natural philosophy.

[34] Socrates, who died by drinking hemlock after being condemned in his trial in 399 B.C.

195 occultum quatiente animo tortore flagellum?
poena autem vehemens ac multo saevior illis
quas et Caedicius gravis invenit et Rhadamanthus,
nocte dieque suum gestare in pectore testem.
Spartano cuidam respondit Pythia vates
200 haut inpunitum quondam fore quod dubitaret
depositum retinere et fraudem iure tueri
iurando. quaerebat enim quae numinis esset
mens et an hoc illi facinus suaderet Apollo.
reddidit ergo metu, non moribus, et tamen omnem
205 vocem adyti dignam templo veramque probavit
extinctus tota pariter cum prole domoque
et quamvis longa deductis gente propinquis.
has patitur poenas peccandi sola voluntas.
nam scelus intra se tacitum qui cogitat ullum
facti crimen habet.
210   Cedo si conata peregit?
perpetua anxietas nec mensae tempore cessat
faucibus ut morbo siccis interque molares
difficili crescente cibo, Setina misellus
expuit, Albani veteris pretiosa senectus
215 displicet; ostendas melius, densissima ruga
cogitur in frontem, velut acri, ducta Falerno.
nocte brevem si forte indulsit cura soporem
et toto versata toro iam membra quiescunt,

205 templo *codd.*: Phoebo *Jacobs*
208 sola GKTU: saeva PAHO: scaeva FLZ | voluntas AFGUΣ: voluptas PΦ   213 Setina *Herelius et Withof*: sed vina *codd.*
215 melius *codd.*: mulsum *Scholte*

---

35 Rhadamanthus was a judge in the Underworld. Caedicius (also at 16.45) is unknown to us.

silent whip, and the mind is a torturer wielding an invisible lash? Yes, it's a fierce punishment, much more cruel than anything devised by stern Caedicius or Rhadamanthus,[35] to carry in your breast your own hostile witness, night and day. The Pythian prophetess once replied to a certain Spartan that he would not go unpunished, sooner or later, for wondering about keeping the money lodged with him and bolstering his fraud with an oath.[36] After all, he was asking to know the attitude of the deity, and whether Apollo recommended this crime to him. So he gave the money back, from fear not from principle. All the same, every utterance from the shrine was true and worthy of its temple, as he proved by his destruction along with all his children and house and extended family, however far removed. This is the punishment suffered for just wishing to do wrong. You see, people who contemplate any secret wickedness in their heads incur the guilt of the deed.

Then what if he carries through his efforts? His anxiety is never ending and doesn't recede even at meal times. His throat is parched, as if he were ill, and the stubborn food expands between his teeth. The wretch spits out Setian wine and dislikes the pricey antiquity of vintage Alban—and if you show him something finer, hundreds of wrinkles gather on his forehead traced by the Falernian, as if it had gone sour.[37] At night, if his anxiety has perhaps allowed him a short sleep and his limbs are now still after tossing all

---

[36] Glaucus was a Spartan who asked the oracle of Apollo for advice on a fraud he was contemplating and was punished, despite the fact that he returned the money (Herodotus 6.86).

[37] Setian and Alban wines (from Latium) were among the best. So too was Falernian, generally sweetened with honey.

continuo templum et violati numinis aras
220 et, quod praecipuis mentem sudoribus urguet,
te videt in somnis; tua sacra et maior imago
humana turbat pavidum cogitque fateri.
hi sunt qui trepidant et ad omnia fulgura pallent,
cum tonat, exanimes primo quoque murmure caeli,
225 non quasi fortuitus nec ventorum rabie sed
iratus cadat in terras et iudicet ignis.
illa nihil nocuit, cura graviore timetur
proxima tempestas velut hoc dilata sereno.
praeterea lateris vigili cum febre dolorem
230 si coepere pati, missum ad sua corpora morbum
infesto credunt a numine: saxa deorum
haec et tela putant. pecudem spondere sacello
balantem et Laribus cristam promittere galli
non audent; quid enim sperare nocentibus aegris
235 concessum? vel quae non dignior hostia vita?
[mobilis et varia est ferme natura malorum.]
cum scelus admittunt, superest constantia; quod fas
atque nefas tandem incipiunt sentire peractis
criminibus. tamen ad mores natura recurrit
240 damnatos fixa et mutari nescia. nam quis
peccandi finem posuit sibi? quando recepit
eiectum semel attrita de fronte ruborem?
quisnam hominum est quem tu contentum videris uno
flagitio? dabit in laqueum vestigia noster
245 perfidus et nigri patietur carceris uncum
aut maris Aegaei rupem scopulosque frequentes

236 *del. Jahn*

over the bed, at once he sees the temple and the altar of the god he has insulted and—the sight that oppresses his mind with extraordinary sweats—he sees you in his dreams. In his terror, your image, supernatural and larger than life, disturbs him and drives him to confess. These are the men who quake and turn pale at every flash of lightning. Whenever it thunders, they faint at the first rumbling in the sky, as if the fire falls to earth not at random or from the frenzy of the winds, but in anger and as a judgment. If the last storm didn't do them any harm, they dread the next one with deeper anxiety, as if it were just postponed by this lull. And another thing: if they have started to feel a pain in the side along with a fever that keeps them awake, they believe that illness has been inflicted upon their bodies by an angry power. They think these are the stones and missiles of the gods. They don't have the courage to pledge a bleating animal to the little shrine or to promise to their hearth gods a cockerel's crest. After all, is there anything that the guilty can legitimately hope for once they're ill? Is there any sacrificial victim that doesn't deserve to live more than they do? When they do something wicked, they have more than enough resolution. It's only long after the crime has been committed that they begin to get a sense of right and wrong. Yet their nature, which is set and incapable of change, reverts to the ways it has condemned. After all, who ever put a limit on their own wrongdoing? When has the blush of shame been recuperated after it's been banished from a hardened forehead? Have you ever seen anyone on earth draw the line at a single outrage? Our traitor will put his feet into the trap, and he will face the murky prison's hook or some craggy rock in the Aegean Sea

exulibus magnis. poena gaudebis amara
nominis invisi tandemque fatebere laetus
nec Drusum nec Teresian quemquam esse deorum.

249 Drusum *Courtney, Willis*: surdum *codd*.

crowded with important exiles.[38] You will revel in the bitter punishment of the man whose name you hate, and eventually you'll happily admit that none of the gods is a Drusus or a Teiresias.[39]

[38] Condemned prisoners were executed in prison and dragged by a hook through the crowds.

[39] Drusus is the emperor Claudius, reputedly very slow-witted; Tiresias is the blind prophet of Greek mythology.

NOTE ON SATIRE 14

Juvenal commences the poem, the longest in Book Five, with a general discussion of the bad example that parents set to their children (1–58), and advocates responsible, moral behaviour: "You should make yourself refrain" (38). He demonstrates how little thought parents give to their children's moral well-being (59–85). Two specific examples follow, of fathers who instil in their sons an obsession with building and the practice of Jewish religion (86–106). At this point, Juvenal shifts into the particular topic of avarice (*avaritia*), which occupies the rest of the poem. (For other poems combining two topics, see Satires 2, 4, and 12.) This is the only vice which is commended by parents as a virtue (107–22). He shows the ways in which fathers instruct their sons in avarice (123–72 and 179–209), pinpointing avarice as the major cause of crime (173–8). As a warning to fathers who give this kind of training, Juvenal argues that their sons will learn the lesson so well that they will quickly outstrip their fathers, with potentially fatal consequences (210–55). He describes as "an exceptional entertainment" (256) the risks people take for money (256–302). That, combined with the difficulties of hanging onto money, suggests that a minimalist life is preferable

(303–16). Finally, he ponders "the amount of wealth that's enough" (316–17): he imagines his addressee as continually dissatisfied with whatever limit he proposes and at last he gives up (316–31).

SATIRE 14

Plurima sunt, Fuscine, et fama digna sinistra
1A [et quod maiorum vitia sequiturque minores]
et nitidis maculam haesuram figentia rebus,
quae monstrant ipsi pueris traduntque parentes.
si damnosa senem iuvat alea, ludit et heres
5 bullatus parvoque eadem movet arma fritillo.
nec melius de se cuiquam sperare propinquo
concedet iuvenis, qui radere tubera terrae,
boletum condire et eodem iure natantis
mergere ficedulas didicit nebulone parente
10 et cana monstrante gula. cum septimus annus
transierit puerum, nondum omni dente renato,
barbatos licet admoveas mille inde magistros,
hinc totidem, cupiet lauto cenare paratu
semper et a magna non degenerare culina.
23 quid suadet iuveni laetus stridore catenae,
24 quem mire adficiunt inscripta, ergastula, carcer?
15 mitem animum et mores modicis erroribus aequos
praecipit utque animas servorum et corpora nostra
materia constare putet paribusque elementis,

1A *om.* PFU, *del. Calderinus*
23–4 *ante* 15 *Housman, Willis*
16–17 utque . . . putet *Buecheler*: atque . . . putat *codd.*

458

SATIRE 14

Fuscinus, there are many, many things that deserve a bad reputation and that fix a lasting stain to shining lives which are actually demonstrated and passed on to sons by their parents. If it's ruinous gambling that is the old man's pleasure, his heir is a player, too, while still a boy,[1] rattling the very same weapons in his tiny dice shaker. And if a young man has learned how to peel truffles, to marinate mushrooms, and to douse floating fig-peckers[2] in mushroom sauce under instruction from his waster of a father's white-haired gluttony, none of his relatives can entertain better hopes for him. Such a boy, when his seventh year has just passed by and before all his teeth have grown again, will always want to dine in lavish style without falling short of the high standard of his grand cuisine, though you bring in thousands of bearded tutors on his left and his right. Someone who revels in the clank of chains, who is extraordinarily excited by branded slaves, chain gangs, and dungeons—what is his influence on his youngster? Is Rutilus teaching gentleness of spirit and a disposition that doesn't overreact to minor lapses? And that he thinks the souls and bodies of slaves consist of the same stuff and elements as

[1] The *bulla* was an amulet worn by children.
[2] A small bird, a delicacy in the autumn.

an saevire docet Rutilus, qui gaudet acerbo
plagarum strepitu et nullam Sirena flagellis
20 conparat, Antiphates trepidi laris ac Polyphemus,
tunc felix, quotiens aliquis tortore vocato
22 uritur ardenti duo propter lintea ferro?
25 rusticus expectas ut non sit adultera Largae
filia, quae numquam maternos dicere moechos
tam cito nec tanto poterit contexere cursu
ut non ter deciens respiret? conscia matri
virgo fuit, ceras nunc hac dictante pusillas
30 implet et ad moechum dat eisdem ferre cinaedis.
sic natura iubet: velocius et citius nos
corrumpunt vitiorum exempla domestica, magnis
cum subeant animos auctoribus. unus et alter
forsitan haec spernant iuvenes, quibus arte benigna
35 et meliore luto finxit praecordia Titan,
sed reliquos fugienda patrum vestigia ducunt
et monstrata diu veteris trahit orbita culpae.
     Abstineas igitur [damnandis. huius enim vel
una potens ratio est] ne crimina nostra sequantur
40 ex nobis geniti, quoniam dociles imitandis
turpibus ac pravis omnes sumus, et Catilinam
quocumque in populo videas, quocumque sub axe,

---

[30] moechum PU: moechos Φ
[38-9] damnandis . . . est *del. Braund*

---

[3] The Sirens' song was sweet and seductive.
[4] Homeric ogres (cf. 15.18): Antiphates was king of the man-eating Laestrygonians (*Od.* 10.80) and Polyphemus the Cyclops ate Odysseus' crew (*Od.* 9).

our own? Or is he teaching cruelty, when he enjoys the harsh racket of a flogging and thinks the lash better than any Siren?[3] He's the Antiphates or Polyphemus of his trembling household,[4] only happy when the torturer has been summoned and someone's being scorched with the glowing iron—all because of a couple of towels? Do you naively expect Larga's daughter[5] not to practice adultery? She could never name her mother's lovers so quickly or reel them off at such a pace that she didn't need to draw breath thirty times. As a little girl she was her mother's accomplice. Now, as her mother dictates to her, she fills her little notes and gives them to the same pathics for transmission to her own lover. That's nature's law. Bad examples in the home corrupt us more speedily and quickly, because they creep into our minds with powerful authority. One or other young man may reject this behaviour, if his heart is fashioned by the Titan with generous skill from a superior clay.[6] But the rest are led along in the footprints of their fathers which they should avoid, and are dragged along in the track of an ancient fault which they've been shown for so long.

You should make yourself refrain, then,[7] to keep our children from copying our crimes. The fact is that we can all be taught to imitate what is disgraceful and crooked. You'll see a Catiline in any nation,[8] under any sky, but you

---

[5] The woman's name suggests she is "generous" with her favours.   [6] Prometheus, who according to one creation story made humans from clay.

[7] Lines 38–9: "from behaviour which is reprehensible. There's one powerful argument for this, at any rate."

[8] On Catiline, see 2.27n.

sed nec Brutus erit Bruti nec avunculus usquam.
nil dictu foedum visuque haec limina tangat
45   intra quae pater est. procul, a procul ite, puellae
lenonum et cantus pernoctantis parasiti.
maxima debetur puero reverentia. si quid
turpe paras, ne tu teneros contempseris annos,
sed peccaturo obstet tibi filius infans.
50   nam si quid dignum censoris fecerit ira
quandoque et similem tibi se non corpore tantum
nec vultu dederit, morum quoque filius et qui
omnia deterius tua per vestigia peccet,
corripies nimirum et castigabis acerbo
55   clamore ac post haec tabulas mutare parabis.
unde tibi frontem libertatemque parentis,
cum facias peiora senex vacuumque cerebro
iam pridem caput hoc ventosa cucurbita quaerat?
    Hospite venturo cessabit nemo tuorum.
60   "verre pavimentum, nitidas ostende columnas,
arida cum tota descendat aranea tela,
hic leve argentum, vasa aspera tergeat alter."
vox domini furit instantis virgamque tenentis.
ergo miser trepidas, ne stercore foeda canino
65   atria displiceant oculis venientis amici,
ne perfusa luto sit porticus, et tamen uno
semodio scobis haec emendat servulus unus:

45 pater PΦΣ: puer A | ite *Markland*: inde *codd.*
48 ne *Ruperti*: nec *codd.* | teneros *Courtney*: pueri *codd.*
51 quandoque P: quandoquidem Φ
52 quoque PFHTUΣ: tibi Φ

won't find a Brutus or his uncle anywhere.[9] Don't let any foul language or sight touch the threshold where there's a father inside. Keep away, keep well away, you pimps' girls and songs of the parasite who parties through the night! A child deserves the utmost respect. So if you're planning something disgusting, you shouldn't disregard his tender years. Rather, your baby son should be a deterrent when you are on the point of doing something wrong. After all, if some day he does something that attracts the censor's anger and proves himself like you not only in his body and face but your true son in his behaviour, too, in every case committing worse offences by following in your footsteps, you'll tell him off, without a doubt, and punish him, ranting harshly—and then arrange to change your will. What gives you the right to put on the stern father's face and authority, when in your old age you behave worse? When that head of yours, empty of brains, has been needing a cupping glass for a long time now?[10]

When a guest is expected, none of your household will get a break. "Sweep the marble floor! Polish the columns till they shine! Get that dried-up spider down along with all her web! One of you, wipe the plain silver, and you, the embossed vases." The master's voice rages as he stands over them, holding the rod. And so you get terribly anxious in case your friend, when he comes, is offended by the sight of your reception room fouled with dog turds or the colonnade splashed with mud, when one little slave boy equipped with just a half-bucket of sawdust can put this

[9] Two Stoic figureheads: Marcus Junius Brutus, assassin of Julius Caesar, and his uncle Marcus Porcius Cato Uticensis.

[10] Used to relieve madness by drawing blood from the head.

illud non agitas, ut sanctam filius omni
aspiciat sine labe domum vitioque carentem?
70 gratum est quod patriae civem populoque dedisti,
si facis ut patriae sit idoneus, utilis agris,
utilis et bellorum et pacis rebus agendis.
plurimum enim intererit quibus artibus et quibus
      hunc tu
moribus instituas. serpente ciconia pullos
75 nutrit et inventa per devia rura lacerta:
illi eadem sumptis quaerunt animalia pinnis.
voltur iumento et canibus crucibusque relictis
ad fetus properat partemque cadaveris adfert:
hic est ergo cibus magni quoque volturis et se
80 pascentis, propria cum iam facit arbore nidos.
sed leporem aut capream famulae Iovis et generosae
in saltu venantur aves, hinc praeda cubili
ponitur: inde autem cum se matura levavit
progenies stimulante fame festinat ad illam
85 quam primum praedam rupto gustaverat ovo.
    Aedificator erat Caetronius et modo curvo
litore Caietae, summa nunc Tiburis arce,
nunc Praenestinis in montibus alta parabat
culmina villarum Graecis longeque petitis
90 marmoribus vincens Fortunae atque Herculis aedem,
ut spado vincebat Capitolia nostra Posides.
dum sic ergo habitat Caetronius, inminuit rem,
fregit opes, nec parva tamen mensura relictae
partis erat. totam hanc turbavit filius amens,
95 dum meliore novas attollit marmore villas.
    Quidam sortiti metuentem sabbata patrem

---

[11] Unknown.   [12] A wealthy freedman of Claudius.

right; and yet you don't make any effort to ensure that your son sees a home that's pure and completely flawless and without reproach? Thank you for producing a citizen for your fatherland and your people, just so long as you make him an asset to his fatherland, capable of farming, capable of action in war and peace alike. The fact is, the habits and behaviour you train him in will make a huge difference. The stork feeds her chicks on snakes and lizards she finds in the remote countryside and they, once they have their wings, seek out the same creatures themselves. The vulture rushes from cattle, dogs, or crucifixions, carrying bits of carrion to its young, and as a result this is the vulture's food when it too is full-grown and feeding itself and already making its nest in a tree of its own. But the noble birds that attend Jupiter hunt for hares and deer in the glades, and that's where the prey they serve up in the eyrie comes from. So too when their offspring reach maturity and launch themselves, hunger goads them to swoop down on the prey that they first tasted after breaking out of the eggshell.

Caetronius was obsessed with building.[11] He constructed the high roofs of his villas at one time on the curving shoreline of Caieta, then again on the heights of Tibur, and again in the hills of Praeneste. With his marble brought from Greece and from far away he outdid the temples of Fortune and Hercules, just as Posides the eunuch tried to outdo the Roman Capitol.[12] The result was that, in this kind of accommodation, Caetronius reduced his property and frittered away his wealth. Yet what was left was not a negligible amount. All of that his crazy son squandered by putting up new villas of even finer marble.

Some happen to have been dealt a father who respects

nil praeter nubes et caeli numen adorant,
nec distare putant humana carne suillam,
qua pater abstinuit, mox et praeputia ponunt;
100   Romanas autem soliti contemnere leges
Iudaicum ediscunt et servant ac metuunt ius,
tradidit arcano quodcumque volumine Moyses:
non monstrare vias eadem nisi sacra colenti,
quaesitum ad fontem solos deducere verpos.
105   sed pater in causa, cui septima quaeque fuit lux
ignava et partem vitae non attigit ullam.
         Sponte tamen iuvenes imitantur cetera, solam
inviti quoque avaritiam exercere iubentur.
fallit enim vitium specie virtutis et umbra,
110   cum sit triste habitu vultuque et veste severum,
nec dubie tamquam frugi laudetur avarus,
tamquam parcus homo et rerum tutela suarum
certa magis quam si fortunas servet easdem
Hesperidum serpens aut Ponticus. adde quod hunc de
115   quo loquor egregium populus putat adquirendi
artificem; quippe his crescunt patrimonia fabris
[sed crescunt quocumque modo maioraque fiunt]
incude adsidua semperque ardente camino.
[et pater ergo animi felices credit avaros]
120   qui miratur opes, qui nulla exempla beati
pauperis esse putat, iuvenes hortatur ut illa
ire via pergant et eidem incumbere sectae.

117 *del. Jahn*   119 *del. Housman*

---

13 The Pentateuch (the first five books of the Bible) was attri-
buted to Moses.

the sabbath. They worship nothing except the clouds and spirit of the sky. They think there is no difference between pork, which their fathers abstained from, and human flesh. In time, they get rid of their foreskins. And with their habit of despising the laws of Rome, they study, observe, and revere the Judaic code, as handed down by Moses in his mystic scroll,[13] which tells them not to show the way to anyone except a fellow worshipper and if asked, to take only the circumcised to the fountain. But it's their fathers who are to blame, taking every seventh day as a day of laziness and separate from ordinary life.

Still, it's by their own choice that young people imitate our other vices. It's only in the case of avarice that they are told to practice it even against the grain. The reason? This is a deceptive fault, with a shadow and pretence of goodness, because it has a gloomy bearing and severe look and get-up. Without hesitation the miser is applauded as if he were frugal, an economical guy who keeps a surer hold of his wealth than if the dragon of the Hesperides or the one from the Black Sea were guarding it.[14] What is more, the public consider such a man as this exceptionally skilled in the art of acquisition. Workers like these, you know, make inheritances grow[15] on their nonstop anvil and in their permanently glowing forge.[16] Anyone who is in awe of wealth and who thinks there can be no cases of poor men who are happy urges his sons to proceed down that path and to

[14] A dragon guarded the apples of the Hesperides and another the Golden Fleece in the land of Colchis.　　　[15] Line 117: "but they grow in whatever way and become greater."

[16] Line 119: "So the father, too, considers misers to be happy in their outlook."

sunt quaedam vitiorum elementa: his protinus illos
inbuit et cogit minimas ediscere sordes;
125   mox adquirendi docet insatiabile votum.
servorum ventres modio castigat iniquo
ipse quoque esuriens, neque enim omnia sustinet
        umquam
mucida caerulei panis consumere frusta,
hesternum solitus medio servare minutal
130   Septembri nec non differre in tempora cenae
alterius conchem aestivam cum parte lacerti
signatam vel dimidio putrique siluro
filaque sectivi numerata includere porri.
invitatus ad haec aliquis de ponte negabit.
135   Sed quo divitias haec per tormenta coactas,
cum furor haut dubius, cum sit manifesta phrenesis,
ut locuples moriaris, egentis vivere fato?
interea, pleno cum turget sacculus ore,
crescit amor nummi quantum ipsa pecunia crevit,
140   [et minus hanc optat qui non habet. ergo paratur]
altera villa tibi, cum rus non sufficit unum
et proferre libet finis maiorque videtur
et melior vicina seges; mercaris et hanc et
arbusta et densa montem qui canet oliva.
145   quorum si pretio dominus non vincitur ullo,
nocte boves macri lassoque famelica collo
iumenta ad viridis huius mittentur aristas
nec prius inde domum quam tota novalia saevos
in ventres abeant, ut credas falcibus actum.
150   dicere vix possis quam multi talia plorent

124 minimas PAFGU: nimias Φ
140 *del. Braund*   149 abeant A: habeant PΦ

become devotees of that same school of thought. Vices
have certain rudiments. From the start he saturates them
with these and forces them to master the tiniest kinds of
stinginess. Soon he teaches them insatiable desire for ac-
quisition. He punishes his slaves' bellies with unfair rations
and goes hungry himself. The fact is that he can't ever bear
to eat up all the mouldy hunks of his blue-green bread. He
habitually keeps yesterday's mincemeat in the middle of
September and, yes, in summer he puts aside his beans
till the next dinnertime, sealed up with a bit of mackerel
or half a rotting sprat, and he puts away the shreds of
chopped leek only after they've been counted. Any beggar
from a bridge[17] who's invited to this meal would refuse.

But what's the point of heaping up money through such
tortures? It's undisputed madness, it's sheer lunacy, isn't it,
to live like a down-and-out just to die rich? In the mean-
time, when your little purse is bulging with its mouth full,
your love of cash grows as much as the money itself has
grown.[18] You'll get another villa, since one country estate is
not enough. You like extending your boundaries, and the
neighbouring cornfield looks bigger and better. This too
you buy up, along with the vineyards and the hill pale with
a mass of olive trees. If their owner is not won round by any
offer, you'll drive some scrawny oxen and famished pack
animals with weary necks into his green corn at night and
they won't go home until the entire new crop has disap-
peared into their raging bellies. You'd think it had been
done with a scythe. You can scarcely describe how many

[17] Beggars often stood at bridges.
[18] Line 140: "and the person who has not wants it less. So you'll
buy yourself."

469

et quot venales iniuria fecerit agros.
sed qui sermones, quam foede bucina famae!
"quid nocet haec?" inquit "tunicam mihi malo lupini
quam si me toto laudet vicinia pago
155 exigui ruris paucissima farra secantem."
scilicet et morbis et debilitate carebis
et luctum et curam effugies, et tempora vitae
longa tibi posthac fato meliore dabuntur,
si tantum culti solus possederis agri
160 quantum sub Tatio populus Romanus arabat.
mox etiam fractis aetate ac Punica passis
proelia vel Pyrrhum inmanem gladiosque Molossos
tandem pro multis vix iugera bina dabantur
vulneribus; merces haec sanguinis atque laboris
165 nulli visa umquam meritis minor aut ingratae
curta fides patriae. saturabat glebula talis
patrem ipsum turbamque casae, qua feta iacebat
uxor et infantes ludebant quattuor, unus
vernula, tres domini; sed magnis fratribus horum
170 a scrobe vel sulco redeuntibus altera cena
amplior et grandes fumabant pultibus ollae.
nunc modus hic agri nostro non sufficit horto.
inde fere scelerum causae, nec plura venena
miscuit aut ferro grassatur saepius ullum
175 humanae mentis vitium quam saeva cupido
inmodici census. nam dives qui fieri volt,

---

[19] King of the Sabine people who joined with the Romans to
form a single state.

[20] The Punic Wars were fought against Carthage in 264–241,
218–201, and 149–6 B.C. Rome fought against Pyrrhus, king of
Epirus (including the Molossians), from 280–75 B.C.

people make complaints of this kind or how many estates
are put up for sale because of damage. But think of the gos-
sip! Think of the awful noise of scandal's blare! "What
harm does that do?" he says, "I'd rather keep my lupin pod
than reap the paltry grain off a minute country estate while
the neighbourhood sings my praises through the entire
district." And I suppose you'll be exempt from diseases and
infirmity, and you'll escape grief and worry, and you'll be
granted a long span of life with better luck from then on—
if only you are the sole owner of a swathe of arable land that
matches the amount ploughed by the whole Roman people
under Tatius.[19] Later, even the veterans of the Punic bat-
tles or of fierce Pyrrhus or of the Molossian swords, broken
by age, received at long last a scanty couple of acres in re-
turn for their many wounds.[20] None of them ever thought
that this reward for their blood and toil was less than they
deserved. None said that their fatherland was ungrateful
and short on loyalty. A clod of earth like that was ample for
the father himself and the crowd in his cottage, where his
wife lay pregnant and four children were playing, one a
home slave and three of them masters. But when their big
brothers got back from the ditch or the furrow, a second,
larger dinner was waiting for them and huge pots steaming
with porridge. These days, we'd regard this amount of land
as not enough even for a garden. That's mostly why crimes
happen. There's no fault of the human mind that has pre-
pared more poisons or gone on the rampage with steel
more often than the savage lust for extravagant wealth.
After all, the man who wants to be a millionaire also wants

et cito volt fieri; sed quae reverentia legum,
quis metus aut pudor est umquam properantis avari?
"vivite contenti casulis et collibus istis,
180 o pueri," Marsus dicebat et Hernicus olim
Vestinusque senex, "panem quaeramus aratro,
qui satis est mensis: laudant hoc numina ruris,
quorum ope et auxilio gratae post munus aristae
contingunt homini veteris fastidia quercus.
185 nil vetitum fecisse volet, quem non pudet alto
per glaciem perone tegi, qui summovet euros
pellibus inversis: peregrina ignotaque nobis
ad scelus atque nefas, quaecumque est, purpura ducit."
   Haec illi veteres praecepta minoribus; at nunc
190 post finem autumni media de nocte supinum
clamosus iuvenem pater excitat: "accipe ceras,
scribe, puer, vigila, causas age, perlege rubras
maiorum leges. aut vitem posce libello,
sed caput intactum buxo narisque pilosas
195 adnotet et grandes miretur Laelius alas;
dirue Maurorum attegias, castella Brigantum,
ut locupletem aquilam tibi sexagesimus annus
adferat; aut, longos castrorum ferre labores
si piget et trepidum solvunt tibi cornua ventrem
200 cum lituis audita, pares quod vendere possis

---

21 Peoples of Italy incorporated into the Roman state, symbols of a rough, simple lifestyle.

22 Literally "oak."

23 The staff was the centurion's symbol of authority. Laelius was evidently the commanding officer.

24 Mauretania (North Africa) and Brigantia (the north of England) were trouble spots early in the reign of Hadrian.

it quickly. But what respect for the law do you ever find, what fear or restraint, in a miser in a hurry? "Live happy with these huts and hills of yours, boys"—that's what an old man of the Marsi or Hernici or Vestini would say long ago.[21] "Let's use the plough to get bread enough for our tables. This is what the country gods approve of. It's with their help and assistance that people acquired their distaste for the ancient acorn[22] after their gift of the welcome ear of corn. The person who is not embarrassed at wearing high rawhide boots in the ice, who dispels the east winds with skins turned inside out, will have no wish to do anything forbidden. It's purple cloth, whatever it is, foreign and newfangled, that leads people to crime and wickedness."

These were the lessons those old men taught the young. But these days, after the end of autumn, the father wakes up his snoozing son by shouting in the middle of the night: "Get your notebooks, boy! Write, stay awake, prepare your cases, make a close study of the red-lettered laws of our ancestors! Or else petition for the centurion's vine staff, making sure that Laelius notices your uncombed head and hairy nostrils and admires your broad shoulders.[23] Tear down the huts of the Moors and the forts of the Brigantes,[24] so your sixtieth year will grant you the eagle that makes you wealthy.[25] Or else, if you shrink from undergoing the lengthy toil of the military life and if the horns sounding along with the trumpets loosen your nervous bowels, you should get hold of stuff you can sell with

[25] I.e. reach the position of senior centurion of the legion, who had charge of the standard ("eagle").

pluris dimidio, nec te fastidia mercis
ullius subeant ablegandae Tiberim ultra,
neu credas ponendum aliquid discriminis inter
unguenta et corium: lucri bonus est odor ex re
205   qualibet. illa tuo sententia semper in ore
versetur dis atque ipso Iove digna poeta:
'unde habeas quaerit nemo, sed oportet habere.'"
[hoc monstrant vetulae pueris repentibus assae,
hoc discunt omnes ante alpha et beta puellae.]
210   Talibus instantem monitis quemcumque parentem
sic possem adfari: "dic, o vanissime, quis te
festinare iubet? meliorem praesto magistro
discipulum. securus abi: vinceris, ut Aiax
praeteriit Telamonem, ut Pelea vicit Achilles.
215   parcendum est teneris; nondum implevere medullas
maturae mala nequitiae. cum ponere barbam
coeperit et longi mucronem admittere cultri,
falsus erit testis, vendet periuria summa
exigua et Cereris tangens aramque pedemque.
220   elatam iam crede nurum, si limina vestra
mortifera cum dote subit. quibus illa premetur
per somnum digitis! nam quae terraque marique
adquirenda putas brevior via conferet illi;
nullus enim magni sceleris labor. 'haec ego numquam
225   mandavi' dices olim 'nec talia suasi.'
mentis causa malae tamen est et origo penes te.
nam quisquis magni census praecepit amorem

     206 poeta PS: poetae Φ   208–9 *del. Jahn* | repentibus
Sang.: petentibus F: repetentibus U: poscentibus Φ
   216 ponere *Markland*: pectere *codd.*
   217 longi Φ: longae PAF

a fifty percent markup. Don't let disgust for any kind of merchandise that has to be kept beyond the Tiber[26] creep over you, and don't imagine that you should draw any distinction between perfumes and hides. The smell of profit is good, whatever its source. Keep this motto always on your lips—it's worthy of the gods and of Jupiter himself, were he a poet: 'No one asks where you got it from —but have it you must.'"[27]

This is what I'd like to say to any father who's insisting on such advice: "Tell me, you brainless specimen, who's making you hurry? I guarantee that the pupil will do better than his teacher. Off you go, and don't worry. He'll beat you, as surely as Ajax outdid Telamon and as Achilles beat Peleus. The young need gentle treatment. The taints of adult wickedness have not yet filled the marrow of their bones. When he's started shaving his beard and taking the long razor's edge to it, then he'll give false evidence and sell his perjuries for a tiny amount, even while touching the altar and feet of Ceres. You have to consider your daughter-in-law already dead and buried if she crosses your threshold with a fatal dowry. Think of his fingers strangling her in her sleep! Yes, a quicker way will give him the things that you think worth hunting through land and sea. After all, a major crime is no great effort. 'I never taught him that!' you'll say, sooner or later, 'I never told him to behave like that!' Yet the root and source of his evil mind lie with you. The fact is that anyone who has incul-

---

[26] Offensive trades such as tanning hides were restricted to the far (right) bank of the Tiber.   [27] Lines 208–9: "This is the lesson ancient dry nurses give to boys before they can walk; this is what every girl learns before her alphabet."

et laevo monitu pueros producit avaros
[et qui per fraudes patrimonia conduplicari]
230 dat libertatem et totas effundit habenas
curriculo; quem si revoces, subsistere nescit
et te contempto rapitur metisque relictis.
nemo satis credit tantum delinquere quantum
permittas: adeo indulgent sibi latius ipsi.
235 cum dicis iuveni stultum qui donet amico,
qui paupertatem levet attollatque propinqui,
et spoliare doces et circumscribere et omni
crimine divitias adquirere, quarum amor in te
quantus erat patriae Deciorum in pectore, quantum
240 dilexit Thebas, si Graecia vera, Menoeceus.
[in quorum sulcis legiones dentibus anguis
cum clipeis nascuntur et horrida bella capessunt
continuo, tamquam et tubicen surrexerit una]
ergo ignem, cuius scintillas ipse dedisti,
245 flagrantem late et rapientem cuncta videbis.
nec tibi parcetur misero, trepidumque magistrum
in cavea magno fremitu leo tollet alumnus.
nota mathematicis genesis tua, sed grave tardas
expectare colus: morieris stamine nondum
250 abrupto. iam nunc obstas et vota moraris,
iam torquet iuvenem longa et cervina senectus.
ocius Archigenen quaere atque eme quod Mithridates
composuit, si vis aliam decerpere ficum

229 *om. Φ, del. Ruperti*   241–3 *del. Markland, Knoche*
247 cavea P: caveam Φ

28 On the Decii's patriotism, see 8.254n. Menoeceus killed
himself to save his city in the conflict with the Seven against

cated the love of enormous wealth and who by his warped advice has produced boys who are miserly in effect gives them licence and abandons the chariot's reins entirely. If you try to call it back, it cannot stop and it's swept along, despising you and leaving behind the turning posts. No one thinks it's enough to break the rules just as much as you let him. People give themselves much more leeway. When you tell your son that anyone who gives presents to a friend or relieves a relative's poverty and sets him on his feet is a fool, you're teaching him to rob and cheat and commit all kinds of crime in the pursuit of wealth. Your love of money matches the Decii's heartfelt love of their country and Menoeceus' devotion to Thebes, if Greece tells the truth.[28] The consequence is that you'll see the fire, for which you kindled the sparks yourself, blazing far and wide and devouring everything. And you'll receive no mercy in your misery. With a loud roar the lion whom you've reared will destroy his trembling teacher in his cage. The astrologers know your horoscope, but it's tedious to wait for the slow spindle. The fact is, you'll die before the thread has been broken. You're already in the way as it is, and you're delaying his dreams. Your long and staglike old age is already a torture to your son. Find Archigenes[29] right away and purchase one of Mithridates' compounds,[30] if you want to pluck one more fig and enjoy roses one more time.

Thebes. Lines 241–3: "It was in the furrows of Thebes that legions sprang up from the teeth of a snake, equipped with shields, and straightaway engaged in dreadful battle, as if the trumpeter had risen up along with them."

[29] The doctor mentioned at 6.236 and 13.98.

[30] On Mithridates, see 6.661n.

atque alias tractare rosas. medicamen habendum est,
255 sorbere ante cibum quod debeat et pater et rex."
Monstro voluptatem egregiam, cui nulla theatra,
nulla aequare queas praetoris pulpita lauti,
si spectes quanto capitis discrimine constent
incrementa domus, aerata multus in arca
260 fiscus et ad vigilem ponendi Castora nummi,
ex quo Mars Vltor galeam quoque perdidit et res
non potuit servare suas. ergo omnia Florae
et Cereris licet et Cybeles aulaea relinquas:
tanto maiores humana negotia ludi.
265 an magis oblectant animum iactata petauro
corpora quique solet rectum descendere funem
quam tu, Corycia semper qui puppe moraris
atque habitas, Coro semper tollendus et Austro,
perditus ac vilis sacci mercator olentis,
270 qui gaudes pingue antiquae de litore Cretae
passum et municipes Iovis advexisse lagonas?
hic tamen ancipiti figens vestigia planta
victum illa mercede parat, brumamque famemque
illa reste cavet: tu propter mille talenta
275 et centum villas temerarius. aspice portus
et plenum magnis trabibus mare: plus hominum est iam
in pelago. veniet classis quocumque vocarit

269 ac vilis PU: a siculis Φ: articulis *Nisbet*

---

31 The temple of Castor in the Forum had security guards.
32 Evidently the Temple of Mars Ultor had recently been robbed. Possibly also a literary allusion to the depiction of Mars that opens Ovid, *Fasti* 3.

You need the drug which fathers as well as kings should swallow before food."

It's an exceptional entertainment that I'm showing you. You won't be able to match it on any of the stages or platforms of the sumptuous praetor. All you have to do is to look at how people risk their lives for growth to their fortunes, for the huge money bag in the bronze-bound treasure chest and the cash which has to be deposited under Castor's guardianship,[31] ever since even Mars the Avenger lost his helmet and couldn't hang onto his own property.[32] So, you can abandon the scene curtains of Flora and Ceres and Cybele in their entirety.[33] Human life is so much more entertaining. Which is more amusing? Bodies thrown from the trapeze and the man walking down the tightrope again—or you, forever lingering and living on your Corycian boat,[34] forever tossed by the winds from the northwest or south, a desperate and cheapskate trader in stinking sacks, delighted to be importing syrupy raisin wine and winejars, compatriots of Jupiter, from the coast of ancient Crete?[35] Yet the person who places his steps with balancing foot earns his living from that work. With that tightrope of his, he avoids cold and hunger. You, by contrast, take foolish risks for a thousand talents and a hundred villas. Just look at the harbours and the sea full of bulky timbers. The majority of humankind is now on the water. Fleets will come wherever hope of profit summons

[33] Three holidays celebrated with theatrical shows: Floralia April 28–May 3, Cerealia April 12–19, and the Ludi Megalenses of Cybele April 4–10.

[34] Corycus was a port in Cilicia.

[35] Jupiter was said to have been raised on Crete.

spes lucri, nec Carpathium Gaetulaque tantum
aequora transiliet, sed longe Calpe relicta
280   audiet Herculeo stridentem gurgite solem.
grande operae pretium est, ut tenso folle reverti
inde domum possis tumidaque superbus aluta,
Oceani monstra et iuvenes vidisse marinos.
    Non unus mentes agitat furor. ille sororis
285   in manibus voltu Eumenidum terretur et igni,
hic bove percusso mugire Agamemnona credit
aut Ithacum. parcat tunicis licet atque lacernis,
curatoris eget qui navem mercibus implet
ad summum latus et tabula distinguitur unda,
290   cum sit causa mali tanti et discriminis huius
concisum argentum in titulos faciesque minutas.
occurrunt nubes et fulgura: "solvite funem"
frumenti dominus clamat piperisve coempti,
"nil color hic caeli, nil fascia nigra minatur;
295   aestivum tonat." infelix hac forsitan ipsa
nocte cadet fractis trabibus fluctuque premetur
obrutus et zonam laeva morsuque tenebit.
sed cuius votis modo non suffecerat aurum
quod Tagus et rutila volvit Pactolus harena,
300   frigida sufficient velantes inguina panni

---

36 The Carpathian Sea was between Rhodes and Crete. Gae-
tulia was northwest Africa. Calpe = Gibraltar. Hercules travelled
beyond the Mediterranean into the Atlantic, where the sun was
thought to dip itself into the sea.

37 Orestes, brother of Electra.

38 Ajax attacked a herd of cattle, thinking they were the Greek
leaders, in his anger at the award of the weapons of Achilles to
Ulysses, "the Ithacan."

them. They'll not only leap across the Carpathian Sea and Gaetulian waters but leave Calpe far behind and hear the sound of the sun hissing in Hercules' deep.[36] It's a grand reward for your effort to go back home from there with a tight-stuffed money bag and to exult in your swollen purse after seeing the monsters of the Ocean and the young mermen.

People's minds are hounded by different kinds of madness. One man in his sister's arms is terrified by the faces and fires of the Furies.[37] Another, when he has hit an ox, thinks it's Agamemnon or the Ithacan who is bellowing.[38] The man who loads his ship with merchandise to the gunwale, with only a plank between him and the waves, needs a minder, even though he keeps his hands off his shirt and his cloak, when the only reason for so much hardship and all that danger is bits of chopped up silver with inscriptions and tiny portraits. Up come the clouds and the lightning. "Cast off the rope," shouts the owner of the grain and pepper he's bought up. "This darkness in the sky, these black bands are no threat at all. It's only summer thunder." Poor thing! This very night he will perhaps fall overboard as the timbers are shattered, and be overwhelmed and engulfed by the waves, hanging on to his belt with his left hand or his teeth. But the person whose dreams were yesterday not satisfied by all the gold rolled along by the Tagus and the Pactolus in its red sand[39] will now have to be satisfied with rags covering his freezing crotch and with scraps of food,

[39] Gold-bearing rivers, the Tagus in Spain and the Pactolus in Lydia, Asia Minor.

exiguusque cibus, mersa rate naufragus assem
dum rogat et picta se tempestate tuetur.
    Tantis parta malis cura maiore metuque
servantur: misera est magni custodia census.
305 dispositis praedives amis vigilare cohortem
servorum noctu Licinus iubet, attonitus pro
electro signisque suis Phrygiaque columna
atque ebore et lata testudine. dolia nudi
non ardent Cynici; si fregeris, altera fiet
310 cras domus aut eadem plumbo commissa manebit.
sensit Alexander, testa cum vidit in illa
magnum habitatorem, quanto felicior hic qui
nil cuperet quam qui totum sibi posceret orbem
passurus gestis aequanda pericula rebus.
315 nullum numen habes, si sit prudentia: nos te,
nos facimus, Fortuna, deam.
                       Mensura tamen quae
sufficiat census, si quis me consulat, edam:
in quantum sitis atque fames et frigora poscunt,
quantum, Epicure, tibi parvis suffecit in hortis,
320 quantum Socratici ceperunt ante penates;
numquam aliud natura, aliud sapientia dicit.
acribus exemplis videor te cludere? misce
ergo aliquid nostris de moribus, effice summam
bis septem ordinibus quam lex dignatur Othonis.
325 haec quoque si rugam trahit extenditque labellum,
sume duos equites, fac tertia quadringenta.

310 aut AGU: atque PΦ

---

[40] Shipwrecked sailors begged for alms by displaying a painting of the shipwreck. Cf. Pers. 1.88.

482

while he begs for pennies as a shipwreck survivor and maintains himself by painting a picture of the storm.[40]

Possessions acquired through such great hardships are kept safe with still greater trouble and anxiety. Protecting great wealth is a miserable business. The millionaire Licinus[41] stations his fire buckets and tells his cohort of slaves to keep watch through the night, terrified for his amber and statues and columns of Phrygian marble and ivory and plaques of tortoiseshell. The naked Cynic's tub doesn't catch fire.[42] Break it and the next day another home will appear, or else the same one will remain, patched up with lead. When he saw that pot with its great inhabitant, Alexander realised how much happier this man was for having no desires than the one who claimed the whole world for himself and who would endure dangers that matched his achievements. Fortune, you'd have no power, if we were sensible: it's we who make you a goddess.

Yet I'll tell you the amount of wealth that's enough, if anyone asks my advice: as much as thirst and hunger and cold require, as much as was enough for you, Epicurus, in your little garden, as much as was kept in old times in Socrates' house. There is never any difference of opinion between Nature and Philosophy. Do I seem to limit you with examples that are too severe? In that case, throw in something from Roman behaviour. Make up the amount which Otho's law ordains as right for the fourteen rows. If this too produces a frown and makes you sulk, take two knights, no, make it a treble 400,000.[43] If I've still not filled

---

[41] See 1.109n.   [42] Diogenes the Cynic philosopher of the 4th century B.C., who lived in a large earthenware pot.

[43] On Otho's law and 400,000 sesterces, see 3.153–5n.

si nondum implevi gremium, si panditur ultra,
nec Croesi fortuna umquam nec Persica regna
sufficient animo nec divitiae Narcissi,
330   indulsit Caesar cui Claudius omnia, cuius
paruit imperiis uxorem occidere iussus.

your lap, if it's stretching wider still, then neither the
wealth of Croesus[44] nor the kingdoms of Persia will ever
satisfy your desire, nor the riches of Narcissus, to whom
Claudius Caesar granted everything and whose commands
he obeyed when told to kill his wife.[45]

[44] King of Lydia, proverbially rich.
[45] Emperor Claudius' rich and powerful freedman who played
a role in the execution of Messalina.

NOTE ON SATIRE 15

The third poem in Book Five is a novel condemnation of anger, anger which manifests itself in the graphic form of religious intolerance, murder, and cannibalism. Juvenal starts by inviting his addressee to join in his amazement at Egyptian religious beliefs which elevate animals to the status of gods and condone the eating of human flesh (1–13), a claim that even Ulysses might have had trouble convincing people of (13–26). In contrast with the uncorroborated stories of Ulysses, Juvenal emphasises that his story, a story of "mob crime," is from contemporary times (27–32). There follows the narrative of the atrocity (33–92), which occurs in the context of a religious feud between the people of Ombi and of Tentyra. The people of Tentyra attack the people of Ombi while they are off guard at a religious festival, and a brawl ensues. When the Ombites chase the Tentyrans away, one man slips and falls, is torn to bits and eaten raw. Juvenal then ponders other cases of cannibalism, but concludes that cannibalism induced by siege, such as the case of the Vascones, is completely different (93–131). He then praises the uniquely human quality of compassion (131–58), a concept which includes fellow-feeling, pity, a sense of community, and concord. This positive quality he finds missing in contemporary humans: he accordingly declares that some people behave worse than wild beasts (159–74).

SATIRE 15

Quis nescit, Volusi Bithynice, qualia demens
Aegyptos portenta colat? crocodilon adorat
pars haec, illa pavet saturam serpentibus ibin.
effigies sacri nitet aurea cercopitheci,
5   dimidio magicae resonant ubi Memnone chordae
atque vetus Thebe centum iacet obruta portis.
illic aeluros, hic piscem fluminis, illic
oppida tota canem venerantur, nemo Dianam.
porrum et caepe nefas violare et frangere morsu
10 (o sanctas gentes, quibus haec nascuntur in hortis
numina!), lanatis animalibus abstinet omnis
mensa, nefas illic fetum iugulare capellae:
carnibus humanis vesci licet. attonito cum
tale super cenam facinus narraret Vlixes
15 Alcinoo, bilem aut risum fortasse quibusdam
moverat ut mendax aretalogus. "in mare nemo
hunc abicit saeva dignum veraque Charybdi,
fingentem inmanis Laestrygonas et Cyclopas?
nam citius Scyllam vel concurrentia saxa
20 Cyaneis plenos et tempestatibus utres
crediderim aut tenui percussum verbere Circes

---

1 A ruined statue, in fact of Amenophis III, from which a musical sound emanated every day at dawn.

488

SATIRE 15

Volusius of Bithynia, is there anyone who doesn't know the kind of monsters that crazy Egypt worships? One district reveres the crocodile, another quakes at the ibis, glutted with snakes. The sacred long-tailed monkey's golden image gleams where the magic chords reverberate from crumbling Memnon[1] and ancient Thebes lies in ruins with its hundred gates. Entire towns venerate cats in one place, in another river fish, in another a dog—but no one worships Diana. It's a violation and a sin to crunch your teeth into a leek or an onion. Such holy peoples, to have these gods growing in their gardens! Their tables abstain completely from woolly animals, and there it's a sin to slaughter a goat's young. But feeding on human flesh is allowed. When Ulysses told the story of a crime like this over dinner to an astonished Alcinous, he provoked anger or perhaps laughter in some of his listeners—they thought him a lying raconteur. "Won't someone chuck this guy into the sea? It's a real, cruel Charybdis that he deserves, for inventing these monstrous Laestrygonians and Cyclopses. I'll tell you, I'd sooner believe in his Scylla, or his clashing Cyanean rocks, or his skins full of storms, or his Elpenor grunting with his fellow oarsmen turned pigs after being

et cum remigibus grunnisse Elpenora porcis.
tam vacui capitis populum Phaeaca putavit?"
sic aliquis merito nondum ebrius et minimum qui
25   de Corcyraea temetum duxerat urna;
     solus enim haec Ithacus nullo sub teste canebat.
     Nos miranda quidem sed nuper consule Iunco
gesta super calidae referemus moenia Copti,
nos volgi scelus et cunctis graviora coturnis.
30   nam scelus, a Pyrrha quamquam omnia syrmata volvas,
nullus apud tragicos populus facit. accipe nostro
dira quod exemplum feritas produxerit aevo.
     Inter finitimos vetus atque antiqua simultas,
inmortale odium et numquam sanabile vulnus,
35   ardet adhuc Ombos et Tentura. summus utrimque
inde furor volgo, quod numina vicinorum
odit uterque locus, cum solos credat habendos
esse deos quos ipse colit. sed tempore festo
alterius populi rapienda occasio cunctis
40   visa inimicorum primoribus ac ducibus, ne
laetum hilaremque diem, ne magnae gaudia cenae
sentirent positis ad templa et compita mensis
pervigilique toro, quem nocte ac luce iacentem

---

[2] In *Odyssey* 9–12 Ulysses ("the Ithacan") narrated to Alcinous, king of the Phaeacians, how he survived Charybdis and Scylla in the straits of Sicily, the clashing rocks (usually Symplegades, but here called the Cyanean rocks), the man-eating giant Laestrygonians (cf. 14.20), Polyphemus the Cyclops who devoured several of his crew, Aeolus' gift of the winds in a bag, and Circe's trick of turning his crew, including Elpenor, into pigs.

[3] Phaeacia is said to have been Corcyra, modern Corfu.

[4] In A.D. 127; Coptus (Keft) is on the Nile in Upper Egypt.

struck by Circe's delicate wand. Did he think that the people of Phaeacia were so empty-headed?"[2] That's what someone might have said, quite rightly, someone still sober, who'd drunk very little liquor from the Corcyrean jar.[3] After all, the Ithacan was reciting his story on his own, without corroboration.

For my part, I shall tell an amazing story of something that happened recently, in Iuncus' consulship, beyond the walls of baking Coptus.[4] My story is of mob crime, more horrific than anything in tragedy. You see, even if you unroll all the robes of tragedy from Pyrrha onwards,[5] in the tragic poets you won't find an entire people committing a crime. Hear what a paradigm of appalling barbarism has emerged in our own time.

Between the neighbours Ombi and Tentyra[6] there still blazes a lasting and ancient feud, an undying hatred, a wound that can never be healed. On each side, the height of mob fury arises because each place detests the gods of their neighbours. They think that only the gods they themselves worship should be counted as gods. So when one of these tribes was holding a religious festival, the chieftains and leaders of their enemy decided unanimously to seize the opportunity to prevent them from enjoying a happy and cheerful day and the pleasures of a great meal: the tables set up at the temples and crossroads and the sleepless dining couches, night and day, which sometimes lie there

[5] See 1.84n.

[6] Two towns in Upper Egypt near Coptus around ten miles apart, modern Negadeh (probably) and Dendera. At Ombi the cult of the crocodile was important, whereas the people of Tentyra hunted the crocodile.

septimus interdum sol invenit. (horrida sane
45 Aegyptos, sed luxuria, quantum ipse notavi,
barbara famoso non cedit turba Canopo.)
adde quod et facilis victoria de madidis et
blaesis atque mero titubantibus. inde virorum
saltatus nigro tibicine, qualiacumque
50 unguenta et flores multaeque in fronte coronae:
hinc ieiunum odium. sed iurgia prima sonare
incipiunt: animis ardentibus haec tuba rixae.
dein clamore pari concurritur, et vice teli
saevit nuda manus. paucae sine volnere malae,
55 vix cuiquam aut nulli toto certamine nasus
integer. aspiceres iam cuncta per agmina voltus
dimidios, alias facies et hiantia ruptis
ossa genis, plenos oculorum sanguine pugnos.
ludere se credunt ipsi tamen et puerilis
60 exercere acies, quod nulla cadavera calcent.
et sane quo tot rixantis milia turbae,
si vivunt omnes? ergo acrior impetus et iam
saxa inclinatis per humum quaesita lacertis
incipiunt torquere, domestica seditioni
65 tela, nec hunc lapidem, qualis et Turnus et Aiax,
vel quo Tydides percussit pondere coxam
Aeneae, sed quem valeant emittere dextrae
illis dissimiles et nostro tempore natae.
nam genus hoc vivo iam decrescebat Homero,
70 terra malos homines nunc educat atque pusillos;

64 seditioni *H.Valesius*: seditione PΦ

until the seventh dawn finds them. (Egypt is uncouth, for sure, but in terms of extravagance, as far as I can tell from my own observations, its barbarian mob matches scandalous Canopus.[7]) Another factor is that it would be an easy victory over people sozzled and stuttering and reeling from the wine. On one side were men gyrating to a black piper, with perfumes (of a sort) and flowers and many garlands on their heads. On the other, ravenous hatred. So first of all, insults start to sound: when tempers are blazing, these are the bugle call of the brawl. Then both sides shout and charge, attacking with their bare hands instead of weapons. Few jaws are unwounded, hardly anyone, or no one, in the whole fight has an uninjured nose. Through all the ranks you could already see mutilated faces, features unrecognisable, bones gaping through torn cheeks, fists full of blood from eyes. Yet they think this is just a game, a childish practice fight, because there are no bodies to trample. And after all, what's the point of a brawling mob thousands strong if no one is killed? So the attack gets fiercer. Now they look for stones on the ground and start hurling them with arms bent back. These are the home-grown weapons of rioters—not the kind of stone that Turnus or Ajax wielded, and not as heavy as the one the son of Tydeus used to strike Aeneas' hip,[8] but the kind that modern-day hands, unlike theirs, can manage to launch. The human race, you know, was already declining while Homer was still alive. Nowadays the earth produces

[7] Juvenal distinguishes the native Egyptians from Hellenised Canopus, the fashionable resort of Alexandria.

[8] Turnus: Virg. *Aen.* 12.896–902; Ajax: Hom. *Il.* 7.268–70; Diomedes: Hom. *Il.*5.307–8.

ergo deus, quicumque aspexit, ridet et odit.
a deverticulo repetatur fabula. postquam
subsidiis aucti, pars altera promere ferrum
audet et infestis pugnam instaurare sagittis.
75 terga fugae celeri praestant instantibus Ombis
qui vicina colunt umbrosae Tentura palmae.
labitur hinc quidam nimia formidine cursum
praecipitans capiturque. ast illum in plurima sectum
frusta et particulas, ut multis mortuus unus
80 sufficeret, totum corrosis ossibus edit
victrix turba, nec ardenti decoxit aeno
aut veribus, longum usque adeo tardumque putavit
expectare focos, contenta cadavere crudo.
hic gaudere libet quod non violaverit ignem,
85 quem summa caeli raptum de parte, Prometheu,
donasti terris. elemento gratulor, et te
exultare reor. sed qui mordere cadaver
sustinuit nil umquam hac carne libentius edit;
nam scelere in tanto ne quaeras et dubites an
90 prima voluptatem gula senserit, ultimus ante
qui stetit, absumpto iam toto corpore ductis
per terram digitis aliquid de sanguine gustat.
    Vascones, ut fama est, alimentis talibus usi
produxere animas, sed res diversa, sed illic
95 fortunae invidia est bellorumque ultima, casus
extremi, longae dira obsidionis egestas.

75 fugae POT: fuga Φ | praestant instantibus ombis O: prae-
stant instantibus omnes U: praestant instantibus orbes LZ: prae-
stantibus omnibus instans PFGK: praestantibus omnibus instant
AHT

humans who are nasty and puny, so any god that takes a
look is filled with laughter and loathing. I must recall my
story from its diversion. After they've been joined by rein-
forcements, one side has the audacity to produce weapons
and to renew the fight with hostile arrows. As the people of
Ombi chase them, the inhabitants of neighbouring Tentyra
with its shady palms turn their backs in rapid retreat. One
of them slips while speeding his departure in mad panic—
and gets caught. He's immediately chopped into hundreds
of hunks and morsels—to get enough portions from one
dead man—and completely devoured by the victorious
mob, even gnawing his bones. They didn't cook him in a
blazing pot or barbecue him. They thought it was far too
long and tedious to wait for the hearth: they were content
with raw corpse. At this point, I'd like to celebrate the fact
that they didn't desecrate fire, your gift to the world, Pro-
metheus, which you stole from highest heaven. I congratu-
late the element—and reckon you're delighted, too. But
people who could bring themselves to chew on a corpse
never ate anything more willingly than this flesh. Let me
tell you, in such a colossal crime, so you won't ask or be in
doubt whether it was only the first gut which experienced
pleasure, the last man standing there watching, once the
whole body had been eaten up, dragged his fingers across
the ground to get a taste of blood.

The story goes that the Vascones prolonged their lives
with this kind of sustenance. But the situation was differ-
ent. In their case, it was fortune's malice and the extremi-

---

77 hinc PO: hic Φ   85 Prometheu *Griffith, Willis*: pro-
metheus Φ: promethea P   86 donasti *Griffith, Willis*:
donavit *codd*.   90 ante *Lond.BM Add.11997, Housman*:
autem PΦ   93 usi Φ: olim PFOTU

[huius enim, quod nunc agitur, miserabile debet
exemplum esse tibi, sicut modo dicta mihi gens.]
post omnis herbas, post cuncta animalia, quidquid
100   cogebat vacui ventris furor, hostibus ipsis
pallorem ac maciem et tenuis miserantibus artus,
membra aliena fame lacerabant, esse parati
et sua. quisnam hominum veniam dare quisve deorum
ventribus abnueret dira atque inmania passis
105   et quibus illorum poterant ignoscere manes
quorum corporibus vescebantur? melius nos
Zenonis praecepta monent, [nec enim omnia quidam
pro vita facienda putant] sed Cantaber unde
Stoicus, antiqui praesertim aetate Metelli?
110   (nunc totus Graias nostrasque habet orbis Athenas,
Gallia causidicos docuit facunda Britannos,
de conducendo loquitur iam rhetore Thyle.)
nobilis ille tamen populus, quem diximus, et par
virtute atque fide sed maior clade Zacynthos.
115   tale quid excusat Maeotide saevior ara
Aegyptos? quippe illa nefandi Taurica sacri
inventrix homines, ut iam quae carmina tradunt

97–8 *del. Guyet*   98 tibi G: cibi PΦ
104 ventribus *H.Valesius*: viribus Φ: urbibus PU
107–8 nec enim . . . putant *del. Francke*

9 A Spanish people, the modern Basques, whose main town
was besieged by Pompey and his followers until it fell in 72 B.C.
Lines 97–8: "The fact is that this example, which is now my topic,
you ought to pity, just as the people I have just mentioned."

10 Founder of the Stoic school of philosophy. Lines 107–8:
"after all, some think that not every measure should be taken to
preserve life."

ties of war, a desperate crisis: dreadful need caused by a long siege.[9] It happened after they'd eaten every plant and every animal, whatever they were driven to by a raging empty belly, when even their enemies were pitying their pallor and emaciation and skeletal frames. Hunger made them start tearing one another's limbs, ready to eat their own too. What human being or god would refuse to pardon bellies that had suffered such dreadful and monstrous things? Even the ghosts of the people whose bodies they were devouring could forgive them. We know better thanks to Zeno's teachings,[10] but how could a Cantabrian be a Stoic, especially in the time of ancient Metellus?[11] (Nowadays the whole world has its Greek and Roman Athens. Eloquent Gaul has been teaching the lawyers of Britain. Thule is already talking about hiring a professor of rhetoric.[12]) Yet that people I just mentioned was noble, and so was Zacynthos, equal in courage and loyalty, but victim of a worse disaster.[13] What self-defence of this kind can Egypt offer, more barbaric than the altar at Maeotis?[14] After all, the Taurian inventor of that ghastly rite,[15] assuming for now that poetic tradition can be reliably believed,

[11] The Cantabrians were in fact from a different part of Spain from the Vascones. Quintus Caecilius Metellus was a general sent to Spain in the 70s B.C.

[12] The furthest place imaginable, precise location unknown.

[13] Saguntum in Spain, besieged and razed by Hannibal in 219–18 B.C.

[14] Lake Maeotis is the Sea of Azov, northeast of the Crimea, where Artemis/Diana was worshipped.

[15] The cult of Artemis/Diana practised by the Tauri involved the sacrifice of strangers; Lucian *Dial. Deorum* 16.1 alleges cannibalism too.

digna fide credas, tantum immolat; ulterius nil
aut gravius cultro timet hostia. quis modo casus
120 inpulit hos? quae tanta fames infestaque vallo
arma coegerunt tam detestabile monstrum
audere? anne aliam terra Memphitide sicca
invidiam facerent nolenti surgere Nilo?
qua nec terribiles Cimbri nec Brittones umquam
125 Sauromataeque truces aut inmanes Agathyrsi,
hac saevit rabie inbelle et inutile volgus
parvula fictilibus solitum dare vela phaselis
et brevibus pictae remis incumbere testae.
nec poenam sceleri invenies nec digna parabis
130 supplicia his populis, in quorum mente pares sunt
et similes ira atque fames.
                       Mollissima corda
humano generi dare se natura fatetur,
quae lacrimas dedit: haec nostri pars optima sensus.
plorare ergo iubet, [causam dicentis amici
135 squaloremque rei] pupillum ad iura vocantem
circumscriptorem, cuius manantia fletu
ora puellares faciunt incerta capilli.
naturae imperio gemimus, cum funus adultae
virginis occurrit vel terra clauditur infans
140 et minor igne rogi. quis enim bonus et face dignus

---

[124] brittones AHL: bristones F: bistones OU: Teutones *Markland*   [134–5] causam . . . rei *del. Knoche* | amici *codd.*: amictus *Courtney*

---

[16] A city in Lower Egypt. Juvenal implies that the cannibalism is designed to shame the Nile river god into fertilising Egypt with his flood waters.

498

does no more than sacrifice humans. The victim fears nothing more or worse than the knife. But in this recent case, what crisis drove them to it? What hunger so terrible, what weapons threatening their defences forced them to commit such an abominable outrage? Was there some other way of making the Nile feel ashamed for refusing to rise, if the land of Memphis were parched?[16] Never have the terrifying Cimbrians or Britons, the fierce Sauromatians or monstrous Agathyrsians[17] raged with the frenzy of this effete and useless mob, which likes hoisting tiny sails on their earthenware boats and leaning on the miniature oars of their painted crocks. You won't devise any punishment for the crime or provide retribution suitable for these peoples who assimilate and identify anger and hunger.

Nature declares that she has given the human race the gentlest of hearts by her gift of tears. This is the finest element of our sensibility. She accordingly urges us to weep for[18] the ward who summons his defrauder to court, with his girlish hair making indeterminate the sex of his face, streaming with tears. It's by Nature's command that we sigh when we meet the funeral of a marriageable virgin or when a baby is buried in the ground, too young for the pyre's flame. The fact is that no person who is good and worthy of the mystic torch, who behaves as the priest of

[17] All militaristic tribes: the Cimbri were Germans; the Sauromatae were from further north; the Agathyrsi from Transylvania wore war paint like the Britons.

[18] Lines 134–5: "the case of a client, the squalor of a defendant."

arcana, qualem Cereris volt esse sacerdos,
ulla aliena sibi credit mala? separat hoc nos
a grege mutorum, atque ideo venerabile soli
sortiti ingenium divinorumque capaces
145 atque exercendis pariendisque artibus apti
sensum a caelesti demissum traximus arce,
cuius egent prona et terram spectantia. mundi
principio indulsit communis conditor illis
tantum animas, nobis animum quoque, mutuus ut nos
150 adfectus petere auxilium et praestare iuberet,
dispersos trahere in populum, migrare vetusto
de nemore et proavis habitatas linquere silvas,
aedificare domos, laribus coniungere nostris
tectum aliud, tutos vicino limine somnos
155 ut conlata daret fiducia, protegere armis
lapsum aut ingenti nutantem volnere civem,
communi dare signa tuba, defendier isdem
turribus atque una portarum clave teneri.
        Sed iam serpentum maior concordia. parcit
160 cognatis maculis similis fera. quando leoni
fortior eripuit vitam leo? quo nemore umquam
expiravit aper maioris dentibus apri?
Indica tigris agit rabida cum tigride pacem
perpetuam, saevis inter se convenit ursis.
165 ast homini ferrum letale incude nefanda
produxisse parum est, cum rastra et sarcula tantum

[143] ideo *codd.*: adeo *Nisbet*
[145] pariendisque OU: ***iendisque P: capiendisque ΦΣ

Ceres wishes,[19] considers the distress of others irrelevant to themselves. This is what separates us from the herd of dumb creatures. So we are the only ones allotted a disposition worthy of respect, who can comprehend divinity, who are equipped to practise and invent the arts and crafts; we are the only ones to derive a sensibility sent down from the height of heaven, something missing from the four-footed creatures that face towards the earth. To them, at the beginning of the world, our common creator granted only the breath of life. To us he gave souls as well. His intention? So our mutual feeling would urge us to seek and offer help, to draw together scattered individuals into communities, to migrate from the ancient woodland and leave the forests inhabited by our ancestors, to construct homes, with another house adjacent to our own hearths, so that combined confidence would make our sleep secure, thanks to a neighbour's threshold, to protect with our weapons a fellow citizen who has fallen or who is reeling from a mighty wound, to give the signals on the community's bugle, to be defended by the same towers, and to be contained by the single key of the gates.

But these days, there is more harmony among snakes. The wild beast with similar spots spares its relatives. Have you ever heard of a stronger lion robbing another lion of life? Or of a forest where a boar breathed its last under the tusks of a greater boar? The Indian tigress lives with frenzied tigress in everlasting peace. Savage bears agree among themselves. But for human beings it is not enough to have beaten out lethal steel on the wicked anvil, al-

[19] A reference to religious cults such as the Eleusinian mysteries in honour of Demeter/Ceres.

adsueti coquere et marris ac vomere lassi
nescierint primi gladios extendere fabri.
aspicimus populos quorum non sufficit irae
170   occidisse aliquem, sed pectora, bracchia, voltum
crediderint genus esse cibi. quid diceret ergo
vel quo non fugeret, si nunc haec monstra videret
Pythagoras, cunctis animalibus abstinuit qui
tamquam homine et ventri indulsit non omne legumen?

168 extendere PAT*Sang.*: extundere Φ: excudere LO

though the first blacksmiths spent their time and effort on forging rakes and hoes and mattocks and ploughshares only. They didn't know how to produce swords. We are looking at peoples whose anger is not satisfied by killing someone but who think his torso, arms, and face are a kind of food. What, then, would Pythagoras say? Wouldn't he run off, anywhere, if he now saw these horrors? Pythagoras was the one who abstained from eating all living things as if they were human and who didn't treat his belly to every kind of bean.[20]

[20] Pythagoras advised a vegetarian diet, although some types of bean were off limits because they caused flatulence.

NOTE ON SATIRE 16

The incompleteness of this poem precludes an analysis of its structural and thematic features. The stated programme is the advantages of military life (1–2), and in the 60 lines which survive the emphasis is on the immunity and privileges enjoyed by soldiers in legal matters (7–50), with a movement into the topic of financial advantages in the last few lines (51–60). To this extent, the poem appears to continue the earlier themes of the book: crime, punishment, the courts; money, gain, and greed. How the poem continued is open to speculation.

SATIRE 16

Quis numerare queat felicis praemia, Galli,
militiae? nam si subeuntur prospera castra
2A ⟨nil tibi di possunt donare optatius. ergo⟩
me pavidum excipiat tironem porta secundo
sidere. plus etenim fati valet hora benigni
5 quam si nos Veneris commendet epistula Marti
et Samia genetrix quae delectatur harena.
    Commoda tractemus primum communia, quorum
haut minimum illud erit, ne te pulsare togatus
audeat, immo, etsi pulsetur, dissimulet nec
10 excussos studeat praetori ostendere dentes
et nigram in facie tumidis livoribus offam
atque oculum medico nil promittente relictum.
Bardaicus iudex datur haec punire volenti
calceus et grandes magna ad subsellia surae
15 legibus antiquis castrorum et more Camilli
servato, miles ne vallum litiget extra

post 2 *lacuna Jahn, suppl. Housman*
10 excussos studeat *Nisbet*: gaudeat excussos *Markland*: audeat excussos *codd.*

---

[1] I.e. the hour of a person's birth.

SATIRE 16

Gallius, who can count the rewards of a successful military life? After all, if you join a top company ⟨there's nothing more desirable that the gods can bestow on you. So⟩ I'd like to enter the camp gate as a nervous recruit, with the stars smiling. A moment of generous fate[1] is more powerful, after all, than a letter of recommendation to Mars from Venus or from his mother, who loves the sands of Samos.[2]

First, let's deal with the advantages shared by all soldiers. Not the least of these is that no civilian will have the nerve to beat you up. Instead, if he gets beaten up himself, he'll pretend he wasn't, and he won't be eager to show the praetor his teeth that have been knocked out, or the black lump on his face with the swollen bruises, or the eye he still has, though the doctor isn't making any promises. If he seeks redress for this, he gets a hobnailed boot[3] for a judge, with huge calf-muscles sitting at the big bench. The ancient military law and the rule of Camillus have been maintained, forbidding soldiers from attending court out-

[2] Juno, who had a cult centre on the island of Samos. When young men joined the army, they had letters of recommendation from powerful connections.

[3] I.e. a centurion. The Bardaei were Illyrians who provided Marius' bodyguard and gave their name to the military boot.

et procul a signis. "iustissima centurionum
cognitio est" inquit "de milite, nec mihi derit
ultio, si iustae defertur causa querelae."
20   tota cohors tamen est inimica, omnesque manipli
consensu magno efficiunt curabilis ut sit
vindicta et gravior quam iniuria. dignum erit ergo
declamatoris mulino corde Vagelli,
cum duo crura habeas, offendere tot caligas, tot
25   milia clavorum. quis tam procul adsit ab Vrbe
praeterea, quis tam Pylades, molem aggeris ultra
ut veniat? lacrimae siccentur protinus, et se
excusaturos non sollicitemus amicos.
"da testem" iudex cum dixerit, audeat ille
30   nescio quis, pugnos qui vidit, dicere "vidi,"
et credam dignum barba dignumque capillis
maiorum. citius falsum producere testem
contra paganum possis quam vera loquentem
contra fortunam armati contraque pudorem.
35   Praemia nunc alia atque alia emolumenta notemus
sacramentorum. convallem ruris aviti
improbus aut campum mihi si vicinus ademit
et sacrum effodit medio de limite saxum,
quod mea cum patulo coluit puls annua libo,

[18] *del. Nisbet* | est" inquis "de milite, *Housman, Willis*: est
igitur *codd.*: exigitur *Buecheler*: agitur *Kilpatrick*
[21] curabilis ut sit PSAFU: plorabilis ut sit *Guyet, Cramer*: ut
cura tibi sit *Housman*
[25] adsit *S. T. Collins*: absit Psit F

side of the rampart, far from the standards.[4] "The centurions' jurisdiction over soldiers is absolutely fair," you say, "and I'll have my satisfaction, if the case I bring before them is a justified complaint." But the entire cohort is hostile, and all the units act with one mind to ensure that your redress needs medical attention and that it's worse than your original injury. Since you have only two legs, it must be typical of the ranter Vagellius' mulish understanding[5] to offend all those heavy boots and all those thousands of hobnails. Besides, who'd accompany you so far from Rome? Who'd be like Pylades[6] and venture beyond the massive Embankment?[7] Let's dry our tears at once. Let's not bother our friends who will only make their excuses. When the judge says, "Call your witness," suppose the person who saw the attack has the nerve to say "I saw it," I'd think him good enough for the beard and long hair of our ancestors.[8] You can more quickly produce a false witness against a civilian than someone to tell the truth against the property and honour of a military man.

Let's now take note of some other rewards and benefits of swearing the military oath. Suppose some scoundrel of a neighbour has taken from me a glen or a field from my ancestral estate, digging up from the middle of the boundary the sacred stone that I have honoured with my yearly offer-

[4] The establishment of a standing army in the time of Marcus Furius Camillus (4th century B.C.) put soldiers under military rule at all times.   [5] The declaimer mentioned at 13.119.

[6] The devoted friend of Orestes, the classic loyal friend.

[7] The praetorian camp was less than half a mile outside the Embankment.

[8] The hairiness of the ancient Romans was associated with their moral integrity.

40 debitor aut sumptos pergit non reddere nummos
vana supervacui dicens chirographa ligni,
expectandus erit qui lites incohet annus
totius populi. sed tum quoque mille ferenda
taedia, mille morae; totiens subsellia tantum
45 sternuntur, iam facundo ponente lacernas
Caedicio et Fusco iam micturiente parati
digredimur, lentaque fori pugnamus harena.
ast illis quos arma tegunt et balteus ambit
quod placitum est ipsis praestatur tempus agendi,
50 nec res atteritur longo sufflamine litis.
     Solis praeterea testandi militibus ius
vivo patre datur. nam quae sunt parta labore
militiae placuit non esse in corpore census,
omne tenet cuius regimen pater. ergo Coranum
55 signorum comitem castrorumque aera merentem
quamvis iam tremulus captat pater. hunc favor aequus
provehit et pulchro reddit sua dona labori.
ipsius certe ducis hoc referre videtur
ut, qui fortis erit, sit felicissimus idem,
60 ut laeti phaleris omnes et torquibus omnes . . .

41 *cf.* 13.137
42 inchoet Φ: inchoat PU
56 favor *Ruperti*: labor PΦ

---

9 The festival of the Terminalia took place on February 23rd every year in honour of Terminus, god of boundaries.

10 The court year ran from January to October.

11 At 13.197, Caedicius is a *iudex*.

12 There is an orator called Fuscus at Martial 7.28.5–6.

INDEX TO JUVENAL

INDEX

521

INDEX

INDEX TO PERSIUS

535